Buried Treasure

Buried Treasure

Jack Downs

Apprentice House
Loyola University Maryland
Baltimore, Maryland

First Edition
Printed in the United States of America

Paperback ISBN: 978-1-934074-83-1
E-Book ISBN: 978-1-934074-49-7

Cover design by: Allison Focella
Cover photo by: Jennifer M. Downs
Published by Apprentice House

Apprentice House
Loyola University Maryland
4501 N. Charles Street
Baltimore, MD 21210
410.617.5265 •410.617.2198 (fax)
www.ApprenticeHouse.com
info@ApprenticeHouse.com

Dedication

For Jen

Acknowledgements

I would like to thank especially the members of The Eldersburg (MD) Critique Group, who plowed through chapter after chapter, offering sage and frank advice, as well as my brother Chris and sister Teresa, who slogged through significant portions and put in their two cents. Grateful thanks also to Alice, Kristy, and Ashley for the additional eyes. Props also to Eric Silvester, fellow Gymkanite and long-time friend, who offered invaluable structural and proofing assistance. Errors of fact are none but my own.

A special shout out to Penny Hartmann of the Eastern Shore Writers Association for her help and advice on items relevant to the Eastern Shore in the 1960s. Also, to the unsung drivers who shepherded me for countless miles as a hitchhiker, back in the day, and provided so much inspiration for this tale.

Thanks to the design team from Apprentice House – Allison Focello and Chloe Germain, for their unflagging good humor and expert advice. Thanks also to Alisa Piotrowski for help with the maps, and to Allyson Watt for assistance with the cover!

Finally, thanks to my family: Jen, Brendan, Collin, and Devin, for lending so many of my hours to the craft. Hopefully, it was time well-lent.

Fact and Fiction

Crane Ridge, MD is a fictional town. I tried to stay faithful through research and interviews to life and times on Maryland's Eastern Shore in the 1960s. The lynching of Matthew Williams described in Chapter 33 was a real event, occurring in Salisbury, MD in 1931. I obtained the details from Wicomico County History, Peninsula Press, Salisbury, MD (57).

Darien, GA is a real town, quaint and picturesque. I took some liberties with establishments and street names, while attempting to maintain the geographic characteristics of the mid-1960s. Cat Head Creek and the Butler Plantation are real. The depiction of practices of the *Church of God with Signs Following* is based on research.

Incidents similar to the broken-bat episode in chapter 12 have actually occurred in the major leagues. Most recently in Game 4 of the American League playoffs of 2012, pitcher Joba Chamberlain was forced to leave the game when a broken bat at the start of the 12th inning smashed into his elbow in the Yankees' 2-1 loss in 13 innings to the Baltimore Orioles.

1 / Sam's End

Berlin, Maryland 1954

The sun rose above the trees, lighting the day in a blaze of early spring brightness. The darkest chapter of Sam's life opened on that day, a morning somewhere between ordinary and promising. He coaxed the baby carriage across the tracks traversing Washington Street on the east side of Berlin. David, his two-year-old, was asleep as soon as they'd started out from the house. David was more a mystery than James, his older son. The tot made Sam uneasy, as if he possessed a time bomb. The baby's fair hair and skin, so light in contrast to James's, belied his temper.

"James, slow down boy! Stay where I can see you!"

Sam's voice carried no bite. It was spring, finally. The equinox was almost two weeks past, but the cold had clung, raw and stubborn as a soggy wool coat. Now a temperate front bullied its way up the close Atlantic coast, trumpeting a promise of balmier weather. Berlin, Maryland, was awakening from a long chill, casting aside its foggy slumber. Sam shrugged off the nagging sense of unease that had plagued him. Today no delusions of somebody following him, no paranoia about his wife's strange behavior.

James pedaled down the sidewalk toward the playground, pumping the shiny three-wheeler Santa had brought—Maureen wept at the expense—tassels streaming from the handles. In the short travel from the house, James had spilled twice from the bike and righted himself, to pedal again like a demon. His last visit to the playground had been November, around the time Sam was laid off at the chicken processing plant. Yet this morning, James flew there unerring, like a leatherback hatchling to the surf.

His wife, Maureen, had suggested the outing. Insisted, really.

"You'll do fine. I know you've a lot on your mind, but the boys need air, and so do you," she'd said, slipping on her gloves. "Just don't let James out of your sight. He tends to never look back." She'd smiled enigmatically, kissed him, and left for the bus stop.

Just beyond the train tracks, two routes led to the playground. The shorter path cut through the hedges that fronted the Bomberger's stately home, at the corner of Washington and Hyatt Streets. The longer path followed the sidewalk around the corner and down Hyatt to the far side of the home, where it passed between the Owings and the Magid's to the small playground. Inez Bomberger periodically blocked the shortcut with yarn or baling twine. The neighbor kids found some use for the string, for it would disappear, and the tracks of youth-sized sneakers would emerge again in the permanent mud of the passage.

Sam waved a greeting at Mrs. Somers across the street. She braced astride her porch, gardening implements in hand, her fists on her hips like the captain of a warship. A hundred pots of various sizes assembled neatly before her, all waiting their assignments.

"Hello to you and yours, Sam Paxton," she said. "And another on the way? Did I hear right?"

He nodded, tipping his hat. "Afraid so, Miss Ellen. Maureen's in a family way again."

She snorted and turned back to her patient pots.

It was a glorious morning. Sam felt light, for a change not consumed by worries about work. Spring meant new life and renewal. Careers could founder in the bleak fall. Optimistic owners hired come spring. Sam straightened his shoulders and glanced down at his angel, his son, lacking a care.

At a clatter up the street, Sam raised his head. James's bike was on its side, the high wheel spinning. He glimpsed the red sweatshirt hood disappearing into the hedge in front of Miss Inez's. Sam picked up his pace to circle around the Bomberger's the long way. That would be at least a couple minutes. What if there were older boys at the playground? Or worse, a responsible mother, like Judy Owings? She would have this or that to say about letting a boy run unattended.

Sam called out, blending disapproval with plea. He was hollering because Mrs. Somers would expect it. He glanced again at David, innocent in his slumber. He turned to ask Mrs. Somers to watch the carriage for a moment, but she'd disappeared. He looked up and down the street. No one. Sam stepped across the grass and saw a child's shoe in the lumpy mud between the bushes.

"James!"

He felt his anger rise. *Think.* He hadn't been out of the house twenty minutes yet. Sam glanced back, and then burst through the opening, jogging toward the playground. It was further than he remembered. He saw James clawing up the ladder to the slide.

"James Patrick!"

His eldest son smiled briefly before resuming his climb, one foot dangling a muddy sock. Sam swiveled. The street was invisible beyond the hedge.

Sam raced to the playground and positioned himself at the bottom of the aluminum slide. "Down. Now, young man."

James leaned forward, a hand on each rail, a muddy shoe tapping the metal. He flashed a quick smile.

"Where's David?" he asked.

"Out on the sidewalk, where I left him to chase you. Down! Now! I told you not to run out of sight! Down! Now!"

"Where's my bike?" James asked.

"Come down here, young man, right now!" Sam could hear his mounting tone. "We'll go get your bike, and your brother," he relented. "Now, please!"

James started to cry. Sam reached up and grabbed James's ankle. He pulled his son down the slide and picked him up. Resting James on his hip, Sam made his way back to the hedge cut.

"We gonna get my bike?" James sniffled.

Sam, winded from two packs of Marlboros a day, puffed.

"Yes, and your brother better be sleeping."

Sam heard a car screeching around the corner in front of Bomberger's, down Hyatt. Could the carriage have rolled into the street? He'd eased the front wheels off the sidewalk into the spongy spring grass. The area was flat. The carriage could not have rolled. Sam drew a deep breath, relieved.

He twisted sideways through the hedges and bent to pull his son's shoe from the muck. The carriage stood where he'd left it. His arms were aching from carrying James, who now had his own small arms wrapped tightly around his father's neck. In one of his last completely sane thoughts, Sam reflected that James already understood that nothing staved off anger like a child's affection.

He chided himself for losing his temper with his son on such a peaceful morning. Blessing on blessing, not a peep from the buggy. They shuffled across the lawn, James with his muddy sock hanging from his foot.

Sam strode up to the carriage, his eyes taking in what his mind couldn't.

It was empty.

***

When had the world shrunk to such a dark and cold place? How had something as light and magical as love become a sword that cut down good people to writhe, without the mercy of death? Deep in her head, she peeked out through her own eyes, listening but not reacting, hearing but not falling. She loved him more than she could comprehend. Lovers do what lovers must, for love.

Those seared by the insanity of passion will recover, given time. That was her new faith. Lovers regard only their beloved, else the love withers and chokes. Strong as the fiercest will to live, love fights not to die. Nothing dies in spring, least of all love. Once, she had thought she loved. Silly now, it seems. Real love is beyond thought and reason. Intractable in its insisting. In another time, in another world, it might have been different. But there is only this time, in this world, and so it is *this* way. She tenderly stroked the small mattress where her child had so recently lain, but would never again.

2 / Dylan

Crane Ridge, Maryland 1962

The ride back from the courthouse was quiet. From the deep back seat, Dylan Paxton stared at the stubble springing from Mr. Thompson's head beneath the hat brim. The same color as the sky, sponged and sturdy gray.

The boy sighed and bounced his new shoes. Once, Mr. Thompson jerked at a kick against the back of his seat. Next to him, Nana turned and dropped her chin to her chest, her eyes narrowing. Dylan stilled under her gaze.

He turned to stare at the landscape out the Dodge's window. A sign loomed and whooshed past. *Now Leaving Salisbury, Maryland. Jewel of the State's Youngest County,* courtesy of the Rotary. As far as Dylan could see, hoary stumps of corn stalks stood sentry in neat rows. Flocks of geese mashed the edges of feed ponds dotting the fields. Winter wasn't much to fuss about here. Today though, a close sky framed a landscape drizzled with a white icing of snow from last night.

Fallow late-winter fields yielded to farm spreads, silos, and clusters of one-story frame houses. *Welcome to Crane Ridge.* Poor sister to Salisbury, to the west on the Wicomico River. Salisbury straddled the placid waterway, while Crane Ridge hugged the southeastern bank, upriver from Salisbury five miles or so as the geese fly.

Dylan slid across the seat to gaze at the river as they drove along deserted East Ferry Street, near the War Memorial at the center of town. He was surprised the stone abutment marking the old ferry landing was deserted. Usually it would swarm with kids he knew pelting the thin river ice with rocks. Then he remembered school was still in session today. Last evening his friend Billy Bergin had been busting to skip Miss Marsden's class and travel to the courthouse with him, but Nana just tssked and shooed him home. Dylan had been surprised his brother James wasn't going too.

"Why is it just me going to the-" he'd struggled for the word.

"Disposition," his grandmother said. "It's called a disposition."

Dylan had waited, as the front door whooshed closed in Billy's wake. Nana busied herself over a pan of corn bread muffins.

"James," he repeated. "Isn't he going tomorrow too?"

Nana had turned and said abruptly, "You are eight years old. Your brother is thirteen, and can't be made to..." her voice trailed off. She had turned the pan to slide the steaming muffins into a wicker basket. "He's old enough to make his choice, and he chose not to go. That's the end of that."

Mr. Thompson eased the car onto Nash Street. Dylan listened for the dog as Mr. Thompson slowed to ease into Nana's drive. Dylan heard Buster barking from the roof of the garage. Whenever Nana drove somewhere, Buster would bound onto the woodbox at the end of the porch, and then up to the slanted roof of the garage, pacing the peak, gaze fixed on the driveway. Nana didn't pay any mind to the old dog, but Buster was devoted to her. Dylan was sure he could hear Buster barking a welcome long before he could see the car and Nana. The Dart crunched up the driveway and eased to a stop in front of the garage. The snow had melted on the drive, but a thin white sheen still glazed the grass.

"Here we go," Mr. Thompson said. He shoved the shifter into first, and pulled at the parking brake. "Just let me get the door now."

Mr. Thompson's car lived in Nana's garage. Nana didn't have a car. Mr. Thompson had a car, but no garage. Sometime back before Dylan and James had come to live with Nana, a deal had been struck. On weekly trips for groceries, or on infrequent occasions Nana needed to go over to Salisbury, Mr. Thompson would drive her. In return, he garaged his car here.

Dylan and Nana climbed out and stepped onto the walk. Buster greeted Nana, head lifted as if to bay, then sweeping the grass with his huge tail, dousing Dylan's good pants at the knees. Mr. Thompson strode to the solid garage door and bent low, his white socks gleaming from his trouser legs and his shirt cuffs telescoping from his sleeves. Dylan thought it was a funny sight, but when he giggled, Nana gave him a glance to set geese to flight.

The compact man pressed the garage door high, his arms rising like a preacher exhorting his flock. He turned, shot his cuffs back into his dusty black coat, and marched to the car. He eased the Dodge carefully into the opening, and cut the engine. Nana rested a hand on Dylan's shoulder as their neighbor lowered the door and clap-wiped his hands. Mr. Thompson tipped his hat and limped down the driveway toward his home across the street. He lurched a bit, and Dylan thought one leg might be shorter. They both gave a slight wave to his back.

"Dylan, mind you don't step in that puddle. Step 'round, look where you go." The sidewalk up to the front steps was cracked and canted. Years of runoff, freezing and thawing, had lifted and split the slabs.

Dylan clicked up the sidewalk behind Buster. His nostrils tickled with the inhale of sharp cold air, and the welcome smell of wood smoke from houses along the street. The smell would thicken in the later afternoon, as children clattered in from school, and wives warmed homes for their husbands.

"Hold up at the stoop, son."

Dylan turned, offering his shoulder to his grandmother. But she gestured for him to take a seat. He glanced up, surprised. On warmer days, she would often settle on the stoop watching the street and snapping her beans, or reading a Harlequin romance. She wasn't partial to cold though. Even in summer, she'd move inside when the sun went down. She looked tired, and something else too. Dylan sat down at the top stoop, feet out, heels together, liking the weight of the new shoes when he wasn't standing in them. He was surprised his feet now stretched over the edge of the third step down. All summer his bare toes had hung over the second step, not quite touching the third.

Nana was stocky, made more squat by painful rheumatism that lent her a bowlegged waddle. She rested a hand again on his shoulder and eased down next to Dylan, smoothing the fabric of her dress. Dylan didn't think she owned a pair of pants. *Slacks*, his grandma called them, with a look reserved for a knotted sack bound for the garbage pail.

They sat in silence, the river's far bank visible in the distance beyond Mr. Thompson's drive. Barely lunchtime on a school day. It felt weird to be home, like a dream where he and his friends are in the middle of a baseball game at Mass. He reached down and worried the fur under Buster's upraised chin.

"Dylan." Nana rocked back and forth on her bottom. "You understand what happened in the courthouse today?" She looked up at the distant scraping sound as Mr. Thompson dragged his empty trashcan from the curb.

"Well, is James still my brother?"

Nana started, staring at the boy. "What a question. Yes, of *course* he's still your brother."

"Why was daddy crying? Is he still my father?"

Nana sighed, lightly smoothing her dress in a gesture familiar. "You know your father's been through a bad time. Like a long sickness with no end. Or more like an amputation than being just sick. When you're ill a long time, you get well, or.." She plucked at an invisible thread on her knee. "He did not deserve such a thing, in a hundred hundred years. Neither of your parents did," she rushed. Nana stopped, and Dylan wondered what today had to do with that old knot of pain.

"It just broke him," Nana sighed, as if he'd asked aloud. "And after, when your mother saw your father, she only saw the brokenness, I guess. It wasn't right for him to leave, but then it wasn't right to suffer such a thing. Your father maybe hurt deeper, with the blaming. He loves you and James. But it just gets crowded out by the other. Not knowing. That's unnatural. I wonder some he hasn't just blown up like a bad bottle of moonshine and drifted away on a hard wind."

Nana picked at her Sunday dress, her mouth creased.

"Sometimes I think that'd be more the blessing." Nana spoke to the middle distance, her voice soft and bare. "He's my own, and I will always love him. I just hope he can make his way back somehow. Blaming himself for something nobody ever could've imagined. He loved that boy...well, like he loves you. Like he loved air. Little David went off somewhere, along with your father's peace."

Dylan pressed close to his grandma's bosom, wishing she'd talk about something else. Buster too looped in a tight circle on the bottom step, ready for a change of subject.

"His precious son. All these years. It would've been more charitable to just shoot Sam, that is the truth!" Nana's tight hair bun bobbed up and down beneath her floral pillbox hat.

Dylan felt the hurt rising up. He was eight, but he felt older sometimes, trying to understand the sorrow around him. He never knew David. The second of Sam's three sons had vanished without a trace the year Dylan was born. David was two years old then. He'd just be turning 10. But James was the only brother he'd known. As long as Dylan could remember, he had lived here with James and Nana. His father had lived here too, until a couple of years ago. Dylan couldn't recall his mother's face. He could not remember the house in Berlin, Maryland where he'd been born. He'd been two when Maureen left, and three or four when they'd moved in with Nana.

No one ever talked about his mother. Dylan suspected Nana viewed her poorly for leaving her other two sons. Not because of anything that was said. It was just this unseemly quiet around the subject of her. James would up and leave the room if someone asked after her. Of course, he did the same when someone mentioned his father, Sam. Seems James was leaving a lot.

Nana plucked at a thread on Dylan's shoulder and smoothed the spot with weathered hands, gnarled fingers accustomed to hard work and no shortcuts.

"Your father did something for you today that he thought needed doing. He understands that he is too sad to raise you proper right now, and he knows how important..."

When Sam had lived here too, after David disappeared, Dylan felt like he lived in the front parlor of a funeral home. He had been to one once, for Mrs. O'Driscoll down the block. He remembered the way people nodded very somber, faces set and heads slowly shaking, edged up on the front of their chairs. If they spoke standing, they stood close, voices hushed like church.

Dylan sensed immense sorrow about the past, all the important stuff never spoken. It had to do with his brother David being gone. He never did seem like an older brother. He just stayed two years old. Dylan stared ahead, feeling the strong hand close tight on his shoulder, and hearing the quiet catch in her voice.

"...how important it is to have someone to care for you. So he and I went to the courthouse today to make sure everybody knows that for now, you are in *my* care. You will always be safe here. Do you understand, Dylan?"

"Yes'm. Does that mean he's not my dad anymore?" He turned on the stoop, breath clutched, knees drawn up and pressed to his chest.

"Come closer. Keep your Nana warm, child. Your daddy will always be your daddy, 'til the day you die. Lots of things change in this world. Some of the change makes no sense if you muddle it a hundred lifetimes. But one thing can't ever change—Sam Paxton is your daddy. Will be. Always."

Nana squeezed him tight to her side, kissing him atop his head. "Time for another trim, already," she mused, tousling his thick brown crew cut hair. He made a face.

"Today was just to make sure everybody knows, for now, I am your guardian."

"Like an angel?" Dylan slipped under Nana's arm, and watched a squirrel clamber across a snow-flecked branch in the front elm.

Nana's mouth formed a happy *Oh*, her eyes shining.

"Yes, young Master Paxton. Like an angel. Your guardian angel. We will make do. And we sure do hope," she said, now talking to the top branches of the naked elm, "that someday soon my son will be fit to be a father again. Make him well, if you're awake up there, would you please?"

Nana and Dylan rose, turning to the door. She kept her eyes aloft for another moment. "Seems like you owe him that much," she muttered.

"Sorry?"

Nana looked down at her grandson.

"Let's go get us some cocoa, and maybe a cookie for you. And a biscuit for that silly dog."

3 / The Hobbitmobile

Crane Ridge, Maryland 1966

The light from the midsummer sun shimmered off a cloud of gnats darting above the sparkling coffee-tinted river. The far bank looked like a living thing, a vivid emerald garden draped in a pulsing silver veil. Here, where the river skirted the north edge of Crane Ridge, it ran wide and slow, gurgling over polished rocks that poked close to the surface. Nana called this time the *depths of summer*, when butterflies and fireflies enjoyed their brief and spectacular reign, and the rich tang of a trimmed lawn was the sweetest smell under heaven.

A noise like a stick drawn along a picket fence disturbed the soft buzzing and the river's murmur. Twelve-year-old Dylan whirled, along with his friend Billy Bergin. Ryan Daggert arced over the crest of the slope beside Mr. Thompson's house, pumping his ten speed in low gear. The playing card clipped to the frame of the Schwinn Continental thrummed like a hummingbird on strong coffee. Ryan brushed close around the trunk of the massive oak that shaded half an acre of the backyard in the afternoon sun.

Buster, startled from his lazy recline, leapt up woofing. Near the bottom of the hill, Ryan leaned the bike in a slow, sideways slide, his uphill Chuck Taylor All-Star tennis shoe scuffing a long rut in the trimmed lawn. In a grind of torn grass, Ryan lay the bike down at Billy's feet and stepped out over the frame. He punched his glasses up the bridge of his nose and smoothed his hair back in a single sweep Dylan always admired, though he'd sooner give up his *Frank Howard* card than admit it looked cool. It was Ryan's trademark *bike dismount and hair rake*, doubtless practiced for hours on some quiet back lane.

"You're gonna land in the middle of the river one of these times," Billy whooped. Laughing, he pushed at Dylan, who snorted, "Idiot! You scare all the fish with that god-awful racket!"

Billy looked down at his hands, and mimed flipping over a judging card. "Russian judge says four point five, outuff a possible ten," he said with a guttural accent.

Ryan ignored Billy, and addressed the meandering river.

"My partner's Bill Gannon. My name's Friday," Ryan deadpanned. "We were working bunko out of Nash Street one steamy afternoon, when a call came in, claiming one Dylan Paxton and one Billy Bergin couldn't steal a fish from the whole Wicomico, even with the aid of dynamite."

"You know, Ryan, that thing on the bottom of your bike frame? It's called a kickstand. It's so you don't have to be laying it down like that everywhere you go." Billy checked his bloodworm bait, and flicked it back out into the sluggish current.

"For the ninety-fourth time, if I lay it down, I don't have to worry about some yokel bumping it over and scratching the paint."

Dylan rolled his eyes. Ryan's bike was caked with dried mud. Clods of earth sporting brown grass clung to the axles on the "lay-down" side. Lisa Haggerty called the bike *The Hobbitmobile,* because she said it looked like produce from Frodo's garden.

Billy and Dylan both rode three-speed stingrays, the bike of choice for most of the sixth-grade class at Crane Ridge Elementary. But Ryan loved his ten speed. It was fast, though not much good for the bike-jumps down by the quarry.

Ryan had tried "catching air" exactly twice over the bridge culvert and out into the woods behind the school. Both times Ryan had spent the afternoon in the infirmary. Mrs. Vactor warned him if he tried to jump the culvert again, she would confiscate the bike. Dylan suspected Ryan was glad of the excuse not to break his neck.

"Seriously, kids. Are you using those minnows on that string as bait?" Ryan chewed a piece of grass. "I mean, you got a knife small enough to clean those infants?"

"Funny yuck yuck," Dylan grinned.

"You going over to the school later, play some catch or Five Hundred or something?" Billy flicked his rod, glancing at Dylan.

"I guess. I'll see if James wants to come over too."

"Ask him if you can bring his glove, if he doesn't come with you." Ryan and James were both left-handed, and James had the only lefthander's glove. Ryan dug a stone from the caked bank and side-armed it skipping across the water.

"Hey! You just scared the last damn fish away!" Billy glared at Ryan. A bell tolled richly in the afternoon haze.

"Suppertime already?" Billy turned to Dylan.

"Too early," Dylan answered, puzzled.

The bell tinged again. "Uh oh. Nana rang twice," Ryan said, smiling. "What's that mean?"

Dylan's brow furrowed, and he slipped the limp worm off his hook and flicked it in the water. He clipped his hook onto his reel bar, and hefted his small tackle box.

"Two bell peals means come quick," Dylan answered curtly. "See you guys up at school. Come on, Buster." Dylan started up across Mr. Thompson's yard toward Nash Street.

His brother James was sitting astride the top step of the porch, his arm resting on one bent knee. A lemonade glass dangled from his fingers. Buster loped up the steps, paced off a circle, and flopped down.

"Come set a spell, Dylan." Nana patted the glider at her side.

Dylan set his fishing rod against the railing and his tackle box on the gray porch deck. He sat on the glider next to his grandmother, and smiled at the pitcher of lemonade sweating on the upturned milk crate. She poured him a glass. Buster lifted his head from his paws for a fraction before returning to dreams of bounding rabbits.

"Fishing good today?" Nana handed a glass to him, and he sipped, nodding yes.

"You let Billy take them all home again?"

"You know I hate to clean those things." Billy was the third of seven children. Mr. Bergin drove trucks when Eastern Shore produce was moving, and drank when it wasn't, so the fish would be welcome at the Bergin table. And Dylan really *hated* cleaning them. But he liked fishing with Billy.

Nana smiled briefly, looking from one boy to the other. James and Dylan might both be called serious boys. James was lean, despite his round face. Dylan was stockier with wide, swimmer's shoulders. Most people, if they saw Dylan and James together, would see the resemblance. They both had crew cuts over high, intelligent foreheads, and the ruddy rounded cheeks of their Gaelic Northwest Ireland ancestors. There was a trace of those fierce, fragile island people in their deep-set, dark brown eyes. They were both good students, and avid readers, though James had not adjusted well to high school. They shared a devotion to boy's mystery and detective stories. One or the other was likely to receive a *Hardy Boys* mystery, or *Tom Swift*, or *Encyclopedia Brown* book for their birthday, and it was not long before both had read it. The books often came in the mail a day or two before their birthdays, from their mom.

They liked to argue about the stories they read. "Anyone would know she was the murderer," James might say, or point out a twist in the story as being too farfetched. "Tom Swift wouldn't be all that great without his father's money." Dylan liked heroes, and James liked attacking them. Dylan liked the way James challenged him, Nana could tell, and the brothers were close, despite the difference in their ages. But sometimes James could be harsh.

"Nobody's all good," he would say to Dylan. "The sooner you get that straight," he'd continue, tapping the side of his head lightly, "the easier it'll be on you."

Nana sighed. James and Dylan were sipping their drinks, watching her.

"Boys, I have some hard news." Nana set down her glass with care. "I don't know how to tell you in pieces, so I am just gonna tell you. Your mother—I guess she was real sick." She placed a hand on Dylan's arm. "I didn't know. Even your father-" she glanced at James, pausing to catch her breath. ""Your father didn't know until just a little bit-"

Nana gulped at her lemonade, her look a cross between anger and frustration. "She was real sick, and now…she is in a better place. Your momma has passed."

A sound like an owl screech escaped James, and he turned his back on them, rigid on the top step, facing down the sidewalk.

Nana turned to Dylan. He looked dumbly at his glass. He had an idea he was supposed to be sad. He guessed he might be a little. He nodded, as if he understood. But he didn't.

Nana was funny about pictures. She kept photos of her family in the front room–ancient black and whites of smiling young people, most dead now. Dylan's father was in a couple of the pictures, along with Sam's three older brothers, and Nana, and Nana's own husband, Walt Paxton. But there were no pictures of Dylan's mother.

In a drawer in the sewing room were several of Maureen, smiling and holding James. There were also a couple of Maureen posed with James, David, and Sam. She was thin, with bobbed light brown hair, much like his, thick and well-mannered. The light had done a funny thing in the pictures. He couldn't make out her eyes. That was pretty much how he pictured her. A woman in her twenties, before and after David disappeared, with a dark blur under her bangs where her eyes must be.

Each year, James and he would receive a gift from her on their birthdays, along with a short note. Nana always said the same thing— "This came for you."—and Dylan had followed his brother's habit of opening the gift and note in private. Once he had asked James about the notes he got, and James had replied, "It's always the same stupid 'How are you? Miss you. Hope you like the book.'" James had never mentioned the notes, but Dylan had once seen the stack of them at the bottom of a desk drawer under a cigar box.

No one ever said much about Maureen's leaving, and David's disappearance. Nana once, maybe fearing that Dylan would blame himself for his mother's departure, tried to explain. But her words sounded like she was at the far end of a tunnel. He couldn't make them into something he cared about.

James mumbled something, his back still to them.

"Sorry, son?" Nana responded.

"Where is mom—where was she?"

"Your mom was somewhere around Houston, Texas. I got a call from your father, from California. She got real sick, and she talked to your dad just days before she died. Then another man called your dad to say yes, Maureen Paxton had passed. She was only 39 years old."

Nana rocked, her face clouded. Dylan watched his grandmother out of the corner of his eye. For a second, she looked much older, like her neck had collapsed into her shoulders, and she was shrinking like the evil witch in the Wizard of Oz. He turned to her, startled, and she was normal again.

A puzzled look crossed over her face. "She told your father she was sorry and wrong. Over and over. I think it really helped him. He sounds—so different now. I guess she finally healed up enough to see how other people must hurt about it too."

This last elicited a bitter snort from James.

Nana patted Dylan's hand. "I am sorry too. Sorry for her short, sad life. But she did accomplish some mighty good work."

"She did? Like what?" James turned for an instant. His face was twisted and deep red. Dylan swung his legs to coax the glider to move, and drained his glass.

"Why, she made you of course." Nana smiled, and bent to pour them more lemonade.

Nana had another piece of news.

"Your dad is coming home."

4 / Superman's Rocket

Seasons changed, but James's life was still. In the place where his mother used to live, James had draped a dark shroud. Not a lifeless, droopy thing, but a breathing, expectant shadow. It pulsed with anger and hurt, and he stoked it like a furnace. For James, the world was forever tilted since that April morning.

"My bike fell over. My bike fell over. Let me go. My bike fell over." He chanted in a cadence to distract his father, who already was traveling to a different place on a ride without controls that was picking up speed.

Mrs. Somers had been only too glad to let his dad use her phone. She'd set James down on her porch glider, trying to calm him. He remembered not breathing, and the hiccoughing terror, and snot pouring down his chin. James hadn't understood what was wrong. But he sensed his father fleeing after the baby, and the screeching was his own voice. It lasted until his air was gone, then a viscous sucking. Dying. First his mother, waving goodbye, smiling, to live at *bus*. Then David. How did he climb from the buggy? And his father, eyes empty, licking the lips in a hollowed face. The sound of the sirens, piercing between his cries. His father stumbling off the porch and back across the street to stand beside the carriage.

His father seemed to shred like Superman's rocket from Krypton. Pieces of his dad flaming up in his own wake, ripping away. Two police cars arrived together. The first pulled up alongside his father, the second nosed to the bumper of the first. Four police heaved out of the cars, stepping slowly toward his dad, glancing down the empty street.

"You Mr. Paxton?" That's how it started. Before his father stopped answering questions, he was a broken and much older man, a pebble that finally dropped, spent and gray, to the surface of the earth. Superman blasted to tiny bits.

His mother never looked at him again, not directly, not after David left. He understood David had been taken. Then he was furious at David for getting lost when James was naughty. David's leaving made his mother leave, and then his father. James wanted to go where they'd gone, but he couldn't find the way. Nana wanted to make him hers, and that would've been all right. But his father wanted it too, and James simply couldn't bear it. He'd refused to leave his father, even when his father left him.

Then there was another baby, and he was not alone. But he wanted his mother to come back, and his father to come back, so they would not be mad at him anymore. He waited, and he tended the anger and hurt that kept him from being ripped apart too.

5 / Tale of a Fateful Trip

Dylan picked his path up the sidewalk, avoiding the cracks. Lightning-bolt fissures caused by tree roots, shifting ground, freezing and thawing water. Dylan paced the same route daily. Patterns kept the world aright. He stopped and gazed up at the neat exterior of Nana's home. The dormers looked like the hooded eyes of a friendly troll. The roofline of the porch was the troll's crooked smile. All appeared normal, but there was a rumbling disquiet. He did not want to go in.

His father had arrived Monday. Today was Thursday, when Nana went shopping with Mr. Thompson down to the A&P. It was the day when Dylan and James and Billy, and sometimes Ryan and Tink, watched *Gilligan's Island* at four o'clock. But that was before. What would happen today?

Before his father had arrived, Nana had told him "it" would take time. Dylan wanted to ask her what "it" was. What she had *not* said also made him uneasy. Nana didn't say, "He's coming to visit," or "He's coming to see you." Dylan knew that Sam had lived here as a boy, and remembered Sam being here for a time after he and Maureen stopped being married. So this had been his home once. But was he coming home to stay?

When Sam left, Dylan wondered where he had gone, and why, and if he was coming back. No one had told him, maybe because nobody knew. James was the only one who asked questions. But he asked with a boy's wounded snarl, as if he already knew the answers. After a while, James would say, "Good riddance the bastard," by way of opening and closing the book on his dad, anytime Dylan mentioned him. For his part,

Dylan was sad, but he noticed that kids at school didn't bother James about it the way they did Dylan.

"Your mother *and* father just *left* you. What kind of parents just move away without you?" "With Dylan, his mom warn't willin'. "

When he cried to James about the teasing, his brother said, "Act like it doesn't matter. Kids'll get bored, and find someone else to pick on about something else." He wasn't as good at it as James was.

Dylan squared his shoulders and strode up to the front steps. His father nodded at him through the open window to the right of the door. Dylan gave a little wave and hopped the steps, two at a time.

"Hi. Um."

"Hi. Your brother's upstairs."

Dylan slipped his book bag off his shoulder. He patted Buster, who stood in greeting, tail wagging, then plopped back down sighing on the cool porch deck.

His father cleared his throat. "Mother—Nana—is off to the store with Mr. Thompson. She was all morning in the back yard, still trying to call forth the dead. Rhododendrons, I mean."

Dylan nodded, looked back at the street. "Billy and a couple others usually come over to watch the TV on Thursdays. With James and me."

"Nana mentioned you boys get together. I'll be out of your way." Sam slid his chair back as Dylan entered the front room. Dylan raised a hand. "It won't be till four o'clock."

Sam nodded, settling back down. Dylan started to thank his father, but Sam's expression closed. It was as if the effort to talk had taxed him.

Dylan moved down the hall and clunked up the stairs to his room. He greeted his brother with a nod, then laid his book bag atop his desk and opened it.

James and Dylan shared the upstairs. Nana would not tolerate anyone calling it the *attic*. The room was bisected by the stairwell, which was gated with a balustrade on three sides. Dylan pulled his books from his bag and glanced out the window. Both dormer windows looked out over Nash Street and Mr. Thompson's house across the way, with a glimpse of the river beyond. He remembered fishing with his father and James at the foot of the Thompson property, before his father left to head west.

After Sam moved out, Nana reared them with just enough discipline—vinegar, she called it—that they understood that practice and application would yield results. She was not harsh in their upbringing. Lately though, she seemed at a loss in coping with James. It had gotten more pronounced since they knew Sam was coming home. He was increasingly withdrawn and often would disappear at all hours, returning with no explanation.

Billy clutched the throw pillow and rolled over, his knees drawn to his chest. "Tell me Ginger isn't such a *babe*," he moaned. Billy made *babe* a three-syllable word.

Ryan craned to peek out the front window. Satisfied that the porch was deserted, he hunched down, his expression serious. "Lisa Haggerty told me the Professor doesn't *like* girls. *That's* why he never fools around with Ginger."

Dylan considered this. Lisa was in their class, but she knew more than he and his friends did about grownups. She knew that Jackie Gleason made all the girls who wanted to dance on his TV show strip for him in a private room. She whispered this fact to him one day on the jungle gym at recess.

"Well, I feel sorry for him then, the jerk." James swung his feet down on the floor. "If I was on a deserted island with Ginger and Mary Ann, first thing I would say is *"Our clothes are gonna fall apart sooner or later anyway, so let's just wear coconuts!"* He laughed, heading down the hall. Dylan heard the door to the stairs open and close.

"Maybe if you're really smart like the professor, there's no room left in your head for sex stuff." Ryan was talking to the TV scrolling the *Gilligan's Island* closing credits.

Dylan made a face at Ryan from his perch on the sofa. The subject of sex always made him feel stupid. He was starting to feel like he wanted to know much more than he did.

"Well that's a bite." Billy flicked his ball glove in the air end over end. It bounced from his outstretched fingers and tumbled to the oval carpet. Billy lunged to grab it. "So if you aren't real smart, then you'll think more about sex, and have *more* impure thoughts, and end up with even *more* penance. What's fair about *that?*"

"Well, one thing's for sure," Ryan said, heading for the front door. "I bet the Professor always eats fish on Friday."

6 / James

James stared at the picture he'd taken from his drawer. This was never going to work. Even if Anne continued to like him, her father would never let her date a boy like James. When he saw *Two Little Savages* under her arm, he should have kept his mouth shut. But it had been one of his favorite books—ironic, since his father left it behind when he headed west, perhaps to start a new family he could ruin. Turns out she was reading it for the second time.

"I think it's dumb that girls can't be boy scouts," she'd said to him at the checkout desk. The librarian had smiled, and Anne glared at her. "Everyone knows boys have all the fun," she'd said, her eyes glittering. Though Anne had a ready smile, James was drawn to her fire. Lots of girls had liked him—they joked in high school that he was the JD of WiCo High. He'd seen James Dean in a movie, and didn't think they looked at all alike. James had not met a girl who interested him until Anne. She knew what she wanted. And, at least for now, she wanted to be with James.

For all his mystique, James had no skill with girls. His friends assumed that because girls liked him, he must be experienced. He was aloof, and some girls took that as a dare. Mostly though, he just wanted to be left alone. Until Anne. James wasn't worried about Anne's feelings for him, but he didn't trust his feelings for her. *They* could be dangerous. He could stand being hurt. He was not sure he could tolerate her leaving, if he let her get close to him.

She had given him this picture of her at their last meeting, in the library. "Something to keep the rats at bay," she'd smiled. He'd fingered it, feeling her eyes on his face. Anne was beautiful. In the picture she was standing next to an elm. She wore shorts and a sleeveless blouse, and her light brown hair was pulled back from her face, her hands clasped in front. Her gaze was steady and sure, her smile confident. He could feel himself falling into her eyes. When he looked up from the picture, those same eyes gazed straight into his. He couldn't trust himself to speak. Finally she giggled and turned away.

Now, in the quiet of his room, he mulled the changes in his life. His father had returned, but he was different somehow. He didn't drink, for one thing. It didn't make James hate him any less. James had watched his father fade, beginning with the clear morning on Washington Street. No one else had seemed to notice, in all the ruckus of David's disappearance. But James had watched in anguish as his father grew fainter, like the dot on the TV screen after it's turned off. When Nana had asked him about the guardianship, he'd brushed it off the way he'd shrug about what to do with his father's old hat. *No difference to me.*

James had steeled himself to be cruel to his father in return for Sam's coming back. But Anne had happened, and it was hard to remain focused on his anger. Instead, his reaction to his father had been more of a polite indifference. A distraction. He was delighted and worried with Anne's attention. Was this the way life worked? Good and bad things happened together? First David disappearing, then his mother leaving— those were bad. Because of his confused feelings for his father, he was actually glad when Sam left. Since that period, he had tried to find his own peace with just Nana and Dylan for his family.

Father Mullenix down at the church had assured him, when his mother left, "Time... takes time." He'd been right, of course. James liked the quiet, confident priest, who always seemed to be waiting when James would create an excuse to visit. Over time, James became a fixture at the church during the week, doing odd chores around the rectory and grounds. But never on Sunday. He resisted Father's coaxing to come to mass, and he respected the priest for not pushing it.

James liked the older priest and the times they sat and talked passed naturally. At first, he'd expected Father to ask about his dad, or to lecture him about giving his dad a break. But the priest hadn't mentioned Sam. He had thought about talking to Father about Anne, and his concerns about Anne's father. But Anne was Methodist, and he was sure that would be the end of it as far as the priest was concerned.

James slipped the picture back in its hiding place at the sound of Dylan on the stairs. Time for baseball.

7 / Safe Passage

Sam didn't talk much to Dylan, and even less to James. He seemed tentative, as if a phrase could somehow go off like a bomb. But he did talk to Nana, and to Dylan's surprise, his father and Mr. Thompson seemed to be renewing an old friendship.

When Dylan's dad returned, Mr. Thompson had come over to welcome him. Dylan at first thought it was about the car in the garage. Mr. Thompson had assured Sam he could move the Dodge across the street to his own house. Sam had allowed as how there was no need for a change just because he was here.

It was funny to Dylan how two quiet people could become friends, when that didn't seem to happen with two loud people. Mr. Thompson never said much to Dylan, but he always had a way of making Dylan feel like he was listening when Dylan spoke. Maybe that was the reason Sam too felt comfortable with Mr. Thompson.

Dylan would sit on the porch and watch his father in the company of Mr. Thompson in the driveway, both bent under the hood of Mr. Thompson's car, one or the other with an oily rag and some tool in hand. Or they might be in one front yard or another, gazing with bemusement at a lawnmower in need of attention.

The dad he remembered had been much taller, and more talkative. Of course, the other dad had a way of never getting around to the end of a sentence where the period is put. That dad would blurt, rather than speak, sometimes with wild eyes darting in company with the words. But Dylan also remembered a stretch of time before he finally left, when his father would lapse into silence, and the funeral-home pall would descend on the house. People who did not know him well would wait on him, expecting him to finish a thought. Often they just waited.

Now, Dylan found himself waiting. Would he get along with this other version of his father?

***

Stinger Owens lived on the south side of Crane Ridge. Sam had said once that in just about every town he'd been in, the south side was the bad side, and he wondered why this was so. Dylan had thought of Stinger then. Not that the south side of Crane Ridge was particularly dangerous. But Stinger was. The boy was large, and lumbered rather than walked, but somehow he could move across the school hall with blurring speed to slap an unsuspecting student. He was two years ahead of Dylan, so he was in the junior high.

Stinger's beefy right hand had a heavy ring on it. When he slapped the back of your head, it hurt worst where the ring connected with your skull. The first time Dylan realized that James and Stinger were acquainted was this past summer on a hot afternoon, when Dylan was coming back from the library the long way, rounding the corner by Wilson's Drug Emporium. Stinger had his back to him as Dylan passed, talking to one of his pals, Scooter Morris.

"—Can't take a joke is all. We'll fix him good when—"

Scooter's eyes widened when he saw Dylan.

"Hey, little man! What brings you down to this part of town?"

Dylan slowed, out of range of Stinger.

"Just come from the library. Heading home."

Dylan watched Stinger's eyes. Something about the way Stinger furrowed his brow made Dylan's skin crawl. His sloped white forehead bulged with a fatty thickness, and when it wrinkled, Dylan wondered what seismic effort it required to sort through the range of responses for the appropriate one.

Stinger's forehead relaxed. He stepped toward Dylan. "Let's see what the bookworm picked up at the library store."

Dylan wondered if Stinger thought a library was like a store because he had never set foot in one. The calm on Stinger's face worried him. He eased along the sidewalk, keeping between Stinger and the open street. He glanced down at the pile of books in his arm, dismissively. "Just some stuff on planes, and a Tom Swift book. You like Tom Swift?"

Stinger paused in his shuffle to consider the question. Dylan wondered if anyone had ever asked Stinger about his literary preferences.

Stinger cocked his head and studied Dylan. "What's it about?"

Dylan gulped. "I can't say I know. I just got it. But I read the first couple pages—" Dylan tried to remember what he'd read, but couldn't.

"Why don't you let us help you carry some of them?" Scooter eased off the wall toward Dylan.

"Guys, look, I gotta get home now, or Nana'll raise a ruckus."

"I guess when you got no real mom and dad, you can't afford to piss off the people that'll have you." Scooter grinned.

Stinger swung his pumpkin head around, and grinned at Scooter. "Good one."

Dylan took advantage of the distraction to turn on his heels, preparing to start running. Instead, he came face to face with his brother. Dylan shrugged his books under his arm, and ran a shaking hand under his nose.

"What's up, Dylan?" James smiled, his eyes unreadable. Dylan sensed faint disapproval.

"I'm just going home is all." Dylan's own voice sounded plaintive.

Scooter chortled. "We was gonna help Dillie carry his books. Who could read all that in a year?" Stinger reached out and Dylan backed away. Dylan noted the sidelong look James gave Scooter.

"Now now, we just want to see what the professor's reading," Stinger said slowly, as if to a child. He reached out again, a smolder in his look.

James casually stepped between Dylan and the two other boys. "You're expected at home, Dylan."

Scooter slipped off the wall, easing down the sidewalk in Dylan's direction. Stinger rubbed his fist in his other hand pondering his response, and then brightened.

"Safe passage will cost you Tom Swift," he said, holding out his hand.

"It's not mine to give you."

"Call it a loan," Scooter volunteered helpfully. Scooter froze as James pressed a hand up to the brick wall, blocking his advance.

"Go on home, Dylan. I'll be along shortly." Dylan nodded and turned, sighing with relief. He hurried down the sidewalk toward Nash Street.

"Stinger, I think James wants to rumble again." Something in Scooter's liquid voice made Dylan turn and stop. James had turned on Stinger, fists clenched, but low, at his sides, and Stinger was stumbling back, hands raised, palms out.

"I just wanted to see the books. What are you in an uproar about? Jeez."

Dylan turned back in the direction of home, and quickened his step.

8 / Note in the Newspaper

Dylan's father stopped Mookey Geiger, the boy delivering the *Daily Times* one morning, and asked to have it delivered to the house. He would scan the paper over breakfast. Nana would not read the paper, but she was fascinated with the items Sam shared with her. Dylan was passing through the dining room to the front door on a crisp and vivid morning, the very air expectant. The hydrangeas burst with blue outside the window. Dylan stopped at his father's side.

"I'm heading for the library this afternoon. Want to come along?"

Sam's face was ashen. He was staring at a single sheet of white paper, apparently from the envelope lying on top of the newspaper. The envelope said simply, *SAM.*

His father was sucking thin breaths, almost like a whistle in reverse. He kept glancing out the window, and then at Dylan. After a moment, Sam made up his mind about something.

"Best you be off, or you'll be late for home room."

"Everything all right?" Dylan followed the man's gaze out the front window. The street was deserted.

"I'm sure it will be. Just a bit of hard news, I'm afraid. Want me to walk you down to the school today?" Sam's eyes looked a bit bloodshot, and he was licking at his lips as he tapped the edge of the refolded note on the envelope.

"Wait. Forgive me boy. I have some things to attend to this morning. See you after school?" Sam wiped his mouth with the back of his hand.

"Sure. Okay."

Dylan went out the door and down the sidewalk. He was almost to the corner when he remembered his father had not answered about the library. He turned back up toward the house. Dylan saw his father trotting across the street toward Mr. Thompson's. Instead of heading up the sidewalk to the door, his father ran across the lawn, heading to the far side of the house—the path used to access the river.

Dylan broke into a run back up Nash Street. He followed the route Sam had taken. His father's footprints were outlined on the light dew in the yard. Dylan hesitated when he reached the corner of the house. His father clearly knew what he was about to do when Dylan left, and Sam had not seen fit to mention anything to him. His curiosity pushing him, Dylan turned the corner.

At first, he saw nothing. But he heard a man breathing hard. Stepping out around the corner of the house, Dylan looked down the hill. Sam was struggling with the end of a rope, which was looped several times around the trunk of the large elm, several feet from the ground. The rope traveled up behind the house on a diagonal. It was drawn taut, like the cord on a bow. A light breeze rolled up from the river. *Buster pooped in Mr. Thompson's yard. Buster never poops over here*, Dylan thought, his nose crinkling.

Dylan trod halfway down the slope, gingerly picking his way to avoid sliding on the slick grass. He stopped, looked up again, and saw Mr. Thompson swinging slightly at the other end of the rope. Dylan froze in shock.

Sam called, "I need a...hatchet, or an ax. A big knife. Hurry boy. And tell Nana to call the police. Mr. Thompson's had an accident."

Dylan understood Mr. Thompson had taken his own life. The image of the rigid form swaying at the end of that rope. The panicked expression on his father's face. When Dylan dashed breathless through Nana's front door, excited and very afraid, Nana looked as confused as he felt.

He'd demanded that she call the police, and then had grabbed her butchering knife from the shelf beneath her butcher block. She set her jaw firmly and stepped in front of him, her hand out, uncompromising. Dylan had started to sputter something and she waved her other hand, palm up, slowly. Dylan understood. He placed the handle of the knife in Nana's palm. She gestured at the chair.

Sitting down, he blurted, "Mr. Thompson's had an accident. He's hanging in a tree out back of his house. Dad said fetch a knife to cut him down and call the police." His voice quavered, but he managed to get it all out.

In the middle of his account, Nana picked up the phone, waited a beat, and said "Melba, it's an emergency. I need to talk to Walt or one of his men." While she waited, Nana cupped her hand over the phone.

"Tell your dad not to touch Mr. Thompson. What's done is done, and the police will want to—"

She paused, listened, and turned away to speak in a lower voice. She still held the knife in her free hand. Dylan sat, waiting. He lifted his hand to his mouth to wipe it. Stuck to his damp fist was a folded piece of paper. He glanced back at Nana, who was fussing with whoever she was talking to, her voice hushed.

Dylan peeled the paper from his fist and laid it back on top of the newspaper, opening it.

May 16, 1967

Sam —

Sorry for putting you in charge. By the time you see this, I will be dead. Unless the paper is late today. But it usually is right on time, that boy is a good one. You can find me at the big oak out back. I will be hanged. If anyone is bothered by it, it can be cut down and hauled away.

If the rest goes right, John Latham will contact you soon. It's a good car. I am glad you came back. You can be proud of your boys. Your mother favors shopping on Thursdays.

Dylan was folding the note back in thirds when Nana turned to hang up the phone. She glanced at the clock, said, "Maybe you can go at lunchtime," and then rested a hand on his shoulder.

Softer she said, "Did you see Mr. Thompson just now?" He nodded. Nana bent to drape an arm around him, and drew his head to her ample middle. She rocked gently for a moment, humming an unfamiliar song.

"I need to go talk to your daddy. Why don't you come sit on the porch?" she bent and looked out the window, then apparently satisfied herself about something. "It is going to be a day around here."

"Okay," Dylan muffled from the folds of her dress. He shifted to rise from the chair, but his grandmother was squeezing him tightly. Dylan looked up. The old woman's eyes were red, her face for a moment all open sadness. Then her jaw hardened and she released him and turned to the door, moving as fast as he had ever seen her move. She flung the screen back and stepped across the porch, not waiting for him to catch the door.

"Sit right there," she gestured at the top step, "where I can see you son. I'll be right back."

A police car pulled up in front of Mr. Thompson's a few minutes later. A single officer spoke into his radio microphone for a moment. Then he hitched himself out of the car, and noticed Dylan as he closed the door. He looked like he was going to ask something, and Dylan pointed at the side of Mr. Thompson's house. The officer tipped his hat and moved quickly on.

Several minutes passed. The officer huffed back to his car, spoke into his microphone, and then went back around the house. Soon another police car arrived, along with an ambulance. By this time, Nana was back. Even though Dylan had had breakfast of sorts, Nana insisted on making him french toast—a rare treat. Nana was carrying Dylan's plate to the table when his father walked in.

He had his jacket draped over his arm, and hung it over the back of his chair in the dining room. Nana said, "Would you like some french toast?" He gave her a puzzled glance.

"Um, I have to go back for just a minute. That poor old soul—" Dylan followed his father's gaze in time to see Nana give a slight shake of her head. Sam fixed his eyes on Dylan.

"Son, are you alright?"

"Sure. Is Mr. Thompson…?"

Sam glanced up at Nana, then back at Dylan. "Mr. Thompson had a kind of an accident, and…" his voice trailed off. His father pulled the envelope with his name on it across the table to himself.

Nana spoke up. "Dylan, Mr. Thompson got hurt real bad. When the doctors came, they couldn't make him better. He's gone to be with God. In heaven. It is a hard thing on such a pretty morning."

They all turned to look out the window. Dylan wondered how anyone could choose to leave the earth on a morning like this. The day's sun was soft on the lawn, the trees, and on the vehicles gathered across the way. The air was so electric, the flashing lights seemed more like a parade stopped on the street, waiting for the majorettes to move along past the review stand. He could practically smell the cotton candy.

After school in their room, Dylan told James all he could remember. James was mad that it had happened just after he'd left that day. Dylan hadn't intended to say anything about the note. But James was so eager to hear every detail. So Dylan told him.

"Dylan, I have to see that note."

"Well, I'm pretty sure he put it someplace safe."

Then James's eyes shone with a new brightness. "I got it! I know how to get him to show us the note."

James rolled off his bed and headed for the stairs. "Let me do *all* the talking," he said. Both boys made their way out toward the porch where their father and Nana were sitting on the glider.

"What would possess a man…?" Sam's voice trailed off.

Nana's high tone suggested anger. "Well, now that is at once a mystery and no kind of secret at all. What *always* possesses men who are perfectly—" Nana stopped mid-sentence when James opened the screen.

Dylan and James settled in their usual spots, James lounging on the rail, one knee resting on it, his back leaning against the modest pillar. Dylan perched on the porch, feet on the top step, braced against the opposite pillar. The four of them sat silent, the only sound the glider tracks squeaking like a protesting seagull.

"Been quite a day," James led off. He almost never talked during the infrequent times he would join them on the porch.

"That it has," his father replied.

"Mr. Thompson was an awful nice man," Dylan said. James nodded.

"He was always good to us," Nana said.

"How did you know what he'd done?" James asked his father.

"How's that?"

"Well, Dylan said that as soon as he left for school this morning, you ran over to Mr. Thompson's. Did he call or something?"

His father looked uneasy. Nana turned to look at Sam. It was clear the question had not occurred to her. The glider squeaked a little faster.

"Somehow he managed to get a note in my newspaper this morning. I guess he figured I'd see it."

"He put a note in your paper? Saying *what?*" This time Nana was asking.

"Well, I don't remember it all. It was short. I guess he said he was dead. He told me where to find him." Sam scratched his chin now, trying to recall.

James turned to face his father. "Can we see it?" Nana leaned forward as if to protect Sam, and rested a hand on his knee. But she didn't say anything. They all waited.

"I don't have it anymore. The police wanted to know how I found him. When I mentioned the note, they asked me to fetch it right away. I gave it to them."

James slumped on the rail, his face a mask of frustration. "What else did it say?" he asked.

"Well, I was just trying to remember. Somebody was going to contact me in a few days, but I can't remember the name. Lannam. Something like that."

James turned again, voice pleading. "Did he say *why* he..." Sam shook his head, looking into the middle distance. "Did he say why *you?*" Again, Sam shook his head. The group settled into a sort of buzzing silence. So many questions, so few answers.

9 / What's in a Name

The evening of Mr. Thompson's funeral, Nana served a Sunday dinner. It was a pleasant change for a Tuesday, which was always baked hot dog and mashed potatoes with melted cheese on top. Tonight, it was roast chicken and baked potatoes, and corn and fresh-baked bread.

James looked around the table. *Looking in our window, you might think we were normal. Mother's probably in the kitchen fetching the butter dish.* He smirked, smoldering.

"What made you decide to come back?" he said, stirring his crushed potato.

His father had been back now since before Thanksgiving. James tried to be gone most of the time.

"Hmmm." It was plain that though James had asked the question, his father was preparing to answer everyone.

"I always *wanted* to come back. At first, when I left, I just thought that even though it'd be hard for you, you'd be a lot better off without me around, because of what I was becoming. Had become."

James rested his fingertips lightly on the edge of the table. He studied the fingers of each hand in turn as they tapped a quiet cadence on the edge of the smooth maple wood.

"So let's see. I lose my brother. Stolen." He glanced up at his father. "And… it makes you feel bad too, and so you leave, because that somehow is better than you staying."

James's eyes locked again on his fingers. His father's eyes were dark swirling pools. James plowed on. "David was your son. He was my brother. I guess because I was a kid, I didn't have the choice of cutting out and drowning my pain."

He could feel his eyes reddening, and the vein throbbing on the side of his head. "You say you left because of David." His mouth set, and he lifted his eyes to stare back at Sam. "But you still had a son, you bastard."

His dad continued to look on James as if his son were describing a football play, or an accident downtown. Outside, a blue jay squawked, chasing the smaller birds off the feeder just beyond the window. James didn't think anyone else noticed.

"How. Do. You. Think. It. Made. Me. Feel." James spit each word in a low growl. Separate and distinct. His own quiet fury made him think of a leg-trapped possum he had seen once on the far side of the river.

"I'm sorry, son." His father's voice was low, as gentle as a mother coaxing her infant to sleep. "There is nothing I can do to change what's passed." Sam dropped his head. "I wish I could, but wishing won't change any of it."

Nana moved to lay a hand on Sam's, but held back when he raised his head, chin firm. "I can only try to do the next right thing." He paused. "When I talked to your mother last, when she was…she asked me if I remembered how it was, back before…" His father's eyes misted and he shook his head, as if trying to rattle the right words loose.

"You boys are entitled to a father. Doesn't mean I'm entitled to be one. But…" He gave a slight smile. "I'm likely the closest you're gonna get. So if you'll have me, I'd like to stay." At these last words, Nana's hand covered her son's, and she patted his lightly.

"Well, don't you think it's a little late for me?" James said. "I could be gone next year." His tone had softened a fraction.

"We are free to start over again, anytime we like. Maybe time isn't all there is." Sam shifted in his chair, leaning forward over the table. He continued: "We all have had some hard lessons. Thing is, maybe we learned some things that can help each other. Maybe we need each other some."

Sam looked out the window at the sound of the ice cream truck crawling down Nash Street, Buster tailing it in joyous pursuit.

"I want to tell you a little about your mother, too. Some things you don't know." His father somehow knew better than to move toward

James, who had quiet tears rolling down his face.

"Your mother was a big James Brown fan. The colored singer? His voice would just get her swooning." His mouth curled in a small smile, remembering. "She always said she just liked the name. I always told her I didn't believe her."

"So who named me?" Dylan asked.

"Ah, Dylan was my idea," His father replied, smiling. "Do you recall," he asked Nana, "How Mo fought me on that one?" Nana nodded.

"Mo?" Dylan asked.

"Maureen. Your mother. I called her Mo. No one else was allowed to. She was not big for nicknames." His father was more at ease than James ever remembered seeing him. Funny, considering how the talk had started. James knew there were tough things, not yet discussed.

"For reasons that escape me now, I was a fan of the poet Dylan Thomas. Seems like I used to understand his poems, and now I don't anymore. He was quite a drinker too, in his day. I still like the name, though."

"He's dead?" Dylan asked.

"I'm afraid so. He was not yet forty. The booze I think got him."

James stared hard at his father. "If drinking made him die, didn't you think about that when you drank?"

"I didn't think about the dying part, though I did think the way he drank was sort of...tragic and heroic, all in one." Sam looked down at the table's surface, rubbing his jaw. "It's a little hard to say. In the beginning, I drank so I would understand his poetry. I thought it was the secret elixir of the gods."

"Who named David?" James asked quietly.

Sam pursed his lips, watching his own fingers tap the table in cadence. Maybe it was like the way Dylan avoided the sidewalk cracks. Patterns that gave assurance. Then it struck James. Sam tapped just the same way he did.

"The name *David* was your mother's all the way," he said to the middle of the table. "Don't know where it came from, really." Nana set a tray service down in the center of the table. It held two cups for coffee and a small pot, and two tall glasses of lemonade, along with a plate of

Oreos. His father ran a hand along the side of his head, and then sniffed a bit.

"So David it was." He leaned the chair back on its two back legs, balancing with his knees on the side of the table. Dylan waited for the reproof from Nana—*four legs on the floor, that's why they give a chair four legs, for the floor*—but she sat quietly, sipping at her cup.

"I kind of think your mom always wanted a girl. Not instead of either of you," he hastened to say. "I just think probably every mother wants a little girl. Is that so?" He raised his face to Nana.

"I was happy enough with you," she said shortly. "Of course," she sighed, as she poured a half cup of coffee, "I suppose it would've been nice to dress up a wee little lass. I never did hear that woman mention wanting a girl, though." There was a disapproving edge to her comment, and she seemed to sense it.

"Oh, she spoiled you boys something awful." She smiled, amending. "I thought that was a grandmother's solemn job." She winked at Sam.

"As I recall, you did a fair amount of spoiling on your own," he said.

"Not after mommy left," James said, without malice. "You got a lot stricter with us when we came to live here."

"So what do you boys remember?" Sam asked. Dylan knew he was referring to Maureen.

James looked at Sam, shrugging. "I remember when it was just me and David, how she loved to play with us. It was almost like having a big sister sometimes." He looked at Dylan. "She used to take us on walks around the block, with other ladies from the neighborhood, and their kids. She never yelled and hollered like the other moms would."

"I remember her smoking, us sitting in the kitchen mornings," said Dylan.

"Yeah, I remember that, now that you say it. She smoked a lot." James shrugged. "I remember she didn't talk very much. Not like Nana." He glanced over at Nana. 'I don't mean you talk too much. I mean the *way* you talk to me. Mom didn't seem to…care." He had a feeling like he was rolling in a drum. The floor didn't seem as solid as it had earlier.

Nana looked uncomfortable. "Losing David seemed to just drain the heart of your mother. I don't know how else to say it. She went into a kind of shock that she never came out of."

Sam laid his hands on the table. "And I was no help. None at all. When David first disappeared, things went crazy. Not just with us. With the whole town of Berlin. There was this...panic. Understandable. Nothing like that had ever happened in these parts."

Sam's face clouded at the memory. "Every moment that went by cut our chances of finding him. Maureen needed to care for you," Sam raised his eyes to James, "and so she was alone. All alone, while the rest of us were out looking. I had the search to distract me."

"Distract you from what?" James asked.

"The pain. It was unimaginable, worse than I would ever have guessed. Wanting like Jesus—sorry, mother—wanting 'til you almost bled, to turn back the clock. To choose over again."

His father rubbed at the slight stubble on his chin. He seemed to be recounting the sad story of a stranger, pitiful and mystifying.

"But I was going through the motions. From the beginning, I knew he'd been taken, and whoever ran with him was not going to stop running for a long time. Berlin was too small a town for it to be anyone who lived there."

He sighed. "The town was just so...enraged. And scared. Everyone felt so violated. They needed for it to be...fixed, and there was just no fixing it."

Sam looked out the window, recalling a time seared in his memory. "By the time I came back home to pick up the pieces, your mother and I were complete strangers. No arguments, no tears. She just walked out and headed west. I can't blame her. I hope you don't either, though it must be hard to understand."

James snorted, but didn't speak. In the gathering dusk outside the window, an owl hooted a mournful question, over and over.

***

A week or so after Mr. Thompson's funeral, Dylan and James walked up the sidewalk from a baseball game in the waning evening. Their father was sitting with Nana on the porch.

"Boys, supper's in just a few minutes," Nana said. Then she glanced at Sam.

"I was hoping I could hold you up a second to tell you some news." Sam spoke to James, his tone a question. He seemed to be steeling himself for James to march inside. But his oldest son rested his hands on his hips.

"Sure. Let's hear it. What's up?"

"I have some things to tell you. It may come as a surprise, some of it. It sure did to me, anyway."

"Is this gonna be bad?" James sighed, slumping in his chair.

"Well, I don't think so," Sam replied, "But it is a little sudden. I went down to see a lawyer today. The one Mr. Thompson mentioned in his note. Seems that Mr. Thompson wanted us to have some things."

Nana gasped, covered her mouth, and glanced across the street. She dropped her hand and shook her head as if she'd spoken out of turn. Sam paused, bemused. She bit her lip and waved a hand in front of her face.

"What kind of things?" James asked.

Sam scratched his chin. "Well, his car for one. He wanted us to have his car."

"My goodness," Nana said in a hushed tone. "What a generous thing."

"There's more. He left us his house."

James whistled. "Say, what do you mean he left it to *us*?"

Sam spoke as he studied the dark house across the street. "Mr. Thompson left a will, and in it, he left the car and the house to me. But he was pretty clear that it was for the use of us all."

"The car's cool, but we already have a house." James said. He sighed impatiently. "Are we moving across the street? What do we need a house for?"

"He intended for me to sell it, I guess." Sam shook his head slightly. "Shouldn't say I'm guessing. Elmore—that's Mr. Thompson—was quite plain on that point."

James listened in amazement. Mr. Thompson was just the friendly old man who lived across the street, until a month ago. Then he had become somebody they'd never really known. And now, he was back in their lives.

His father looked again at James. "Well, there you have it. You don't have to decide anything now. But I know you're graduating this year. If you want to try college, we can help with at least some of it. If we can sell the house, of course. But I'm sure somebody will want to buy it."

James looked down, his forehead creased. "Um, that's something, alright. I'll have to think it over. College wasn't part of my plan. Do I have to use the money for that?"

Sam looked at James. "What were you thinking you might want to do with it?"

"Well, lots of the guys have cars. I don't need something new. But I could work at the Dash-n-Go for a hundred years and still not be able to afford much. Some money for a car would help."

"So you're going to sell his house?" Dylan asked.

"I am," said his father. "I have an appointment with a realtor fella this week. While you boys were in school the other day, I met with Mr. Latham over at the house. It seems to need very little. Mr. Thompson kept it pretty much up to snuff." Sam looked out the window as he talked, gazing across at the house. "Mr. Latham did suggest I have some painting done, and take the old wallpaper down. He said the realtor would know best in that regard. I'll probably do it myself, if it comes to that kind of thing. I used to be fairly handy with a paint brush."

James saw a look pass between his father and grandmother. Did adults really think they were so clever that no one noticed them?

"Well, boys," his father started. "I have one other bit of news. I've been doing some talking with folks around here about what I might do with myself. Fact is, I talked to Elmore—Mr. Thompson—about it a few times."

James and Dylan glanced at each other, and Sam continued. "I'm pretty good with cars, I guess. It's what I did when I was in California, and I kinda got used to it." Sam hesitated and then plunged on. "With some of the money from the sale of the house, I could start my own garage. Thing is, we're a little off the beaten path here to take advantage of traffic to the beach." He looked up at Nana as he chewed his lower lip, but she was bustling around the table, wiping it clean. "Somebody suggested I consider Virginia. There's a new bypass opening up soon near Richmond, to skirt people around the downtown area."

James nodded slowly, trying to follow.

Sam laid his hands on the table. "This is just in the talking stage. We haven't even put Mr. Thompson's place on the market yet. And truly, I don't feel I have the right to come in here now and tell anybody what they ought to do."

James's head snapped up. He shot a look at Dylan, but his brother's face was unreadable.

"It got me thinking a new highway might be a good place to open up a service station. I wanted to get an idea of whether you'd be open to a move yourselves. To Richmond."

James turned around to catch Nana's eye. She had risen to stand in the doorway.

"Whatever you boys decide is best, I'll go along. If I'm invited, that is." She smiled at his father, and James sensed this wasn't the first time Nana had heard about the possibility of moving.

James had thought Nana would object to this whole discussion. But as she stood there, she was the image of tranquility. James was confused. Was this all about Mr. Thompson's gift, or Sam coming home? Or his mother's passing?

His father brushed his hair back along his temples, a habit he had whenever he was mulling something over. "Nana, you wouldn't mind leaving this old house? Just pulling up stakes and having to start all over?" His gaze swept over the boys, as he addressed his mother, still standing in the kitchen door. "You sure you're okay with this?"

Nana's eyes sparkled. "I think it might be nice."

James had been staring at his father for the last several minutes, and felt oddly like he was seeing him for the first time. Sam's eyes dropped to lock softly on James. "Well, boy. What do *you* think?"

The porch felt fluid to James, the chair not solid, the railing a prop that could vanish if he let go. His life was mutating at a giddy pace, and he felt dizzy with the speed of it.

"I guess it might be okay," he heard himself say. He instantly felt betrayed at his own hand, but his life was veering in a direction he felt powerless to stop.

***

Later in their room James dropped into his bed, and grabbed *The Sinister Signpost* from the Hardy Boys mystery series. He had just finished *Treasure Island,* and handed it over to Dylan. "See if you can find the hero buried in this book."

He tried to focus on the words on the page, but they made no sense. He rose and went to the bathroom. Running water in the sink, he squeezed toothpaste over the bristles of his brush. James looked in the mirror and saw a dismal dread in the eyes staring back. His life was here in Crane Ridge. But it had been in an uproar since his father came back. Things were a lot less confusing when Sam wasn't around. Calmer. He wasn't calm at all now. He flicked the light out and made his way back down the hall. Tomorrow, he decided, he would talk to Anne.

10 / House of Secrets

The Saturday morning looked bright outside Dylan's window, but he had a grayness in his head that wouldn't shake loose. Things had been good with just Nana, James, and him. Then his dad came home. Now Mr. Thompson was dead and they might be moving away. How many more Saturday mornings would he get to sleep in, in this bed, in his room?

Dylan lifted his arms slowly over his head and stared at the ceiling. His ceiling. Directly above him, his latest craft, the Cessna 150, hung by a thin piece of sewing thread, angled in a shallow descent. He and his dad had collaborated on the 150. Dylan had never bothered to put on the little decals that came with the model airplane kit. He thought they just made the models look cheap. Like they were store-bought, made-in-Japan.

But when Dylan was nearly complete with the 150, his father had appeared at the foot of the stairs to Dylan's bedroom with several small bottles of modeling paints and a couple of small brushes. Dylan waved Sam up the steep stairs.

"Thought you might want to jazz up the fuselage a little," his dad had said, handing Dylan the paints and brushes. "Never seen one fly overhead that had quite that dry-putty look to it."

Dylan had held up one of the small glass bottles, inspecting it with a dubious expression. "Think you might be able to give me a hand?"

Almost as if this recollection had summoned Sam, there was a light tap at the door. Dylan called, "Come ahead." His father clumped up the stairs and took a seat at Dylan's desk.

"Happy Fourth of July, son." His father glanced over to James's bed, and Dylan had a feeling there was another reason Sam had wanted to come up.

"Your brother out and about already?"

"I guess he is."

Sam rubbed his chin. "You know what time he left out of here this morning?"

"I didn't hear him leave. So, no."

It was not unusual for James to be gone when Dylan woke up. But it was just a week or so ago that Dylan started out of sleep at some noise, in time to see James slipping out the bedroom window. He almost spoke, but the way James turned and slid the screen back down, he was clearly trying to move quiet. Dylan was a little hurt. James and he, as two boys without either a mother or a father, had had a tight bond as long as he could remember. It felt like James was growing away from him.

"See you downstairs?" Dylan turned to go.

"Right behind you," said Sam.

Sam and Dylan tramped into the kitchen just as Nana set down their plates. A stack of pancakes sat in the middle of the table, along with a bowl of scrambled eggs and a small plate of toast.

"I'll be going over to Mr. Thompson's house this morning, if you want to come along." Sam forked up several pancakes and passed the plate to Dylan.

"I'd like to have a look, sure."

Nana bustled in and took a seat on the window side of the table. "That poor man. My guess is you'll find his house neat as a pin." She sipped her coffee, glancing over her shoulder.

"Me and that lawyer fellow walked through it quick." Sam scooped eggs out onto his plate, set the bowl in front of Dylan, and reached for the pepper. "He even said we may just want to leave the furniture in case somebody needs that too."

Nana nodded.

Sam glanced at her. "Do you want to see if there's anything you want?"

She shook her head vigorously before he finished his sentence. "I'll just keep the memory of a good man. There's nothing we need from the house, I don't suspect." Dylan knew that was the end of that subject.

After they finished eating, Dylan and his father rose. Sam gave Nana a light kiss and squeeze, thanked her for the meal, and turned to Dylan.

"Ready?"

"I'll be along in just a minute," Dylan said, avoiding his father's eyes.

Sam stepped out the front door. Nana drew the plug from the bottom of the sink and dried her hands on the towel hanging from the bar on the stove front. She turned to Dylan. He was surprised they were nearly the same height.

"I know things are changing, maybe a little fast for you." Nana pursed her lips. "It sounds silly, I know. But home *is* where your heart is. It's not a square of land. It's where you're happy."

Dylan stared at Nana. He felt an odd discomfort at Nana's words. She was not talking to him as she would a child. Another change that felt somehow...wrong. He had a disorienting sense of being mistaken for someone else. He also had a feeling that Nana was not simply who he'd always imagined her to be: the elderly woman in the constant monochromatic dress who ran the affairs of the house. Nana was someone with wishes of her own. That also made him uneasy.

She patted his arm, glancing down. "You are going to tear that cap asunder, the way you work it, boy. And don't fret so. He's made some mistakes, but he is your daddy, and he won't let anything bad happen."

They stepped out into a quiet, radiant morning, the sun still low and the day cool, but with the promise of a baking later. A summer Saturday was the best, because it held mystery and promise. It made him giddy sometimes, to think the day was a thinking thing, quietly planning how to surprise him.

Nash Street was beginning to stir. Mr. Geise, two doors down, was out collecting dead twigs from his yard. His lawn always reminded Dylan of a buzz haircut. It was thick and clipped tight to the terrain, like the hair of the Kelly boys at school. Mr. Geise was as much a fixture on his lawn as the little jockey with the lantern, which he repainted every year. His father waved at Mr. Geise, who lifted a stick in return. When Mrs. Geise was alive, she had been the one who tended to the bushes and flower groupings in the yard. Only occasionally would the husband be seen, lugging some plant ball to this or that corner, and digging another hole to plant another bush. After Mrs. Geise passed, he had taken over tending the yard. This apparently endeared him to Nana. At least once a week she would shuffle down the walk with a dinner dish draped in a red cloth for Mr. Geise.

"I feel bad for the poor man," she'd say. "The men should go first. Did you ever see a man try to care for himself?"

Together, his father and he crossed Nash Street and strode up the walk. Sam dug in his pocket and extracted a small white envelope. He shook a key from it. Unlocking the door, he eased it open, stepping soft over the threshold.

Sam bent to pick up mail strewn on the floor from the mail slot. They stood together in a neat foyer, with an old, polished entry table in front of them. A small pile of mail rested on the table next to a dish with several small rings of keys. Some of the pieces of mail had little white notepaper clipped to them. These Sam kept on top of the pile as he added the mail from the floor.

Dylan followed a step behind as they entered a well-appointed sitting room on their left. A dark wingbacked chair and matching footstool sat catty-corner to a stuffed sofa, both kneeing up to an ash coffee table. The room had the look of a doctor's waiting room without the magazines. There were no pictures on the walls, except for an oil of a fruit bowl above the sofa.

Dylan turned to watch his father, who glanced briefly at the furnishings and then moved a slow eye across the walls and ceiling. Sam eyed the carpet under the coffee table, and the wood floors, critically. He also stepped to the window, unlatched it, and lifted it. It gave a brief resistance, as if it had not been opened in some time.

Sam and Dylan moved through the house room by room. Sam spent some time in the kitchen, turning the stove and oven on and off, and opening and examining the icebox. He also checked the walls, doors, and windows as he went, and occasionally made a note on the little envelope, with the stub of a pencil from his shirt pocket.

Upstairs, they glanced into Mr. Thompson's bedroom, and a smaller bedroom that was nearly empty. Everything was spotless.

"It probably needs a fresh coat of paint, though the walls are in good shape. A little plastering in the hallway upstairs. You ever have occasion to paint? Or should I assume based on your model planes that you don't have much experience?"

Dylan turned to see his father grinning at him.

"Well, Nana had James and me try to paint her porch last summer. But somehow..." his voice trailed off.

"So that's your work?" Sam grinned again. "If you want, I can show you some of how it gets done, and there may even be a little money to pay you."

"That would be fine." Dylan followed Sam down the second-floor hall. "Nana ended up finishing the porch, but I don't think she knew more than James about painting. And James couldn't tell one end of the brush from the other."

Sam flipped on a light switch and leaned into a shadowed room at the back of the upstairs hall. The brick chimney jutted out into the small space and the room was barely bigger than the bathroom downstairs. It must have served as an office, dominated by an old desk with a rolling chair tucked into the leg well. A dark four-drawer filing cabinet stood next to the desk. Sam turned to go, then reconsidered and stepped into the room.

"I feel like an intruder, but I guess we'll have to decide what to do with all this." Sam drew open the top drawer of the filing cabinet.

"I guess Mr. Thompson trusted you to do right by it." Dylan flipped open a dusty thin cardboard box on a low table by the door. It looked like it hadn't been touched in years.

"Watch your way with Elmore's things," Sam reproached, then sighed. "I guess it won't matter a lot. I still can't fathom what provoked him."

A glint caught Dylan's attention. "Hey! Look at this!"

He stepped back to show Sam the cluttered display of medals, pinned to a velvet backing. Sam stepped over and fingered one of the larger medals, attached to red, white, and blue ribbon.

"The Bronze Star. These must all be from Double U Double U Two," said Sam. "Mr. Thompson would have been too old for Korea."

"What's the Bronze Star?"

"It says here, on the back: 'for Heroic or Meritorious Achievement.' I remember him mentioning being in France once, during the war." Sam set the medal back in the box.

"How come he never marched at Memorial Day? I thought all the old soldiers are in the parade." Dylan ran his fingers over another ribbon, attached to a heart-shaped pendant. "Say, do you think this is from a girl?"

His father picked up the medal gently. "This is the Purple Heart. See George Washington there? It's for soldiers who are wounded or killed in battle. I wonder that's what his limp came from."

Sam turned back to the open filing cabinet and Dylan pulled the chair out slowly. He had never seen a chair on wheels before. He sat down slow and gasped when it started to turn.

Sam grinned. "It won't bite you. That's the way it's supposed to be. Swivel chair. They are pretty common in offices of big executive types." Dylan spun the chair a little, surprised at how quiet and smooth it was.

"Hmm. Tax forms for the last few years. Copies of the bills. Well, what is this?"

Dylan looked up at the change in Sam's tone. "What did you find?"

"It's a file with your brother's name," Sam's voice was puzzlement and wonder.

"What would Mr. Thompson want with a file on James? What's in it?"

Sam drew the folder out slow, then stopped, and eased it back so it was only halfway out. The folder was thick and worn. Sam cocked his head to examine the contents as he riffled what looked like old newspaper clippings, attached to note paper.

"Um, it's not James. It's your brother David. Looks like the articles that they put in the *Daily Times* back then. But why would...?" Dylan studied Sam's face as his voice trailed off. Sam drew the folder out, glanced at Dylan, and laid the file open on top of the cabinet.

"He made notes. I wonder why. Says here, 'Check when Godfrey Winter left town.' Godfrey was my shift mate down at the plant when

I was laid off. He got moved to nights, but then he had to leave out of Salisbury to go be with his folks. Nice enough fella—"

They both turned at the sound of Nana's voice, calling from downstairs.

"Sam! You had better come now. It's James!"

Dylan emerged from Mr. Thompson's house just ahead of his dad. Nana stood on the porch, her apron front splotched where she'd wiped her hands hurriedly. Sam started to speak, then saw the Crane Ridge Township police car idling in front of their house. Two uniformed police stood talking at the front of the car. A shadowy figure was hunched in the back seat. Dylan guessed it was James.

Dylan started down the sidewalk.

"Child, why don't you give me a quick tour around Mr. Thompson's kitchen? We'll see if there's anything we want for a keepsake."

Dylan looked at Nana, puzzled.

"There might be something we want to remember Elmore by. He was good to us," she said, her eyes fixed on the scene across the street.

Dylan glanced again at the police car. He reckoned he would learn soon enough what mischief his brother had gotten into. He looked at his father, who was rubbing his chin, his other hand on his hip, frowning. Gazing across the street, his dad said, "I'll see you back at the house shortly, mother." He hitched up his pants and headed down the sidewalk.

***

Dylan raced up the stairs to his room. At the top landing, he stopped at the sight of James sitting on one tucked leg on the sill of the dormer window. James turned, his chin resting on his fist, and gave Dylan a cold look. He swiveled his gaze back out the window. Before James had turned away, Dylan saw something in his eyes that was frightening. It was a kind of sadness, almost like grief. Dylan realized he had missed whatever James had said.

"Pardon?"

"You and Sam must have had quite a chat about things."

Dylan stood by the stair top, trying to remember what he'd come for, and puzzled by the statement.

"Me and Sam? He invited me to go over to Mr. Thompson's with him. Did you know Mr. Thompson was in the war? A soldier?"

"Didn't know. Don't care. What I want to know is what you told Sam about me sneaking out." James's head swung slow to face Dylan. Dylan saw that James's eyes were red and watery. This was the scariest. James never cried. Dylan took a step back. He tried to look thoughtful, but what he felt was a fear. He didn't trust himself not to shake, so he leaned against his desk. Dylan didn't ever remember being afraid of his older brother before.

"Is that why the police came for you?"

James swiveled to turn his back on Dylan, gazing down on Nash Street. He didn't answer.

"He asked what time you left out this morning. That's all."

James turned back, his jaw set, lips thin. His gaze burned. "What did you tell him?"

"I said I didn't *know!*" Dylan heard his voice slip on the last word, like an inexperienced skater.

James's look softened a fraction. "They don't arrest people for sneaking out. Something happened down to Wilson's Store last night. They think I had something to do with it. But I didn't."

Dylan waited. Finally, he said, "All right. I believe you. But why does anybody think it was you?"

"I picked up something I shouldn't have, and it makes it look bad for me. That's all."

"Well," Dylan said lamely, "I'm sure it will all work out okay. Going to the fireworks tonight?"

James flashed a brief smile and turned back to the window. "One way or another, I'll be there," he said quietly.

11 / Anne

The black sky exploded in a pinwheel of bright green twinkles. Delighted screams and laughter bubbled from the throng arrayed on the shore of the Wicomico. James squeezed Anne's waist, stroking her new red, white, and blue tee shirt. She turned, her face aglow for an instant in the gleam of the fireworks. She glanced around, and kissed him, soft and possessive, as the darkness enveloped them again.

The crowd was relaxed, smoke wafting the air from a thousand cigarettes, tips glowing in the dark. The threadbare pasture of the fairgrounds transformed with the arrival of the Cook Brothers Circus, the centerpiece of the Crane Landing Fourth of July. Along with the fireworks, of course. The town paused in its labors at the dock and the fields to celebrate, and neighbor reacquainted with neighbor over watermelon and smoking grills. The Lions Club had its booth with the roulette wheel. The Methodist Church was selling something this year called tie dye tee shirts—multicolored, whimsical splashes created on a plain white tee shirt, no two patterns the same.

Back in May, there was a good deal of discussion about selling the shirts, at the annual planning meeting, according to Ryan, who heard it from his mom. She, like most of the parents, thought the shirts were too flashy. But the newly installed minister, a Michael Dennis from the mainland, convinced parents that red and blue die on a white background was a fine means to encourage patriotism among the young people.

James glanced around at his neighbors, gathered in family clusters or couplings of sweethearts on old blankets covered with picnic remnants. His dark mood was in contrast to their smiles and carefree comments. Anne seemed to sense his turmoil and turned again, gazing seriously at him.

"I told you, my mom never comes to the fireworks 'cuz of the noise, and my dad won't leave her home by herself. Relax, would ya?" She kissed him again, lightly, and pressed back to him.

"It's not that. I just... I'm thinking of leaving for awhile." Under his fingers, he felt Anne stiffen. The crowd stilled again with the muffled *whoosh*, signaling a canister launch. High above the river, a great explosion of blue and red sparkles preceded a series of concussions, gasps, and scattered applause. From the fairgrounds, the raspy hawking from the Volunteer Fire Department's dunking booth echoed faintly.

"But *why*? Where would you go?" she whispered. "How long before you come back to Crane Ridge?"

James drew a deep breath. "My dad said my mom was living in a little town called—" A screeching whistle interrupted him, and they both turned to gaze out over the river.

The crowd oohed and aahed, and James turned back to Anne, his mouth close to her ear. "She was living in a town in Texas." He smiled. "Sugar Land. That would be my mother."

Anne hugged him and kissed his cheek. "What makes you say that, James?"

He kissed her soft, in the glow of a blossoming rocket. "Before... she was so full of life. So happy and so much fun to be with. Not like a mother, really." He dropped his gaze. "Imagine how crushed a woman would have to be, to..." he shuddered and she gripped him tightly.

"I've been thinking of her lately." He laughed softly, as a *thwump* signaled another launch. "That's not right. I've never *stopped* thinking about her."

In the bright bloom of light, he sighed. "And just the thought of her dying out there, alone."

He noticed Anne eying him oddly. "What?"

Anne cleared her throat. "Didn't your mother leave you? I mean, didn't she leave you and Dylan? And he was no more than a baby?"

"She left because of *him*! What *my father* did!" He said hotly. A few feet away, heads turned at his tone. Anne raised a finger to her lips.

A breathtaking flash drew everyone's eyes skyward. "So you want to go to Texas? To do what?"

James sighed and slipped his free hand in hers. "I want to see where she's buried." He felt her steady gaze. "It's just something I have to do. This seems like as good a time as any."

Anne rested her head on his shoulder. "Gosh, I'll be crazy missing you. When will you be back?"

"Well, that's a little harder to say." He waited through a series of bursts. "Everyone thinks I broke into Wilson's store, and the chief tried to pin me with beating some boy real bad over in Millwood."

"You have to stay and defend yourself, James!" Several hushes sounded in the dark. Anne lowered her voice. "Or it will never be better for you here."

"Well, since my father came back I just don't fit anymore."

"I want to go with you."

James started. "I don't even know what *I'm* going to do. But it won't be clean sheets and Nana doing my laundry. I don't plan on being back for the start of school, and—"

"Jimmy Paxton. You think you're the only one has a yearning to get off this stupid peninsula?"

Mr. Geiger on the next blanket over glanced their way, and then looked more closely at the two, twined sinuously on the blanket James had lifted from the linen closet.

James buried his face in Anne's neck, and inhaled her raspberry fragrance. The crackling tune of *Windy* by a group called the *Association* grated in the temporary pause of concussions. As if Anne's response weren't surprise enough, he found his own feelings betraying the resolve he'd worked on since this morning. What he had rehearsed saying was *eventually maybe they'll catch the guys who really broke into Wilson's Hardware, and I can come back quiet.* Truth was, he didn't really plan to return at all. If it weren't for Anne, and for Dylan, what was keeping him here?

Now it sounded like his family might be fixing to move away. His father could mess things up by being close or far away. It didn't really seem to matter.

But what he found himself saying was, "How will we travel? Where will we go?"

She kissed him quick and hard, breathing, "Shhhh...not here," into his mouth. He started to speak, and she kissed him again, her face in the darkness appearing soft, and wiser than he felt. One thing that attracted him was the way Anne moved so comfortably in the world they inhabited, as if she belonged here. As if she had a say in her life. He closed his mouth and eyes, and melted into the safety of her.

12 / Freak Play at the Mound

Dylan raced in the front door and hurried down the hall. He bounded up the stairs, to discover James, sitting quietly. A game was starting down at the school. He was always misplacing his glove, and it wasn't on his desk now. James saw his glance around the bedroom.

"Your glove's on the closet shelf. If Stinger pitches, expect him to buzz you. Especially if you somehow manage a hit off him." James turned his gaze back out the window. Dylan grabbed his glove.

"You're not coming?"

"Not now. Maybe later."

This was Dylan's first summer playing ball with the older kids. James had taken him several times to play up at the school. James usually made sure they were on the same team, where he could back up Dylan discreetly in the field.

"You sure?" Dylan tried not to sound whiny. He really wanted to play, but was not excited about going alone.

"Ryan will probably be there. Maybe I'll come up later," said James.

The game started with Ryan Daggert pitching for the other side. Everybody on the opposing team liked to see Ryan on the mound. He would work hard to find the batter's box, and the way he screwed up his face in concentration, you could usually tell where Ryan at least *intended* the ball to fly. Ryan was actually a good pitcher. The slower he threw, the more accurate he was, to a point. So he was also easy to hit. Since the other team usually ran up an early lead, Ryan was what one would call a starter, rather than a finisher. At some point, watching the other team wear down the base paths, his team would call for a pitching switch.

Halfway through the game, Stinger came from the catcher's position to pitch. As he toed the rubber, his teammates smirked. It was fun to be on Stinger's team. Stinger could be hit, but if you hit him once, he was like as not to "hit" you back.

In his first ups against Stinger, Dylan eked out a sickly grounder that snagged the grass at the feet of the third baseman and darted past him. The next time Dylan was up, he looked into the eyes of the pitcher and didn't like what he saw there.

Stinger couldn't distinguish a continent from an ocean, but he had no trouble keeping tally of the other team as they rotated to the plate. Stinger tossed two easy pitches wide. In his own way, Stinger's intentions were as transparent as Ryan's. But where Ryan was eying an imaginary box, Stinger was studying your profile.

Stinger nodded—to himself, Dylan was sure—not to any signal from the catcher. Then he launched into his windup. This was the *lesson* pitch, Dylan knew, and he fought the urge to step out of the box. The only thing Dylan didn't know for sure was whether to duck, leap, or dodge. Stinger grunted as the ball left his paw. Dylan's brain registered that it was in a straight line with his gaze. At the same moment, a whispered *shit* came from behind and below. Dylan closed his eyes and swung. He felt, rather than heard, the crack just above his grip, and his palms instantly tingled like they had been shocked.

He didn't realize he'd closed his eyes until he popped them open. He was on one knee, genuflecting on the plate. His teammates were on their feet along third base, pointing at first. Dylan had been smashed, hard. But where? What remained of the bat dropped from his numbed grip. Dylan knew he was expected to lunge at Stinger, screaming and cursing. He crouched and turned, hoping his team would get to the mound right when he did. Startled, he saw Stinger curled on his back, knees up, eyes squeezed tight, his mouth gaping in a wide *O*.

Inexplicably, the other end of the bat lay placidly on the mound in front of Stinger. Dylan turned to his teammates, dumbfounded. The roaring in his ears focused.

"Run! Go, Dylan!"

Dylan looked again at Stinger. The large boy looked like a fish at the bottom of a johnboat, fresh caught and unhooked. Dylan could now see the bulging whites of the bully's eyes. Dylan stumbled toward first base, tripping over the dropped bat-handle. He was standing with both feet on first base moments later, when it dawned on him the game was over.

***

The trees along Nash Street swished in a hot wind as Dylan and Ryan turned off Clarence Street. At the sight of Stinger gulping on the mound, everybody suddenly had something to do. Dylan had mumbled a half-hearted "hope you're okay" before Ryan's firm grasp swung him toward his bike. Dylan pulled away and Ryan shoved Dylan's glove against his stomach.

"Trust me. Send a card," Ryan hissed.

As soon as they had bicycled onto Clarence Street, out of sight of the field, Ryan had rounded on Dylan, cackling. "Man oh man, did you see his face? He looked like he was swallowing live electricity!" Ryan sucked his lips tight, imitating Stinger gasping. Despite his guilt, Dylan grinned, looking over his shoulder.

"I still don't see how you got a hit trying to get out of the way," Ryan laughed, and they pedaled racing away from the school. As they slowed on Nash, Dylan turned to his friend.

"Ryan, you know anything about what James has been up to?"

Ryan shrugged. "What do you mean?"

Dylan wondered how much to say. He didn't want Ryan thinking bad about James. But James was in some kind of trouble. The boys slowed to walk their bikes.

"He's been leaving out at night—or in the early morning—I don't know." Dylan palmed his own ball and flipped it behind his back, and up over his shoulder to Ryan.

Ryan snagged the ball with his outstretched hand. His glasses glinted when he turned back. "Daggett goes to the warning track, aaaaannndd PULLS IT DOWN, robbing Mickey!"

"I take it you mean Mickey Mouse. Mantle is washed up, in case you hadn't noticed." Ryan wound up, as if to bean Dylan. Dylan laughed, ducking. Ryan worshipped Mantle, the *Commerce Comet*.

"I hear some stuff, but you know. Guys might say a lot of stuff that's just wind. But I tell you, I don't get why James is wasting his time with Stinger or Scooter. Scooter! That guy's a chop! And James keeps hanging with them, he's down the tubes."

Ryan's tone dropped as they turned up the sidewalk at Dylan's house.

They looked up at the sound of voices from inside.

His father's low, steady voice was saying, "It wouldn't do any harm to have left him stew in there for a day or two. Nothing you say seems to register—"

Nana's voice interrupted. "My boys—our boys—are not going to be locked up like animals! I am surprised you would even consider letting that happen!"

They lay the bikes on the lawn and stepped up on the porch just as Sam pushed open the screen door. His expression was a dark scowl. His brow furrowed, and his lips were set in a thin line.

"Hi," said Dylan. Sam paused at the door, as if he might have forgotten something inside, or as if he might have wished he'd forgotten something. Then he sighed and shrugged the screen door closed. The three stood on the porch in an awkward silence.

Sam nodded to the boys and licked his lips. He ran fingers through his thin hair. "Ryan." Sam nodded at the lanky boy.

Dylan glanced at Ryan, then back to his father. "Is everything all right?"

Sam wiped a hand on his pants leg, and for a second, Dylan wondered if he'd been drinking. Dylan had never seen a person drunk—at least he didn't think he had. But he had sometimes wondered about it, after his dad confided that he used to drink a lot.

"How was the game today?" Sam asked. He rubbed the back of his neck.

The boys grinned at each other, and Ryan started to speak. "Dylan kinda decimated the pitch—"

"I need to talk to you for a minute," His dad interrupted, addressing Dylan. "Maybe you boys can get together later."

Ryan nodded. "Catch you on the flip side, Hondo!" He handed Dylan his baseball and swung the bat onto his shoulder, glove shoved on the fat end of the bat. Ryan straddled the *Hobbitmobile* and pedaled back down Nash Street. Dylan watched him lift a hand to wave at Mr. Geise, who was tending his azaleas.

"Hondo?" His dad raised an eyebrow and gave a thin smile.

"Frank Howard. Left field. The Senators?"

"Oh. Of course! Hondo. So how was the game today? Did I ask you that already?" Sam stood sideways to Dylan at the top step, his hands jammed in his jeans.

"It was okay. Some guy got hurt. I tipped the ball, and somehow it ended up in the pitcher's...uh, groin." Dylan sat in the glider, watching Ryan's back as he disappeared around the corner up Stockton Avenue.

"Game called on account of...the pitcher got racked?" His father chuckled. Dylan grinned, embarrassed.

"Something like that. Something exactly like that, I guess."

"Friend of yours, this poor fella?"

Dylan looked back down the street, at Mr. Geise wrestling with a bundle of azalea cuttings. "Not really. The guys call him Stinger."

Sam grunted, easing down onto the glider. "I hear that boy is bad news. I hear he's also a friend of your brother's."

Dylan watched the expression on his dad's face change. How did Sam know about Stinger and James? Dylan untied and retied the rawhide knot on his baseball glove.

"You say Stinger was at the game today. He was the boy you..."

Dylan nodded, looking up.

"You talk to your brother?" Without pausing, his father looked out over the street, lowering his already-quiet voice another notch. "He tell you he got himself arrested?" Sam said the last word like it was coated with lemon juice, sort of spitting it out.

As the words settled, Dylan wasn't surprised. He felt like he was living with a boy he hardly knew.

"What did he do?" Dylan asked.

Dylan suddenly wished he could take back the question. Not, "Why was James arrested?", but "what did he do?" He felt guilty assuming his brother deserved to be arrested.

"They say he broke into the back of Mr. Wilson's store and tried to haul the safe out the door. Mrs. Potts across the street heard noises and called the chief." Sam said the words quiet, his chin resting on his chest, his hands in his pockets.

Sam's choice of words sounded odd to Dylan. He asked, "They say?"

Sam plucked invisible threads from the knee of his pants. "James was walking down Stockton towards home early this morning when the police stopped him. He had a screwdriver in his back pocket. Chief Munro says it looks like the jimmy marks on Mr. Wilson's door frame might have been made by that screwdriver."

"So what's going to happen to James?"

Sam raised an arm to wave to Mrs. Duncan as she strolled down the far side of Nash with her dog Gemini. Right on cue, Buster shot from under the porch, loping across the yard. Buster and Gemini had a ritual as old as time, involving the sniffing of each other's rears.

"We don't know yet." Sam sighed and shoved a stray lock of hair back off his forehead. "Chief is pretty sure they got enough to charge him, after they finish running fingerprints. Seems everybody in the world has touched the Wilson's front door." Sam sighed. "James swears he had nothing to do with it. No alibi though. He was caught on the street well before sunrise."

Buster trotted back from his visit with Gemini and bounded up the stairs. Dylan sat up to nuzzle the panting retriever. "They going to put James in jail?" Buster scooped his snout under Dylan's hand when the boy paused.

His father shifted on the glider as Buster's tail swatted his knee. "I honestly don't know what will come of it. I kinda think a little time in the pokey might get his attention, but mother is adamant that he be home until..." Buster moved to Sam to nuzzle his hands, which were clasped now in front of him. "As if he'll stay home," Sam said under his breath.

Dylan didn't know what to say. He too was worried about James and the way he'd been acting, as if a dark wind blew the friendly brother away, and left a brooding, defiant boy in his place. Of course, James wasn't really a boy anymore, not like Dylan and his friends. James was old enough to drive, certainly old enough not to cry when he got in trouble. And yet, James had been crying today. What was going on?

"I know it's not my business, but does James ever lay a hand on you in anger?"

Dylan swiveled to look at Sam. "No. Never. We argue some, but that's it. Why?"

"Chief told me he thinks James and some of his friends might have beaten a boy over Millwood way. A few nights ago. I just wanted to make sure you're okay?"

"Yeah." Dylan sensed he should say more, but he didn't trust all his thoughts just yet. They seemed to be running in different directions. He wanted to blame his father for coming home and upsetting the ways things were. But James had been angry for longer than just the time Sam had been back. Maybe it had to do with when Nana had told them their mom had passed. Maybe before that.

His father said, almost to himself, "James doesn't act like he has the sense to know when to lay low. I don't know this girl of his, but I hear she's nice. And if he'd just keep his nose clean, he might have some money coming his way from Mr. Thompson's."

Dylan nodded, not knowing what to say.

"Lacking the good sense God gave a woodchuck." Sam smiled without humor. "Remind you of anyone you've ever known? Apples don't fall far from the tree."

Dylan colored. Sometimes he felt like his father was more honest than was fitting.

Dylan started to rise. "Um, is there anything else?"

His dad looked at Dylan, seemed to ponder something for a moment, and reached over to pat Dylan's knee. "I don't want to worry you. Boys will be boys sometimes. If you ever, you know, just want to talk..." Sam's voice trailed off.

Dylan paused, and turned back to his father. "James can be kind of, I don't know, moody. But I know he would never beat up some kid just for fun."

His dad looked up at Dylan over steepled fingers. "I hope you're right. What makes you say so?"

Dylan thought for a moment. "Because he's a good fighter. Really good. And he knows it. Most times, guys like that don't need to prove something. And they don't just go beating up folks."

Sam nodded slowly. "I hadn't considered that," he said.

13 / Moon Launch

James eased the screen door closed behind him, lifting up the handle to silence the grate of jamb on door edge. The house felt occupied, but not warm. *Am I already a visitor here?* A distant relative, like—well, like his father was at the beginning of this summer? He felt the tension engulf him. *If only...* James felt a tiredness he had seldom known. It wasn't just that dawn was minutes beyond the edge of the horizon. His head swirled with the new plan. *Who was he kidding?* There hadn't been an *old* plan. Just some vague idea about getting out of Crane Ridge, probably by hitchhiking.

Now, the girl he'd thought of mostly for her ability to arouse his passion had pushed him to really look at his life—and admit that he didn't have a clue. They had not been able to meet often in the last couple of weeks, but each time they did, he felt drained.

Prompt on the heels of her critique of his non-existent plan, she constructed a scheme that left him feeling queasy. One thing was sure. If there were some obstacle to leaving Crane Ridge, it would not be Anne's ability to think ahead and to make some hard decisions.

"A body doesn't just walk off into the sunset. That's ridiculous. We have to have a car." Anne spoke the last part almost to herself, her soft words mixing with the humming of crickets in the darkness.

The quarter moon shone milk-pale across the river. Anne leaned back thoughtful against James. When the crowd had dispersed last week after the Fourth of July fireworks, Anne and James had cut across the sea of departing townspeople to stand on the edge of the river. The crowd had thinned to a trickle. Officer Munro passed by on foot for the umpteenth time, looking harried and official. They had spread the blanket down on the bank beside the river, and sat motionless, comfortable in the silence, as the crowd's chatter transitioned to the sounds of summer when the town slept.

Anne had turned to search the darkness, and spoke in a low voice. "Jimmy, I have to get home soon, or daddy will wonder. He already thinks you and I…" James had been watching the water gurgle by, but he looked up at Anne.

"Anyway, we have to talk. A week from tonight, here. Do you have that much time before they…?"

James shrugged. "I don't know what's going to happen. My father said maybe they'll have to talk to Scooter, and he's visiting relatives with his dad 'til Friday."

"I'm worried my father will get suspicious, but if I tell him far enough in advance…" Her voice trailed off.

"Tell him what?"

"Leave that to me. I have an idea." James nodded. He was beginning to suspect Anne had lots of those.

Now in the noisy stillness of the deepening night, James sat enthralled as Anne laid out her plan to leave Crane Ridge—prepared to ensure they were well away before any alarm was sounded.

When she asked about Father Mullenix's Plymouth, at first James thought she had changed the subject. Sure, he did chores around the rectory. Though Nana didn't think much of the good Father, he had always gotten along with the priest. That's why the idea of stealing the pastor's car was so shocking. While James had a reputation as a hell raiser, he usually went out of his way to play by the golden rule.

"This is our chance," said Anne. "Maybe our only chance. It only gives us a start. When we can, we can arrange to get the car back, and… fix the rest of it."

"I still don't like it," said James.

"It's the only car you've ever driven. What we need more than anything is a head start. Time."

Once again, James felt his smoldering anger at his father. This all was *his* doing. James wouldn't be in this mess if Sam had just stayed gone. Stayed dead, really. That was the way James had come to view Sam. Lost at sea, or killed in a war far off. He had still burned with humiliation when Scooter had challenged him a few days after Sam's return. "Thought you said the old man was croaked!" Scooter had shoved his face in James's, in what passed for a grin.

Anne stroked his shoulder. "We have a chance to be together. But not here. Not in Crane Ridge. Is there anything we forgot? I won't be able to talk to you again before we leave."

"I hate the idea of stealing Father's car. I'm in enough trouble already." James drew the chewed tip of grass from his lips and tossed it in the water. "Besides, he's been pretty decent to me."

"Look at me," Anne said, in a tone both fierce and compelling. He turned and searched for her eyes in the shadows. "Do you really think that next week, or Christmas, or next year, we just get to waltz back into town like we went for a soda? If my father finds us he will *kill* you. And don't count on him to sit here on his porch rocker, his gun on his lap, waiting patient for us to come scootin' back up the walk."

"Okay, okay. When can we meet again, Anne?"

"We can't. Not until we leave. It'll be too dangerous." Anne thought for a moment. Then she outlined how they would communicate up to the morning they ran away.

"Do we really have to do all this, Anne?"

She exhaled, her bangs fanning up like netting in the darkness. Maybe it was his imagination, but even the chirping night creatures seemed to hush for a moment, expectant. "Roy Sampson *will* come looking. If we head south, he can't know that." In the dim moonlight, James could see her eyes pool and shine. "My daddy is a proud man. He will never *ever* forgive you. Or me."

As if the night was suddenly more dangerous, they huddled closer. She trembled, though the air was warm and weighted. "Where do your parents think you are now?" he asked. James hadn't wondered about that until this moment.

"I told them I was spending the night with Cherie. Cherie's parents think that's where I am too."

"But how—"

Anne giggled and kissed James. "Cherie is the best kind of friend! First, I can absolutely trust her because I've covered for her and Rudy Mello twice now. Second, her bedroom is on the first floor!"

***

Heading north over the Bay Bridge on to the western shore seemed crazy at first. If they were headed south, why go the wrong way? But Anne's plan was to head north, then west for a while, to create a false trail. James stopped in to Ledbetter's Service Station on Canal Street to purchase a Pennsylvania Highway map. Doogie Owens, Stinger's kid brother, was working in the bay.

"Planning a trip to the western shore? I hear that new bridge is high as the moon!" Doogie ignored the red rag in his hip pocket and smeared his hands on his caked jeans.

James shelled out 50 cents. As if just recalling something, he said, "I'd better take one for Maryland and Ohio too."

Doogie handed back change and the maps. His greasy thumbprint stamped the front of Pennsylvania's smiling Governor Scranton. Doogie picked at his nose and wiped his finger down his front.

"So what're the maps for?"

"I'm thinking of taking a drive up to see Pete." He opened the Pennsylvania map casually and glanced toward the western corner above Maryland.

"Pete Minsk? Where's he now?" Doogie started at the clang of the air bell, and moved around the counter to pump gas for Mr. Geiger, easing out of his flaming red Falcon. When he came back, James had tucked the maps in his back pocket and sipped a Nehi, spinning his quarter on the crusted counter.

"Yeah, so..." Doogie had a disconcerting trait. His eyes did not track together, but tended to wander separate, like twin infants that are fascinated by everything but each other.

"Right. Pete Minsk. He moved up to Waynesburg, Pennsylvania. Near the turnpike. I got a letter from him and he says fishing is awesome on some river." He tried to pronounce the name from memory, but it come out sounding like he'd drank a soda with a bee in it.

"Yock? Like yock yock?" Doogie grinned, one eye fixed on James, the other at some spot above him. James spoke slow, steady, trying to will the word onto the slippery walls of Doogie's rodent-sized brain.

"How you going?"

James shrugged. "Not sure yet. Maybe the bus. You ever heard of that town?" James prodded.

Doogie looked puzzled. Doogie *always* looked puzzled. "Yock?"

"No. Waynesburg. Waynesburg, Pennsylvania. Like Wayne Feed. Only Waynes*burg*."

Doogie shrugged. "Nope." He brightened. "I heard of Cambridge though!" Cambridge was approximately 45 minutes away. James wondered if, even with the prodding of Chief Munro, Doogie would be likely to remember this conversation. Oh well, it wouldn't do to overplay it.

***

James crept up the front steps of the Sampson house, stepping over the squeaky third tread. A corner of pink stationery peaked from the newspaper in front of the door. A note was folded in the newspaper, just as there had been every other morning since they'd last met in person. He knelt and slid the note out, then stepped back slowly, facing the door. The curtain behind the glass panel dropped silently back into place. He lifted a hand, turned, stepped over the third tread, and headed homeward.

James paused under the streetlight on the corner and unfolded the note.

Moon Launch 17 Monday 5 am.
Corner River and Elm. √√ XOXO

James refolded the note and walked slowly home. He smiled at Anne's code. *Double check everything*, she had said. *This is a moon launch. Whatever we forget, we can't go back for. So check and double check.*

The town slept. James swiveled his head as he walked, alert and calm, listening to the crinkling silence. Sometimes he imagined he was the sentinel of Crane Ridge, patrolling the streets while the town snored and dreamed. He felt safe in the enveloping night, when the mask of toughness he wore was laid aside.

The moon rested on his shoulder, following close. It draped the full boughs of the trees that lined the street in warm gold plating. He ran his fingers along the picket fence rounding the familiar darkened corner on to Nash Street. In a few days, he would be a memory ghost, a cipher that the night recalled, more and more faintly, until some future dark gloom, when another angry, lonely boy stepped out and walked these streets, walked through his ghost, and scattered it.

14 / Charcoaled Grill

Dylan pushed open the screen. "Don't forget this," His father said, tossing Dylan his baseball glove. He slowly mounted the stairs to his room. It was true what he'd said about his brother. James *was* a good fighter, but did it help or hurt James to tell his dad that kind of stuff? Halfway up the stairs, he heard Nana's voice, soft as she passed on her way to the front porch. "—butter and banana" was all he caught. He grinned and bounded up the last of the steps.

The fan in the window was silent and the heat in the top bedroom settled on him. James was in his customary spot by the window. Dylan wondered how much of the porch conversation James had heard. Dylan slipped his glove under the bed and sat down. "How come you're not outside?"

"How'd the game go?" James responded. Dylan described the highlights, and they both laughed. It was the first time Dylan remembered his brother laughing in a long time.

"You're not mad I racked up Stinger? Accidentally?" Dylan hastened to add.

"Stinger and I have common enemies. That sometimes makes us allies. It doesn't make us friends. He's a bully, and I wouldn't turn my back on him. Facing him, he's not so much. You watch, he'll likely leave you alone. Unless he's with his jerk friends."

Dylan nodded, weighing his brother's words.

"What is that *smell*?" James sniffed at the wafting oily odor.

"Nana said be prepared for peanut butter and banana sandwiches for supper again. Dad's decided he wants to be the grill king of Nash

Street." Dylan grinned.

The first time Sam had used the grill he'd purchased at Wilson's, he'd set it up on the cardboard box that the grill had come in. Just as Sam was adding cheese to the flaming black lumps on the grill the box below had burst into flames. In a second, the grill was enveloped in a pyre, sizzling for a moment, and then tottering over with a harsh clang as its platform disintegrated in fluffing black cardboard chunks.

Nana, Dylan, and James had looked on from the porch, working hard not to laugh. Helpfully, Nana had said, "I just bet that's why they make those grills black in the first place. That sort of thing probably happens a lot."

Sam had given his mother a look that was part amusement, part frustration. He had let the fire burn itself out on the driveway at the side of the house. Afterward, he'd wiped and cleaned the grill, and set it back up again. That night, they had dined on peanut butter and banana sandwiches, along with potato salad and corn Nana had already prepared.

"Dad and I are not going to be bosom friends," James said, with a soft smile. "He thinks it might be better if I confine myself to the house until... I don't know. Until hell freezes over, I guess. The real deal is he'd rather I was in jail. The last thing he wants is me around—the second to last thing," James amended.

"He told you that?"

"Not so much as he told the Chief that when Munro released me. I expected him to rake me bad, but dad didn't say much at all. I could tell he was pretty mad though."

"Dad said you—" Dylan stopped at the look James shot him. "You didn't break into Wilson's, did you?" Dylan tried to hold his brother's gaze, as if he already believed whatever James said. But he couldn't quite do it.

"I was out in the middle of the night, and the hardware store gets broke into. Two plus two makes..." James tucked his knee under his chin and picked at the dust motes on the window screen. "And the only person who can say where I was wasn't supposed to be out either. I'm supposed to rat her out to save my hide?"

Dylan sat without breathing. It was clear now. There had been talk of James and Anne all through the school year. Anne was, after all, the daughter of Mr. Sampson, the Geography teacher. Dylan sometimes wondered why he never saw his brother with Anne. Now he suspected he knew.

"Not a word of this to anybody. Me being in trouble is one thing. But she... just keep your mouth shut." James stared hard at Dylan, and then softened. "Picking up that screwdriver from the sidewalk in front of the store turns out to be not one of my finest ideas. Who knew?"

"You found it?" Dylan blurted.

"It was just lying by the mailbox. They say it was the one that—" James turned back to Dylan. "But I guess you already heard that part."

"Dad told me some. He didn't say he didn't believe you."

"Well, there's a heartwarming endorsement," James said with a hollow chuckle.

"I think dad is..." Dylan searched for a word. "...trying."

"Trying to what?" James snorted. "Leave it. I know what you're saying. I think he doesn't know what to do with me, and I think I have a way to solve his problem."

Dylan lifted his eyes to his brother, searching James's face for more. The memory of Mr. Thompson's silent solution was still fresh. James noticed his younger brother's look.

"I'm not going to do something stupid. I mean, I'm not going to hurt myself, or anybody else. I just think it might be best if I start fresh. You're getting along okay with dad. That's not in the cards for him and me. Maybe I remember more things than you do. I don't know. But..." his voice trailed off.

15 / Pre-dawn Flight

James tiptoed into the rectory and silently lifted the key to Father Mullenix's Plymouth. A few minutes later, in the utter stillness he turned the ignition, his eyes glued on the second floor of the house. He held his breath, waiting for the lights to blaze on, and all hell to break loose.

The car started up, and purred quiet. James creaked it in reverse down the sloping driveway. He knew the car ran a little rough, but at least the brakes didn't squeal. The car sagged out onto the street and James eased the column gear into first, let the clutch out slow, and flipped on the headlight beams as he glanced back once more to the darkened, brooding rectory.

He glided down the street toward the rendezvous, every sense alive. Would Anne be waiting in the shadows at the corner? Would anyone be out at this deep hour to witness their flight? He pondered what he would say if he had to return the car in an hour, when the sun began to claw its way up from the near Atlantic. No plausible story came to mind. He tried to calculate the mythical point of no return. In his soul, he knew Anne would be there, unless something had gone terribly wrong. *When she eased into the Plymouth, and closed the door, that was probably the point.* From there, they could race to the edge of town and point their way toward Cambridge, unless Chief Munro was in hot pursuit.

James shook his head at his own imaginings, as if he were shaking droplets off after a swim. *Don't get cold feet on me now.* Ten minutes to liftoff and counting. *And don't start talking to yourself, under any conditions.*

Spotting Anne standing back in the shadows two blocks from her house, he eased the car to the curb and clambered out to unlock the trunk.

They drove in silence out of their hometown. She slid over next to him and they linked hands. James often had to retrieve his hand to shift on the quiet lanes of the Delmarva Peninsula on the back approach to Cambridge. The relentless flat land stretched as far as the eye could see, a bounty of staple crops that fed the livelihoods of these taciturn, God-fearing people, along with the other major source of income, the crab traps stacked high alongside one-story cottages.

The sun dappled the road and strobed the interior of the car as the orange globe peaked up from the east, through thin forests of juniper pine. They drove north, toward the legendary gateway to the mainland, the Chesapeake Bay Bridge. North to head south. And the unknown.

16 / Trips to Cambridge

Dylan awoke to the phone ringing. In the dream that ended so abruptly, Dylan had been poised on the riverbank, tugging hard at his fishing rod. The rod was arced like a giant hook, bent nearly in two, and the line darted like a strange water bug, slicing the surface like the unwavering sword of his hero, Aramis.

Dylan is pivoting and side-stepping, eyes locked on the churning water and his enemy, the great cat known as Ironsides, when the alarm rings, the alarm- the phone? Aramis the Musketeer blinks, twice, and the bright sun becomes soft morning, and muffled voices condense into clear words, and then sentence fragments.

"—Of course he's here. Where else would he—" Nana's voice, strident, with a touch of doubt. "I can check, but you just hold on a minute. Saaaaam! Sam, can you come quickly?"

Something about Nana's voice propelled Dylan out of bed and to the stair railing just as his father stuck his head through the door at the foot of the stairs.

"Is your brother up there, son?"

Dylan turned and saw the empty bed. In fact, it was made up. The boys never made up their bed 'til after breakfast, though the rule was the beds had to be made before they left to go outside.

"No sir. He's not here."

"Was his bed...?"

Dylan shook his head.

Sam slammed his palm against the doorframe and closed the door soft. Dylan stared down at the dark paneled wood door. Was he supposed to stay up here? He certainly wasn't going back to sleep now. He went to the bureau and grabbed a pair of jeans and a tee shirt.

"What? Where—" Dylan froze at Nana's words. It wasn't what she was saying. It was the fear he heard. What had his brother done now? Dylan strained to hear his dad's voice. He realized Sam must have taken the phone from Nana.

"No, he is out already this morning."

Silence for a few moments.

"I don't know anything about that. We just found out he isn't here. No, I was surprised he was up and gone."

More silence. Dylan heard the faint whistle of the bobwhites in the elm out front, chattering as they did every morning. He had a feeling this morning was going to be different.

"Yes, I'll do some checking. I think it's a little early to be calling the sheriff." Dylan felt an icy nail slowly rake down his spine, even though the August morning already promised swelter. He unbuttoned his pajama top, and shrugged it from his thin shoulders. "James would never harm your daughter. Of *that* I am sure. There is probably a very simple exp—"

Dylan slowly pulled his tee shirt over his head, and eased off the pajama bottoms.

The phone clicked into its holder, even though Sam had not said anything before he hung up.

"Mr. Sampson's daughter Anne was gone this morning. Do you know anything about James and her?" His father sounded as if he were working hard to sound as if nothing was wrong.

Nana said something Dylan couldn't hear.

"Well, are they dating? James is only..." Sam's voice trailed off.

"Seventeen," Nana sighed, louder now. "Older by two years than you were when you and Maureen were doing your night walking-tours of town."

Dylan stepped into his jeans and slowly pulled them up. They were his favorite pair, but they were getting harder to button. He left the tee shirt hanging out over the waistband and plucked a pair of white socks from his top drawer.

Sam must have given Nana a look, because her next words were softer. "James has always been restless. You can't blame yourself. Sometimes there is a roaring river right under your nose that runs deeper than you can imagine."

"You mean like Elmore Thompson." Dylan froze where he sat, one sock half on. "You care to tell me what you didn't tell the Chief?"

Nana's voice now, with an uncustomary wariness in tone: "Son, I'm not sure what you mean."

"You are my mother. I can tell when you are surprised, and when you're not. Elmore's death shook you. It made all of us sad. But you weren't surprised. It's none of my business, but you said something about what gets normal men in trouble. He never mentioned a girl to me."

There were another few moments of silence. Dylan fetched his Converse sneakers from under the foot of his bed and sat down quietly to pull them on.

"Elmore came to me," Nana finally said. "He told me he was cashing in his life insurance surrender value. After, I realized he knew suicide would forfeit the insurance. Anyway, he told me he put that money into an account he'd set up to be left to the Church."

"But *why?*" His father persisted. Dylan pulled his laces tight, straining to hear.

"Elmore had a lady friend out Cambridge way," Nana sighed. "It was not what you would call an um, *exclusive* arrangement. Cambridge, or here for that matter, doesn't tolerate any practice on the part of ladies of the evening. But the world's oldest profession is also one of the world's most adaptable, apparently."

"Are you saying that Elmore...?"

"She was a retired school teacher, so she said, who lived in a quiet house. She provided comfort and solace to a select group of men. I never knew her name. But every few weeks, Elmore would come over to take the car and head for Cambridge. He was always dressed up extra nice on those occasions. He also smelled of—" Nana said something Dylan couldn't hear. Dylan stood and stared at his reflection in the bureau mirror. His perpetual cowlick pointed to the sky like Chicken Little.

Dylan thought he heard his father laugh gently. "Mr. Latham, that attorney fella, was of the opinion Elmore hanged himself in the tree, instead of completing the deed inside, so it wouldn't diminish the value of the house. I guess if new owners were offended by having a hanging tree, they could just cut it down and have it hauled away, or burn it."

Dylan heard a chair scrape across the dining room floor, then the familiar creaking of the chair's back.

Nana: "Elmore came back from a trip to his lady friend, not long before he... He was as sad as I've ever seen a soul. You were down at the library with Dylan." Dylan lifted his head, and looked into his expressionless eyes in the mirror. "You know how I would ask him for tea—or maybe you don't. He wouldn't accept often. He was always on some mission or other."

"No thanks, mother." Sam responding to some unseen offer of food or coffee. Dylan could see Sam waving his hand up, simultaneously thanking and declining. Dylan noted his own stomach rumbling and wondered if it was okay to go down. But he didn't want to interrupt the two adults. He was still trying to puzzle out what in the world Nana was saying about Mr. Thompson.

"But that day he came in," Nana went on. "When I asked him if everything was alright, he looked down at his plate, and I thought the man was going to weep."

Dylan could picture Nana biting her lip, gazing across the table and out the front window over to Mr. Thompson's house. She would be twisting her apron, as if she'd misplaced something in its deep folds.

"Elmore said his lady friend had decided to marry one of her other suitors."

Sam chuckled. "I guess that's a word for it. Sorry."

"Well, the upshot was his 'friend' wouldn't be able to provide any 'services' to him or to her other clients, from that day on."

Sam let out a low whistle. Dylan wet his fingertips, and futilely worked the cowlick that pointed unerringly at his model A-6 Intruder, suspended over his head.

"They had known each other long?"

"Near as I can recollect, Elmore had been going out to Cambridge for almost ten years now, and it did seem as though he always came back in a good mood. That day, he told me he didn't know how he was going to do without those trips."

"Well, mother. So Elmore tidies up his affairs, writes me a note, and catches the next tree out of town."

"He saw what he wanted to see." Nana sighed. "That was enough for him. But I guess the thought of her not being there was just too much."

Dylan studied the mirror, pondering the ways of people he loved, and wondering if he'd one day be as certifiable as some of them became— his dad, his brother, Mr. Thompson. He thought the answer might be more discernible on a full stomach. Sighing, he headed for the stairs.

17 / World Beyond the Bay

For James, the first day on the road was like the feeling at the peak of the roller coaster that came in with the carnival, just before it plunged straight at the dead grass below. The drive across the bridge was unlike anything he'd ever experienced. Anne told him several times to keep his eyes on the lane, but his head snapped to left and right, looking at the glistening flat Bay far below.

He felt like he'd been living in a small room, and had stepped out a door he'd never noticed to find the room was part of a mansion with ceilings and halls that stretched unimaginably far. The great and mysterious Chesapeake Bay shimmered with the sun now at their backs, lifting to mid-morning radiance. Steamer ships and large sailboats, like toys in the endless blue, hinted of shores far beyond the horizon.

Next to him, Anne sighed, dazzled too at the immensity of the bridge and the grand parade of water that blurred from deep blue under their feet to a gunmetal sheen far in the distance. She squeezed his hand tight and for once he felt that this woman at his side, so often an incomprehensible stranger, felt just what he did in this moment. It was a sensation so singular that he wished they could just drive the bridge forever. But the tiny chill between his shoulder blades reminded him that somewhere behind them a storm was forming that would chase them, and must not be allowed to overtake them.

Anne was not too keen on ciphering a map, so while she had a general idea of how to track west in the company of the arcing sun, when it had clouded up in the afternoon, they had somehow crossed a large river and glimpsed the dome of the nation's capitol. Each time they spotted it, first dead ahead, and then a little to their left, it appeared to be getting closer.

"This can't be right," he'd moaned, slapping the steering wheel. "We're driving right into someplace probably bigger than Salisbury. Can't you get us out of here?"

18 / Parting Note

Dylan bounded down the steep steps, his Senators cap tucked in his back pocket. Nana fussed if the boys (including his father) wore hats in the house. As he entered the kitchen, Nana stood in front of the stove, spatula in hand, regarding the flapjacks on the griddle. She looked up with a soft smile that did not quite reach her eyes, and his dad rustled the paper on the table as if he had been reading it all along.

"How did you sleep, son?" Nana slipped a plate down from the shelf, and flipped several flapjacks onto it.

"Okay." Dylan busied himself drizzling syrup on his plate. Sam was looking steadily at his mother, as if he were trying somehow to speak to her with his mind. But Nana was busying herself scrubbing the white enamel stove top until it seemed she were going to scour the white right off.

His father finally turned to Dylan.

"Did James say anything to you about where he might be headed today?"

At the mention of James's name, Dylan shoveled a large wedge of flapjack in his mouth. He nodded at Sam, gesturing needlessly at his occupied lips. At last he swallowed, his mind made up.

"James didn't say anything to me about going out. What's the matter?" It was the truth, after all.

"Did he ever say anything to you about... North Carolina?" From the corner of his eye, Dylan noticed Nana's head snap up. He glanced at her. She turned back to the stove, but not quick enough to hide her puzzled look.

Dylan scrunched his brow. "No, I can't say he ever did."

"Are he and this Anne...?" Sam's lips pursed, and again he shot a glance at Nana, but her back was turned. "Are they boyfriend and girlfriend?"

Dylan had never really considered what to call James and Anne. They were just... "I guess you could say that. They like being together. They just don't like other people prying."

Sam drummed his fingers on the table. "There are some folks thinking your brother has run off." He looked at Dylan expectant.

Dylan dropped his eyes first. "Run away?" Suddenly it occurred to him. "I didn't notice if any of his things are missing."

Sam slapped the table and rose, heading for the hall. Dylan sighed in relief. He was not comfortable answering questions about his brother's business. At the kitchen door, his father turned. He looked at Dylan for several moments.

"I'm going to need your help. I won't know what's missing, unless it's obvious. You know your brother." Sam's voice trailed off.

"Let the boy finish his breakfast," snapped Nana. Her voice softened. "Can you help your father? It's important, son."

"Yes, ma'am." Dylan wiped his mouth and laid the paper napkin on his plate.

Upstairs, Dylan could tell right away. Some of James's things—his bowie knife, his hiking boots, his fishing pole, nearly all his clothes—were gone. Dylan checked the back corner of the closet. The duffel bag Mr. Thompson had given them several years ago was not in the corner. Dylan looked up at the clinking sound the empty hangers made as his father moved his fingers lightly across them. Sam looked down at Dylan.

"Any idea where he'd head if he was in trouble? James ever mention a favorite place?"

"Not that I can think of, no. He—" Dylan stopped in mid-rise, staring at his desk. Leaning against his ball glove was an envelope. It said "Dylan" in block letters. How had he missed it? Sam turned at Dylan's pause and followed his stare across the bedroom.

"Dylan, I know it's not my business what your brother might care to tell you, but I'm asking you to trust me. Things will go better if I find him first."

"I don't know what it says. I didn't see it 'til right this minute." Dylan stepped across the room, torn between wanting to know what James would say, and not wanting to defy his father.

Sam caught Dylan's arm, gently. "I don't need to read the letter, let's say. But after you read it, I need to talk to you again. Fair enough?"

His father spun and headed down the steps. Dylan noticed how easy Sam strode down the steep stairs. But then, this had been his room at one time, too. He lifted the white envelope from the glove. He tapped it, staring at his name, written in James's confident, hurried print. Then he shoved it in the back pocket of his jeans.

19 / First Night

Though it was only mid-afternoon the sky was darkening, a brooding roil of pan-gray clouds that dipped low. James could not tell east from west, but guessed they were still east of the Capital. He aimed to keep it off his left shoulder and skirt it to the north, but he was only guessing at directions. A huge cemetery climbed a slope to their right. As the first ham-sized drops tapped the hood and windshield, on impulse he eased a right turn through the massive black gates.

James eased the car slowly on a winding drive that climbed, traversing the slope. He and Anne gawked at strange structures, part of the cemetery architecture. White and grey buildings the size of small houses loomed back off the road, with giant marble tiles adorning the front, in uniform rows and stacks. Anne glanced at him, and he shrugged. "You got me."

A gray statue of Abraham Lincoln, seated, greeted them without surprise, and James suddenly knew where they were spending their first night. Today had been the first time in his life when he had awakened and eased out of the only bed and life he had ever known, having no idea where he would lay his head that night. As he eased the car to the edge of the drive, he wondered at the new sensation, and thought that he liked it. As if in acclamation, Anne moved close and laid her head on his shoulder. They jumped apart for a moment to crank the windows tight shut as the sky split to baptize their first night.

20 / Lois

Dylan loped down the stairs and swung right. He patted Buster, said, "Come on boy, let's go scare some fish." At the word *go*, Buster wagged his tail with gusto. The two stepped onto the back porch and Dylan eased the screen door closed, grabbing his bamboo pole. Buster wagged at the low fence gate, and shot through the opening when Dylan unlatched it. Buster moved down the back fences of the neighbors, hitching in to sniff at things. He looked up as Dylan walked past, wagging expectant. "What?" Dylan asked, his voice low.

"Oh. You are a smart dog all right." Dylan laid the fishing pole over his shoulder, rifleman style, and started whistling. As a joke, he, Billy, and Tink would whistle Opie's "fishing pole" song when they were headed for the river. The song was the only one Buster was keen on, and he would howl at the high parts.

Dylan grinned despite the churn in his stomach. James and he hadn't been close recently, and he missed it. The thought of his brother gone saddened him immensely. Dylan was warming to the reality of having his father around, but Sam—well, Sam wasn't family. And Nana, she was more like a mom. A boy didn't talk to a mom about some things.

Why did things have to get so upside down? When his father came all of a sudden, it felt like everything was changing. A small voice reminded him that James had been acting distant before Sam ever arrived. But back then, at least, James had not run away.

Dylan's eyes stung and his Opie-whistle faltered. Buster slowed and turned to look at the boy. Glancing around, Dylan wiped at the corner of his eye, and lifted his shirt hem to wipe under his nose. This was stupid.

Dylan turned out of the alley, around the tall hedgerow in Mr. Geise's lot, and almost ran smack into Lois Mast. She gasped and dropped the armload of books she was carrying.

"Dylan Paxton! You scare a body half to death! Is that dog friendly?" She bent to collect her scattered library books. Buster sniffed at the books and wagged as she and Dylan collected them.

"What happened to your eye? Is fishing fun? Do you catch anything?"

Dylan opened his mouth, then shut it again, like one of the fish he was intent on catching. He still had not spoken.

"I go to the library Mondays and Thursdays. I already filled up two reading wheels. Do you like to read?" He handed her back Trixie Belden's *The Mystery of the Emeralds.* "That one's new. It was so spooky! I bet you don't read these. You read the Hardy Boys, and Superman, I bet!"

Lois wiped at a smudge on the corner of *Trixie Belden.* "Mrs. Fletcher would bean me if I brought back her new book all messed up." She eyed it and applied a light daub of saliva from her fingertip. "Well, I hope you're having a good summer. You don't talk very much, do you?" Lois' eyes took on a mischievous look. "Maybe that's why she likes you."

"Who?"

"Lisa Haggerty, of course. Boys don't know anything. Her paper chain is the longest in the class, she's going to burn it the last day of summer, and she says it's for you! It's longer than the Wicomico, she says."

"Paper chain?" Dylan's head swirled. *Lisa Haggerty? She never even looks at me. Never says hi.*

"—seen those Wrigley wrapper chains? Like the one that Daggert boy did for Susan Opsosnick? Well, Lisa made hers out of scrap paper, and Jennie Worth said she saw it and it takes up two A&P bags!"

Dylan called for Buster, who was sniffing at a pile of something. Lois wrinkled her nose and went on.

"Do you want me to tell her you like her?"

Dylan stuttered, shaking his head vigorously. "No. I mean, what would you say?"

Lois looked at Dylan as if he'd just asked directions to his own house.

"I would send her a note. What do you think?" She sighed, as if continually baffled at the mechanism of a male brain.

"A note. Sure. But what would you say?"

"I don't know. 'Dylan Paxton thinks you're gross.' What do you *think* I'd say?"

"Lois, if you're going to send a girl a note about me, I want to know what you're going to say! Aw, forget it. She doesn't even know me." Dylan bent to stroke the back of Buster's large head as the dog snuffled his knee.

"Suit yourself, Mr. Shy Man. I don't really know why she likes you anyway. I want a boy who will at least talk to me. Ryan talks to me, but he likes Susan. Only he never talks to her. What's the point of liking somebody and then not talking, tell me that? Why was your brother driving Father Mullenix's car this morning?"

Dylan stared at the collar around Buster's neck, the way the short fur bunched around the ancient leather. He waited for Lois to catch her breath and start her perpetual monologue again. But the only sound was the blue jays bullying the finches over Mr. Geise's scattered toast crumbs in the back yard.

"James does some work up the parish now and again. Maybe he was running..." Dylan's voice trailed off. He drew a hand down Buster's sleek spine, as the dog licked at his face. "What time did you see him? Where?"

"I get up ever so early summer days. I just don't want to miss a moment. Some girls hate summer, can't wait to get back to school. *Ugh* I say. I don't think spelling and all that are such great shakes. I like walking summer mornings more than anything."

Steadily, Dylan looked up. "So it was early you saw James?"

She stared down at him in exasperation. "Didn't I just say... didn't I? Oh!" She smiled and for the first time Dylan thought how she could be cute if she just smiled more. "It was right before sunrise. I was on the porch having Cheerios. My mom lets me get my own breakfast summers, as long as everything is put away. Even french toast if I want, but it was cereal today. And bananas, of course. He was driving down

Stockton Lane just as casual as you please, his arm draped out the window. I waved, but I guess they didn't see me."

"They?"

"I couldn't tell who was he was with. It was still dark. Somebody was in the front seat with him."

Dylan lifted a stringy earthworm from under the fieldstone on the edge of the bank, and slipped the hook twice through the wriggling creature. The envelope weighed in his back pocket like a big river rock, the kind he would skip just to make a large splash. He flicked the line out over the lazy brown water and sat on the steep bank alone.

James was gone. Dylan let the thought creep in, like a mist, soft and relentless. He was quite sure he hadn't seen the last of his brother. Even at 12, he understood that James was not likely to get far with nothing but anger and fear to fuel him. Dylan didn't really know Anne, but she didn't strike him as particularly resourceful either.

But the brother who shared the room at the top of the stairs, the brother who taught him sports and looked out for him, the brother who gave him a sense of family, was gone. Something had shattered, like a vase in the front room that was one of the only links to the Paxton past. Shattered so as soon as you saw it, you knew that no amount of glue could ever make it whole again.

The tears on his eyelids blurred the river into a wide, rust-colored lane. At this moment he wanted nothing so much as to step out and just walk, keep walking that lane, out in the middle where nothing could touch him. He shoved his fingers in his back pocket.

His name across the crinkled envelope was just three letters. Addressed by someone in a hurry. Or someone who remembered only one person ever called him that. Like a final breath of how it was when it was just them, and good. Dylan stared at the limp fishing line glistening in the sun and gently loosed the gummed fold.

July 17, 1967

Hey. Guess you know by now I left. Dad will never be family for me. One of us had to go, so it is me. But with only Sam and you it might be good. I will always be your big brother. As soon as I get settled, I will contact you. Not everything you hear about me is true. This is just something I have to do. Watch Stinger's fastball.

J.

Dylan started to ball up the paper. Instead, he smoothed it out and folded it carefully. He slipped the paper back in the envelope. The scribble word on the front blurred. He tucked the folded envelope in his back pocket, laid his elbows on his knees, and wept.

The evening that James and Anne vanished, her father came to see Nana and Sam, with Chief Munro. Nana shooed Dylan out onto the front porch. He sat with the pie she had hurriedly sliced for him—the men had arrived near the end of a quiet dinner.

Nana ushered the men into the front parlor, but Mr. Sampson said, "I'm not here for a social call." Chief Munro said something in a voice too low for Dylan to hear.

"He knows who I am, "Mr. Sampson said harshly. " Sam and I went to school here before he moved over Berlin way." It sounded like Mr. Sampson said this last with a sort of snarl.

"Roy." Dylan heard his father's soft voice.

The Chief spoke up. "Father Mullinex's car disappeared sometime last night or early this morning from the rectory parking lot. Seems somebody came right into the rectory and lifted the keys off the hook they keep in the kitchen. The priest reported it missing first thing."

"Like father, like son, I told you!" Mr. Sampson's voice raised several octaves. "I told him to keep away from my Anne. He was always looking to bother her."

From the sound of the voices, everyone was standing in the small parlor. Dylan could picture them, and felt guilty again that he'd not told Sam about the car. But Sam had only asked if there was anything in the letter he ought to know. Dylan said *no*, the letter had given no hint where James was going, or what he planned to do. It also did not mention Anne.

Chief Munro cut in. "Sam, whether Anne went with James voluntarily or not—"

Nana's voice: "What's *that* supposed to mean, Walt?"

Mr. Sampson: "Walt, this is getting us nowhere. We need to know where that boy took my girl. NOW!"

Dylan heard Chief Munro's clear voice: "There is no proof they're even together, but I think we have to assume they are. And there is certainly no proof she was taken un—"

Mr. Sampson's voice cut in. Near panic, he sounded a little like the deputy Barney on the Andy Griffith Show. "She would never leave on her own with the likes of that boy!" His voice dropped an octave. "It's not the first time somebody just up and vanished with a Paxton nearby!"

Dylan heard Nana gasp. Chief Munro: "I warned you if you came, you had to keep a civil tongue. Sam, I'm sorry about this."

Mr. Sampson: "Sorry? Do you know who you're talking to? This... MAN!" Mr. Sampson's words were chopped, like when Nana sliced up potatoes for scallops: "Let. His. Own. Son. Be. Stolen! His own wife! And her—"

Chief Munro: "Now just hold on. Turn around. We'll be going right now!"

Sam, his voice in halting wonder: "No Walt. Let Roy speak. What do you know?"

Mr. Sampson was spitting out words, a little hard to follow. "You could not have been that blind. Maureen was not exactly the Flying Nun! I mean, she flew all right. Flew right out of town. People talk, and where there's smoke there's usually a flame of truth!"

Sam said something quiet. It ended in a question, but Dylan couldn't hear what he said, and Mr. Sampson made no response.

Dylan felt the porch spinning under him. Adults were hard to follow sometimes, but this took it. What did James's leaving town have to do with David?

The screen door suddenly swung open. Mr. Sampson strode out, shaking off the Chief's hand on his arm, and clomped past Dylan. The Geography teacher looked odd in jeans, work boots, and a plaid work shirt. Odder still, and sad, it was evident he'd been crying. His face was puffy and distorted, like a lightly singed marshmallow on a stick. His cheeks were a lacy pink. Dylan watched the back of the teacher huffing down the sidewalk. The man reached the end of the walk where it joined the street, and looked up baffled, as if he'd just landed on another planet. Then he headed toward Chief Munro's squad car across Nash and looked back, his face a mix of fury and grief.

The Chief turned back from speaking quietly to Sam. He stepped out on the porch and rumpled Dylan's hair as he passed by. "Be good now, hear?" At the bottom of the step, the Chief turned, twirling his hat on the fingers of his free hand.

"Your dad said James left you a note. I need to see it."

Dylan swung around looking for Sam, but the door entry behind the screen was vacant. Dylan reached in his back pocket and drew out the creased envelope. He withdrew the note with shaking fingers and extended his hand, as if he was approaching a flame. The chief lifted the note from Dylan's fingers and made a point of opening the folds with care.

"Do you have to keep it?" Dylan watched the Chief's eyes move, his brow wrinkle, and then finally he looked at Dylan.

"No, son." The chief sighed, and handed the note back. "If you hear from, or about your brother, I need for you to tell me. He's in some trouble, but the longer he's gone, the worse it'll be for him."

The Chief slipped his hat back on, smoothing the back edge of it over his crown. He raised a hand, palm up, to Mr. Sampson, who was marching back up the walk as if he had something else to say. Dylan folded the note and slipped it back in the envelope, watching the men settle into the car and ease away from the curb.

21 / George

George, neatly stitched in red thread on the smeared gray oval background of petroleum-stained overalls. *George*, wiping his meaty paws on the maroon garage cloth, blackened and greasy from innumerable conversations, James suspected, like this one.

George, reasonable and assured, right up to the moment when he said, "Nothing for it but a rebuilt transmission. Don't see the sense in throwing good money after bad."

George when he talked had a way of screwing up his face so his eyes disappeared deep in his ruddy veined cheeks. *George*, jaw set tight when James responded that not only were they not affording a rebuilt tranny at $510, but they were not affording dropping the engine back in for sixty-five dollars.

He had suspected ever since Waynesburg that the Plymouth was not going to last all the way to Texas. To convince any pursuers of their travel due west, James and Anne had driven out through western Maryland and veered north to Waynesburg, Pennsylvania. James had stopped in to see his friend Pete Minsk, after locating the address in a local phone book.

He first dropped off Anne in a coffee shop on Greene Street. Even though she knew Pete as well, they decided not to complicate things further, especially because Pete's parents might object. The plan was for James to make it clear he was headed west—maybe mention Denver—and then to be on his way. He also asked Peter to mail a letter from him to Nana—but to wait five days before he sent it.

Pete's parents were home when he called and he accepted a dinner invitation for that evening. When the Minsk's asked him about his travels, he said he was on an errand for Father Mullenix, and couldn't really say more. He wasn't sure if the Minsk family was Catholic or knew Father Mullenix. Turns out they didn't. But it was as good a cover as he could think of. Besides, James was counting on Doogie Owens from the Crane Ridge service station to point any pursuers to this household.

Pete invited James to spend the night, but he begged off, saying he had to make up some time. He finally picked up Anne around 8:30 pm, and they left Waynesburg to wend their way south.

From Waynesburg they drove to Front Royal, Virginia, and traveled the length of Skyline Drive through a national park. They spent two days in the park, enjoying the peaceful scenery and each other. When they reached Waynesboro, Virginia, they backtracked southeast to Richmond, where they picked up the main route south. Their plan was to drive to Florida, and then head west. But around Fayetteville, North Carolina, the car had started shifting hard. James had finally pulled into this garage, just inside Georgia.

James had liked *George* at first. Maybe it was the way George addressed him man to man. They stood talking in the steamy close garage, a collection of ghost-cars barely visible through the sooty back window. The rusted shells might have fallen from the sky like some science fiction invasion of dead metal.

Anne in contrast flared her nostrils when George's jaw relaxed, his eyes darted to the ground, then to the ceiling of the gritty garage, and he proposed a solution. He might be willing to give them twenty-five dollars and a lift to the bus station in exchange for their "rollin' parts wagon." He chuckled at his own words. Anne reacted as if he'd called her a horse's rear end. Her Irish eyes had arched, her eyebrows lifted.

"The tires are nearly brand-new! And she only has fifty-five thousand miles. She's worth at least a hundred!" Anne's reddish-brown bangs shook when James laid a hand on her arm.

"I can't sell the car! It isn't even—" Anne shrugged his hand off as if it were one of the innumerable black flies orchestrating the low-grade hum in the dank garage bay. She turned on *George*, who stood now, paws on his wide hips. George glanced at James, an ugly storm passing briefly over his fleshy face. "No title to sign and you want me to give you a Benjamin? I'll go thirty-five, Missy—"

"Don't call me that. That's—not my name." Not for the first time, James marveled at the way a girl who was supposed to be keeping a low profile seemed to revel in flaring up so. James only made matters worse, he suspected, when after some give and take, George glanced openly at him and rolled his eyes. Involuntarily, James shrugged a "what-can-you-do" reply, and Anne spun without a word and stormed to the car trunk, wrenching it open. She jerked her two bags out and marched into the relentless sunshine.

When James turned back, the owner of *George's Auto* gave him a look that was two parts leer, one part pity, and then motioned James to follow. George stepped up from the service bay to the tiny office store and set aside several greasy copies of *Car & Driver*. He raised the lid of a cigar box, reached in, and grabbed two twenties. James extended his hand, and George drew his paw up against his chest.

"You gotta give me five," George said. The way the man said the word *five* chilled James. It sounded like rotten swamp gas escaping. James felt a cold rock drop down his spine.

"Five?" said James.

George winked at James, glancing knowingly in the direction Anne had fled. "Thirty five for the car, that's the deal. All's I got is two twenties. So, you give me a Lincoln, or five minutes with your high-and-mighty girlfriend."

James clenched his fists. His first urge was to smack the smile off this joker. But he was in a strange town in a situation out of his control. He forced himself to breathe slowly and reached into his back pocket, withdrawing his wallet. He pulled out a five. In gestures mirroring their mutual distrust, each man slowly reached out for the other man's money. Just before James could pluck the two twenties from the man's beefy hand, George froze.

"Just one set of keys to that heap?" He asked, eyes narrowed.

James nodded.

"Sure you won't save yourself the five for a coupla minutes with your girl?"

Maybe it was the way James's eyes narrowed, his gaze glittering. For an instant, something seemed to fall from George's face, revealing a reptilian grin, naked and cold. In the next moment, *George* was the friendly mechanic again, with an *aw shucks* smile.

"Happy birthday, lover boy," George said, and handed over the two greasy twenties. James grabbed the rest of his things out of the trunk of the car, and pivoted out the cave opening of the garage after Anne.

22 / News From Billy

It was the kind of summer day so bright that you had to squint or keep your eyes downcast. Blustery and dazzling, lifting and stirring the upper branches of the trees, and coaxing swing sets to sway as if friendly ghosts were enjoying a rare daytime play. The clean sharp odor of lilacs wafted over lawns and fields. It felt like summer had laid a welcome siege that would last forever. Dylan's friend Tink bit down on the split shot and tied a quick knot to keep it from slipping on his line. He pinched the red and white bobber back on the string, and stood to cast. "Mrs. Hanley said her nephew uses flour balls for bait."

Ryan worried a large bit of wild grass in his teeth, and grunted. "I think she meant her Stinger Owens uses flour balls for brains." He chomped on the wild grass.

"Did Stinger ever catch up with you for smacking a single into his crotch?" Tink grinned at Dylan and reeled his line back in slowly.

Dylan stood straight on a stone at the edge of the water, his pole tucked in the folds of his arms. It was a stance *The Rifleman,* Lucas McCain, had taken when he'd been held at gunpoint one episode, and Dylan thought it looked cool. He really missed that show.

"The Stinger man must be on the road with his dad. I haven't seen or heard from him since that day." His voice trailed off.

"I am sure Stinger's forgotten all about the hardball in his knickers by now," Ryan snickered.

Tink grinned at both of them. "How do you forget a thing like that?"

Dylan hitched up his jeans and leered at Ryan. "Are you trying to ruin my day, jerk wad?"

Ryan gawked at Dylan and slapped his thigh, laughing. "Jerk wad! Good one!"Dylan grinned, but the smile froze on his face when he saw the look Tink gave him.

"What's with you?" Dylan flicked his hook out over the muddy passing water.

"I just never heard you talk like that," Tink turned back to reel his line in slow, dancing the rig across the surface with a snap. "For a minute, you sounded like James."

Dylan turned his back to the two boys, and the silence hung.

"Any idea where James might've gone?" Ryan broke the awkward quiet.

Dylan considered. "Nope. I guess he plans to be gone awhile. He took the important stuff."

"If he was alone, I'd be guessing Texas." Ryan shrugged at the look Dylan gave him. "He told Cammy once he was mad he didn't get to go to your mom's...you know...funeral."

Dylan stared at Ryan. Cammy and Dylan had almost been friends, once, back before Cammy had started hanging out with Stinger and Scooter. This after a bloody one-sided fight between Cammy and Stinger—life never ceased to surprise him. He'd been thinking the same thing about James, that maybe he was headed for Texas somehow. It hurt that James would tell Cammy but not him.

Ryan looked back at him shrugging, and Dylan said, "He was pretty mad about not being able to go," as if he and James had discussed it.

The boys fished, laconic as the sultry day. Dylan bit off a piece of taffy and rolled it in his teeth, softening it.

"Anybody seen Billy lately?" Tink dug at the moist bank with his sneaker heel and plucked a worm from the muddy mix.

"Psyche, I was just wondering the same thing." Dylan snapped off another chunk of taffy and looked at Ryan. Ryan and Billy lived two houses apart. Ryan shifted and shrugged.

"Billy's old man is being weird."

"Billy's old man *invented* weird," Tink huffed.

"I saw Billy this morning, hanging sheets on the line out back. I had to talk to him through the fence. He said his dad told his mom he's not to see me. Or you. Or you."

"For how long?" Tink asked. Dylan looked at Tink, as he too asked "Why?"

"Because his old man is a total nut job!"

"But what's got his panties in a ball this time?" Tink persisted.

"Mr. Bergin doesn't want Billy *associating* with us. He does a lot of work for Mr. Sampson."

Dylan stared at Ryan, started to speak, and looked away, over the water.

"You got any more taffy, Paxmax?" Ryan tossed his mangled grass straw into the riffle at the edge of the water.Dylan reached into his pocket and drew out the crumpled wrapper. Tink reached out his palm too.

Ryan started at the bobbing of his pole tip. "Shit. Something hit me!" He rose and stepped up to the riverside, snapping his pole tip back over his head to set the hook.

"Just a dog-gone second. This is GOOD!" Dylan and Tink watched as Ryan stilled, and cocked his head at a slant. After a moment, his shoulders slumped.

Dylan smiled. "Do you twist your gourd like that to listen to the fish? You *are* good!"

Ryan flipped his middle finger at Dylan, once more flicked his pole tip back in a final check, and sat down again, shoving the taffy in his mouth.

"Hold on," said Dylan. "I want to hear what Billy said about his dad. Why can't Billy hang out with us anymore?"

"Cuz everybody knows you're faggots," a voice spoke from behind them.

Billy Bergin laughed and sidestepped down the hill. "Who's taking care of Old Man Thompson's place?" he asked.

"My dad's looking after things," Dylan replied. He didn't elaborate, but Sam had been working in his spare time over at Mr. Thompson's, and had just cut the yard down to the river this morning.

"Hey. Where you been, BB?" Tink and Billy slapped palms.

Billy slipped his hook from the bottom eyelet of his rod. "Didn't

Ryan tell you?"

Dylan shook his head. "He was just starting to when he caught a big old hunk of snag."

"You guys caught anything else?"

"A couple serious horsefly bites." Dylan slapped the top of his head, and another fat black fly fluttered to the weeds.

Billy grinned. "Step aside, gentlemen. Let a pro put on a show!"

"Hold up. Why's your dad so mad at us?" Dylan slipped the taffy pack into his back pocket.

"Man, it's not you. Mr. Sampson's ready to crucify James like Christ himself. You think the man would calm down just a little. My dad's been mending his back porch, and he says everyday he goes over there, the Sampson are screaming and crying. Crying I guess would be *Mrs.* Sampson. So my dad said I can't hang out with you, because you're James's brother."

Ryan snorted. "So what's it got to do with me?"

Billy crinkled up his nose, thinking. "I guess cuz you're friends with Dylan."

"So what are you doing here?" Ryan still chewed on the hunk of taffy, garbling the words.

Billy flicked his line out into the middle of the placid water. "I think my dad's afraid to ask Mr. Sampson for any of the money for his paint work, since he's not done yet, and because Mr. Sampson is homicidal. I was hoping to catch something for supper."

The four boys turned to landing some fish.

23 / Clancy

"Let's just give it a try. The worst that can happen is we don't move from this godforsaken spot." Anne craned to look back over James's shoulder at the garage in the distance, and back-pedaled several more paces down the gravel on-ramp.

"Anne, we can't do this. We're supposed to be lying low. Maybe we should walk." James turned, following the girl's gaze, as Anne's grin brightened, and she lifted her outstretched arm higher, thumb pointing skyward.

An elderly woman in the passenger seat of the Rambler gave them a look like she had just come across an animal carcass on her porch. She slapped the aged driver on the shoulder. After an almost imperceptible pause in the car's engine, James heard the *whoosh* of shoe-on-gas and the couple roared past, the woman's expression fixed and disapproving.

James looked back to see Anne's smile dissolve like sand swept clean off a tile floor. Just as quickly, her smile reappeared, neon and gleaming. "I still feel like I've been pawed," she murmured. James heard the squeal of brakes and turned to see a farm truck, dragging a cloud of road dust. He glanced back once to the garage they'd just left. Father Mullenix's old Plymouth sat silent, drooping, judging him.

Anne knocked her bags against his side. She was speaking breathless, nodding, and smiling to the driver.

"Darien? Sure! That's south, right? Sure, cool. We came up for the weekend and the stupid car...As if we're not in enough hot water back home!" Anne smiled and chattered and hopped up on the bench seat of the sputtering Ford pickup, weaving a story that fit the scenery.

"My brother said the car would be fine. So *I* say don't be dropping out of Savannah State to take up carriage repair quite yet. He's going back in September." James slid in next to Anne and jerked the door tight to his side, easing his right elbow out the open window. In the rearview mirror the garage shrank. He had always intended to return the car. Now, that seemed unlikely.

The last few days, their plan had included finding work and a place to stay, and arranging for someone he would befriend, who could drive the car back up, close to the Eastern Shore. James would then send Father Mullenix a note...*Plymouth in Bowling Green....keys on back wheel... Father, forgive me, it's been about 10 years since my last confession...I gave myself a thousand* Our Fathers *and ten thousand* Hail Mary's, *and I already feel closer to Jesus, though I am not a quarter of the way done yet.*

"This is my brother Roy," she said. "And I'm Betty. Thanks for stopping. It'll be good to get back home. Hot, isn't it?" James turned to the driver, a sunburned hayseed in a dusty straw cowboy hat. Perhaps five or six years older than himself.

Pressed to James's side in the small cab, Anne talked a streak. The driver, Clancy, was as taciturn as Anne was chatty. He was headed to Darien, Georgia, a town 50 miles or so to the south.

He seemed nonplussed by the female chatterbox in his cab. All the same, James noticed how Clancy had sat up and shoved the paper coffee cups off the seat and onto the floor, joining oily newspapers from past sandwiches and a well-thumbed *MEN* magazine. While Anne had slipped in beside him, James had noticed Clancy's attempt to heel it under the bench.

The sun shone brilliant on the macadam as the miles slid under the battered hood of the Ford. James marveled at his partner's ability to spin words in a lyrical fiction. At various bits of Anne's narrative, James's mind would spin off the swirl of phantom words. She described his days at Savannah State, studying for his law degree in accord with *daddy's* wishes.

James stared at the flat rows of summer peas and soy clipping by, their geometric alignment presenting a steady visual metronome. Anne's raising and lowering tone harmonized with the engine of the truck, and he easily imagined another life, with a too-authoritarian father, and books tucked under his arm. Georgian-style buildings were his habitation during gripping lectures and razor-edged intellectual debates. In this life, his father was mustached of course, thin like Sam, but with a sharp, judging gaze, and much taller than James, always looking down at him.

This father engaged him in heated discussions about points of law and important civic concerns. In his daydream, as he was excused from this father's dark-paneled office and turned with his books to leave, this father would rise, come around his desk in a suddenly convivial mood, and lay a warm, fraternal hand on his shoulder. *Mano a mano. Son, you do warm an old man's heart. Don't ever be afraid to come to me and speak your mind.*

James felt the sharp jab of Anne's elbow in his ribs. "Roy? Isn't that something?"

"Hmm... Sorry. How's that again?"

James turned to look at Anne. Clancy was leaning forward, looking over at him. She had dropped her chin a little to shield her face, and was glaring at him.

"My brother. I do believe college has made him even more scatterbrained." She laughed a high giggle, and cut herself off in the middle, nodding over her shoulder to the back window.

"Did you hear *any* of Clancy's story?" James glanced around out the back window at the large oil drums standing in the truckbed. "A renderer! A body would never ever guess all the things that come from such a..." she turned to Clancy for help.

"Byproduct," he offered.

"Yes! Byproduct!"

James stared at her, uncomprehending. She nudged him again as Clancy looked on, a slow, fixed smile settling on his face. James looked more closely at the driver, noticing now that his eyes were a little glazed, his facial muscles soft and doughy, like a rising loaf of bread. Clancy reminded him of kids in the special education classes.

"Um, tell again what you do, Clancy. Sorry, my mind was drifting," James said.

"Silly! Clancy here goes all up and down the state, collecting fat from farmers when they do their butchering." Anne turned beaming to Clancy, as if she'd just recited the Pythagorean formula correctly in class.

James could see by the smile on Clancy's mug that she'd gotten it right. "So these barrels in your truck..." again James glanced out through the rear glass. His nostrils flared and caught the oily engine smell, and his mind returned for an instant of stabbing guilt to the Plymouth—his responsibility—now in *George the Mechanic's* clutches. James had a vision of George strapping the car to the lift, like a victim of Doctor Mengeles, and lifting the protesting car, honking and bleating, high to probe at its underbelly.

There was no odor of dead animal. James was no farm boy, but he thought that he, now prompted, should smell something bad. The lighter out-of-place scent was Anne's perfume. She had told him several times what it was, and James felt another ping of anxiety. She had mentioned she was nearly out of it, and James had promised himself, back in the early part of the trip, that he would manage to get her more. Had it really been just three weeks since they'd left Crane Ridge in the pre-dawn of a still July morning? Three weeks of rinsing in service station bathrooms, and the one sneak into the college gym at the University of Maryland?

James focused on Anne as she acted the place of Clancy's interpreter. Clancy would speak in *33* speed. Anne would nod and click it up to *45* for James. Her head moved back and forth. She seemed to enjoy her role as go-between.

"Clancy says it never smells. The animal parts. He takes *everything* the farmer has left over. The head, the hoofs, bones...all of it! And Clancy says they make it into soap, and perfume, and even lipstick!"

Maybe it was the lurching, protesting gears each time Clancy slowed, but James felt a little light-headed. They eased up to the outskirts of what appeared to be a sizeable town.

"He says lots of guys out here make their living rendering. And he never has to go inside the plant. He said you would not *believe* the stink. He would never work inside." Again, Anne swung back to Clancy, beaming. James suspected Clancy wasn't following all of what Anne was saying, even though they were his own thoughts cranked up to normal speed. But he was clearly enjoying the attention of this peppy young girl in his cab. James wondered if there had ever been another girl sitting close to Clancy like this, pressed to him in the truck. James suspected not.

Anne leaned close to Clancy to hear something. James noticed that Clancy had abandoned any attempt to talk to him across Anne. Clancy might be dim, but he seemed to realize that talking to this angel over the clank of the truck's motor was a singular opportunity.

"So once your rendering plant is done with whatever it uses, does someone like you come and take *their* byproduct?" James grinned at his own wit, but his smile faded as Anne gave him a warning look. Clancy leaned forward, his frozen half-grin thawing into a semblance of furrowed thought. Anne leaned forward, and she and Clancy were talking again—or rather, she talked, and James could see an occasional nod over her reddish-brunette bob.

He turned to look over his elbow again at storefronts and parking lots increasing in number. He must have missed the name of the town. It appeared they were entering the commercial area. *Darien Staples and Feed. Don's Esso Service and Petrol. Here in the Peach State, We Chew Mail Pouch!*

Truth was, James was grateful to have Anne as a companion. He was by nature quiet, and on the occasions they'd had to talk to folks on the road, Anne was as natural at it as a duck on the river, navigating the eddies and swifts with a deft ease. Not that she went out of her way to talk to others—she seemed very comfortable when it was just the two of them—but she had this ability to slip in and out of conversation that James would never possess.

It was a gift. Not high on his personal list, but a valuable skill in their present circumstances. The last several weeks had been a kaleidoscope of new sights, sounds, and smells. When they first discussed running away, Anne was all for heading for Norfolk, down across the new bridge and tunnel via Route 13. She was also worried though that Roy would probably catch them before they made it into North Carolina.

James had been the one to suggest they travel north and west, over the Bay Bridge onto the mainland. Anne had thought to make bogus entries in her diary and leave it behind, to be discovered. James enjoyed having a partner, for once, in his intrigues.

"Are you sure they'll find it?" James asked.

She looked at him as if he'd asked if Johnson was still president. A mixture of wonder and pity. "By the time Roy gets done with my bedroom, it'll look like it was tossed by April Dancer. Now there's somebody you would not want to cross!"

James looked at her, shrugging.

"Stephanie Powers?" She prompted. "*The Girl from Uncle?* I guess you probably didn't watch it. I don't think she'll be back this season anyway. Mark Slate is the dreamiest."

James rolled his eyes. "I do like that guy Illya Kuryakin. He's got some pretty cool moves."

"Maybe so," Anne said coyly. "But don't you think Mark and April had more fun than Napoleon and Illya?" That night at the fireworks was when Anne had hatched the plan for staying in touch, since they couldn't meet in person before they finally ran. Her father spent his summers working on a highway crew for his brother to supplement his teaching income. Her mother slept late summer mornings. Anne suggested he retrieve notes from her, and leave notes if need be, in the Salisbury Times after Jesse Clemens delivered it in the morning. James pointed out how risky it was to get as close as Anne's front porch. Why couldn't she just sneak out and meet him?

"Jimmy, would Napoleon Solo do anything that foolhardy? Now pay attention." James sometimes felt he was living *The Adventures of Huckleberry Finn*, where Tom Sawyer got it into his head to bust the slave Jim out of a shed, following an excruciating and convoluted prison-break code that only Tom could decipher.

From the beginning, he hadn't felt right about taking Anne along. He had enough to worry about with just himself. But now he trusted her. He was pretty sure that was love, but he liked knowing that she knew more than he did. He was okay with letting Anne step out first on this path of adventure. James was less afraid than he thought he'd be. Every day since they'd pulled out of Crane Ridge in the dead of dawn, he'd felt a rush of elation. Excitement and fear, they were so much alike, and he liked that each morning now, he didn't know where he and Anne would lay their heads that night.

"Roy? Isn't that right?" James shook himself. He had to pee badly and the truck was slowing. Were they making a stop? He swiveled his head to look at Anne, pressed up to his side.

"Sorry?"

Maybe it was Clancy's eyes. They reminded him of Doogie from the service station, the way they flitted, one apparently unaware of the other. The truck was pulling over to the side of the road.

"Clancy was just saying if we're headed on south of town, this is where he's turning off. We are heading south, right, Roy?" Anne winked at him, and he wondered where she'd gotten *Roy*. Did she have a made-up name too? Shit! Oh well, they were parting ways here, so what did it matter?

"Y'all sure you have someone will come out this far for you? I could take you over and show you the rendering operation, if Mr. Nelson's not around. He's kinda grumpy, but he should be gone—" This was the longest speech Clancy had made over the 50 or so miles.

In the idling truck, James pulled the inside handle back, and eased his shoulder against the door. He turned in time to see Anne lay her hand on Clancy's thigh, light. The look in the boy's eyes was a storm of grief and joy. Softly, she said, "You have been very kind to Roy and me. If you are ever in Brunswick, please do look us up."

James once again admired Anne' ability to think quickly. As Clancy had described his route, he had mentioned *Darien, up above Brunswick*. When she'd asked him earlier if he knew if that's where they make the bowling balls, Clancy had allowed as how he'd never actually been that far south. After that, Anne worked it so Brunswick was their home and destination. She could think like lightning sometimes.

James pulled their bags from the back. He examined them with care as he lifted them over the wall of the truck bed. It did not appear anything had splashed from the battered drums. He paused to wave to Clancy, who still looked at Anne with the aching gaze of a pup watching the school bus pull away. Clancy revolved his head to nod at James, and

Anne closed the door gently.

She turned to James and walked to him. He could tell from the lift of her chin and the distance in her gaze that she had already forgotten the renderer. She nodded, agreeing with herself.

"We need backpacks. We can't lug our truck like this. We look like Ma and Pa Kettle."

24 / Ambushed

Dylan usually loved early autumn, when the leaves brittled and the wind cut sharp and cool across the newly shorn fields of corn. But James's flight had cast a pall over the late summer. Everybody in the small town speculated on their whereabouts.

Dylan was harassed regularly by Stinger and his sidekick, Scooter. He wanted to hate the boys, but most of his anger was toward his brother. How could James have left him by himself, to face this?

Coming back from the library one afternoon, Dylan rounded the corner of Wilson's Hardware and ran into Scooter Morris. Scooter's eyes were big as saucers. Then his mouth formed an "O." Out from the alley stepped Stinger Owens, with his brother Doogie.

"Well, look what we have here. The littlest Paxton! Heard from your thieving, girl-stealing brother lately?" Stinger and the younger copy of the blond bully laughed. Dylan stepped back and tripped off the curb. He put his hand down to catch himself, but Scooter reached out his own hand as if to assist him. Scooter gave Dylan's shoulder a slight shove, and Dylan sat down on his backside. The other boys roared. Mrs. Kirby appeared a moment later at the front door to the store.

"You boys scoot now! I'm sure you have better things to do than hang out on the street corner!" She disappeared back inside.

"You know, the old coot's right. What say we move down the alley and show Dylan a new game!" Stinger grinned.

"Uh, what game you talking about?" This from Doogie Owens, Stinger's younger brother, a boy whose face always reminded Dylan of the cartoon coyote on *Roadrunner*. He had a perpetual snivel, and his closely shaved head bore the light pink gashes of a barber who occasionally went awry. Dylan was staring at a scar that reminded him of a broken spear when a high voice pierced the summer afternoon.

"You boys stop being bullies!" Lois Mast, on the opposite corner, emerging from the Ben Franklin store. With her hands clutching a large brown store bag to her chest, she looked even smaller than usual, Dylan thought.

Stinger glanced up and grinned at the fuming girl across the street. He looked back at Dylan. "So you got a sissy girl to protect you?" Scooter grabbed Dylan's arm and lifted him up.

That was when Dylan noticed Cammy, sitting on a trash can lid, his arms crossed loose across his chest. Cammy Harris had arrived in Dylan's class late in the year. Dylan had noticed how skittish the thin, olive-skinned boy looked the morning he'd been brought into the class by Mrs. Andrews, the school principal. His teacher, Mrs. Wakefield, had smiled at the boy, and moved him to the center of the room to introduce him. Dylan remembered thinking how weird that must have been, to be the new kid in the school.

Mrs. Wakefield sat Cammy behind Dylan, near the window. Dylan had turned to nod at the boy, who had returned a thin smile. At lunch, Dylan introduced himself. Cammy had moved from Chicago. He was the oldest of three boys, but Dylan learned later that Cammy really lived with his older sister and her two boys, and that his parents had died together in a car accident.

Dylan had liked the quiet boy with the smoldering grey eyes. They walked home from school together several times, since Cammy lived on the far side of town beyond Nash Street. One day on the playground, Dylan noticed Scooter and Doogie talking to Cammy. Then the talking had turned to something louder and more vicious. Cammy had said something to Doogie, and Doogie had pushed him, hard. Then Doogie was on top of the smaller boy, shouting and swinging his fists. Dylan had raced over to help his friend from the dirt as Mr. Sampson pulled Doogie up, swinging and cursing. Cammy's face was caked with dust, and his eyes were venomous. Oddly, though, he seemed unafraid, while Doogie, a thin cut over his eyelid, had hot tears welling in his eyes.

Cammy's lips were curled tight.

Dylan touched Cammy's arm. "Hey, are you okay? That guy's not worth—"Cammy shoved Dylan hard and stormed toward the school building, scraping at his face with the back of his sleeve. Dylan stared after him in shock.

After that, things changed. Cammy drew inside himself for a time, even avoiding Dylan. Word got around that Stinger was gunning for Cammy for cutting his younger brother. Dylan at least saw the irony in this, for Stinger was constantly tormenting his slow-witted brother. Word also got around that Cammy, even though he was two years younger and a grade under Stinger, would fight him.

The hype for Cammy's fight with Stinger was on a level with Liston's second fight with Cassius Clay. Everybody in the school knew about it. The drama had spilled into a second day because Stinger had a detention in Mrs. Chalmers' class that went well beyond the usual sixty minutes. Some speculated that the administration had kept Stinger inside while they tried to reach the parents of one or both boys. Putting off the fight for a day only contributed to the carnival atmosphere.

All arranged fights took place near the water fountain on the municipal field, down the hill from the school grounds. By fifteen minutes after closing bell that Wednesday, it seemed the whole student body was gathered in the little valley, milling around. Usually the kids who brawled were not very popular to begin with. Often, they were egged on by other kids who had more sense than to ever fight. Many of the students didn't even know who Cammy was.

Dylan watched his former friend move down through the groups of kids gathered on the hill below the school. Someone would point at him, and the group would turn and stare. Stinger was waiting at the fountain. He was throwing circus punches into the outstretched palms of Scooter Morris. Scooter was doing his best impression of Angelo Dundee, Clay's trainer. Dylan spotted Ryan and Tink at the top of the hill.

Dylan had managed to claim the back side of the stone fountain, leaning on the wire backstop that loomed behind home plate on the opposite side. A stone that jutted out from the wall of the fountain gave him a foothold, and he had a view several feet above those gathered in front of him. Though later he wished he hadn't, Dylan saw the whole thing.

The one constant was the look in Cammy's eyes. It wasn't anger, or fear. It wasn't really—anything. Dylan had the thought that Cammy had no clue what was going on, or the role he was expected to play.

The only kids talking were Stinger's little gang. They were taunting Cammy, but Dylan could tell that they too were confused by the look on the boy's face. Stinger had a huge grin as the smaller boy made his way to the fountain. He made a show of mashing one fist into his other palm, as if he were applying pressure to a sudden scrape. His face twisted into a leer. The effect was to make him look a little nauseous.

Cammy walked up to Stinger and stopped. Stinger looked back over his shoulder at Scooter, and Scooter jabbed at Stinger, grinning, and then gestured at Cammy.

"Murder him," Scooter said. To Dylan, the words sounded like the way Laura Petrie talked to Dick Van Dyke when she really wanted something badly. Throaty and teasing.

Stinger turned to Cammy. "Today, you'll find ou—"

So fast Dylan thought he must have blinked, a red blotch formed at the corner of Stinger's mouth, and his head snapped back. Cammy no longer was slouched, hands at his sides. He had turned his side to Stinger, a fist covering his face, and another cocked back. Loaded, Dylan thought.

Dylan had watched the first Cassius Clay/Sonny Liston bout, with his dad and James, on their RCA. He had been surprised at how much his father seemed to know about boxing. He remembered what Sam said while watching the young, unknown Clay.

"That is one heck of a coach." At first, Dylan didn't understand. What did the man in the corner have to do with the chaos in the middle of the ring? Sam patiently pointed out the way Clay maneuvered to stay clear of Liston's famous fists. Clay never looked at Liston's legendary scowl, but instead focused on Liston's torso. What at first seemed like Clay's steady avoidance of any kind of exchange began to form, after several rounds, into a very calculated, artful dance on the part of the younger, lean fighter.

As his father had narrated, Liston slowed, leaning back on his heels, his scowl replaced by a look of pure frustration. In the fifth round, Liston chased Clay like a demon, his fury unleashed in a vain attempt to pulverize the young lion who could *"float like a butterfly, sting like a bee."*

"Look at Liston. He's turning into an old fighter, right in front of your eyes, son."

Dylan was mesmerized. He turned to Sam, puzzled, following the seventh-round bell. Liston was shaking his head, the anger of the early rounds again on his face. But now, the champ was also saying *I'm through*, and in fact he was. Though the two would fight again, fifteen months later, this fight had mattered most, to both boxers.

In response to Dylan's look, his father had shrugged. "He's whipped, son, and he knows it. That's not always a bad thing."

Now, watching Stinger staring in shock at Cammy's scraped fist, Dylan knew what was going to happen, no doubt at all. Cammy looked like he was watching a western at the Crane Ridge Cinema, his eyes still unfocused and soft. But he had put a look in Stinger's eyes that told Dylan all he needed to know.

You can't win unless you think you can, Sam had said after the Liston fight. *Sonny gave up. The rest was just filler.* Stinger had given up in the moment Cammy landed a blurred right hand hard on his cheekbone.

Cammy jabbed Stinger several more times, lightning quick. He slammed his fists with a meaty whack into Stinger's upper right arm, then sidestepped and smacked his other arm, up high, hard. Stinger tried once to wrap the smaller boy in a bear hug. He was rewarded with two quick chops to his chin.

After that, Stinger circled cautiously, but the large boy had no more experience with defensive fighting than Mrs. Crowley did. Everyone close enough could see desperation spreading across Stinger's face. Cammy smacked powerful jabs into Stinger's beefy shoulders, until Stinger's fists lowered to hover around his midsection. A merciful judge would have rung a bell. But this crowd did not trouble to gather in order to confer mercy.

Cammy started unloading his right hand at Stinger's face, ignoring the open midsection. *The rest was just filler.* To his credit, Cammy stopped landing blows as Stinger's pudgy body finally got the message to collapse. His knees buckled and he swooned to earth like the Hindenburg, awkward in demise.

A lone cry lofted from somewhere in the crowd, a shout of triumph. No doubt a child who had suffered one or more humiliations at the end of Stinger's ring finger. Most kids called him *Stinger* behind his back, a tribute to his proclivity to smack one on the skull with his ring finger. Whether it was because one's skull reverberated like a tuning fork, or one's eyes would burn with tears at the sudden sharp pain, Stinger was what most boys called him. Stinger had visited most of the male population of the school in this fashion.

But except for a few croaking cheers, the gathered crowd was hushed as Stinger's bloodied face smacked the thin grass. Murmurs rose from the outer edges of the throng. Those near the back of the crowd were trying to find out what happened. Though it seemed to Dylan like Cammy had punished Stinger a long time, it had all happened quickly. Ryan was just now edging his bike through the back of the crowd, still talking to Tink.

In the unwritten rules of afterschool fights, the victor is expected to acknowledge, through his own various badges of bloodied disarray, the adulation of those in attendance. The first problem was that the last glimpse Dylan had of Cammy, the thin boy did not appear to be winded in the least, much less showing any effects of a struggle. The second problem was that Cammy had melted back through the crowd the same way he had arrived, turning his back to Stinger before the big oaf had even hit the turf.

Dylan marveled at how a person could be so gifted in certain respects, and so retarded in others. Cammy clearly had been taught to defend himself by someone with advanced fighting skills. Didn't that same teacher understand the rules of victory? Cammy could have shown a deference and humility in victory that would have made him the school's unanimous choice for student body president. Like Dorothy in the Wizard of Oz, he had defeated the evil—well, Stinger.

But somehow, leaving as abruptly as the boy did, Dylan felt let down. Betrayed almost. If Cammy himself took no pleasure from his victory, was it right for anyone else to? Dylan worried it for several days, never able to put it just right.

In the weeks that had followed, Dylan noticed that Cammy was no more approachable than he'd been before the fight. Worse, the other kids seemed to go to some lengths to avoid contact with him. Dylan thought about it a lot. Hadn't Cammy done what most of them would have loved to do to Stinger?

One day, Dylan turned away from talking to Ryan on the playground at recess, and saw something that chilled him. Cammy, Scooter, and Stinger were all sitting atop the jungle gym, talking together. The jungle gym was the unofficial headquarters of the bad boys. The top level of the jungle gym, to be precise. And there was Cammy, drawn from his usual retreat on the center bar of the seesaw.

After that day, the three boys were always together. The increase of their number by the one scrawny olive-skinned boy seemed to act like a negative magnet. Now an even wider circle of empty space surrounded them. Dylan noticed that even the youngest kids avoided the lower reaches of the jungle gym.

Now, Dylan looked hard at Cammy, and Cammy looked away, as if a spot on the brick wall in the alley was suddenly fascinating. Dylan felt a shove between his shoulder blades, and he stumbled down the alley.

"Come with us, squirt. I think you'll really like this game!" Stinger shoved Dylan toward the mouth of the alley, and Doogie laughed and punched Dylan hard in the shoulder.

Dylan whirled, but too late. Stinger grabbed up Dylan's elbows behind him, and slammed him into the brick wall.

"Hey, take it easy," Dylan heard Cammy say in a low voice.

"This jerk's had it coming for a long time. Take 'em down."

Dylan felt hands at his belt buckle. A cold terror gripped him. He arched violently back against the boys, but with his arms pinned, he could do little but swing his head. His skull did crack against another boy's, and he heard the squelched cry of someone who's been smacked in the nose.

"Jeez, he does have some fight in him." Scooter moved around in front of him, trying to shove his jeans down over his hips. Without thinking, Dylan shot his foot out and caught Scooter in the midsection. The boy doubled over, exhaling "shit." Scooter curled on the filthy floor of the alley, in a too-little too-late effort to protect his belly.

"Here, hold him," Stinger said. As he relaxed his grip, another set of arms enveloped him, pinning his arms again at his sides. *Cammy.*

"Let me go let me go," Dylan brayed, his voice hitching, his red eyes spurting large, hot tears.

"Cry baby, this'll be over in a minute. Next time, maybe you'll think twice about messing with me," Stinger said, his tone malevolent.

Dylan was spun hard into the jowled face of Stinger. Without thinking, he spit in Stinger's mug. The heavy boy roared and buried a fist in Dylan's stomach. Doubled over, Dylan would have fallen face first, but Cammy held him up. Blinded by the pain, Dylan again felt hands at his waist, and then his pants were ripped down. His feet were pulled out from under him, and down he went. Now horizontal, he opened his mouth to cry out and a soft cloth was cinched between his teeth, peeling his lips back. His eyes opened wide, and his head jerked from side to side. He felt fingers working at the back of his head, and a sharp rap of knuckles on his temple.

"Let's toss his underpants out in the street": Doogie's high-pitched, excited chirp.

"What if he tells?" Scooter's low, urgent tone.

"He won't tell. He knows better." Cammy's first words since the nightmare scene started.

"See how he likes his pants now." Stinger's hoarse, guttural words, overlaying the sound of water streaming. An awning somewhere pouring out a small pool of gathered rain, or a garden hose lifted and dribbling out its dormant contents.

"Ah Christ, what are you doing?"

Against the pain in his stomach, Dylan pushed his fists up as best he could, fighting the weight straddling his torso, Doogie and Scooter both pinning him to the grimy, trash-strewn concrete. Dylan winced, feeling a small, hard object jammed against his bare thigh. Cammy's voice again, a throaty hiss: "That's too far, man. Quit it and put your pencil peck back."

"You gotta go when you gotta go," Stinger answered, followed by a self-conscious snicker.

"Let's get the hell outa here," Scooter said.

"What about—"

"Leave it. Baby Boy Paxton will find his way home," said Stinger. In the quiet of the alley, above the boys' heaving breaths, Dylan heard a— zipper? The weight on his chest and middle evaporated and Dylan curled into a ball, knees drawn up. His head lifted, his ear having encountered something soft mashed into the asphalt and dregs in the shadowed alley. The sounds of a quiet Crane Ridge summer afternoon drifted into the dim passage. The swish of Mrs. Kirby's broom sweeping across the sidewalk. A dog barking far off, and another dog picking up the chorus even further away. The smooth ratcheting of someone trimming a lawn. The slow drip of a drain at the back of the alley.

Dylan rolled onto his back, satisfied for the moment to lie in the filth, and feel the comfort of real tears tickling his cheeks.

A few minutes later, Mr. Wilson stepped cautiously into the alley, calling *Hallo* in a low voice. A young girl had grabbed his shirtsleeve, panicked, but he'd been in the midst of a big order with George Simonson on the phone. Now he studied the dark form, lying amid the refuse in the alley, and shook his head disapproving.

25 / Lost in Love

"Jimmy, we are far enough away, and we have to get off the road. We'll find work, and a place to stay. We have to. So we will." This was by way of Anne explaining how they could take some of the proceeds from the car to buy a used backpack. James knew Anne well enough now to know this was her cue that the subject was done. Truth was, he was glad to hear they would soon stop running. He felt unsettled. He was still getting used to the sensation of not planning each day. It was strange not to know, from one moment to the next, what was coming up. He had always thought of himself as flexible, rolling with the punches. But losing Father Mullenix's car had depressed him.

James followed Anne as they lugged their bags down the four-lane boulevard through town. "So why are we buying backpacks if we're going to stop hitchhiking soon?

"One, we have to have the right props for our story. *We are two orphans, and we were living with relatives, but it got too crowded.* Two, we might have to just up and run fast sometime, if my father tracks us down."

Anne spotted a thrift store. "You wait here. *I'm going backpacking with some girlfriends, but I'm not sure I'll like it, so I don't want to spend an arm and a leg.* Sound good?" James grinned and waved her away.

Anne emerged again a few minutes later. She carried an odd metal frame like a suitcase, smiling and lifting it slightly as he watched her approach.

"A dollar seventy-five!" She set the rig down on its end. Zippers and empty pouches dotted the outer edge.

"I'm not sure, but I think it's upside down," he said laconically, enjoying Anne's exuberance. Once they'd satisfied themselves on the bag's orientation, they began filling it with the contents of Anne's bags. They were able to stuff all of her clothing, two books, and her girl-things in the bag, as well as his books and extra shoes. She tried to lift it, and groaned.

"I can carry the pack," he said. "Can you handle the red bag for now, if we rig a shoulder strap for it from my duffel bag's strap?"

With his Bowie knife, he cut two slits through either end of Anne's travel bag, to slip the belt through. After a couple of attempts, they were able to fashion a shoulder strap for the bag.

Anne lifted it and shrugged the strap over her shoulder. "This will work," she nodded, as her eyes focused on something in the distance. She turned to James, in a now-familiar set.

"Now what are you plotting, April Dancer? You have that look," he said.

"Well, it's funny you should mention her, Mister. How would you like to be my Mark Slate tonight?" She glanced meaningfully across the highway.

Traveler's Roost. Rest a spell. Free TV. $12.95 single.

James looked back at her. "Think they'd have a bathtub?" He was amazed to feel his cheeks flame when the words passed his lips. Anne seemed suddenly shy too, as if she'd walked into a dance where she wasn't sure she knew anyone.

"If it isn't too much more than that... a shower is more likely. I've only stayed in a motel once, when we took the ferry to go to Williamsburg last year." She stopped.

James felt the stillness between them, even as the breeze lifted the leaves on the lone tree in front of the thrift store. He rose to shove the duffel bag into a trashcan at the corner. As he walked back, he noted the darkening sky, and the currents of air flapping the canopies along the other storefronts.

"It would be cool to sleep in a real bed for one night. And clean up. Maybe there's a laundry mat nearby." He sat down next to Anne.

"Also looks like it may rain. Maybe hard." Then she turned to look at him, her eyes a mix of passions, at once wet like a youth and glittering like a woman.

She took James's hand, and he squeezed hers in return. "So what's our cover, April?"

Anne grinned shyly, and then reverted to her schoolteacher tone, instructing him on the story to offer the clerk at the motel. James returned a few minutes later, his heart pounding. In answer to her unspoken question, he said, "The man never asked. He looked at me funny, but when I said *my sister, and me* he just asked for the money and the registration. It was fifteen dollars and twenty-five cents, check-out noon." James chortled. "He did say if we're in town on Sunday, we should come on down to his church for "Jesus-centered" worship. I told him we were Catholic. What are you, anyway?"

"I am Methodist, James Paxton. Catholic, indeed!" She shouldered the bag, and shaded her eyes against the rising wind, to glance up the thickening clouds. "Is he from the Methodists?"

"Naw. Something I never heard of. Church of Signs Following or something." He shrugged.

"Do you mind if I run in the market, and get something for us to eat later? Maybe crackers and cheese? Grapes? A couple Nehis?"

"No. You go. I'll keep an eye on things." He shoved the green-tagged room key in his back pocket and watched her walk away, his mouth dry. He felt the subtle shift of their roles. Anne was deferring to him, and something primal in him responded. In this one area of their joined lives, at least for this time, he felt her stepping back to let him lead, and he liked it. Unless he was wildly mistaken, they were about to participate in the most ancient of rites, and his palms felt clammy at the prospect. He was curious, afraid, and excited.

A minute later, she returned, fisting the grocery bag at her side.

"Ready?" She breathed.

He nodded, not trusting his voice. James lifted the backpack. Anne had to help him position it on his back. It felt heavier than he had imagined, and he wondered how he'd manage.

"Use the belt," she said. "It has a belt that puts most of the weight on your hips."

After a few gyrations, he was able to connect the two ends of the belt, and cinch it tight. Immediately he felt the lightness in his shoulders. "Hey, this isn't bad!" He grinned sheepishly at her. "I guess I can do this for a hundred feet."

She glanced across the street, her chin down. He reached out to take her hand, and then stopped.

"Are we brother and sister?"

She stepped close and scooped her fingers into his, squeezing his palm. "Not today, Mr. Slate."

The crackers and cheese sat untouched on the small round table in the room. They lay in the warm darkness to the sound of pelting rain tapping the windows. It was a soaking summer storm, with the occasional thunder boom, at first close, then drifting off to the east. James cradled Anne in his arm and stroked her back. The light seeping through the places where the curtains refused to join painted an undulating pattern of grey and black on the wall next to the lone mirror.

Anne sighed. He sensed, rather than saw, Anne lift her head, and sensed her smile as well. She kissed him light, but wet, on the lips, lingering.

"This is why I ran with you. I couldn't bear the thought of never doing this with you. Just this." She shifted to lay her leg over his, and slowly drew his thigh between her own.

Sometime during that too swift, unforgettable night, James remembered the small packet he'd picked up in Mount Rainier. In the dark, even after the raw intimate exchanges, they blushed, fumbling. He almost threw the tiny capsule aside, in frustration.

He marveled at the manner in which Anne took over, at the crucial moment. She seemed to sense the pain that awaited her, but it was she who soothed him. She stroked his face, even as tears seeped from her eyes. He made a mild attempt to pull away, but she clutched him, breathing hard into his neck.

"I love you," she murmured, soft as a beach cloud.

26 / Skipping Stones

Nash Street was ablaze in late summer morning sun. The soft golden rays dappled all the unshaded areas with bright warmth. Dylan stared out at the street, his jaw clenched. It had been several days since the attack. He replayed it repeatedly, hating himself for reliving the fright and the shame. He vowed there would never be a next time. Never again would he get into a spot where he was so completely helpless. He would die first.

Absently, he noticed his body rise to its feet, its shuffle through the act of dressing and slipping on sneakers. As if observing a stranger, he saw his body walk downstairs and then left toward the front door. Nana called out something, but he had tuned his mental receiver to scramble all incoming messages for the last several days. Without a plan, he headed across Nash Street toward the river.

Dylan had overheard Nana and Sam talking last evening on the porch, from the sanctuary of his room. Something about the end of summer, and boys, and moodiness. Nana was trying to explain Dylan to his father, not for the first time. He admired and loved Nana a lot. But he could not understand what she thought qualified her to explain his complex life to anyone, much less a man who had quit the job of being his father years ago.

If his dad had been around, like Stinger's dad and Billy's dad, Dylan would have learned how to take care of himself. Never mind that those other dads also had a nasty habit of periodically beating their sons nearly to death for serious infractions such as forgetting to close a door. No, Dylan had been raised not by his dad, or even by his mother. Nana was nice enough, but she was not really a parent, was she?

He had heard Nana and his father last night harping again on the question of why Maureen seemed so sorry as she neared death. The last time his father had talked to his mother had been by phone, shortly before she passed. She had said repeated how sorry she was. She had done something, she was sure, to harm him. When he had tried to tell her that he understood, she had responded with *No No No you don't. No one could.* But even dying, she would explain no more.

"Of *course* I hoped that Dylan's birth somehow would help ease the pain in our lives. But by then, I think she was spent, or she was afraid to allow herself to feel, because she just never showed an ounce of affection for that child. Truth be told, for James either, after David…" His father, in a soft, sad tone.

Dylan thought he understood the anger James felt. On that one quiet morning, his father had not only let David slip away. It was when James lost his mother too, and eventually his father. All because Sam made a bad choice.

These thoughts ran through Dylan's head as he settled on the bank of the Wicomico, staring unseeing at the muddy swirls around the log stump occupied by the smooth-backed water turtles.

After a while, Dylan rose, stiff and feeling the bruises. He felt the weight in his right hand, and lifted the three smooth river stones. Where had he collected these rocks? The *why* was readily evident. Skipping rocks was a boy's whole purpose on the banks of a river. That and fishing. He dropped two of the stones into his left hand, and cocked the remaining one in the trigger finger of his right.

If this stone skips six times or more, I talk to Sam. Hand him his job back on a trial basis. Dylan side-armed the stone, which arced only slightly before ricocheting off the surface in its first skip. It stayed flat, skimming the muddy water for several more bounces, before skittering into a dribble of smaller skids, and sinking into the river near the far bank.

Dylan considered this. *If* this *rock skips at least twice, and lands on the far bank, I'll talk to Sam.* Dylan arced the second stone out over the water. As soon as it left his hand, he knew it flew true. The rock glinted in the bleached morning sun, darkened wet as it skipped once and twice, and landed with a pffft in the wild grass of the opposite bank.

Dylan straightened. The rocks had spoken.

27 / CeCe

James held the restaurant door open for Anne. They passed from the steamy, dusty August outdoors into the cool shadows of the A & W Diner. The waitress led them to a booth by the window.

Anne stirred her coffee, glancing out the window of the café. James thought he had never seen her so beautiful. Maybe it had been so long since he'd seen her hair washed and shining just so. She looked different. Or perhaps it was he.

"Sure you won't try some, Jimmy?" Anne lifted her cup, her eyes sparkling. The late-morning sun dappled her in the red and blue colors of the diner's window advertising. A large *E* danced across her left breast as she lifted and replaced the cup.

He shrugged, smiling, and took the proffered cup. He sipped as she watched.

"I guess it's an acquired taste," he grimaced, handing the cup back. "Nana never drank it until my father came back." His face darkened for an instant. "So we never had coffee in the house."

"I just started this year. Drinking it. My mom wouldn't let me."

James raised his eyes from his drumming fingers at the hitch in her voice. Her eyes were wet, glimmering in the sun's bright reflection. She dabbed casually at her cheekbone, intent on something out the window.

"More orange juice or coffee?" the waitress asked. She reminded him of Nana, with her quiet manners. *It doesn't hurt to show a bit of Emily Post's etiquette*, Nana would say. *We're not beasts, after all.*

Across the table, Anne covered the cup gently with her hand. "That was very good, thank you."

Emily Post reached across the table, grunting, to adjust the shade. "Don't want y'all getting blinded with such a pretty day waiting for you." Her voice had a lilt that reminded James of the way Sam used to converse, well into his cups.

"Food'll be up in a jif," she said, and moved to the next booth.

Emily arrived again with their plates. James started to reach for his knife, and paused as she set the plates down, toast on the side.

"More orange juice, honey?" she asked, though he had hardly touched it.

"No. No thanks, this is fine." As soon as the waitress turned, James said quietly, "What is this white stuff?"

Anne had a soft scoop of it on her plate too. "I don't know. I asked for eggs and sausage. Which I got." They both stared at the mounds on their plates, a consistency of crushed corn, but lighter in color.

James lifted his fork and slipped a dollop on the end. He tasted it. "It's like...oatmeal? But not oats. Got me." He moved on to his own eggs.

"Do you like it?" Anne asked.

"Not even a little bit," James replied.

"You were wonderful last night, Jimmy," she leaned forward over her plate, smiling.

He blushed red as Christmas.

"Jimmy!" Anne lifted a hand to her mouth, then bent close over the table. "Did you ever collect that trash like I told you?" she whispered.

James groaned. He was supposed to collect the wrappings from the condoms, and the condoms themselves, before they'd left the hotel room.

"Oh well. Guess somebody's going to realize we are not really brother and sister." He whispered back quietly. She did not return his discomfited grin.

"Oh well," she said, shrugging. Then she looked around, and leaned forward again. "Are you sure you never..." she smiled, and rubbed the side of his calf with her bare insole, up under his jeans cuff.

He withdrew his leg, banging it against the booth base, and a police officer who'd just entered paused on his way to the counter stools.

James looked up as Anne fixed him with a sweet smile.

"'Morning," she beamed, as if she'd known him all her life. The officer glanced at James, and then smiled back at Anne. He tipped his hat and then removed it, the *Georgia State* insignia gleaming at the peak. He turned to the server behind the counter, a willowy girl with flat blonde hair, who'd just arrived, a little breathless.

"'Morning to you also, Daisy Ritter. Or did I miss the wedding?" he raised a hand in greeting to the young waitress. "Cuppa joe, when you have a moment."

"Where you been keepin' yourself?" the waitress asked. James followed her automatic movements as she slipped her purse into a shelf below the register, shrugged out of a sweater, and knotted a small apron around her waist, all at the same time, it seemed, while managing to nod back at the officer. Her smile could have been arranged by a mortician, with eyes that were as disconcerting as seeing a dead person with the lids open.

The officer turned back to Anne, with a brief nod to James. James noticed his glance at their packs, resting inside the benches next to them.

"This hot where you're headed?" he said, looking now at James.

James froze, and again felt Anne' toes on his shin. This time, she was lightly tapping. *Think*, the toes said.

"This isn't so hot," he replied, his mind racing.

"We're headed back to school in a couple weeks, then we'll be wishing it was still summer," she said.

The officer spun his hat in his meaty hands. He was not tall, perhaps James's height, and thick in the middle. His shock of brown hair was graying at the short sideburns, and one eye rested distractedly lower than the other. Maybe James just imagined, but it seemed he cocked his head in the other direction to compensate.

The officer nodded at Anne, clearly expecting her to say more.

"Ever since my brother Roy and I got the letter," she nodded at James, "We've been looking forward to seeing this part of Georgia." James noticed how she said *letter* with no discernible *r*, and he thought it best to let Anne do the talking.

"But we had to get through the funeral and meeting with the lawyer and all, and turns out mom had nothing but the house—which is really a lot, I guess, except not until it's sold…" Anne's explanation seemed to mesmerize the officer, who continued to twirl his cap, his eyes and smile fixed on Anne.

"And when—well, do you know Judith West and her family, out Odessa Way?" Anne paused, and James marveled at her calm. He remembered seeing a sign for Odessa coming into town yesterday. Somewhere off to the west, he thought.

"Sorry, miss. I'm out of the Riceboro Barracks. I don't get down this way as often as I used to. These folks kin of yours?"

Anne looked at the officer, and then dropped her eyes. For a sickening moment, James thought she was about to confess all. Then she looked at the officer again.

"Judith and my mother served in the Army Nurse Corps in France together. They both agreed that if there were ever anything one could do for another…"

The officer spun his hat, looking into the middle distance for a moment.

"I was almost sent over, and then it all ended," he said distantly. "This might sound strange, but I'm sorry I missed it. But…" he grinned, "The military made me a policeman, so here we all are."

Anne smiled her most radiant smile, and said, "We told Judith we would come down and visit her as soon as things settled a bit. The house is for sale, but money's tight 'til it happens. So we decided to leave Chicago for a week, and come down visiting!"

The officer mulled this over, and seemed satisfied. Daisy the server's flat voice rang out that his coffee was up. He listed to one side to adjust his belt, and said, "Have a nice visit here," and moved off to the counter.

James wiped his damp palms on his thighs, hunched low over the table. "I hate cops," he said.

Anne gave him an exasperated look. "Jimmy Paxton." She glanced away. "It doesn't pay to get so angry."

"And I don't want to be *Roy*. You called me that yesterday too."

"Who would you like to be?" she said, then hushed as *Emily* stopped to offer her coffee.

"And how is everything?" *Emily* asked.

"Wonderful, thank you," Anne replied.

"Can I get you anything else, dears?" She beamed at their clean plates, but seemed to pause over the small mound remaining on each.

Anne nodded no, and *Emily* drew the receipt book from her apron pocket. She tore off the check, and laid it between them.

"Make a memory then, this glorious day," she smiled.

James paid at the register. The trooper was having his ear bent by a grizzled farmer in ancient overalls.

"Coming out of Chestnut's store, bags of vittles, like he just bought the place. You ever seen a darkie *ever* in Chestnut's?"

The officer was nodding absently, stirring his coffee, as James waited for Daisy to compute the change. She stared at the numbers displayed on the register, then down at the money in her hand, and back again.

"I guess Baker's ain't good enough for the colored around here anymore. They be all up in Chestnut's clutching at fruit and vegetables and what all, and looking decent folk in the eyes."

James noticed the trooper wipe at something on his cheek, as the old codger turned once again to exclaim in his face. James grinned to himself and took the change Daisy offered. Amazingly, she got it right. He pocketed all but fifty cents, and walked back to the table.

"Ready?" he laid down the tip and helped Anne to her feet. Together, they slung their packs, and headed out into the day. The late morning sun already had folks walking the shady side of the street, as James and Anne made their way back to the highway. The heat shimmered on the sidewalk, and they hiked from shady spot to shady spot. At the end of the commercial area, they had to step off the walk and set out again on the dusty asphalt.

"Hey. What do you think that's about?" James shielded his eyes, pointing ahead on the side of the road. Anne followed his gaze. A figure was crouched on the gravel of the wide shoulder ahead. It appeared to be a woman, dressed in a flannel shirt, jeans, and gardening gloves.

"Is she planting something?" James asked, from the side of his mouth.

"I can't tell," she said under her breath.

The woman turned at the sound of their steps on crunching gravel. A girl, really. She was young, perhaps 13 or 14, and she wore a straw farm hat which she pressed to her head as a large truck whined past them on the highway. She occupied the center of a pull-off notched in the shoulder of the highway, set back in a stand of loblolly pines.

James could see now she was bent over a makeshift memorial, with a cross rising from a pile of stones, adorned with flowers, faded scraps of paper, and several yellowed photographs.

James and Anne would have walked by, but the girl raised a trowel in greeting.

"Howdy," she said, in a friendly Southern lilt.

They nodded, and Anne said, "Nice day," with a rolled timbre to the word *day* that told James she was preparing to strike up another conversation. Why did she have to talk to *everybody*?

The girl bobbed her head up and down, and sat back on her haunches in the dust. She smiled and wiped her palms on her dusty jeans. "I'm CeCe Delikat. Short for Cecelia. It sure is. Where you two off to?"

Anne introduced the two of them as Stephanie and Mark, sister and brother. James nodded, wondering why those names sounded familiar.

"So Miss CeCe, what are you doing out here?" Anne asked.

"Oh, just tending. I come out here every week or so. There....was an accident here."

Anne looked down at the scant offerings below the cross.

"It was my mom and my little brother. She was coming to pick me up from a sleepover, and a big truck had a flat tire, right when she was trying to get onto the highway."

James blanched. "Are they right here?" He blurted, gesturing at the makeshift monument. A passing truck raised a swirl of gray dust that settled on the flowers at the base of the white picket cross. The girl lifted a rag and wiped at them absently.

"Goodness no. They're in the town cemetery west of here. Pastor said it was the biggest turnout he'd ever seen. Seems like more people was there than live in the whole town. Stores closed. The Negroes came, the school closed. It was the biggest thing around." CeCe looked from them to the small pile of mementoes as she narrated the events.

"I'm awful sorry for your loss," Anne said quietly. James nodded. "When did all this happen?"

"Thanksgiving vacation last year. Momma let me spend the night with my best friend Julie Rose the Friday after. It happened Saturday morning." CeCe bent and straightened a crooked stem, and James realized the flowers, once brightly colored, were plastic.

"So they...it happened right here?" James felt a little squeamish.

"Yes," said CeCe. "The car caught fire, and nobody could get near for a goodly time. But everyone said they'd gone to see Jesus before any of that happened."

CeCe plucked a sheet of plastic from beneath a stone. James peered at the cutback in the side of the road. He sniffed at the air; no lingering trace of smoke. But high on the trunks of several trees, he noticed scorched skin, and stumps of branches, charcoaled at their ends. While nature had restored things quickly, he could imagine the scene less than a year ago, as townspeople and highway drivers would have gathered, the way people do.

He felt guilty that he'd been so impatient just a moment ago. He stepped forward and looked at the low monument more closely. A *GI Joe* with chipped paint stood next to a vase filled with the only real flowers, and a small sunflower plant with dusty leaves was rising from a mound of dark soil.

"My mom loved sunflowers more than anything." CeCe reached out to James with a picture, taped inside the plastic.

"Jerome was a real pain, truth be told. He was the whiniest creature. A tattle tale too." James looked at the faded photo of a gap-toothed boy with tousled hair the same shade as CeCe's, squirming on the knee of a young, harried woman who was saying something to him, not looking at the camera.

James felt Anne lightly brush his side, and they both stared. James tilted the photo to block the glare of the nearly straight-up sun. "My mom was Susan Delikat. She was going to be a dancer, but she fell in love with my daddy, and didn't go off to Atlanta after all. She always said the dancing could wait. But sometimes when she was cleaning, she would put on this record—some Russian man's music—and she would dance for Jerome and me. She was real good."

James handed the picture back. For the first time, CeCe's voice cracked. Next to him, Anne slipped her arm in his. She said, "It must be hard, losing your momma and your brother together like that." Then Anne stiffened, and eased her hand from under James.

CeCe looked away from them, pressed the plastic carefully around the edges of the picture, and laid it back down next to the cross.

"It was hard on my daddy. He loved my mother so. And Jerome..." CeCe shook her head slowly, gazing into the middle distance. Then she brightened.

"We get along okay. The neighbors still bring food, and Julie Rose's mom says I'm like a daughter, and Julie Rose says I *am* her sister." CeCe peaked up at them from under the brim of the straw hat. "My daddy's still pretty lonesome. 'This too shall pass,' Miss Wetzel says. She's my teacher at school. I think she might be sweet on my dad. But he doesn't notice much of things."

Anne nodded. "So... is it just your dad and you now?" she said quietly.

"Why yes, when daddy's here. He drives trucks for the lumber company, and seems like he has to go further and further to pick up wood." CeCe peered up at Anne.

"Where do you stay when you're not at home with your father?" Anne asked. James cleared his throat, but she ignored him.

"My grandma and grandpa—my momma's parents—I stayed with them pretty often in the beginning. Now over to Julie Rose's sometimes, when school's out for summer holiday. I know her from church. Where're you and your brother staying?"

"CeCe, you ask such intelligent questions, and I would feel more intelligent myself if I knew the answer!" Anne gave an exaggerated shrug. "Our parents, well, before they passed..."

"My goodness! Y'all haven't got either of your parents?" CeCe pressed her hat down on her head. For a moment, James thought she was going to whoop or something. He already had turned away from the young girl, hoping Anne would follow suit, but he could tell his companion had an idea percolating.

"We're orphans. Mommy and daddy died together, and that was probably a comfort to each of them." Anne laid a hand on CeCe's arm. "But it was a long time ago, and we don't know all the details. We...well to tell the truth, by the time people seemed inclined to talk about it, I just didn't want to hear about it anymore. I like the memories I have... just the way they are."

CeCe nodded, absorbing this older girl's words with appropriate solemnity. "It might seem strange. Daddy tells me I'm gonna get myself killed out here by a car. But I come out here to...where they...were last, because it feels like I can catch them on the way out the door, or something like that. I never do. I always miss them—even Jerome. But I don't mind. I know I'll come again, and who knows?"

James thought he saw the sense of her young logic. He couldn't know for sure, but he guessed that her mother's and brother's presence would somehow seem more real here than in some anonymous plot of ground where empty shells of skin and bones lay moldering.

"I am about to burn up in this sun," Anne said. "Can we move back in these trees and cool ourselves a bit?"

James looked at her with growing resentment. Whatever she was up to, he could not fathom. She clearly was ignoring his attempts to get her moving. Instead, they ambled past the small cairn to the back of the cleared space. A pine-needled path led back into the loblolly pine stand. James felt immediately cooler in the quiet shade.

"Where does this trail go?" James asked, as he set down his pack heavily.

"Almost all trails around here end up at Cat Head Creek." CeCe smiled.

"You sure it's not Cattail Creek?" James asked, feeling contrary.

"I should be sure, shouldn't I? I've lived here pretty much all my life. So what's wrong with Cat Head Creek anyway?" She blinked at James.

"I just never heard of a Cat Head anything before. That's all. I suppose one could catch catfish from Cat Head Creek?" He smirked at her.

"Only from a catamaran. Otherwise, it's a catastrophe." CeCe leered back and Anne burst out laughing. James grinned widely.

"You are a bright girl, CeCe of Darien," Anne giggled. "I started to tell you, my brother and I—um…what?"

CeCe had crossed her arms and was rolling her eyes. She dropped her hands and shoved them deep in her pockets, studying them. "If you are brother and sister, then I'm a caterpillar in a catalog."

James and Anne gaped at the girl. "Why, what do you mean, CeCe?" Anne said.

"Since when do a brother and a sister make goo goo eyes at each other?" CeCe's eyes narrowed. "I won't tell anybody. But you look at him—" CeCe looked from Anne to James, "like Miss Wetzel looks at my daddy. And there isn't any *sister* about it."

"If we tell you you're right, will that do for now, CeCe?" Anne pleaded. James watched, fascinated. He was beginning to understand just how good Anne was about reading people, and he could see that her affected emotion touched CeCe, who instantly softened and smiled.

"Of course it will, Stephanie. Is that your real name?" she asked, grinning.

"You said…." Anne looked at James for help.

"Okay. If you say you are Stephanie and Mark, I believe you. But I'm probably not the only person around who watches *Girl from Uncle.*

James glanced at Anne. "Our friend should be a detective." He sighed. "I'm James. This is Anne." And that is a *big* secret for the time being." CeCe nodded seriously.

"One more thing," CeCe said, her face now somber. "Are your parents alive?"

Anne looked at James, who spoke. "My mom died recently. I didn't really know her. But we…" he looked at Anne, and she shook her head imperceptibly. "…will tell you more another time. Maybe."

CeCe smiled. "So I suppose you're looking for someplace to…stay? Do you camp out?"

James looked at Anne, who shrugged, a confused expression on her face. They watched CeCe turn down the path, and they hitched their packs up once again.

"Maybe. So Miss CeCe, how do you know about where this goes?" Anne wiped at her brow and slipped her hand in James's.

CeCe retrieved the straw hat that a low pine branch had snagged. A long red piece of ribbon dangled from the back of the hat, and CeCe drew it through her fingers, combing needles out of it.

"Momma used to carry Jerome through these woods, me following, to retrieve herbs, in the manner of *her* mother." She stroked at a blooming pink plant at the side of the trail, and then moved on.

"That's a useful plant y'all will likely become friends with out here," she said, over her shoulder. "You won't find it down by the river. It doesn't favor shade."

James and Anne glanced down at the bush with the crimson buds. "What is it?" asked Anne.

"Eucalyptus," James and CeCe replied in unison.

"What will we use it for?" Anne continued.

"Mosquitoes," CeCe called back.

28 / Pugilistic Guidance

Sam tinkered under the hood of the Dodge Dart. He had pulled the car out of the garage and into the shade of the front elm. His hands were streaked with oil, but the car's engine gleamed under the propped hood.

Dylan stood for a few moments and watched his dad replace the oil cap and wipe the manifold cover with a light blue rag.

Finally, Dylan said, "I need to learn how to fight."

Sam paused in his wiping but did not speak.

"I'm not going to be beat up because my brother is a dumb jerk."

His father gave a slight nod, to register the words.

"I can learn on my own. But I don't know just where to start."

Sam eased out from under the hood and straightened, stretching his back with his hands on his hips.

"I guess I can show you the basics. It will be enough to keep you alive, maybe." Sam winked.

Dylan nodded, grateful his dad wasn't asking a bunch of grownup questions. Though Sam didn't act like Dylan thought a father should, that wasn't entirely a bad thing.

"I'd appreciate it if you could—when you have some time, sir."

Sam wiped his hands with the oil-streaked rag, studying Dylan for a moment. "How about we take some time before supper? In the back yard."

***

Dylan felt his father's strong hands position his shoulders. Then Sam bent and coaxed Dylan's left leg back a foot or more from his right. "Most folks think boxing is all about your hands. Let's hope your challenger thinks that way too."

Fists raised in imitation of how he remembered Cassius Clay, Dylan swung his head to follow Sam as his dad stepped in front of him.

"Consider that your legs are like having two more arms. Wouldn't that be helpful in a fight?"

The image of Cammy pinning him while Stinger smirked just inches from his face burned in Dylan's memory. "How does that work though? Two more arms?"

"I'll show you. Drop those hands. Clasp 'em behind your back."

Dylan did as instructed. He instantly felt exposed, facing Sam on.

"Now," his father said, his own hands at his side, "if you wanted to shrink yourself as a target, what do you think you'd do?"

Dylan studied the problem. "Shrink myself?" Like Atom Ant? I guess I'd scrunch. Like this."

Sam smiled. "Good. Since you're thinner sideways, present just your side to me. No, keep the hand—your writin' hand—away from me."

Dylan turned his shoulders. His hips were now squared over the feet Sam had positioned.

"Remember how Clay ducked his head in, kept his body down low 'til he fired?"

Dylan ducked his neck in like a turtle hiding.

"Good. It won't feel so awkward when you get your arms in the game too, but you got it so far. Now, I'm going to poke at you in slow motion. Since you got no arms, you'll have to dance."

Dylan grimaced. "I thought I said it was fighting lessons I was after."

His father grinned. "Who won the Clay-Liston fight? Bear or butterfly?" He cocked a brow at Dylan. "For now, we assume whoever you're up against is also right-handed. But you'll want to be sure to inquire, before you undertake pugilistic combat."

Dylan scratched his head. 'Puga- what?'

"Just a fancy word for fisticuffs. Boxing. Sparring. Bouting. Come to think of it, there's a bunch of words in the language for braining your fellow man."

Dylan smiled. "Fighting. Rumbling. Slugfest."

Sam nodded. "Well, yes. But those aren't always done with as many rules as boxing includes. Hands behind your back again."

Dylan reached behind himself, clasping his hands together. "Boxing has rules?"

His father turned Dylan's shoulders again to present a side view. "Of course. Else, there'd be no need for the zebra man. The referee."

Sam studied Dylan for a second, and then raised his own fists. "I am going to spar a little now, with my lead fist. The left one, out front here. When you see me let loose with it, move to your left. To the back of the hand. Try stepping sideways, not back."

"But what if you hit me?"

His dad smiled. "This is a fight. Less I am one of the neighbor ladies, who you are not allowed to fight anyway, then you are going to get hit. Sometimes hard. The idea is for you to hit back, harder. And a little more often."

Sam poked at Dylan like he was jabbing underwater, and Dylan easily stepped sideways, watching the back of Sam's fist move past his chin. Dylan noticed the blotches of dark skin on the back of his father's rough hands.

"Now, I throw a little faster. Most street fighters aim for your head. The boxer's version of a home run. It's easier to move your head out of range than to move your middle."

Sam jabbed several times at Dylan's face. Dylan swiveled out of the arc of Sam's fist. Then Sam cocked his elbow low, and fired at Dylan's stomach, easing up on the punch as Dylan swung his hands up, too late to cover.

"Another thing. Don't watch my eyes. Watch my middle. My eyes will lie to you, so I can take you out. Now, fists up."

Dylan raised his fists, and rocked up on his toes. Sam smiled. "Remember too. Street fighting, you sometimes have to make your own rules, to accommodate the situation you find yourself in."

"What do you mean, *make your own rules?*"

"Say Clay is boxing Sonny, and all of a sudden Sugar Ray jumps in the ring. Do you think Cassius is going to box by the regular rules?" Sam tucked lower, and jabbed at Dylan's middle, grunting his approval when Dylan covered and shuffle-stepped sideways.

"You mean like what happened to me?"

Sam nodded, his face darkening. Dylan hadn't told him everything, but he'd told him enough. "So watch what I do when the fight turns mean."

29 / Cat Head Creek

In twenty minutes, the three hikers came to the edge of a sweeping river, visible beyond a thick stand of cattail. They turned east along the bank, until CeCe suggested they were doubling back a little too close to town.

"Townsfolk out fishing will spot you within the day. I'd guess y'all would prefer folks not be traipsing through your site." She led them back west and south, to a spot at the base of an awning-like oak at a tiny jutting where the river hooked south.

"Most people just follow the deer path past this spot." She pointed back at the barely-visible trail they'd hiked in on. "If you're quiet during the day and careful to not overuse the trail, y'all should be good for— well, how long y'all staying?"

James shrugged his pack down and walked slowly around the base of the tree, noting the flat area on the river side of the giant oak, and the traces of a deer path down to the river. The plants that grew in such profusion along most of the river's edge were absent in this small section of riverbank.

"We're not exactly sure. How far are we from town, you reckon?" he jammed his hands in his pockets.

CeCe pressed her hand to her hat as a small breeze lifted off the lowland. Her blonde hair danced under the brim. "A mile, give or take. An easy walk, but most won't bother coming this far out. Fishing's fine closer in." She gazed down the bank and the water that lapped at it. "Y'all be easy spotted from the river itself, depending, and this might be a place for fishermen to come ashore and tinkle. Not that most of them bother. If I were y'all, I'd toss some dead branches down to block the path up the bank."

"What about canoe campers?" Anne asked.

"Possible," Anne nodded. "Today's um...Wednesday. Y'all might see some campers the weekend. Most boaters favor the Altamaha, especially up in Wayne County. Y'all can see an old paddlewheel boat in the muck up by Jesup. Y'all going to be here long?"

James looked at Anne. She shrugged.

"I was thinking I'd like to go to a church on Sunday."

CeCe smiled. "I took you right off for a Christian girl." James noticed she did not refer to his religious inclination.

"How do we get to town from here?" James asked, kicking away large branches at the foot of the tree.

"Y'all just follow the river path back east. It gets wider as you approach town. Don't get confused by the river direction, though. It's a tidal river, sometimes running north, sometimes south." Cece bent to lift the leaves of a small two-leafed plant.

Anne walked to the edge of the small cleared area, looking down at the river flowing lazily by. "I guess we can fish."

James smirked. "Did you bring your pole? Don't worry," he said. "I brought a reel. But I need tackle."

Anne turned to CeCe. "Are you headed back to town?"

CeCe nodded. "Yep. Y'all want me to call you by your real names?"

James shook his head behind CeCe, but Anne set her face in a decision. "CeCe, you must promise never to use them, except right here, in this spot, with just us."

CeCe nodded solemnly. "I've no wish to get you in more trouble. Are you in some kind of trouble?"

"Just the running-away kind," Anne smiled. "I'm close, but not quite, of age."

CeCe waited. Anne drew a breath. "Anne and Jimmy are fine here. Maybe it's best somebody knows. Jimmy goes by James too. If you ever here of somebody asking after us..."

"...I'll tell you right away. Promise."

James slowly pivoted, surveying the scene. "We need some things.

I'll hide the packs, and we can hike back with you."

CeCe straightened her shoulders. "I'm not one to tell you your business, but Darien's not exactly what you'd call a big town. If you are trying to stay low, it might be best to avoid going in too often. People around here have lots of time to talk. Especially after planting, and after the boats come in in the afternoon."

James glanced at Anne. "We need some kind of tent. Or at least a tarp. Fishing tackle. Bait. Food. Water." He shrugged. "A can opener."

"I can help with some of that," CeCe said slowly.

Anne touched her arm. "What are you talking about, CeCe?"

CeCe walked to the edge of the clearing, looking out over the river. "My parents used to take us camping. Over to Okefenokee, and Lake Lanier. We have all the gear."

James considered. "That's great, but how do we get it here?"

CeCe paused, thinking. "I can get stuff out of the house. My dad would never miss it. He doesn't notice much anymore."

"You don't think anyone else will wonder about you walking through town with an armload of camping gear?" James sighed. "What do you have, anyway?"

"Everything you'd need. Tent. Lantern. Sleeping bags. Cook pots." CeCe looked thoughtful. "Let me think for a second."

Anne studied the clearing. James could see her imagining a camp. A tent pitched, door facing the meandering river. A fire in the middle of the clearing. Once again, he felt helpless. He was supposed to be the man. But here he was, nearly penniless, without a clue, while two girls worked out what should be done next. He turned, annoyed, and kicked at the dust. He stared out over the placid water and the gently fanning cattails. His attention was snared by an obelisk, jutting above the trees in the blue mid-day sky.

"Hey, what's that brick tower?" he asked.

Without glancing up, CeCe said, "that's the old Butler Rice Mill chimney."

"It's a chimney?" James asked, impressed.

"Yes. This whole area was dotted with rice plantations before the war, and many of them had their own mills. That chimney is all that's left of one of them."

"War?" asked Anne.

CeCe took a stick, and bent to draw in the dirt. "The Civil War, silly. 'Course we like to call it the War of Northern Aggression. Where are y'all from, anyway?" She sat cross-legged in the dirt, laying her straw hat aside. James stared for a moment longer at the redbrick tower. The lower portion was clad in ivy, dark in the shadowed side of the square shaft.

Anne sat down on the carpeted forest floor, near CeCe, at the edge of the dirt clearing. "Up north of here. You look like you have an idea, young miss. How old are you, anyway?"

"Almost sixteen, come October. October 30, just before Trick or Treat. I might have a way," CeCe smiled. "Benjamin, son of Jacob. Or, in this case, son of Millie."

James looked at CeCe. "Not to be rude, but are we changing the subject?"

"Benjamin. He can help by doing what I can't. But we'd have to let him in on your secret."

"I already don't like it," James snapped.

CeCe scratched at the dirt. "I've know Benjamin since I was born, almost. His momma, Missus Millie, tends our laundry and cooks once a week for us. More than that now, seems." She leaned back on her hands, one foot slowly tapping. "Missus Minnie brings Benjamin after school and summers. He could carry your stuff without notice."

"This boy is colored?" James snorted. "And you want to tell him about us hiding out back here?"

"I don't see as we have much choice if we want shelter out here, Jimmy," said Anne.

"Why don't we just publish a little piece in the Our Neighbors section of the paper?" James swore, and kicked at the base of the tree. "Besides, this wasn't our plan."

CeCe swiveled to face him, her young jaw set. "Benjamin is my friend. If I ask him to keep a secret, he will keep a secret. But if you'd rather not..." she shrugged.

Anne laid a hand on CeCe's arm. "We won't last out here without help." She turned to CeCe. "Jimmy's just not used to being a cheerful receiver."

"Mosquitoes out here are known to pick up visitors and just fly right off over the swamp." CeCe nodded. "It can be harsh." Anne's head was turned from him, but James saw Anne grin at CeCe.

"I'm glad you think this is funny. It's not you has to worry about..." His words faded at the warning look from Anne. He looked away in anger, and grabbed a thin reed, lifting it to his lips to chew the end.

"A nigger. I don't like it one bit."

"James!" The word was spoken soft, but Anne's voice was clipped, sharp. She almost always called him Jimmy.

"I don't mean nothing by it. But where we come from, colored aren't exactly given keys to the city. They're lazy and they steal stuff. We don't have much to start with," James sighed, sitting down next to the girls.

Anne started to say something, but CeCe swung on James. "I know plenty of white folks I wouldn't trust with an old fry pan. I don't know about where you come from. If it's so great, it makes me wonder why you had to run."

She raised a hand as Anne made to speak again. CeCe spoke slowly, her jaw set. "Benjamin is a Negro, I guess. Tell you the truth, I don't pay it any mind. I don't think he does either, when it's just him and me. What on earth does it matter anyway?"

The wind lifted as the three sat quiet. James sniffed a hint of something earthy and moist wafting from the ancient water.

"If you trust me, you can trust Benjamin. I am his best friend. I am just trying to help y'all. I don't know another way." CeCe spoke with a surety that made James marvel. She was a younger version of Anne. James wondered what it was like to be so sure of things.

Anne spoke. "We trust you. And if you trust Benjamin, that is all we need to know." She glanced behind CeCe's back, meaningfully, at James. James tossed the reed into the bushes, but did not object.

"We should be okay here for a few days, while we decide what to do. But we can't stay out here too long. We're pretty exposed." James shrugged.

Anne and CeCe nodded and exchanged a glance. A rushing sound made them all turn to the horizon of the river. A large bird flapped low over the coffee-colored water following the thin tidal current.

James looked at CeCe. "Heron?"

"Ibis," CeCe replied. "Herons are thinner."

"How do you know so much about what's out here?" Anne asked.

"Momma. Me and Jerome would help her collect things for the household. When she passed, I kept coming out here because I wanted to remember what she taught me."

CeCe pointed to another plant growing in a clump near an eddy on the river. "See those bees hovering? Watch." The three moved to the edge of the clearing, and sat looking down at the scene. Small wood bees dropped to the flowers, then disappeared inside.

"The bees are after the pools of water in the stalk. But that'll be the last drink they have," CeCe said quietly. "The stalk has these prongs that point down, and the way in doesn't allow getting out."

"What does the plant do with the bees?" Anne asked.

"It eats them. Some kind of acid inside the plant. And not just bees. Anything that fits, it eats."

"Yum," said James, making a face. "What's it called?"

"Pitcher plants. That one's a parrot pitcher."

James turned to stare at CeCe. "Well jeez, how big do they get out here?"

CeCe laughed. "I never heard tell of any humans or small dogs getting gobbled. That's about the normal size. Lucky they don't grow like the Bald Cypress."

Their gaze followed CeCe's to the canopy above them. The mysterious trees were draped in a gray shawl that hung still in the afternoon air.

"That's where all these needles come from, and what makes the floor so soft out here," CeCe continued, gathering a handful of pine needles at her side. "Bald cypress shed their needles come fall. Don't know why. It's also why the water's the color of tea sometimes."

"Is it drinkable?" asked Anne.

"Sure," replied CeCe. "Lots of critters survive off it, and in it. Wouldn't hurt to boil it first though. I'll see to it Benjamin comes with a pot and lid first trip, as well as the shelter tent."

James crinkled his nose. "Does it always smell that way? Smells like... "

"Roadkill?" suggested CeCe, grinning.

"Well, yes. Something dead."

"That's actually that plant running up the tree trunk there." CeCe gestured behind them. "It's a stinky old thing."

"That's the *plant*?" James asked, incredulous.

"Yes indeed. It's called a green-briar. The ibex, which you met before, favors those red berries." CeCe gestured with a nod. "And the flies you see are drawn by the stink. Just don't pitch too close to the bush, and they shouldn't trouble y'all."

"Green-briar," said Anne slowly, scratching at her shoulder. "And bald cypress. Does that gray hanging stuff have a name too?"

"Spanish moss," said James, promptly. He looked at CeCe. "I know a thing or two about the woods myself."

"I can see you do," CeCe said. She paused a moment, then looked at him levelly. "But be cautious thinking that when you know the name of a thing, you've learned all there is to know. Like," she glanced at Anne, "Negro."

30 / News From James

As they walked to the back door, Sam rumpled Dylan's hair. Dylan bounded through the screen door. He looked up at Nana. She had an unreadable expression.

"Mail is in," she said. Dylan and Sam both paused on their way through to wash for supper. The arrival of post was not generally a cause for comment.

"Did you open it yet?"

Nana nodded at Sam. Dylan looked at his grandma, confused.

"Did he say where he is?" His father asked.

Dylan realized what they were talking about. "James wrote? What did he say?"

"You both go and wash up. I'm sure you must be heated up from your exercising. I'll pour some lemonade." Nana dried her hands on her apron.

Dear Nan-

First, I am sorry for causing you worry. You know I can take care of myself, and I owe most of that to you . The trouble that caused me to leave in a hurry- I never said it out, but that was not my doing down at Wilson's store.

I think I know who and what, but I also don't' think Chief or Mr. Sampson were of a mind to listen to me. I have never expected to not come back, I am just not sure when or how. So you don't have to tell any fibs on my account, the place where this is posted is not where I am anymore. But if you could, it would be better for now if you make the envelope disappear.

I am fine, and so is Anne. I know you don't approve of her coming with me, but she wanted to, and it is not the best circumstance for starting life, but she also says this is the best chance we may get for now.

She is wonderful, and a good companion. But I sure do miss you, and even miss my little brother. Please tell Dylan and Dad that I am fine, we are fine, and when we figure out a way, we will come back.

Love,

James

Dylan chided himself for the hot tears that trickled from the edge of his eyelids. But his father and Nana seemed not to notice. Sam stared out the kitchen window, his face blank. Nana, expressionless too, folded the note carefully, and tapped it lightly on the table. Dylan noticed there was no envelope about. He lifted his glass and stared at the surface of the lemonade, vibrating in tiny ovals. The note really said nothing. The boy that wrote it had left Dylan behind to take James's beatings for him. Dylan realized with a slow ache that what he felt was some kind of grief, for himself, and for James. He felt a twinge that it had never occurred to him that James might not be guilty of the break-in at Wilson's. He tried to recall what he could about the details. He remembered what James had told him the next day. How he'd been out with Anne, and how he'd picked up the screwdriver that had been used to jimmy the store's back door.

"What's gonna happen to James if he comes back?" Dylan tried to sound calm, but he felt on the verge of trembling. Nana pursed her lips and glanced at Sam. At first, Dylan wasn't sure his father had heard. Then Sam turned full to the table, and tapped his fingers rhythmically on the Formica.

"Honestly, I don't think if he went to court, there's enough evidence to find him guilty. But he'd probably have to testify, and offer some accounting of what he was doing out at that hour. Of course, now I think we can probably guess what that was."

Nana clucked, and Sam flashed his mother a small grin. "Not behavior we might approve of, mother. But not the sort of thing they generally lock someone up for."

"That's true enough," she said, wiping at imaginary crumbs on the table's surface, the letter now safe in the folds of her apron. "Heaven help those children."

Sam continued. "For the rest of it, that'll be up to James himself."

Dylan watched his father, and waited for more, but Sam looked done. "What do you mean, 'the rest of it'"?

As Dylan watched, his dad seemed to age before his eyes. When Sam had first arrived in Crane Ridge, he seemed quite fit, if a little drawn into himself—like a man with a chill. His father moved with an ease that was not quite grace. More like economy of motion. He had a way of understated movement when he reached for his coffee, or planted his cap atop his head. Sam was not one given to flourishes or effect. But he had never seemed to Dylan to be quite the proper age of a *dad*.

Now, his father seemed to be shrinking a little, like a man on the cusp of old age. His eyes watered, red-rimmed, and his gaze had all the focus of a boy gazing out the school window in May.

Dylan shrugged, and headed for the back door.

"Ever been in love?"

He turned back to his father. "Pardon?"

Sam continued to stare out the rippled glass of the kitchen window. "Have you ever been in love?" he asked again.

Dylan usually felt a swell of quiet pride when this strange man would speak to him as if he were not a child. But sometimes, it was as if the man were speaking across the back fence from a different world altogether, where the summer was cold and winter was fair and human mammals abandoned their young to be raised by *their* parents. This question felt like the other side of the fence somehow. *Have you ever been in love?*

"No," he said automatically. Then more slowly, "I don't think so. Why?"

His father pursed his lips as if here were about to whistle, the veined backs of his hands jutting from his front pockets. "I think James is in love. It creates a kind of temporary insanity. Like sniffing from the gas pump or getting into the moonshine." He looked finally at Dylan. Sam's gaze softened.

"That's all I meant about 'the rest of it.' Love can cause a fella to say and do some crazy things. I guess that may be true of women too," he said cryptically. Sam hesitated, his mind somewhere distant. Then he continued. "But it ensures the extension of the species, so I guess the good Lord had his reasons." Sam ducked as Nana swung her dishtowel at him.

Nana tssked. "If you're going to have *that* talk, maybe I should head for the market."

31 / Camping

CeCe prepared to head home. "I'm expected to my grandma's for supper, and I'm helping Julie Rose and her mom. They are baking for this Sunday's social at church."

Anne smiled at her, then frowned, looking around. "Will we see you again today?"

"Probably not. My daddy's off the road. Leaves tomorrow early, and won't be back until Friday evening." CeCe thought a moment. "It might be best if Benjamin and I don't travel here at the same time. Since he should be with Missus Minnie tomorrow to clean, I can talk to him then. Though she is just inclined to stop by this afternoon with a pie. Isn't that funny? Her last name is Pie, and she makes a fine pie. So I don't know when he'll be able to come. Benjamin."

They agreed that if CeCe could get back out of the house this evening, she would try to bring some food, and water. "The river is fine to clean up in," she said. "Just take turns if y'all go in the water so one of you can watch out for gators."

Anne and James looked at each other, askance.

"For drinking water, raid the pitcher plants. You just might have to pick out bug parts." She laughed. James wondered what they *hadn't* been told about their temporary new home deep in the forest. Yes, they had matches, and a fire this far out would probably be fine at night, as long as it wasn't large. CeCe then took her leave.

James had been collecting branches and laying them across two longer poles, forming a shelter that would also serve as a barrier against prying eyes from anyone trekking the wider path west. It passed perhaps two hundred feet from them. As long as they were quiet, it should be safe.

Anne sat and opened the book she'd brought from home and hadn't started yet. She'd looked up when James asked, and held the brown cover up as she recited. "*Dune,* by someone named Herbert. Cherie gave it to me when we traded gifts at the end of school. I'm just getting started. My mom—"

James turned at the sudden silence. Anne's lips were frozen in a small *purse.* He balanced awkwardly, one knee up to splinter the long stick he held. Today was the first day he'd actually missed home. It was the sight of the lazy river in the afternoon stillness, and the dazzling reflection of hundreds of airborne insects dancing above its surface. He had been thinking of Dylan and Nana, and his friends, and fishing behind Mr. Thompson's house.

He felt the anger rise again. A good and peaceful life resurrected from ashes, and then this man, his father, had returned. To wreck things. Yet again. He looked into Anne's eyes, filled with unwept tears. He laid the stick on the ground and moved to her. Sitting down, he encircled her with his arms, holding her close.

"I...miss her. I knew I would, and I am so happy to be with you. I have no regrets. But I keep thinking of her, sitting on our porch. I am positive that's where she is right now."

"Well, doesn't she clerk down at Wilson's summers?" James asked stupidly, his mind's gears grinding helpless.

She looked at him, her eyes inches from his, drying even as the tears dropped on her cheeks. "My mother has not worked since we left. My mother has not gone to church. I doubt my mother has gone to the store."

James stared at her, feeling the tightening in his middle. "What are you talking about?"

"There's some hurts where you have to be brave, and accept company, take food, and smile. Lose a baby. Lose a parent. I don't know— lose your job." Her chin dropped to her chest, and her shoulders shook. James stroked her back and squeezed her shoulder, but she shook him off roughly, her face a twisted and wet caricature.

"There is a hurt where you hide and don't come out, except to sit on the porch when you're sure everyone is inside or off to work, and you wait." Anne sobbed and said no more. They sat quiet as the woodland around them hummed with deep summer.

"If it rains, we're screwed. But at least it's warm. And the washer and dryer are free." James shook droplets from one of his tee shirts and hung it over a low bush next to the lean-to. The night had been uneventful. A moderate breeze kept the bugs from eating them alive. Today James had worked up a sweat dragging limbs for the sloped roof. He'd also gathered a nice haul of wood for the fire. He hoped the loblolly would burn without too much odor or smoke.

Anne had had her nose buried in *Dune* as the first full morning passed into afternoon. She had not spoken again about her mom. As he was hanging up the last of his clothing across the top of the lean-to, he felt something soft land on his shoulder. He turned, and managed to catch Anne' blouse. She sat grinning in her bra and shorts, her pen in her teeth, the book in her lap.

As he looked down at the bunched top, she said, "There's more where that came from, boy."

James smiled at her. "And just what's in it for me?"

Anne smiled coyly back. "Do a good job and you might just get a scrubbing yourself."

He grinned, and then darkened. "What about the alligators?"

Her smile widened. "If you're nervous about them, we can always cuddle up next to the fire later."

He ached at the thought. "Where are your things?"

***

In one of his trips foraging for sticks, he noticed a downed cypress submerged up against the river's edge, a hundred yards or so upstream of their camp. He also saw dark shadows, large and suspended, against the underside of the trunk. Whether these were river bass or drums, or even snapping turtles, he couldn't be sure. But he was sure he was getting hungrier and hungrier.

He thought about what Daniel Boone and Mingo, Boone's faithful

Indian friend, would do for food. He had his Bowie knife—a gift, ironically, from his father for his last birthday, in February. Mingo had once caught fish by spearing them. There was a thing you had to do when throwing the spear to allow for refraction or something. He couldn't remember exactly. But if the fish were as big as they looked—and if they were fish, not snappers—he might just have some luck. And the way CeCe had talked, the next couple of days he and Anne might have a lot of time to themselves. He chose a slender stick about six feet long and peeled the bark from it. Carefully, he sharpened one end.

***

Anne gently drew a fishbone from her lips and placed it on a leaf between her knees. She smiled and James turned another bass slowly over the fire, using the same spear he'd fashioned earlier to broil his catch.

"I've been calling you *Mark*, sidekick of the Girl from Uncle. But maybe I'd do better to call you Tarzan," she glowed in the flickering firelight. The orange radiated off her shimmering skin. She still wore only her bra and shorts, and James had taken to moving about the camp in his boxers, as if they were a loincloth. They had even been barefoot since early afternoon, gliding across the soft pine-needled forest floor.

When the mosquitoes had started to hum at dusk, Anne remembered CeCe's words and gathered eucalyptus, which was plentiful. They spent a playful few minutes oiling each other in the bare places.

James turned the spit, grunting. "Me Tarzan, you Jane. Makum' *Boy* later."

Anne gasped in mock horror. "I think we have enough to worry about for the present. Don't you?" She looked worried for a moment. "I hope nothing came of leaving those Trojan wrappers behind in that hotel."

James glanced around again at the night and the shadowed forms that surrounded them. Out over the clearing and down the bank, the river gurgled by, pale milk in the thin slice of moon, just three nights now past new.

At a low hiss from somewhere behind James, both of them swung around. They stared into the dark, but all was impenetrable blackness.

James considered the noise. A hiss, like someone shushing. He withdrew the spear from the fire slowly, and turned the tip toward the sound's origin. The fish dripped oil and Anne let out a squeak as a drop or two of the hot grease splashed her. He glanced at Anne, sitting hunched, her knees drawn up against her chest, her face a mask of fear.

James spoke softly, dropping his pitch an octave. "Who's there?"

In answer, a small bundle arced out of the night, and landed with a phwoop between them. It was wrapped in a red-checkered cloth and secured with a piece of red ribbon. The thin fabric looked familiar. Anne gasped and whispered, "I think that ribbon's from CeCe's hat."

James peered intently into the black forest wall, but staring into the fire had shrunk his pupils to pins.

In a hoarse voice, he whispered, "CeCe?" Then, "Benjamin?"

A low voice answered. "Benjamin. Yes, it's me. Don't shoot."

James looked at Anne, baffled. She returned his puzzled gaze, but looked less fearful.

James stared into the night. Again, in his octave-down voice: "Come ahead. Slow." Then realizing Anne had no shirt on, he said, "Wait!"

He crab-walked over to the lean-to and pulled down one of his damp tee shirts, bunched it, and flung it to Anne. She turned and pulled it over her head. Backwards, he noted. As his eyes adjusted, he could see milky moonlight reaching the higher branches of the forest, but the ground level was still pitch dark.

"Are you alone, Benjamin?" James asked.

"Yessuh." Sounding young and nervous.

"Come ahead then."

Much closer than James would have guessed, a form rose from behind a tree several yards away and moved quietly over the ground. At the edge of the clearing, he hesitated. James sized up the boy. Tall and slender, with skin that seemed liquid in the pale firelight, the boy clutched several bundles to his chest.

"Hey." the boy said. "Miss CeCe sent me."

32 / Mister Wilson

Dylan slid into the passenger seat of the Dart and Sam swung his arm over the back of the seat, to glide it down the drive and onto Nash Street. The steady summer rain drummed on the roof as Sam pointed the car toward town center.

"I need to stop in Wilson's for some turpentine and another brush, and I've some books to drop off at the library. Maybe see if the next *James Michener's* in," his father said. "There's a book called *The Source* that nice librarian recommended."

He grinned sideways at his father. "Does that have something to do with why you've been reading a lot lately? Miss Spencer is a nice lady."

Sam shot Dylan a look, but Dylan thought he saw a twinkle in the man's frown. He sat back, gazing out the window at the tree branches lifted by the whipping wind. His father said, "Somebody ought to invent an umbrella that keeps you dry against sideways rain."

Dylan sat up as they splashed past Stockton Avenue and pulled over to the curb in front of Wilson's Hardware. There was no one on the street, except for two of the kids from the elementary school, soaked through, who appeared to be guiding twigs in the racing water along the curb.

"I'll just wait here," Dylan said, peering out through the gray downpour.

There was silence for a moment as the car engine ceased, and the roof pinged in the drumming rain-beat. His father cleared his throat. "Nobody's going to bother you while I'm around, son," he said.

Dylan didn't mean to snort. It came out sounding like a gurgle, and he clarified. "There's nothing I need from the store." He hoped the words sounded final on the subject.

"Well, I've been meaning to tell you, you're becoming quite a boxer. Ask me, I think those boys'll have something to worry about next time."

Dylan groaned. "Stinger and Scooter are older. But neither of them fights as well as Cammy." He winced again, remembering how Cammy had turned on him, and pinned him as if he were a child while the others had assaulted him.

"Well, there's other ways to get the upper hand besides fighting. Seems like boys like that always come to a sour end, and sooner than later." His father patted Dylan's knee. "Besides, I thought you might want to look over some new models Mr. Wilson just got in." Sam's arm lifted ahead of Dylan's gaze, and Dylan eyed the front window of the hardware store. It held a shiny stack of airplane models.

"Wow! Is that the *Senior Falcon?*" Dylan pressed his nose to the car window. "I have the *Falcon 56*, but..."

Sam's door handle clicked, and Dylan turned. "Want to have a look?" his father asked. The street was still deserted. Even the two kids had jumped into a car up ahead, and Dylan heard the scolding of an angry mother, muffled as the door slammed.

Dylan shrugged. "Sure. Why not?"

The bell clanged at the back of the building as Sam held the door for Dylan. They both rushed in, shaking the raindrops from their hair and wiping their shirts.

Mr. Wilson moved quickly up the main aisle, smiling. "What a drencher, aye?" He held out his hand to Sam, who shook it firmly. "Well, Lord knows, we need it."

"Good to see you, Lucas. Just a couple things today." Sam told Mr. Wilson what he needed, and the proprietor nodded.

"I see you spotted my newest merchandise."

Dylan turned back to him, nodding.

"I think I got the *Skylark 56*, and the *Skat Rat*. Oh, that's right," he nodded as Dylan started to speak. "You already got my last *Skylark*. Well, have a look while your dad and I conduct major commerce."

Dylan turned to the front window display and lifted a box from the top. *Riley Wooten's Voodoo* combat plane for $5.95. He turned the box over in his hand, and glanced up at an umbrella moving past the window. It was his teacher from middle school, Mrs. Welsley, and she nodded to him before moving quickly by. Dylan glanced at the door to see if she was coming in, but it didn't open. He noticed the gleaming metal plate on the inside of the door panel, below the windowed top half. It looked new.

"See anything you have to have?" It was his dad, approaching the worn wooden counter, with Mr. Wilson in his white apron right behind him.

Dylan set down the box and shrugged. "Maybe the Scat Rat. It's got a 31-inch span, and it's five dollars." Dylan held up the brightly colored box so that Sam could read the front panel: *Full size plans illustrated step-by-step, plus detailed up to the minute Rat-Racing hints!*

Mr. Wilson looked up at Sam expectantly. "Add it on," his father said with a slight smile. "And get ready to be buzzed walking down Canal Street, from the sounds of it."

Mr. Wilson smiled. "Need any glue or paints today, Captain Dylan?"

Dylan shook his head. "I'm good, thanks. And thank *you*, sir." He glanced at his father. He still didn't know how best to address Sam. *Sam* seemed impolite. *Dad* seemed too familiar. He had settled on *sir* for the time being, and Sam didn't seem to object.

They splashed back to the car and jumped in. Sam set the supplies on the seat between them, started the car, and eased out from the curb.

Dylan looked over at Sam. "I was wondering something."

His father glanced at him, waiting.

"About Mr. Wilson."

"Yes?"

"Well, he doesn't seem to be bothered that my brother is the one people think tried to break into his store."

Sam drove on toward the library, his brow furrowed. Finally he spoke. "You know I grew up in Crane Ridge, right? Before I moved over to Berlin with your mother?" Dylan nodded. "Well, like your brother, I might've raised a little hell too. Nothing too grievous," he added hastily. "Just youthful shenanigans."

Dylan glanced over at Sam. He didn't know if he wanted to know more. But he wondered what this had to do with Mr. Wilson. "Like what kind of things?"

Sam pursed his lips and thought for a moment. "There was a woman here in town, used to go over to the Catholic cemetery nights, singing." Dylan turned to give Sam a wary look.

"If I ever knew her name, it's forgotten now. Seems she had somehow left a child to drown in a washtub. A baby. I guess it put her out of the main house, if you understand."

Dylan looked through the teary windshield at the wipers, sloshing drops away in a losing effort. The rain had picked up and the shower was pelting the car's metal in a staccato rhythm. "So what did you do?" Dylan pressed.

Sam laughed hollowly. "Was not our proudest moment. We never talk about it. But I've a feeling every time he hears *Hush Little Babe*, or walks through a cemetery, he thinks on that night too."

Dylan waited as Sam pulled alongside the library and eased the Dart into first, switching off the key. Sam sat back in the seat, his gaze far off.

"One night, we were in the cemetery. Smoking cigarettes, I guess. Maybe even sharing one of somebody's father's *Natty Bo's*. That's a brand of beer," he offered.

"And this lady was there?"

"Well, we saw her coming from down the lane. A couple of the kids run off—she was just that spooky. But Lucas and I—we were just dumb boys—decided to have some fun." Sam shifted in his seat and reached into the back for a handful of books.

"So we hid behind a gravestone. Kind of laughing, but kinda scared too. But when we heard her start to singing, one of us—I don't *think* it was me, started calling out, in a creepy high pitch, 'momma.' Just like that, and nothing more. 'Momma.' Sam arranged the books on his lap, and considered the rain.

"What did she do?" Dylan asked.

"She just kept on singing, as if she didn't hear. We could see her, and she never did turn to us. But sudden as you please, she just lunged at the ground. She didn't trip, or fall. I am just certain. She had come to stand at this one grave, singing. A pretty song too, it was, some lullaby." He looked at Dylan then.

"She just dropped right down on the ground, and her crying turned into something awful. Something like an animal in a trap might make, if it decided it was never going to get away. It was just that pitiful. But powerful too, like it could rip the very ground."

Dylan thought Sam shivered for a moment.

"What did you do then?"

His father looked at Dylan surprised. "Why we ran like holy hell, is what we did." He turned towards his door. "Coming?"

Dylan laid a hand on his shoulder, lightly. "Wait up a second. I asked why Mr. Wilson doesn't mind us coming in his store, being James's relations and all."

"I went and told Lucas it wasn't James, and that was good enough for him." His father paused. "But even if it had been, I think Lucas would have understood just how stupid a boy can be. And how much stupider he gets when you throw in other boys. Let's go see what's new in the library."

"You just want to say hey to Miss Spencer!" Dylan grinned.

Sam gave him a warning look, with just a trace of humor. "You severely underestimate my literary fondness. It is Michener and Capote that summon my muse."

Dylan rolled his eyes, but his heart felt lighter as they stepped out into the deluge.

33 / Benjamin

Anne and James stared at the collection before them. There were several small piles, each unrolled from a towel or a dishtowel or a washcloth.

Again, Anne thanked the boy. "This is all such a gift right now. This is better than a fancy hotel." She glanced at James, blushing.

"Miss CeCe said say she has to send stuff over slow. Her daddy's home again." The boy shifted where he stood at the edge of the firelight. After he'd laid his offerings down between James and Anne, he'd backed up so fast James thought he would bolt. But Anne had stayed him with her question.

"No ma'am," he'd replied. "The woods don't fret me. Anyone out here is mostly harmless this time of night."

"But how can you see anything out here?" she'd persisted.

The boy had glanced up, then answered, "Moon make it like day 'most." James noticed Benjamin averted his eyes from the fire. Also to his credit, he had not obviously looked around at the primitive camp they'd put together.

"Are there people out here this time of night? Besides us?" James asked.

"Only ones who live out here," Benjamin replied.

As James looked at the bounty spread on the fabric pieces, he thought again about *Daniel Boone*, the TV show. There was a scene where Mingo introduced Daniel to his tribe. The natural suspicion of the chief had been quelled somewhat when Daniel sat with him and presented gifts, much like this.

Anne reached out to touch each object. There was fresh bread, a jar of preserves. A jar of pickles and a small box of eggs. A small pot and lid. There was more soap, and matches, and a can opener. There was a rolled up vinyl tube, about the size of a small sleeping bag, but heavier.

"That's a tent," said Benjamin. "Netting and a rain fly too. Tarp for under is rolled up in it."

Anne lifted an object. "What's this?" she asked.

Benjamin raised his eyes. Since he had arrived, James didn't think Benjamin had looked directly at Anne, which suited James just fine.

"You put it over the coals, you can toast your br-aid."

Anne turned it over in her hands. She looked at James and shrugged. "You know how this works?" she asked.

James took the offered appliance and turned it over, puzzling it. He raised his eyes to Benjamin.

"Can you show us?"

Benjamin nodded. He gestured at the small device. "You flip open that door, and—"

"Jimmy, hand it to Benjamin. And here." She reached over and picked up the bread, and a long knife beneath it, and handed both in one hand to Benjamin.

Benjamin glanced from Anne to James and wiped his palms on the thighs of his worn overalls. He reached out and took the bread and knife, laid the bread carefully on his lap, and drew a flat rock from the fire ring a few inches towards himself. James watched as Benjamin laid one of the dishtowels on the rock and placed the bread on the cloth. The young Negro sliced the bread with the knife and inserted two pieces into the metal contraption. He worried several coals out of the main fire with a stick, and set smaller rocks around the little island of glowing embers. He set the contraption on the ring of rocks. Only then did he speak again.

"It'll toast up quick, don't go off 'n leave it long." His voice was soft and melodic, and deeper than James would have expected just looking at him. The boy's fingers were long, ropey, like the rest of him, sinewy under the flannel shirt and baggy overalls. James nodded.

Anne cleared her throat. "So, Benjamin. What did Miss CeCe tell you? About us?"

Benjamin looked stricken. "Miss CeCe saý y'all needin' help," was all the boy managed.

"Your last name is *Pie*, Benjamin?" Anne asked.

Benjamin nodded, his face serious.

"How did you come to have such an interesting last name?" Anne said, smiling.

Benjamin seemed to relax for an instant.

"My momma says her momma used to be called 'Monro,' after her owner. She married a man with no last name, who asked her to marry while she was baking pies. My momma say her momma so pretty, she have lots men asking for her hand. She called the one 'Pie Man' so she could remember him, and when the preacher asked, she just said 'Minnie Pie.'"

James sat back grinning, amazed at this oratory from the quiet lad. Anne clapped her hands, delighted. Both boys looked at her, smiling.

James became suddenly serious again. "You get around Darien and these parts a lot, do you, Benjamin?" Benjamin nodded, looking up from his downcast, like a dog half-expecting a whipping.

James continued. "Well, we may have some people coming 'round asking after us. If you hear, don't let on, but come tell us quick, you understand?"

Benjamin scooped the metal frame from the coals. "Come tell y'all quick," he said, staring at the frame on the ground before him. He deftly swung the small doors back, using one of the dishtowels on the hot metal, and lay two pieces of toast on the dishtowel, which he stretched to hand over to Anne, as if he were returning a newborn.

James cleared his throat. "So how can we be so sure you won't out us? What if somebody mentions a reward?"

Anne jerked her head at James, but didn't speak.

Benjamin was nodding his head slowly *no*.

"Well, how can we be sure of you?" James persisted.

"Miss CeCe asked me not to tell."

James sighed, trying to think of another tack. "You do everything Miss CeCe asks you?"

Benjamin bowed his head, and then rose lithely to his feet. "I best be getting back 'fore I'm missed."

Anne glared at James as Benjamin turned to go. "Benjamin," she said. He turned back, not raising his eyes. "Thanks so much. For everything. We are grateful for your kindness."

Benjamin scratched at his temple over his ear and smiled shy in the general direction of Anne. Then he turned and was gone.

James and Anne sat quiet. James marveled that he could hear no sound of Benjamin making his way.

He turned at the sharpness in her voice.

"You didn't have to be so rude."

He colored, knowing she was right. Not sure what had stirred his aggression, he sat silent, feeling her steely gaze. He shrugged, held her look.

"Imagine where we'd be without their help. Not just CeCe, either."

James tossed a loose twig in the low fire. "You can't trust a Negro. They hate us for what our grandparents did to their grandparents, or something."

It was a funny thing about silence in a conversation. Sometimes quiet in the middle of a talk was companionable, like Nana and Sam on the porch. Sometimes quiet was cold and harsh, even when the night was sticky hot. He looked over at Anne. Her eyes bore into the fire, refusing to be drawn back to him.

"Jimmy, just so you know..." her voice skidded into a sigh, and he wondered if she'd changed her mind about speaking. She glanced at him once, and seemed to make up her mind about something.

"Did you ever consider why it is that whites seemed to hate coloreds the way we do?" He felt his head recede down into his shoulders. He wasn't sure why, but talking about what had just happened was something he didn't feel ready for. If anything, he resented the colored boy's intrusion. She seemed to read his thoughts.

"I really care for you Jimmy. And I know you have been through some bad times." She shivered in the damp shirt and moved closer to the fire. "But sometimes it scares me to death to know what men are capable of doing to other men. Men like you." She looked at him fiercely. "Men I love."

He tried to hold her gaze, but finally dropped his eyes in confusion. "I'm having a hard time keeping up with you," he said.

"I know." She tossed a stick in the quiet licking flames and sighed.

"When my daddy was a boy, he was the only starting freshman on Wicomico's football team. He loved football even then." Anne shifted and James leaned back against a tree, watching her expression in the dancing orange light.

"One night before Christmas of his freshman year—after a big game against some team from Delaware—Grandpa took my daddy downtown in Salisbury. Daddy thought they were going to the Wicomico Hotel for a dinner that was being put on for the two football teams. But when they got downtown, Daddy said there was a crowd of men on Main Street, near the *Times* office."

Anne looked at him. He shrugged, baffled.

"Have you ever heard of Matt Williams?" she asked.

James shook his head.

"Grandpa told my daddy that he needed to know what the nature of the colored man was." Anne stared through the fire. "He led my daddy downtown, and my daddy saw some of the older boys from his team. One of the coaches. Older men he knew from Crane Ridge."

Something in the story sounded familiar finally, calling from far back in his memory.

"A colored man had killed a white man. That was what the *Times* said. When he and my grandpa got downtown, the crowd got bigger and bigger, and then it proceeded to march to the hospital. Where the colored man was."

James glanced up as her voice hitched.

"Matt Williams. That was the name of the Negro. My grandpa fetched up a rope from the firehouse where he volunteered, while some other men broke into the hospital and took the Negro."

James listened, a memory awakening. He had heard the story, years ago. He hadn't realized anyone from Crane Ridge had been over to Salisbury that night.

"That was a very long time ago," he finally said.

"I think it was 1931," Anne replied. "Obviously in my daddy's lifetime," she sighed.

He sat quietly, waiting for her to continue. When she didn't speak, he thought she was done, and he was about to say something.

"My daddy said that was one of the proudest moments of his life. He said that what separates man from the animals is that 'we have laws.'" She laughed without humor. "I think what he meant was that they didn't just hang that man any old where. They lynched him in front of the County Courthouse. Grandpa let my daddy tie the other end of the rope to a lamp post."

James knew what came next, and wished for the story to be over. He knew where he'd heard the story now. In the manner of boys the world over, one day the talk on the playground had turned to a discussion of the worst ways to die. James didn't like that the tree at his back was so small, or that the moon had lowered and no longer reflected the soft ripples of the river.

He couldn't remember which of the boys had told the story. The Negro had been hanged, but would not die fast enough. So they cut him down, and tied him to the bumper of a car. James remembered sharply that *yes,* it sounded like the worst death he could imagine.

"I did hear about it," he said. "But if he really killed somebody..." His voice trailed off, sapped by the withering look she gave him.

"Yes," she spoke slowly. "If he really killed somebody, let's steal him out of a hospital, and lynch him in the dark of night from a street lamp. Then, because we are so law-abiding..."

James realized her face was wet, even though there was no sobbing.

"Why did your father tell you all this?" James asked quietly.

Anne lifted the bottom edge of the shirt, and rubbed at her cheeks.

"My father was *proud* of what he'd done. Helping to keep the County safe, for all god-fearing people, I guess. Which is why, even though he is my father and I will always probably love him," she bit her lip, her chin set, "I don't respect him, and I don't miss him. Imagine that much fear and hatred."

She drew her knees up, and rested her chin on them.

"I guess there was no trial?" James asked, feeling lame, as though his brain was coated in molasses. He rose to his feet and lifted the rolled tent plastic. Awkwardly, he unfurled it.

"No," she said. "No trial for Matt Williams. No trial for the men who murdered him. The grand jury had names of over a hundred witnesses, but didn't bring a single indictment."

"Well, did he do it?" James asked, feeling as though he were rowing with only one oar.

"Of course he did it! They lynched him, for God's sake! How could he *not* have done it?"

The silence between them now was not the companionable kind, but was the quiet that comes when something big has been dumped. James didn't know exactly what he was supposed to understand now that he hadn't before.

"My father said the only time my grandpa got mad was when the rope holding the Negro to the bumper came loose. Then daddy said my grandpa slapped him. I guess he felt bad about it after, though."

"Why?" asked James, his mind reeling.

"Because after that, he let my daddy drive."

***

The days passed languorously. The oppressive heat made quick movement uncomfortable, and James and Anne adjusted to the swelter. They joked about "going native," moving about in their underwear, and dipping frequently—if only for moments—in the relative cool of the river.

They worked out a signal with CeCe during her next visit, for when she or Benjamin would approach. CeCe had brought another fishing reel, which James could attach to a stick, using some cast-off line to bind the reel, and some paperclips to serve as eyelets. With some of the spare line, they strung a length from out near the public walking path, threading through the trees back to the campsite. One end was tied to a stick, which when pulled, would trip a rock at the other end. The rock would slip off a low branch above a pile of dry kindling, making a soft sound, but one that was very audible in the clearing where they'd set their tent.

CeCe had nodded with quiet approval the first time she'd stepped back into camp. To his own surprise, James felt himself flush with pride.

Anne once again had brought up going to church on Sunday. It was now Friday.

"We can't use our real names. You think we have to lose the *Mark* and *Stephanie* handles?" asked James.

"I'm afraid so," said CeCe, handing James a small bag of flour and a tin. "Bacon," she added, nodding at the tin as James turned it over. He felt his stomach awaken in response. *Would it be rude*, he wondered, *to start a fire and cook it up*?

"If you like, I can show y'all how to make biscuits using flour and grease," CeCe said. "Unless y'already know how to do that." Both James and Anne shrugged a *no*.

"Then, we can use some of this," she smiled, drawing a jar of a red-wine colored substance from her pocket. "Wild raspberry jelly. You will be quite sure y'all have entered heaven's cafeteria." James was moving to slip the pot from the kitchen bag before CeCe finished speaking. Anne bent to construct the fire.

"Heaven's own cafeteria indeed," Anne groaned, content. She patted her tummy and thanked CeCe again for her kindness. As he licked the wet, warm preserves from his fingertips, James could not remember tasting anything quite so delicious. With a pang, he realized it had been about as long as he'd been gone from Nana's kitchen. The three friends sat gazing across the clearing at the rambling Cat Head Creek and the light breeze that stroked the river grass.

"Do you want to help name us?" James asked.

CeCe laughed. "I have to say that would be a singular honor. Let's see. Categorically speaking…" CeCe grinned at James, who waited, bemused.

"Can't think of a name for a boy that begins with c-a-t?" he finally said. "It's not a catastrophe."

Anne blanched. "How did you two get on that kick anyway?"

CeCe shrugged, and smiled. "It's as if we were catapulted."

James flipped a twig at the young girl. "If it's all the same to you two," he said, "how about I be Matt."

Anne arched an eyebrow.

"What? At least it *rhymes* with *cat!*"

34 / Buttercups

"Sure you won't come up to the school for a game later?" Tink stood astride his bike at the base of the steps leading up to Dylan's porch. Dylan was outside reading a Hardy Boys book whenTink pulled in off Nash Street.

"Not today. I promised Nana I'd give her a hand with something this afternoon." Dylan hoped Nana was back in the kitchen, where she couldn't overhear. He knew he couldn't hide forever, but he wasn't ready yet to face Scooter and Stinger, and Cammy. The humiliation burned like a bad rash. The mercy of it was it didn't appear the three had said anything of the incident to anyone else.

"Ryan and me are going to try some fishing later, out by the fairgrounds. Want me to stop by?" Tink shielded his eyes against the sun's glare, looking up at the porch.

"I'll try to break loose and meet you there."

After Tink rode off, Dylan collected Buster to go explore in the woods west of town. He clicked a stick along the picket fence behind Mr. Geise's. Buster pranced like a pup, begging Dylan to toss the stick, but Dylan ignored him. He turned down Stockton Lane towards the river, and almost ran right into Lois Mast.

"Hey stranger," she grinned. "Enjoying your summer? I haven't seen you around town since the other day, and I was wondering how you were. Those boys are impossible, the way they treat people. Are you going fishing? Where's your pole?"

She bent to nuzzle Buster, who wagged furiously at the attention. Dylan stood mute. Lois rose and took the stick from Dylan's hand,

Turning, she winged it down the alley. With a joyous yap, Buster raced down the lane and scrabbled the stick off the packed gravel, returning in an instant to drop the stick at Lois's feet.

"Don't you ever fetch with Buster? Dogs need attention just like humans. Aren't you going to say anything at all?"

Lois turned in the direction Dylan had been heading and looked back as she started walking slowly. All of a sudden, Dylan thought this must be what it was like for a dog to heel. It was not completely unpleasant.

"I've been a little busy." He wracked his head for more. "Helping my father out over at the Thompson house."

She nodded vigorously. "My dad works down at the bank. But you already knew that. He said that the house is up for sale soon."

Dylan caught up the stick that Buster returned, now slippery with dog-slime, and arced it across Canal Road. "Next week, dad thinks. He's been working hard to get the house ready."

"How is it coming?" she asked.

"Well, it's a little slow since we're leaving most of the furniture in the house for now. But it really just needed a coat of paint. A little wall work." Dylan ran out of thought, and they walked quietly across Canal, along the riverbank.

Lois bent to pluck a buttercup from the wild grass. She stood and held it under her chin. "Do you see anything?" she asked.

Dylan bent. "Yes. There's quite a glow. So *do* you like butter?" He straightened and noticed, as he had last time they'd talked, just how pretty she was when she smiled. When she lifted her chin, which she did often, her dimples sharpened. He liked the way her nose curved up at the point. He also thought her freckles looked more defined now that she'd gotten more sun.

"Now you!" she laughed and plucked another buttercup. She caught his look. "Never use the same one, silly. The buttercup loses its power."

"Is that a fact?" he deadpanned. But he dutifully lifted his chin. She stepped close. He was taller than Lois by half a head, so she didn't bend so much as step right to him. "Aha. You're a butter lover too!"

"Got me," he smiled and then looked about uncertainly. But she had already turned to take the path into the woods along the Wicomico.

"I saw you at the fireworks," Lois said, over her shoulder. "With your dad and your grandma."

"They were good this year, don't you think?"

"Oh yes! I love the ones where they shoot off several at a time, and it's pop, pop, BOOM!" She threw her hands wide. Her smile dazzled him.

"I saw your brother with the Sampson girl too, that night. When we were walking home. They looked like they were just waiting for everyone to leave. Don't you think what they did is so romantic? Like Romeo and Juliet?" Lois turned to him as they stepped over a rock outcropping on the shore.

"Careful for cotton mouths," he said, casting his gaze about. "I think you smell cucumbers when you're near one."

"That's copperheads, silly."

He followed her over the stones jutting from the bank. He admired her grace as she stepped lightly over the coarse stone ledge. She had a lithe form, and he found himself enjoying her company. But his face clouded when she asked if he'd heard from his brother. He'd hoped she would drop it. He grunted in response to her question, and no, James hadn't said where they were, or when they'd be back.

"Did they really take the priest's car? I guess they had to do something. Why don't you think they took your father's car? Or her dad's? Everyone says Mr. Sampson's ready to burst. I never really cared for him, and I don't know Anne. But she was always nice enough to me at church. She helped with Methodist Youth sometimes."

Dylan wondered if he could just be with Lois and not say a word. Would she notice? If just one person was capable of holding both ends of a conversation, and the other didn't mind... She reached a bleached tree trunk on the bank and sat down. "It must be hard when people talk about your brother like, well like they're talking about James. Personally, I admire them for having the guts to leave." Lois squinted out over the broad expanse of flatland on the far side of the river, her hand shielding her eyes. For a moment, he thought she might be scanning the horizon for the two runaways.

He waited, but Lois didn't speak again. The silence was comfortable. They both gazed over the mute grassland, stretching off beyond the river to a line of pines at the horizon. A lone hunting stand broke the uniformity, out beyond the river's far shore.

Finally, he spoke. "I miss him." He started at his own words. He wanted to take them back. He had many strong feelings besides missing James, and he was embarrassed that he had blurted it out. But the words hung in the stillness, out there in front of them.

He tried to temper his confession. "He didn't have the right to leave, just because he didn't like things the way they were." A thought occurred to him, and he tried it out. "That was just what he hated my father for, and here he does the same thing."

He couldn't divine the silence that followed. Lois was always full of words. Had he upset her somehow? He glanced at her, but she sat calm, her eyes on the meandering river.

"What would you have done, if you liked someone and your parents wouldn't let you see her?" She said, musingly.

He glanced at her again, but she did not continue.

"Or if you were in trouble, but you didn't do what people said you did?" His voice was soft, and she seemed not to hear him. "Would you just up and run away?"

He glanced down and realized he was still holding the fetch stick. Buster was in the underbrush somewhere, frightening rabbits. He held the stick at eye level and turned it first one way, then the other, like a sapling bending in a wind. "Is there some way you view it," he sighed, staring at the stick, "that it becomes the right thing to do? Running?"

Lois was now looking at her hands, folded primly in her lap. Then she spoke. "*Love* and *sensible* have no place in the same sentence, Dylan Paxton." He noticed now her hands were twisting, knotted and tense. "I think they decided they wanted to be together, and took a look at how they could, and running away was the only way."

"But he left me..." Dylan's words died as she lifted her eyes, her gaze steady and deep.

"I don't know, but I can't imagine he ever meant to hurt you." She took a breath. "I am also sure it hurt you bad—" Her eyes willed him to hold her gaze. "—that you have suffered for his leaving."

Dylan blinked back something, wanting to talk about other things. Lois seemed to read his mind. "Lisa Haggerty and I have been friends since first grade. Do you think I sent her a note from you?" Dylan opened his mouth, but she charged ahead. "She has the biggest chain in town, and she intends to burn it on Labor Day, for you."

Then Lois turned to him, rising as she did so. "I decided I like you too, Dylan Paxton, and I hope any notes that get written are from you to me. So there." She bent and kissed his cheek before he could breathe, turned, and headed back in the direction they'd come.

Dylan watched her, lightly touching his cheek, 'til she disappeared from sight down Canal Road.

35 / Darien Methodist

"Why on earth do you want to risk going inside a church?" James said. "Don't you think your dad will think to ask at churches?"

Anne considered the question. "Truly? No, I don't. My dad will tell you how much he hates the Jews and the Catholics—sorry—but he never sets foot in our own church, even though he likes to think he makes me go."

CeCe shrugged. "It's up to you two. Y'all will be welcome at Darien Methodist. People there are great."

James asked, "Anne, what'll we call you?"

Before Anne could reply, CeCe said, "How about Gwendolyn? You could be Gwen for short."

James nodded, thoughtful. Anne said it aloud. "It's very pretty. I like it. What made you think of it?"

CeCe colored, smiling. "Really? You like it? The short or the long version?"

Anne considered. "Gwen. Gwendolyn. Yes, Gwendolyn, I should think. You don't think it sounds, I don't know, pagan?"

CeCe laughed. "Darien Methodist survived two attempts by the North to burn it down. I think it will survive the name Gwendolyn." She paused. "It is also the name of a poet I really like. Gwendolyn Brooks."

"Is there a Saint Gwendolyn?" James asked.

Anne smiled. "Only a Catholic would wonder that. Remember, you are my brother, and I am definitely Methodist, so you have to be too!"

"I still don't think this is such a hot idea," James said as they walked down Middlesex Lane, approaching the façade of a tall, stately white church. Ahead, CeCe stood alone, waiting for them. The three of them walked up the sidewalk leading to the imposing entrance.

After the service, everyone filed slowly to the rear of the church and down the stairs to a large, friendly hall. The atmosphere was relaxed, and boisterous little girls and boys in Sunday dress raced through the slalom of stiff adults sipping from chipped ceramic cups. The room smelled of fresh coffee and sweet rolls and fresh-baked bread.

A steady stream of congregants moved past CeCe and the two "siblings." James realized that he and Anne really hadn't thought past what to name themselves. He got used to CeCe introducing him as *Matt*. But there was a moment when he panicked as the minister, taking advantage of the girls chatting gaily with his wife about one of the coffee table centerpieces, took him by the elbow, and quietly asked where he was from.

The minister's expression drew in, as James stuttered through an explanation of parents dying and his sister—what was her *name*?—and he traveling, in search of some relative. Thankfully, he heard the minister's wife address *Gwendolyn*. Just then, a lanky, bald man approached the preacher, to introduce his brother and wife, visiting from Savannah. The minister looked back distractedly at James, and said he would be just a minute. James fled.

In the restroom, he dashed water on his face, staring into the mirror. In spite of the near disaster with the good reverend, James felt a thrill. He winked at his reflection and shook his sleeves down.

"I know what it is. I know what makes you people so different!" Anne exclaimed. "Where we come from, people talk *about* you, if you're from somewhere else. They don't talk *to* you!"

James nodded as the three of them stood in a corner of the hall, sipping orange juice from paper cups.

CeCe smiled, and James noticed how grown-up she looked in her pale blue summer dress, her waist belted, with her burnished wheat-colored hair unribboned, tumbling thickly to her shoulders.

"I told y'all you'd get introduced today." She nodded at an elderly couple who smiled back. Then she broke into a huge grin, and waved energetically. Both Anne and James turned. Across the hall, a girl about

CeCe's age, a little shorter and fuller, waved back and glided impatiently through the throng. CeCe turned back to the two. She was still smiling, but she spoke quietly and quick.

"That's Julie Rose. Try to sound true, because she is nice, but she's also sharp."

Anne glanced at James, shrugging.

More loudly now, CeCe turned as the girl eased past several people to stand in front of them, dropping her eyes shyly, her hands clasped in front of her pink skirt. "Julie Rose and I take turns Sundays minding the nursery during services, along with some other girls."

The young girl blushed, and lifted her fingers in greeting.

"But it's really mostly Julie Rose and me. Miss Ellie calls us the *Toddler Tamers.*" Both girls giggled at this and Julie Rose covered her mouth, her eyes alight.

"Julie Rose Walker, this is Matt, and his sister Gwendolyn." They both nodded and she nodded back.

"Welcome to our church. I guess welcome to our town too. Where y'all from?" she asked.

James opened his mouth to speak.

"Down Florida way. At least for the last few years," Anne spoke brightly, and all three turned to her, attentive.

"We were staying with relatives there," she continued, in a burst. "But then they had... twins, and it was just too much for them." James marveled at how smoothly Anne told the lie. He stole a glance at Julie Rose, who nodded seriously.

"So we decided to head north. We *know* we have family in New York. We wrote. And they wrote back." Anne bobbed her head, as she slowed. "But we thought we had family here too. Only we just heard *about* them. Never actually wrote. And now, turns out, we were probably mistaken."

James nodded in assent, sipping his orange juice. It was a clever fib, he thought. As Nana might have said—though never about a lie, because lies were never good—it left doors open. If they needed to leave quickly, it would sound like they were bound north.

"So y'all are...staying with relatives?" Julie Rose was choosing her words with care. Again, James started to speak, and remembered Anne was now Gwendolyn. He looked at her, and spoke her name aloud. She did not react, and he continued.

"Gwen and me, well, our folks are passed on. Mom, then dad…" As he spoke the words, he realized that for him at least, that was more true than not, and he felt his face grow red. "It's been some time now, but we don't want to impose on people, so we've moved about a bit."

"So y'all are originally from Florida?" Julie Rose asked, gently but with curiosity.

Anne spoke up. "Goodness no. The heat was such an adjustment." She fanned herself, her mouth gasping like a fish, to illustrate. "No, we're from upstate New York. Have you ever been to that part of the country?" she asked Julie Rose.

"Why, me? I wish!" Julie replied. "The farthest I've been from Darien is Savannah, for the statewide spelling contest two years ago!"

CeCe spoke warmly. "Julie Rose is the smartest girl in class. The smartest of *everybody* of course, because the smartest boy is about as smart almost as the dumbest girl—" She paused and her face lit again.

"Matt, Gwendolyn, this is Julie Rose's mom, Mrs. Walker." They nodded as the woman slipped an arm around each of the young girls, squeezing them affectionately. The woman nodded, and James, flustered, extended a hand. Bemused, she took it and shook it seriously.

"A pleasure, and welcome to Darien Methodist. Will y'all be in town long?"

There was a short silence, and then Anne said "Oh," as if she remembered something. "You all were going to bake for the social. So what did you bake up here?"

Julie Rose turned to her mother, her fingers again over her mouth. "I forgot completely to offer any, and now I bet it'll all be gone!"

Mrs. Walker patted her daughter's shoulder. "Well let's not fret too early." They all crossed to a table set up near the coffee. They crowded up to the baked goods displayed.

"The cobbler has vanished," Mrs. Walker said pleasantly. "No surprise there. And look! A few brave souls tried our blackberry tapioca!"

"And the best news is, there's a piece left for each of us!" Anne exclaimed, gasping in admiration at the creamy confection in the center of the table.

"I don't know how good that news is," Mrs. Walker said modestly. "This is a new attempt for our little baking club."

She carefully lifted out a piece onto a plate for each of them, and soon they were sucking at their forks. It was hard for James not to go back for seconds. But others, seeing the treat rapidly disappearing, had descended with used plates to sample the light almond-colored pudding.

"The secret is to use some blackberries that aren't quite black, to help the mixture gel," Mrs. Walker said intimately to Anne, as if they'd known each other a long time. Anne nodded, her mouth full.

"Gwendolyn is such a pretty name. Are you named after someone, dear?" Mrs. Walker lightly scraped her plate and then set it down with the fork atop it, in the dish basin at the end of the table.

Anne glanced around to see if James was listening, then said, "I had a grandmother—my mother's mother. Her name was Gwendolyn. She died young too. Like my mom. Well, not the same way..." Anne paused, clearly flummoxed.

Mrs. Walker patted her shoulder. "It's all right dear. I understand. My mother passed before I was ready to let her go, too."

Mrs. Walker turned to the group. "I have to get together with Mrs. Ellie to talk about the Church picnic next week. Nice to meet you, Matt, and you, Gwendolyn." She strode off and called back over her shoulder, "You and your friends are expected for dinner at two, Miss CeCe."

They waved at her departing form. Then Julie Rose said, "I should get back, too. Parents will be wanting to pick up their babies soon. Well, I don't know if 'wanting to' is always the right way to phrase it." She laughed gaily, and squeezed CeCe's arm.

"Want some help?" CeCe asked.

"No thank you. This is the easy part." She smiled at James and Anne. "It was so nice to meet you. Please join us for dinner this afternoon."

James's head was swirling. He was beginning to realize that being on the run was not the same as being anchored to one spot, trying to pass himself off as someone else. It seemed like a powerful lot to keep track of, and it had barely begun. He determined to speak to Anne about leaving town soon.

He turned to the two girls. Their heads were bent in an earnest discussion. Anne looked up. "CeCe can't leave with us. She's telling me how to find Julie Rose's house, if we want to go."

CeCe said, "I think the less we're seen together in public, the better for now. But please do consider dinner. They are the nicest people in town. And you," she nodded once at James, "could probably use the practice. You know," she dropped her voice, "at polishing your story."

Anne smiled. "I think boys are generally good liars. Don't you, CeCe?"

The younger girl grinned. "For the short lies they are fine. You know, where they don't have to remember too much."

They walked slowly back down the quiet streets of Darien. James had been too nervous before to notice the trim, well-kept yards and the small, friendly bungalows tucked under massive oak trees. He felt the familiar ache. It was very much like Nash Street back home, and he half-expected to see Mr. Geise step out onto one of the stoops.

The houses might have been a little closer to the road, and the terrain was even flatter than what he was used to. But the bucolic summer afternoon was so familiar, so...normal. He wondered, if he'd been blindfolded and set down in this spot, and spun three times, would he know when the blindfold was removed that he *wasn't* in Crane Ridge, right off? He thought not. But his discomfort in the church basement was fresh too.

"Anne, I think we ought to stick to the plan and leave."

She looked around casually, as they walked. But no one was in sight. "The plan?"

At first, he thought she was looking for a clarification. But in the next words, he knew it was something else.

"The *plan*, Jimmy? I don't recall there being *a plan*. And if there was, I think Plan *A* ended when we lost our car."

James winced. He had not thought about the car for several days, and still had no idea how to set things right with Father Mullenix back home.

He turned to look at her, and she gazed back, her eyes softening.

"In case this needs to be said, I've never done anything even a teeny bit like this before," Anne said softly. "I don't know what the rules are. All I know this instant is I am dying to hold your hand, and we can't even do that."

He grinned, but she continued.

"This morning, the church, I realized how much I miss it."

He looked at her as they reached the highway and started down to where the roadside marker for CeCe's mom and brother was tucked back off the shoulder.

"What do you mean by *it*?" he asked.

She lifted a hand to her face, and James wondered if she was starting to cry. They walked in past the well-tended memorial for CeCe's mother and brother and into the cool of the pine grove. He led the way. Behind him for a moment he glimpsed a boy he'd seen earlier outside the church, walking the shoulder after them. The boy nodded as he passed by the memorial grove. James waited a moment, but the boy did not reappear, and he turned down into the path leading out to Cat Head Creek.

"I don't know," her voice said to his back. "I keep thinking about mom, and what all this is doing to her. I know—" he heard the hitch in her throat, "—it's like CeCe says. It won't always hurt like this."

They both walked quietly, he reaching back to hold branches as he passed. He wondered if she were finished. But then she spoke again.

"I want to find us a home. I want to be in one place." He looked back at her. He noticed her nose was red, but she was smiling.

"With walls," she said, moving gracefully through the woods, in her best church dress. "And plumbing."

He started to speak, but she cut him off.

"I know it's probably not here. I don't want to be your sister forever. I want *you*."

He colored and felt the familiar stirring.

"And I know you want to get to Texas, and say goodbye proper to your mom." Anne sighed. "But I loved just being myself—" she gave him a look as he turned in surprise. "I know that's not exactly what I mean. But I just—it was fun. And even if it's risky, I want to go to supper at Mrs. Walker's."

They walked the rest of the way in silence back to the camp, slowly looking around for any sign of disturbance. Everything was as they'd left it earlier that morning.

"Anne," he began, in his firmest voice. But she would not let him get started.

"Jimmy, I think I'll know if it's not safe. I don't know how, but I just feel like I'll know." Her eyes softened, and she looked almost, but not quite, pleading. She looked around slowly, looked with her ears and eyes, then stepped to him and turned her back, so he could unzip the dress.

"I'm not asking you to trust me. That'd be too much. But if it turns out I'm wrong, the two of us together can handle my father Roy somehow."

She turned back and touched his lips as he started to speak. Then she kissed him, soft and languid, lingering.

"You think it's okay I am wearing the same dress to dinner that I wore to church?" Anne asked as they stepped onto the sidewalk from the highway.

"I really like that dress, Anne. It goes so well with your...hair," he responded lamely.

"I think you need to call me Gwen, even when we're alone." Anne drew her fingers idly along the pickets of a white fence as they walked down the shaded lane, past the restaurant where they'd eaten—was that only four days ago?

"Does that mean I'm Matt from here on?"

She looked at him, coyly. "I like that name. It'll be hard not to call you *Jimmy,* but—" Anne's face clouded. "There is a lot at stake for us in not slipping up."

He nodded. "As long as you bring it up, I almost got tripped up by the preacher today."

Anne looked around, then back at him. James continued. "He wanted to know where we were from. And I couldn't think fast enough. I was nervous. So nervous, I forgot your name!"

She smiled, but it was thin and thoughtful. "You're right," she said.

"Here is the way of it. We have to tell a story that's simple to remember, and can't be checked. At least, not easily."

James nodded.

"But what have we said so far?" she continued. "Let's see. What have we told Julie Rose, and her mom? I don't really think we have anyone else to worry about. Maybe today will be good practice. Just let me lead, and listen to what I say…"

Anne's voice trailed off as her forehead crinkled in thought. James ached to take her hand or encircle her waist. He wished their story didn't cast them as brother and sister. But it would not be forever.

"I think what I said was that we're from upstate New York. That might have been dumb—I don't know anything about New York. Do you?"

James scratched his head as they turned the corner in the opposite direction from where they'd walked this morning, to the church.

"No, but we should be okay today unless Mrs. Walker's been up that way. I would be surprised if she has. Julie Rose didn't sound like they traveled much at all. And CeCe can help us out if we get tripped up."

Anne nodded. "Thanks for doing this. I know you would rather be long gone."

He nodded. "I'm okay with being here for awhile. We had to stop somewhere, and we should have some time before your father figures out that the western route was a trick."

"I think it's that house up on the corner. The small white one. Yes, they said red shutters. It looks so friendly!" James sped up as her pace quickened. They skirted petunias that burst out from a dazzling collection of odd and mismatched pots bordering the sidewalk.

"Hi!" A familiar voice called. CeCe waved from the shade of the porch and rose from a glider.

They called back, and moved up the walk. CeCe stopped at the top of the steps.

"I said I'd keep an eye out for y'all, Matt and Gwendolyn." CeCe winked, assuring them she'd remembered. "Come in. Julie Rose and her mom are in the kitchen."

They stepped ahead of CeCe, who held the screen door wide,

smiling. Just inside the door was a narrow hall, with a staircase on the left. A front room on the right was cool and dark. The hall was filled with the most delectable aroma medley that James could imagine. His mouth watered, and he felt a prick of guilt. He had not smelled anything like these dueling aromas since home.

They paused in the small space, and CeCe led them down the hall to the back of the house. On the green-papered wall past the entry to the parlor, an assortment of frames greeted them at eye level. The frames were another odd collection of large and small, darkly wooded and light plastic trim. The pictures were an anthology of current and crisp Polaroids along with faded, sepia prints, some water-stained, behind yellowed and cracked glass. The menagerie of portraits reminded James of the flowers outside, and he found the cluttered tributes to nature and to ancestry homey and charming.

As they entered the kitchen, Mrs. Walker and Julie Rose both rose straight, their backs to them, as Mrs. Walker eased the oven door closed, a large mitt on her hand.

CeCe said, "Look who's here!"

"Welcome, welcome," Julie Rose said, wiping at a stray strand of hair, and trying to blow it out of her eyes at the same time.

Mrs. Walker smiled warmly. "The coolest place in the house is outside," she said. Anne looked at her startled, and CeCe grinned.

"Sundays we usually take dinner at the picnic table out back. Come and I'll show y'all," she said.

"Let us help," CeCe said to Mrs. Walker.

"CeCe, take glasses out, and Julie Rose and I will bring along the lemonade and the cakes," Mrs. Walker replied.

CeCe reached into the cabinet over the icebox and handed down glasses to James and Anne. "Put them on that tray there," she said, gesturing to the tray on the counter.

"Matt, can you handle the tray without breaking our priceless goblets?" Mrs. Walker stared at James, and then broke into a smile.

"Julie Rose wishes we had more expensive household things, but the good part is we never fret about breaking something. Isn't that right, dear?" Mrs. Walker mussed her daughter's hair, and the errant strand again dropped down over the girl's face. Julie Rose blushed.

"I think I can manage, Mrs. Walker," he replied.

The three of them moved out the back door. The way the screen shrieked on its hinges reminded him of the back door on Nash Street, a million miles away.

The rear of the house was a riot of colors, with splashes of flowers that spilled out of teetering pots, all manner of buckets, and a variety of devices recruited for holding soil and seeds.

James did a double take at a solemn figure seated in a collapsing Adirondack chair. It was a scarecrow-ish creation, dressed in overalls and a checked shirt, with a wide brimmed straw hat, and a bandana around the neck. But the exposed limbs were entirely formed of terra cotta pots. The face had rosy cheeks under dark eyes and caterpillar-like brows, and a corncob pipe was glued into a set of clay lips that jutted from the surface of the face-pot.

CeCe laughed behind him. "Don't tell Mr. Walker if y'all meet him, but Mrs. Walker and Julie Rose say they keep 'Mr. Potter' here to hold up his end of the conversation when Mr. Walker has to be away."

"I guess Mr. Walker doesn't talk a lot?" Anne smiled as they passed the eerily human figure. Beyond, there was a table bedecked with a brightly colored vinyl cover, and already set out with a collection of dishes. The silverware was in a crystal decanter in the middle of the table.

CeCe lowered her voice. "Julie Rose says it's because her daddy enjoys getting potted."

They all laughed as James set the tray down. He inhaled deeply.

"Something smells really good," he said.

"Hydrangeas," Anne said promptly. "My mom—" She stopped, glancing around, as Julie Rose emerged from the house. James saw the warning look CeCe shot her as Julie Rose struggled with two large bowls of food. He stepped quickly to relieve her of one.

"Thanks so much," Julie Rose breathed, handing him a heaping bowl of potato salad. "I'm so glad you and your sister could join us."

He nodded and set the bowl in the middle of the table.

"Will your—real father," he glanced meaningfully at the figure in the chair, "be joining us?"

She followed his gaze, and grinned. "No. This time of year, he works the shrimp boats off the coast."

"Is there work to be had then?" James followed Julie Rose back to the house as Anne and CeCe set the plates around the table.

"I suppose," she said. "If my *dad* can get work..." She stepped back as James swung the screen wide for her and followed her into the kitchen.

Mrs. Walker glanced up, her hands balancing a carving fork and knife, like a conductor about to exhort the orchestra.

"Young man, do you carve?" she asked.

"I can give it a try," he said without much conviction.

"You have not had the opportunity? Well, let me show you. And don't worry. You cannot ruin ham," she laughed.

She stepped to the side as James approached the ham, unsure.

"Are you looking for work, Matt?" Julie Rose lifted a towel from a bar on the wall, and bent to open the oven. The fragrance of fresh rolls made his eyes water.

"I'm not sure. Gwen wants to stay here for a while. People have been very nice." He took the proffered fork and knife from Mrs. Walker, and studied her mime as she inscribed a line along the flank of the ham with her finger. James sliced uncertainly into the thick meat, as Mrs. Walker watched at his side. He lifted a thick slab of ham onto the platter that Mrs. Walker set next to him. "Gwen and I pay our own way," James added quickly.

"Perhaps my husband could ask around on the wharf," Mrs. Walker nodded approvingly as James's next slice fell thinly to the platter.

"How long do the ships stay out to sea?" he asked, glancing down at the spatter on his jeans.

Mrs. Walker noticed too, and drew in her breath. "Oh my, I should have asked. Son, would you like an apron?"

"That might not be a bad idea."

"Well, they call them boats, mostly. Shrimp boats. " Mrs. Walker retrieved another apron from the back of the kitchen door.

"They all come back each night," said Julie Rose. "But you pull out from the docks long before sunrise."

He turned to Mrs. Walker and ducked, as she draped the spare apron over his head.

"I thought you said Mr. Walker wouldn't be here because of the shrimping. Do they call it shrimping?" he asked. He raised his elbows for Mrs. Walker to reach the apron strings from behind. Mrs. Walker cinched the apron tight and string-bowed it.

"Mr. Walker thinks it's his duty to guard the fleet, so he stays camped on one boat or another, and comes home every so often to change clothes."

She and her daughter shared a private glance and smiled.

"A thief would have to be blind and desperate to want to steal a thing from the fleet," Mrs. Walker clucked, sprinkling a spice over the ham.

"Being unable to smell would be a big advantage too," Julie Rose laughed.

"I'll ask Myron if he thinks he can get you on over there, if you like," Mrs. Walker said.

"I sure would appreciate that," said James.

James bowed along with the others over the savory feast. "…Guide Matt and Gwen along their way—Your Way—and bless our loved ones everywhere. Amen." Mrs. Walker sat back. James started to bless himself and then stopped when he realized no one else did.

Everyone nodded and hands dropped away around the table. For the next few minutes, a clattering and quiet buzz issued as plates were heaped, lemonade was poured into clinking glasses, and Anne nodded to Mr. Potter, then sipped and sighed. The quiet that followed was warm and friendly, interspersed with praise for the potato salad, the beets, the wonderful green bean casserole, and the biscuits. James noticed CeCe drizzle hers with honey from the end of a wooden stick, and followed suit. The taste was bewitching.

After a time, Mrs. Walker spoke, addressing Anne and James. "I don't know what the good Lord has in mind for y'all, but as long as you are here in Darien you are welcome to join us for a home-cooked meal whenever you can. Oh, dear, I didn't mean to…"

James followed the woman's gaze. Anne's eyes were shining, her fork midway to her mouth. Anne shook her head vigorously.

"It's all right, Mrs. Walker, really. This is wonderful. It's just…thank you. You and Julie Rose and CeCe—everyone's been so kind to us here."

James nodded, but something in him shifted with a vague unease. He ate quietly, mulling it over. As the conversation began to buzz more loudly about him, full of words about recipes and flowers, he considered that up to now, he had not possessed a clue regarding their next step.

When they finally said their goodbyes, late in the afternoon, James took the basket that Mrs. Walker handed to him. "It isn't much," she said again, as he hefted what felt like a large bowling ball, tucked under a checkered cloth in the wicker holder.

She invited them back and they thanked her again, and set off down the sidewalk. CeCe had offered to walk them back to the camp, and they'd readily agreed. James wanted to know if she thought they had performed their roles well enough.

CeCe assured them almost as soon as they reached the corner.

"As long as y'all don't get too close to each other, I think you'll do fine," she laughed quietly, glancing around.

Anne nodded. "I think I know what you mean. When we're close, I just want to…" She glanced around CeCe, smiling, and James noticed for the first time that CeCe had positioned herself between them. *Just a couple of simple rules*, he thought to himself.

"I was going to send Benjamin later with some things from home, but looks like you won't need any food for a day or so," CeCe smiled.

James nodded, shifting the basket to his other hand again. Though he was stuffed beyond expression, even now the aroma of the ham and biscuits was a pleasant distraction.

"They are both so nice. Just like you've been," Anne said. "I feel just awful not being honest with them."

"It won't be forever," James said as they stepped off the lane where it curved left, and moved quietly down a well-worn trail toward the river.

"When will it be safe for you?" CeCe asked, over her shoulder.

"I guess when I turn eighteen; I'll at least be legal. My dad won't be any less mad, but maybe he'll give up looking."

"How do you know he's still trying to find you—" James stiffened at the warning hush from ahead.

CeCe was smiling now and waving to several men and boys lined up on the bank of the river, rods in hand. One of the men waved back and turned to smile at them.

"Hey there Joey. Hi, Preacher Waugh. Mr. Beck. Samuel. How's fishing?" CeCe asked, pleasantly.

James saw that both the boys had their pants rolled up to their knees, standing in the shallows. The two men were in dark trousers. The younger man sported a short sleeve shirt, light blue, while the older man wore a white shirt with a collar, like a minister.

The two boys glanced from CeCe to the older man, who turned and assessed the three hikers with a smoldering stare. James noticed the way the others deferred to him. In contrast to the friendly younger man, the older one was unsmiling. Dark age-spots dappled the backs of his hands, and he had a forbidding look under his dress hat. James felt the old man's stare lasted a moment or two past polite, and that it was directed most pointedly at Anne.

The younger of the two men tipped his hat.

"A bit late in the day for any luck with the worms," he said. "The fish apparently have had their Sunday supper too." He grinned. Midway through his remarks, the older man turned his back on them. The boys glanced at each other, and then turned back to the river.

CeCe laughed, turning to her friends. "This here's Matt, and his sister Gwen. They are visiting from up New York way."

The man nodded a greeting and then continued. "How's your pa, young lady? Not driving on the Lord's Day, is he?" He smiled to show he was teasing.

"He's fine, and he's home. He got back in late last night. Out again on Wednesday," she returned.

"Well, it sure is a nice afternoon for a walk in the woods," he called out over the low wineberry bushes that separated them.

The older man did not turn, but tilted his head to the younger, and said something they could not hear. The younger man listened, nodding, all the while glancing in the direction of the two accompanying CeCe. The old man, apparently done, turned back to the river. The younger man spoke again.

"Preacher Waugh said I should mention step cautious west of here. There's a report from over Belle Vista way about some boys' escaped from the work farm. It's a long way off, and they could've gone anywhere, but keep an eye out is the prudent thing."

CeCe nodded, glancing toward her two companions. "Thank Preacher Waugh, and thank you Mr. Beck, and I hope the fishing improves. Y'all take care now."

The three of them waved at Mr. Beck, and continued walking. The sun was overhead, but arcing west, and there was a cool breeze wafting from the river to their right. James shifted the sweet-smelling burden between his arms again, and asked, "Who was the older guy back there?"

CeCe laughed softly. "Preacher Waugh has a church in town, I guess."

Anne glanced at James. "You guess?"

CeCe looked back over her shoulder as she parted branches for James. They were crossing a side-creek, and the trail narrowed to ford the creek and climb the far bank.

"Preacher has services at Harolly's Service Station. He got Harolly to donate the use of the service area on Sunday mornings, since the station is only open for gas pumping Sundays."

"Services in a service station?" Anne smiled at the joke too. "I can see how that could be funny."

"CeCe's face darkened. " Thing is, Preacher Waugh isn't a joke. He's actually very scary."

"Scary how?" asked Anne.

"He doesn't have too many in his congregation, but they get talked about like they were a much larger church."

"How come?" Anne persisted.

"Let's just say he makes the holy rollers look like atheists. You've heard of being *washed in the blood.* Preacher Waugh practically *surfs* in it."

"CeCe! Is that any way to talk about a man of God?" But Anne was laughing. "So tell us what you mean!"

James looked up in time to see CeCe glance around, as if she were worried she might be overheard. "They use snakes. And poison."

"For *what*?" Anne asked.

"It's part of the service," CeCe said, turning to face them grimly, before moving off again down the trail.

"What's part of the service?" Anne asked, sounding a little short. "CeCe, whatever do you mean?"

CeCe rounded a bend in the trail and turned on her two companions. "Julie Rose's cousin used to go to the preacher's church. At Harolly's gas station," she amended. "He told Julie Rose that the men would have rattlesnakes in these boxes, and they would take them out—"

"Real snakes?" Anne gasped.

"Real *live* snakes," CeCe nodded slowly.

James scoffed, but CeCe looked at him seriously. "His is not the only church that does it. You never heard of handling rattlesnakes in church?"

James shook his head. But he stopped grinning. CeCe was clearly not teasing.

"Church of Jesus with Signs Following." That's what the sandwich board says on Sundays in front of the station. And I've heard tell of churches like it over in Tennessee, and Alabama too."

CeCe looked at Anne, who shrugged. "That's a new one on me." She looked at James, who also shook his head, though the name sounded familiar to him.

"What do they do with the snakes?" Anne persisted.

"What kinds of snakes?" James asked at the same time.

CeCe gave a small smile, and began to walk on again. "Here they use rattlers. Sometimes copperheads. As long as they're poisonous, they get invited to church."

Anne touched CeCe's arm, and turned her. "What do people in church *do* with the snakes?"

Anne looked at her crookedly. "Julie Rose's cousin said that the men—and even the women—dance with the snakes. Some put them on their heads, around their necks—"

James shook his head. "What keeps the snakes from biting them?"

"The Lord," CeCe answered promptly. "Oh, don't think I believe in it," she said more slowly. "But there are a number of folks in these parts do."

"Did Julie Rose's cousin do the snake thing?" James asked.

CeCe shook her head. "Julie Rose said he wouldn't say one way or the other, but the last service he ever went to, he came home just beside himself."

"Why? What happened?" asked James.

"I don't know exactly. Nobody talks about it. There was a boy named Wayne. He was relations with a boy that married one of Preacher Waugh's daughters."

"Preacher Waugh's *married*?" asked Anne, askance.

"Not anymore. He's a widower. They say his wife drank poison one night and died." CeCe shrugged. "I barely remember her."

"Killed herself? Well, if she was married to that crazy old man—

CeCe turned to James. "No, it wasn't that way. She drank strychnine one night at a service. Remember I said it's not just poison snakes. They believe they're protected from *any* poison."

"So she drank poison at the service and died?"

CeCe shook her head. "Not then and there. She was real sick for three days. Finally, Doc Warden couldn't stand the reports he was getting. He went down to the preacher's house to call on Mrs. Waugh."

"What happened?" asked James.

"My dad said the preacher stuck a shotgun in his chest and told Doc to get off his porch."

James looked at CeCe close, to see if she was teasing, but she just kept walking.

Anne spoke: "CeCe, you said the preacher had a daughter."

CeCe nodded. "Two, actually. One's married to Mr. Beck, who y'all just met. The other ran off with a boy from Savannah way. I think that's what makes him so contrary. Oh! Sorry..." CeCe blanched, embarrassed.

"Don't worry. It is what it is," Anne sighed.

James searched the surrounding woods, sensing they were getting close to camp. CeCe's words reminded him of something. "I started to ask earlier, but what makes you think your dad is still looking for us?"

Anne turned on him. "You just don't get it, do you? This isn't so much about getting me back. This is about punishing me. And you. We made my father look bad. Really bad. He won't forget. Ever."

CeCe studied the far bank, clearly uneasy. James held up his hands in mock surrender, and then dropped them with a rush. "You know what? Let him come. I'm sick of running anyway."

Anne glared at him. "I don't think you have any idea what or who you're dealing with." Then she glanced over at CeCe. "Sorry. Bet you didn't guess you were in for such adventure when we met."

James sighed too, and turned back to CeCe. "So did that preacher's daughters have to go to that church of the crazy signs?"

"Church of Jesus Christ of Signs Following."

"Did they have to drink poison too?"

"No. Kids at the service aren't allowed to touch the snakes. Not until they're 18 or 21 or something. Wasn't always that way. And they can still go to the services. Julie Rose's cousin took Julie Rose one time."

"What happened?" asked James, easing aside a branch that had fallen across the path.

"Preacher tried to get Julie Rose to renounce the Devil. But she was so scared and she didn't know what renounce was, so she kept saying back, 'I renown the Devil,' and he just got madder and called for a circle of believers to lay hands on her and pray."

She giggled and pressed her hat atop her head as a low-hanging limb threatened to steal it. "One of the circle forgot he was holding a little rattlesnake I guess, and when she looked up at all these hands, there it was, and she went screaming out the door."

CeCe laughed, but James could see Anne shiver, up ahead of him.

"So who is Wayne?" James pressed.

CeCe nodded, moving close in again. "Wayne was a boy in town, not too bright, but harmless enough. Lonely, I guess. He had a baby face that made him look like, well, everyone said he was a ringer for Lee Harvey Oswald, which just made the boy unbearable. A year or so ago, he was at a *Signs* service, and a snake bit him. His face got all swollen, but preacher and the other elders said if he went to the doc, it was a sign of weakness, and would just make things worse."

James and Anne walked alongside the girl, silent, as the path hugged the river. James could see the curve on the river upstream that marked the location of their camp.

"So what happened to Wayne? Did he…" Anne asked, hushed.

"Mr. Walker said he heard that Wayne tried to get the poison out himself."

"How?"

"After the service, Preacher took Wayne to his house. Next day, Wayne's face was all swelled up, and preacher put him out to tend the garden to keep him occupied. Next thing you know, Wayne comes running in, his face all torn apart. First they thought the swelling had burst his skin, but turns out Wayne had tried to lance it."

"With what?" James asked.

"With a steel garden rake."

"Wow. Did it kill him?"

CeCe shrugged. "No one knows for sure. He just run off that day, and no one's ever seen him again. Preacher was all upset for the week."

James pressed. "Were he and the preacher close then?"

CeCe smiled. "I won't say the preacher is *close* to anyone. But he sure missed the shotgun Wayne took with him."

"But they never found the boy?"

CeCe shook her head. "Benjamin told me he thinks Wayne gets by out here somewhere, or maybe over in the Altamaha Swamp. Says he's seen footprints."

James and Anne both looked around. "I could see being able to get by in the woods, but with those injuries…" James looked back at CeCe. "When did Benjamin tell you that?"

"Oh, more than once—he kids me about it sometimes—that I've been meeting him in these woods. Ha! Wayne and he were friends of a sort too. Wayne even asked Preacher once if Benjamin could come to a service, early on. Preacher told him Negroes had no soul to save." She shook her strawberry locks, disgusted.

"Wayne's mother is one of the ladies in town that helps me with medicinal and herb study. She's a healer." CeCe sighed. "People figured when Wayne didn't head home, he must have died somewhere in the woods." She shrugged. "But he knew a lot himself about forest medicines. It is a sad shame."

"How is it that a white and a Negro get to be friends?" James asked.

"Benjamin's dad did some work for Wayne's family, and he'd take Benjamin along when he was little. I guess they didn't notice skin color so much as children."

"Do you think Benjamin is fibbing about seeing that boy out here?" CeCe shrugged.

Anne shivered. "Snakes in church. What would make god-fearin' people carry on so? And why would a boy take a rake to his own face?"

James grinned. "Maybe he just got tired of looking like Lee Harvey Oswald."

CeCe scowled at him. "Well Mr. Beck, he was at the Preacher's house that day for something, he said that it was the awfulest sight he'd ever seen, and it was one of the few times him and the preacher had words."

Anne looked puzzled. "Mr. Beck doesn't go to the preacher's church?"

CeCe laughed. "Gosh no! I guess he loves Mary Louise all right. But he goes to the Methodist Church. He might have been in the office counting collection this morning."

Anne turned an elm branch off the path. "If folks die at the service, why do people believe that they're protected by God?"

CeCe furrowed her brow. "Preacher tells his believers if you don't have enough faith, you can die. Doesn't that sound a little like being in a lion's den and having your guide whisper, 'If the lion senses fear, it *will eat you*'? How do you not totally wig out?"

James walked ahead as they approached camp to lift away some small deadfall that they'd positioned at the trailhead leading off the main trail. He waited for the girls to pass, and eased it back over the entryway, then followed them. Everything in camp appeared to be normal. Anne too was glancing around, looking for signs of disturbance.

It struck him that something was odd at the same time that Anne spoke.

"James," she said slowly, "Did you move CeCe's hair ribbon from the stick next to the fire ring?"

He shook his head. The first full day they were in the camp, Anne was sitting by the fire, and wondered if she could be spotted by someone out on the river before she might hear them approaching. James had driven a stick into the earth next to her and tied the red ribbon on the shaft, at the level of her eyes. They had never gotten around to the actual experiment, and had just stepped around the stick for the next several days.

He looked quickly around the camp, but the bright cloth was nowhere in sight. The stick seemed to be shorter than he remembered. The same thought must have occurred to Anne, for she bent down next to the stick, as if she were sitting next to it. The stick only came up to her shoulder.

James turned slowly in a circle, trying to still his concern, and to coax his memory to note any other disturbances. Everything else seemed to be in its place. He was about to ease down the thin path to the river's edge to look around, when he saw it.

On the pole of their small tent above the entrance flaps, a small cross, woven from a palm leaf, was lashed to the tip.

36 / Affairs of the Heart

The summer afternoon hummed and crackled with myriad insects, enjoying their brief and active lives. Oblivious to all the activity above the surface, the Wicomico River flowed sluggishly past Dylan's perch on the bank, at the familiar fishing spot below Elmore Thompson's house.

In the last few weeks, Sam had been working to prepare the house for sale. Dylan helped quite a bit, and he was impressed with his father's knowledge of home repairs. This afternoon, Sam was painting the downstairs walls. Since the flooring was shiny tongue and groove hardwood, Sam had allowed that fishing or baseball might be a better endeavor for Dylan. Dylan didn't mind the time alone. There was much to consider.

He had attempted several times to pen a note to Lois Mast. His problem was he didn't know what it was supposed to say. Though he knew about notes that passed between girls and girls, and sometimes boys and girls, he wasn't familiar with the contents. And he didn't know whom to ask. So he waited, thinking maybe Lois would write *him* a note, and then he'd have the idea. But in the meantime, was she getting impatient with him? Her last words had been clear. She was hoping for a note from him.

He considered his attempts so far. He was sure there was a fine balance to be struck between friendly and intimate. He could do the friendly part okay. *Did you see* Ed Sullivan *last night? How did you enjoy your* Trixie Belden *book? Do you ever read* Tom Swift? There was a lot of material there. But did that come before or after the mushy stuff? And what was proper anyway? He was sure he didn't *love* Lois. He hardly knew her. But his mouth was dry a lot, and he thought about her, and looked for her when he was outside, or even inside, glancing out the window every time he was near one. Did love have anything to do with *waiting*? Because he felt like he was waiting a lot more than he had ever before. Was this somewhere between *like* and *love*?

Actually, he didn't know what he felt. Some kids he knew would spell it *LUV*. *Luv ya. Luv ya til Niagara Falls. Luv ya til the kitchen sinks.* He was lonely in his self-imposed exile, and Lois seemed to understand that. Was *that* love?

With worrying over running into Stinger and his bunch and worrying over Lois, and missing James, this was shaping up to be the worst summer in memory. Not that he looked forward to the start of school, which loomed in just a couple of weeks. He would be in junior high, his second year. The junior high sat on one side of the elementary school, the high school on the other. Because the playground for the elementary school was adjacent to the baseball and football fields the other schools shared, kids from all three schools mixed during lunch and recess.

The hammering that had emanated from the house on the hill behind him had ceased an hour or so ago, and Dylan assumed Sam was in the middle of his painting. But his reverie was interrupted by steps approaching. When he turned, his father was walking across the bottom of the yard, wiping at his arms with a stained rag. Dylan sniffed the strong aroma of turpentine. Sam's makeshift smock was also damp with perspiration.

"Done already?" He asked, lightly drawing his line in a length, and reeling up the slack.

"In a manner of speaking." His dad smiled. "I got the ceilings done, and I'm using a different color on the walls, so I thought I'd see how the fishing is."

Dylan looked up, puzzled. It was not like Sam to stop in the middle of the day.

Sam shrugged. "So maybe I felt like playing hooky! Fish biting?"

"I suspect they're taking a siesta. So far, I've been feeding the snapping turtles." Dylan turned to cast out over the water again.

"Snappers got to eat too, I guess. I was thinking of taking a plunge. The house is awful stuffy with the air so still." He stepped up to the river's edge. "How's the bottom here?"

"Straight out, it's rocky because of the bend. Out in the middle, it runs deeper to the far back, shale bottom."

"Current?" Asked Sam, flapping the throat of his smock. "I'm not much of a swimmer."

"You'll be fine then, because it's not much of a current." Dylan flicked his line up river a bit, to demonstrate. The line slowly eased down the channel. "It's a little stronger on the far bank, but still manageable, this low."

Sam peeled the smock over his head and then shed his sleeveless tee shirt, looking around. "Want to join me?"

Dylan turned to his father, puzzled. "Um, no thanks. I'd have to go get my bathing suit."

Sam sat to pull off his work boots.

"Shhh," Sam said theatrically, rising. "Some folks think my suit looks like my boxer shorts." With that, he unbuckled his belt, unbuttoned his pants, and shoved them down, stepping limberly out. He folded his pants neatly and drew a small packet from a pocket of the pants.

With that, he stepped out on a rock at the river's edge, and then into the water. Dylan looked, amazed, trying not to stare.

"Aren't you going to take your socks off?" he croaked.

"I'm hoping the white flash will scare off snappers," Sam replied, walking in to his knees, then his thighs. "I have no scientific basis for believing that will work, of course." Sam had been standing facing Dylan, but as he finished his sentence, he slowly tipped backwards, landing with a splash, and gurgling to the surface a moment later, grinning widely.

As if in prudish protest, the airborne bugs buzzed even more incessantly, grouping on the far side of the river. Sam sat where he'd landed, in chest- deep water, and ceremoniously unwrapped a small bar of soap.

"Here," he called, and tossed the bunched wrapper to Dylan.

Dylan grinned, watching his father lather his thin hair, and then his face and upper arms. He glanced around once more, and then peeled down to his skivvies and socks. He laid his fishing pole aside, and stepped out on a large boulder several feet out. "Geronimo!" he whooped.

Sam and Dylan walked out together toward the deeper channel, passing the soap back and forth. Dylan looked at his father. "You don't do this a lot, do you?"

Sam glanced over at his son, and tossed him the soap bar. "What make you say that?" Then he glanced down and grinned. His work shirt's image was perfectly outlined on the white of his body. Below where the sleeve ended, his arms were dark. Above, and over his entire chest and back, and most of his neck, Sam's skin was the shade of a plucked chicken.

"If the color *white* keeps snappers away, you didn't really need the socks," Dylan laughed.

As casual as he could, Dylan broached the subject of Lois expecting a note. Sam nodded as he listened. His response was initially disappointing.

"Son, to be honest, I'm not all that familiar with affairs of the heart."

Dylan reddened, regretting he'd even brought it up.

"Nice girl, is she?" Sam asked.

"Nice enough, I guess. She likes to talk. But I like to listen," he hastened to add.

Sam snapped his fingers. "I do know one thing about the human female."

Dylan waited, lightly scrubbing his arms and chest with the soap bar.

"It's safe to say that there's not a woman alive who doesn't appreciate the effort of a poem."

Dylan looked at his father, dubious. Sam nodded firmly. "Even a bad one. Yes, that's your course. A poem."

"Like what?" Dylan started, but Sam held up his hands.

"Trust me on this. If it comes from you, she'll appreciate it. No, not from me. From you, son."

Dylan wasn't sure this addressed his problem at all. But he told Sam he'd think about it.

A few minutes later, they sat on rocks at the river's edge, drying in the warm sun.

"How's the work on the house?" Dylan asked.

Sam stretched. "There was more than I thought, when I started moving furniture, but you were a big help, so that saved a lot of effort."

Dylan nodded and rose to slip back into his clothes.

"I got a call from Father Mullenix this morning," Sam said slowly, as Dylan dressed. He too rose, and shook out his tee shirt, then pulled it over his head.

"Why would Father call you?"

"Seems his car turned up."

Dylan stumbled pulling on his jeans. "Is James coming home?"

His father studied Dylan a moment. "You miss him too, eh?"

Dylan had no idea what to say. He guessed he might, a little. When he wasn't busy being mad. "Are you going to tell me what happened?" he asked.

Sam looked out at the water, and ran a comb through his hair several times, slow. "The thing of it is, I'm not sure I want your grandma worrying just yet." He seemed to come to a decision.

"Don't you think it's time we took a drive to Richmond soon, you and me?"

Dylan felt a little queasy. "Richmond? Well, sure. But weren't we just talking about James, and Father's car?" he said, a little irritated.

Sam glanced up at Dylan, and finished lacing his shoes. "Sorry son. I shouldn't have brought it up. We just may need to do something, quick. But I don't know what yet."

"What about the car?" Dylan nearly shouted.

Sam rose, and gathered up his turpentine rag. "Father Mullenix called to say his car turned up in a garage. Apparently it had some trouble, and James and Anne ended up leaving it."

Dylan slumped. "So we still don't know where they are?"

His father shrugged. "The trail's almost a week old." He started back up the rise to Mr. Thompson's house. "I'll let you know more when I know more. We may need to take a ride over to Richmond. And points south."

"One other thing I wanted to tell *you*." Dylan called. His father turned. "Stinger Owens."

Sam looked uncomfortable for a moment, and glanced around, then back at Dylan. "That boy been bullying you? Do you want me to have a word with him?"

Dylan shook his head. "No. I just wanted to tell you I'm calling him out."

Sam nodded, looking down at the rag in his hand. "He's older than you. Mean as a snapper."

Dylan nodded, his insides feeling watery. "Whether I beat him or not, I can't keep going worried all the time."

His dad nodded, almost to himself. "What's your lady friend think of it?"

Dylan shrugged. "I wasn't going to tell her."

Sam nodded again. "Better make it a good poem, then."

"Sorry?"

Sam looked down the hill at his son. "Females never, ever understand fighting, unless maybe it's over them." He grinned and so did Dylan.

Dylan retrieved his pole and checked the worm. "I think I'll do okay, if it's just Stinger and me."

Again, Sam nodded, his forehead beading again in the relentless August sun. "I don't suppose you want me in attendance to…" Dylan was shaking his head before Sam could finish.

"I'll figure something out," the boy said.

"Is there a date set yet for this bout?" Sam smiled, but he looked concerned.

"Before school starts. I don't want a circus. I just want him to leave me alone."

His dad turned to go again, lifting a hand in parting. He turned back to Dylan. "Care to practice a little in the back yard later?"

Dylan nodded vigorously.

37 / Mysterious Prank

"Kids," CeCe agreed again, as she took her leave. "Looks like cabbage palm, which is all over here," she said, bending to look at the woven cross. "But stay close, and keep alert." She spoke lightly, as if to mind them to carry an umbrella when the weather threatens. But she was clearly unnerved by the strange visit. That night they kept a low fire, and snacked on some of the cold leftovers from the supper at Mrs. Walker's. Late in the evening, when the first-quarter moon had settled into the trees on the far side of the river, a dim *thunk* alerted them that CeCe or Benjamin had tripped the rig they used to signal an arrival.

James rose to a crouch, and squeezed his eyes shut for several moments, then opened them, staring into the black. He spoke in a hush.

"Benjamin?"

"Yes, Mr. Jimmy. It's me." James saw the paleness of the plaid shirt first, then the dark overalls, and finally, Benjamin's bare feet, hands, and face.

"Come ahead then. And for Pete's sake, call me *Matt*. It's hard enough for *me* to keep it straight." He smiled briefly at the young black, to take the edge off his voice.

James glanced at Anne as Benjamin stepped out quietly into the light of the low fire. The orange glow did not quite reach his face, and James started at the disembodied effect. It looked like a set of grungy overalls and boots was standing to the side of him.

Before Benjamin could speak, James snapped, "Do you know anything about us having visitors in camp?"

Benjamin started. "Visitors? No sir. Who—"

"That's the problem, Benjamin," Anne spoke up. "We don't know, but somebody knows we're here." She pointed at the small cross on the stem of the tent pole. They all stared at the woven image, willing it to whisper a hint of its secrets.

Who had left the odd calling card? Not for the first time, James clenched his fists as the anger boiled in him. Sparks rose in a spray from the low fire as a thick log burned itself through and split. James noticed Benjamin and Anne watching him over the low flames. Had someone asked him a question?

And what was he so angry about anyway? Angry that this was one more place he wasn't welcome, he supposed. They hadn't been here long but it felt familiar, this wooded home, and the indolent river, with danger lurking below a tranquil surface. Just like Crane Ridge had felt like home. When he'd first walked into Nana's, he felt so safe he never even considered that it might not always be that way. He longed for the return of that feeling of safety.

Yet here, in just these few short weeks, Crane Ridge was a steadily receding memory. He wasn't bitter, exactly. He knew he liked Anne a lot and he liked being out on his own, testing his ability to get by. But he felt like a patient with a fresh wound, where the dressing is working loose before the wound has properly scabbed over. He turned from Anne and Benjamin to look again at the flame-reflecting shimmer of the woven cross. He was not ready to be driven away again. Not again. Not yet.

Anne spoke to Benjamin: "When we were on our way back from Mrs. Walker's today, we saw an old man and some others fishing. They said something about men escaped from a jail somewhere. Did you hear anything like that, Benjamin?"

The boy eased back on the dirt, his bare feet crossed in front of him, his arms loose around his knees. "Heard some boys talkin' at church. What you said. You think that's who came calling here at yo' camp?"

Anne bowed her head and lay it on her knees, as if she were about to sleep. Or weep. Then she raised it, and dusted non-existent dust from her shorts. "Somehow, this doesn't feel like grown men. I don't know why, kids aren't usually given to religious pranks, but this feels more...I don't know. . . playful."

James snorted. "Playful, huh."

Anne looked at him.

James continued. "You think someone walks into the camp of people he's never even met, because he wants to *play?*" Anne shrugged and Benjamin shifted uncomfortably.

James tossed a stick into the small fire. "Another example of southern hospitality?" He shook his head, grinning with a glaring stare. "Well, if they want to play, next time I'll be happy to..." he paused. This was not like him. So what was going on?

Anne turned again to Benjamin. "Did CeCe send you out here?" she asked.

Benjamin nodded, his adam's apple bobbing. "She wanted me to say she'll probably be away a couple days, her daddy's in town, and not to fret if y'all don't see her."

James and Anne exchanged glances. They both already knew that CeCe's dad was in town for a few days. This in itself had not prevented her from coming before. Was CeCe just worried about them?

James looked at Benjamin, and he worked to keep any emotion from his voice. "Anything else?"

Benjamin shifted, and scratched his head. "Somebody come talk to CeCe's father."

"About what?"

"About y'all."

James glanced at Anne. "Who was it? What'd they say?"

Benjamin shrugged. "The minister's wife from CeCe's church, I think is who she is."

Anne broke in, keeping her voice composed. "She seemed like a nice lady. Missus Ellie, I think is her name. So what did she want to talk to CeCe's dad about?"

"I wasn't there when she was. Fact is, she was leaving when my mom and me was returning this week's wash, after supper."

James turned. "Then how do you know she was there to talk about us?"

Benjamin's face swiveled back to James. "Mr. Walker said so. He said 'Benjamin, you know the kids CeCe's been introducing at church?'

I said as how I'd met you and he asked, simple as you please, where did I meet you?" Benjamin shrugged.

"What did you say?" James asked.

"I said as how I didn't recall exactly, just seen you here and there, and knew'd you was friends with Miss CeCe."

Anne bent to squat near the fire, staring into its center. "Did they seem satisfied with that, Benjamin?"

Benjamin shrugged and rolled his shoulders. "Hard to say."

Anne looked at James, and he could see the fear in her eyes. James turned to Benjamin, and drew a deep breath, trying to sound unconcerned.

"Benjamin, just what *are* you doing here? Is CeCe worried about something?" James asked.

"CeCe thinks you might want to move camp. Not far, but..."

"Does somebody own this land we're sitting on?" James clipped the words, staring into the flames.

"Well, no, not so far's I know—"

"Then we'll just stay here. Truth is, I'm in the mood to meet someone who wants to make us leave." James realized he meant it. He was sick of the enemy he couldn't see. Or the enemy who was too big, too arrogant, to challenge. Like his father. He stiffened, feeling like the lone lawman stepping out in the street at high noon.

"Do you really think that's a good idea?"

James turned on Anne. Who was she to talk like this in front of a— stranger? He studied the look on her face, willing her to soften, or turn away. But she stared at him in a way that made him slightly dizzy, as if he'd spun head over heels down a hill and stood up quick. He wondered who she was becoming. Why did it always seem like just when things were good, they got lousy again?

He pressed his lips together and rose, turning his back on both of them. His anger smoldered. The only sound was the crackling of the small flames in the fire ring and the incessant buzzing of the night swarm just outside the circle of orange glow.

James stared into the darkness, his eyes slits. He felt the pressure of his jaws clamped together, and lifted his chin defiantly. If there was an enemy out there, watching, James wanted him to know he wasn't afraid. On the contrary, he welcomed the chance to strike back at a world that seemed to have him at the top of the "humans to pester" list this month.

Behind him, Benjamin cleared his throat. "I best be on my way. Miss CeCe wanted to know y'all need anything?"

There was a pause, and James imagined Anne wagging her head *no*. But then she spoke, perhaps for his benefit.

"We're fine, Benjamin, really. And thank you for coming out here in the dark to check on us. James and I will certainly think over what you said."

James could feel this last part spoken directly at his spine, but he did not turn to argue. He heard the quiet rustle of Benjamin rising, and almost turned, but settled for a muttered "See you later," over his shoulder. He listened to Benjamin move out of the circle, and marveled again at the way the woods almost instantly blanketed the boy's retreat.

In the stillness, he let the anger pour over him. If someone were to step from the dark into their small space now, he was quite sure he would attack without mercy. Truth was, it felt good to be so furious.

Anne retired to their makeshift tent shortly after, without a word. Much later, after banking the fire, he slipped into the dark tent. He lay down and stared at the thin translucent ceiling, awash in a milky moon glow. He was bone tired, but after his burst of adrenaline, and Benjamin's departure, the rage had slowly dissipated, and he'd considered CeCe's words, spoken by Benjamin: *Move your camp. Not far…*

His jaw clenched at the recollection and he felt his fists ball. But when he forced himself to think clearly, he had to admit the suggestion had merit. Ever since they'd found this site, he had suspected it wouldn't remain a secret long. After all, he was sure that at least some folks in town would wonder what he and Anne were up to with no adults to answer to, and no car or other visible means of getting by. He had just hoped that they would be able to stay for a while. The irony was that he'd not wanted to stay at all at first. But after he'd resigned himself to it, he came to see this small bump in the riverbank as their haven for a time. A too-short time, it now appeared. To make things worse, he felt distant from Anne and didn't know how to make that right. Why wasn't she angry too? And what made her look at him in that awful way, when he said or did certain things? Wasn't a fellow entitled to get mad? After all, it wasn't as if he was mad at *her*. He slipped into a shallow sleep and dreamed of a steady stream of strangers moving through their camp, nodding and waving and pointing, but not speaking.

38 / Gauntlet

The streets of Crane Ridge were quiet. Stinger, for reasons Dylan didn't fathom, despised James. He knew the attack had come primarily because Stinger believed James wasn't coming back, and so Dylan was unprotected. Dylan was certain the attack in the alley was just the start, unless he ended it somehow.

Dylan turned north from the town center on Canal Street and trudged up the hill towards the schools. His stomach felt like he'd swallowed something disagreeable as soon as he heard the shouts of playing from far off. His knees felt rubbery as he walked, but he didn't think it showed. He just had to get this over before he wet himself.

He rounded the elementary school and saw most of the kids he knew gathered here, playing or watching the game. Several raised a shout of greeting, and he waved faintly.

He noticed a group huddled behind the third-base bench, and instinct propelled him in their direction. The first person he recognized was Cammy. The lanky boy stepped back from the group, eying him curiously as he approached. Dylan ignored him and spotted Doogie. He walked purposefully up to the group, and tapped Doogie, who turned around, irritated.

"Where's your brother?"

Doogie's eyes widened, and he stuttered, his one eye dancing wildly. "What do you—"

"Where is your brother?"

Doogie glanced over his shoulder and Dylan followed his gaze. In the middle of the group, Scooter Morris stood, a *Playboy* magazine in his paw. But for the moment, he was more interested in Dylan.

"Stinger's on the road. With his dad. Why?" Said Scooter.

Doogie seemed to remember suddenly that he was a tough, and reached a hand up to tap Dylan in the shoulder. "Who wants to know?" he started, but Dylan knocked his hand down.

"He started something that needs finishing," Dylan said slowly.

Scooter considered him for a moment, and started to speak. He apparently changed his mind, and nodded, once. Then he stepped forward, shoving Doogie effortlessly out of the way.

"He'll be back Wednesday. Two days from now. Want me to tell him Thursday? Right after last bell?" There was a flicker in Scooter's grin. Dylan couldn't tell if it was respect or pity. There would be no bell, since this was summer. But everyone in hearing knew the fight would be at three o'clock.

"Thursday. Last bell." Dylan turned on his heel before Scooter could say anything else, and started back the way he'd come. On impulse, he turned left around the backstop, and strode over to where Billy Bergin, Ryan, and Tink were bunched on the bench, waiting their ups.

Tink turned to him. "We on for Thursday? The usual?" Dylan had forgotten about their ritual TV watching at his house on Thursday afternoons, four o'clock. He thought for a moment.

"Sure. I should be home by then."

39 / Moving Day

James awoke slowly, grateful to see the familiar nylon above him and to hear the soft gurgle of the river lapping around some fallen trunk. He realized with a start that the sun was high enough to be reaching the tent over the trees at the water's edge, and he raised up on an elbow.

He found Anne a hundred yards or so from the camp. He spotted first the light green sweater against the russet of the flowing water. As he approached, he could see she was sitting, hugging her knees, head bent. Her shoulders were shaking, and he could feel his anger lance out of him, replaced with a guilt that was even more bothersome. Why did girls have to cry? He considered tiptoeing back down the path and returning to camp, but she seemed to pause, expectant, and he realized he was stuck.

"Hey." He moved in closer, and eased down next to her.

"Yourself," she responded, turning slightly to present him with the back of her shoulder. He could almost feel the temperature drop, and he fought the urge to lash out first.

He took a deep breath. "Listen." He paused, waiting for a sign that she might obey. Almost to mock him, an uncharacteristically chilly breeze lifted across the water lightly slapping his cheek. He barreled on. *In for a dime…*

"Look," he tried again. "I know you're mad."

"You don't know anything."

James dropped the arm he'd been lifting to encircle her. He had no idea how to get back to where things had been good.

"So tell me then. Tell me what I need to know. Because you're asking a lot of me here."

"I haven't asked you anything." Anne whirled on him, her reddened eyes startling him.

He inched back, and stared at her. "You're asking me to *run*. You're asking me to let some yokels chase us away from what's ours. I am *sick* of running."

He stared back at Anne, their chins both set, eyes hard. Then something changed in her eyes, not a softening so much as a dissolving and she turned away, her chin down. He wanted to reach out and tell her how much she mattered. He wanted desperately to tell her what a debt he owed her. And how grateful he was to be right here, right now, in the soft and heavy Georgia stillness. With her.

He realized he *was* afraid. Afraid if he let his guard down, some nameless pain would roar up to swallow him. Again. His mind reeled to the time when Daddy'd been gone for days, and come home drunk and distant. Somehow, James had survived, but he realized it wasn't over. It was never over. Surviving meant never letting himself be led again to the place where it could hurt so much he'd wished for death as a mercy.

They sat in silence, spectators to the soft morning mist and the river that wended its way slow to Darien and beyond. Did the river have any better idea than he did where it was headed? Did it really matter at all in the end?

On the way back to camp, neither of them spoke. The silence felt stiff and awkward, almost noisy to James, like trying to work out a math problem next to a rushing waterfall. As they entered camp, James noticed her glance around, scrutinizing the area for anything out of place. His eyes followed hers as he did the same.

She finally broke the silence. "I want to move the camp. "

They passed the day searching for a new site. They considered and discarded several places. James grew impatient, wondering how they would be able to move today if they didn't find something soon.

"What in particular...you looking for?" He tried to keep the edge out of his voice. He didn't want to make any more bad blood between them, and something told him she was raw.

"I just had a feeling we were in some kind of danger. I don't know what else to say about it." She looked at him reproachfully, and he did his best to maintain a serious expression.

"Nothing specific though?" he pressed. "I just need to know what to expect, if there really is something—"

"I know what you mean," she sighed. "And no, there is nothing. I'm sure I'm just being a panicky girl." Anne dissolved in tears. Late in the afternoon, they finally returned to their camp. They'd found a site about a mile further from town.

"I think it will be at least two trips. CeCe has loaded us down here." James had considered and discarded several different ways to move it all at once. He had really liked the idea of building a raft and floating it down the river using the tide. Besides, as Anne pointed out, there really wasn't ready deadfall to build a raft, and they lacked an axe, as well as time for the effort.

The next morning, as they stepped gingerly across the camp space, eyes searching for articles to take on the first trip, he wondered what other changes might be around the river's bend. He felt the familiar knot in his gut. Trouble was, he had this geyser of anger and didn't know where to direct it. Who, or what, kept pulling his world right out from under him?

When they had collected as much as they could carry, James thought they had more than half the camp loaded. "Anything we shouldn't leave, in case we don't get back tonight? There's probably enough of a load for one more person."

Anne turned in a slow circle, looking over the remnants of their camp. "Maybe we should have waited for Benjamin."

James shrugged. "He wasn't sure he could get back today. I hate to leave any of it. But it's just for tonight." He hefted the backpack, and tucked the bedroll under his arm. She stepped close, and slipped her hand in his.

"Thanks," she said softly, as they turned down the narrow path to head east.

40 / Cammy

After supper, Dylan sat on the porch reading *Treasure Island* by the soft light from the kitchen, and listening to the symphony of a deep summer evening. The sounds of the bullfrogs were commanding, even at this distance from the river. Dylan liked to imagine that the frogs and the fireflies were practicing to make their sound and light in synchronous code humans could not decipher, unless one was very clever.

Suddenly Dylan noticed a figure, unmoving, at the end of the sidewalk. It was too dark to tell who was there, but he had the sensation whoever it was was looking right at him. As if to assure him, the figure nodded, and then stepped slowly up the sidewalk. Halfway to the steps, Dylan recognized Cammy's gliding stride. Dylan froze, the porch glider easing to a stop under him. When Cammy reached the bottom stair, he nodded again. His expression, though now clear, was unreadable.

Dylan waited, his hands gripping the seat and the arm of the glider tightly.

"Go for a walk?" Cammy inclined his head down the sidewalk.

Dylan rose, feeling his cheeks flush. In an instant, he was gripped with an anger that consumed him. "What do you want" He managed.

Cammy didn't lift his hands from his pockets. Again, he inclined his head back in the direction of the street. "Go for a walk?" he said again.

Dylan fumed. "You alone?"

Cammy nodded. "Just me."

If that was supposed to assure Dylan, it didn't. In a fight, Stinger could beat him. But he was quite sure Cammy could hurt him.

Dylan shoved his own hands in his pockets and walked down the steps. He stood close to Cammy, intending to stare him down, but Cammy turned on his heel and started walking slowly down the walk.

At Nash they turned left, toward town, without speaking. When they reached Stockton Lane, they turned left, side by side, into the darkened residences.

"Saw what you did today." Cammy spoke slow, and Dylan thought about how long it had been since he and Cammy had exchanged words as friends. Dylan didn't answer.

"Sometimes guys do stupid shit."

Dylan whirled on the smaller boy. "Is that supposed to be some kind of apology?"

Cammy stopped, eying him coldly. "I don't apologize."

Dylan turned to go. "This is a waste."

Cammy had said something, soft, and Dylan turned back. "Give me two minutes," Cammy repeated.

Dylan stopped, but made no effort to close the distance between them.

Finally, Cammy shrugged, and walked to him. "Thursday, I'll make sure it's just you and Stinger." Dylan looked at him, and finally nodded. "Nothing cute from anybody else." Cammy glanced away and said, "That fool never learns."

Dylan managed an "okay."

Then he had a thought. "Can I ask you something?"

"Shoot."

"You beat Stinger to a pulp last year, but it's my brother he hates. Any idea why?"

Cammy furrowed his brow, as if Dylan had just asked for the capital of Pennsylvania. But then he spoke. "That was all before my time. Stinger used to ride James about your mother leaving town, and one day he said something about your mother going off to be with his uncle, and James just went insane. James got over it, but I don't think Stinger ever did." His eyes twinkled. "Maybe there's always a special place for the first guy to really kick your ass, like James did to Stinger."

Dylan stared at Cammy. He had never heard any of this. "My mom went off? With who?"

Cammy shrugged. "Got me. Some guy that moved to Texas around the time your other brother disappeared."

Dylan sighed. "My mom did move to Texas. But that wasn't til after I was born."

Cammy grunted. "There you go. Stinger being a dick. There's something else. James wasn't anywhere near Wilson's that night, 'til long after we totally hosed the job."

Dylan stared at Cammy. "Why are you telling me this?"

Cammy looked up at Dylan. "Because it's true."

"Yes, but I mean, why tell me? And who would ever believe it?"

Cammy took a breath. "Why doesn't anybody take that screwdriver to Mr. Owens, and ask him if he's missing it out of his truck tool kit?"

Dylan stared at Cammy. "Look," the boy sighed, "I'm not suggesting anybody does that, unless your brother's ever actually charged. I doubt he will be."

Dylan felt confused to his core. He hated this boy, but Cammy was also offering his brother a ticket home. Cammy nodded and turned to go.

"Wait." Dylan said. "Do you know anything about that boy got beat up in Millwood?"

"I know why they think your brother did it, if that's what you mean."

Dylan thought back. He never had heard just why James was considered a suspect.

"Why?" he asked.

"Scooter the criminal mastermind." Cammy laughed softly to himself. "Some guy over Millwood way was snakin' a girl Scooter'd asked out. She said something he didn't like, and he got his knickers twisted."

Cammy looked uncomfortable for the first time. "Since this was a couple days after your brother got picked up for Wilson's break in, Scooter had the bright idea of having Stinger and Doogie address him as *James* when they went over to rumble this guy." He looked away for a moment. "With a *Paxton* or two thrown in for insurance. I guess things got out of hand. Amateurs."

Cammy wilted under the look Dylan gave him. "Hey," he raised his hands in protest, "All he needs is an alibi. He has one of those, doesn't he? Sheesh, I missed that party completely."

Dylan waited, and then said quietly, "You don't miss too many parties, do you."

Cammy shrugged, and turned to go. "A guy's gotta do…"

"Go to hell."

Cammy paused, looking down. "Sometimes it feels like I'm already there."

Dylan walked away, his shoulders aching from tension.

Cammy called after him, "Thursday. Don't let him hit you first."

Dylan kept walking.

41 / Preacher Waugh

Around noon, James and Anne reached the new camp with their load. Anne wiped at her brow as she shrugged off the backpack. Her blouse was stained dark with perspiration. James sat heavily on the ground and eased out from under his own satchel.

They spent some time organizing the new camp. The view was actually more dramatic from this vista. The camp was on a nubby point, with a projection of glitter-bejeweled shale that jutted out high over the water, like a ship's prow. James scrambled up the shore side and stood atop it.

"This will be our foc'sle," James exclaimed. "You can see in every direction up here without being spotted."

Anne shielded her eyes, craning up at him. "Our what?"

"It's the bow of the ship, where the lookout's posted."

"This from the man who couldn't manage a raft?" She laughed, but kindly, and he stuck his tongue out at her.

The two worked for several hours clearing ground, collecting firewood, and putting the new camp in order. "Do you want to head back to get the rest of our stuff now?" He asked. James held a tent pole as she tamped down the corners of the tent and then looped the eyelet over the point's tip.

She looked up, blowing a shock of blonde hair out of her eyes. "Do you need my help? If not, I can keep working here."

"I think I can handle it. But will you be okay?"

She nodded, a small smile playing across her face. "Does Tarzan worry about his Jane?"

"Of course. I mean, *Oongowah*."

"Why don't you have some of the leftover ham and pie with me before you head out?" She carefully lifted the wrapped basket from the backpack. "This won't keep any longer without being cooled, and the ice has all but melted from Sunday."

They ate in companionable silence, gazing out over the sinuous river. The current was noticeable here, and he wondered if this were also affected by the tides, like the waters of the Wicomico where it approached the Bay. It occurred to James how much like the Wicomico this languid river was. Right down to the glittering insects flying over the surface of the water. He thought about Nana and Dylan, and wondered what they might be doing. On the heels of those thoughts, he considered Father Mullenix, and his car, and he winced again. He hoped one day to set things right.

***

As he picked his way over the terrain, James kept the river on his left and looked for familiar signs. He realized he had not been paying attention as they'd looked for a camp. Now, he was a little turned around, but he figured if he moved carefully, he could manage to find his way back. The sun wasn't high, but it should be up for another couple of hours or so. He paced more slowly, just in case. He didn't want to miss the hidden branch of the path that ran to their former camp.

In the distance, he heard voices. The river bent here, and there was a gurgling where the water splashed around an upturned tree ball. He stopped, but heard nothing else. Slowly, James moved forward. From time to time, he would hear a strident tone. Male. Angry. He recognized the forest here. He was close, he thought. The voices were louder too. One voice, raised above the others.

"—are you doing here, nigga?" Something that sounded like a cuff. A protest. Muffled. James slowed more, debating, then bent and crept forward. Ahead of him, an ancient fallen oak blocked his view but also shielded him. He crept up to the dark bark wall, and lay his cheek against its rough surface, listening.

There were several males. Boys, and at least one man. The one was shouting, the other pleading. There was something about the boy.

Benjamin!

"No suh no suh! Don' know nothing about the boy and girl you lookin' for—" A loud crack, echoing off the stately trunks near the river. James eased his head up over the fallen tree. A thick growth of low brush blocked his view. Swearing softly, he eased down the length of the fallen tree to the giant root ball, the highest point of which loomed above his head.

James slipped off the empty backpack he'd carried to transport the last of the camp supplies and leaned it against a clay-smeared root. He peeked around the edge and then ducked back quickly, willing his mind to register what he'd seen.

It was the preacher they'd passed on Sunday, the one with the smoldering eyes. Only now, those eyes flamed at Benjamin. At least James assumed it was Benjamin. The same red flannel shirt Benjamin wore most of the time. The shirt hung limp off one shoulder, exposing the dungaree strap. The boy was Negro and the voice sounded like Benjamin, but ratcheted higher in fear.

James felt the sheen on his forehead. He was breathing rapidly. He remembered the times he'd ridden his bike with other kids down at the old Crane Ridge sand pits out by the Wicomico. Whenever they built a new bike ramp, the other boys expected him to try it first.

The kids would start chanting *Evel, Evel,* after some stunt rider Billy and Ryan had seen on *Joey Bishop*. James would stand astride his stingray bike and close his eyes briefly, long enough to picture himself doing the stunt. Sometimes though, when he tried to see himself flying over the rickety ramp, there would only be a dim blur. When that happened, he would feel his gut knot. Not that it was a bad thing. He would just lean forward, pumping the pedals, and aim for the center of whatever boards anchored the jump.

He felt the same now. He could not see the way ahead, but he knew that in a moment he was going to launch himself. James straightened up, and wiped his brow. Reddish clay smeared his fingers. He reached up again and felt the grit on his cheekbone. He stretched out and dug his fingers into the root ball, then lifted them to his face and smeared more of the terracotta dirt over his cheeks, chin, and throat. Warpaint.

A strange calm settled on him, even as the voices reaching him raised louder, one snarling and the other pleading. He smeared reddish clay down his arms and over his forearms and the back of his hands.

"Fetch me that cooking stick!"

He closed his eyes and saw the stick, lying on the lip of the fire ring. He'd sharpened one end to cook small game. The command was followed by a low groan and a shaky demurral. Two voices. Both younger than the raspy-voiced old man.

James slowed his breathing and eased around the root ball, moving in time with the light evening breeze rustling the underbrush. He saw the old man towering over the cringing black boy, his arm raised in a threatening pose. But the man's eyes and attention were on the boys next to Benjamin. James remembered them from the other day. Samuel, Joey, something like that.

The shorter boy bent to lift something, handing it slowly to the old man. The man raised the stick like the very staff of Moses, as if he were going to strike the boy who gave it to him. Then he turned back to Benjamin, recoiling at the end of his other outstretched arm.

James was moving before he had time to register a decision. He had a short, thick stick in his hand. He wondered briefly where he picked it up, but that question ripped away in the vortex of his launch. Somehow, his feet were shed of his *Converse All Star Chucks*, and he was flying over the forest floor like a scudding cloud of vengeance. He launched himself into the clearing. As the preacher turned towards him, startled, James slammed into him, mid-chest. His body was his fist, and the preacher flew back, smacking the old oak's trunk heavily. James grunted in satisfaction.

James was rolling shoulder to back to feet, and his velocity rocketed him out the far side of the clearing. He was perhaps 20 yards away when the sounds of shock, fear, and rage reached him.

The woods poured beneath his naked feet as he fanned away from the river, in a wide arc, to strike again, from the quarter-hour this time. But out of the corner of his eye, he saw the familiar flannel shirt streak past, and the fear-flooded eyes of the black boy, wide above his pumping arms, the flannel still drooping off his shoulder. James slowed to the speed of the wind, and noted with wonder that his breathing was normal. He felt the same quiet thrill he experienced each time he cleared an impossible hurdle down at the gravel quarry, and noticed that he'd completely circled the clearing, arriving back at the felled tree with the giant root ball.

He heard shouts of dismay and a strangled sound, evidently from the preacher. He eased his head around the clump of earth, and saw the preacher slowly rising, with the aid of his young companions. He watched as they limped out away from the river toward the public trail. He didn't think they'd be in any mood to go searching for what hit them. Not without more help, at least.

For the first time, he considered the possibility that the preacher and the boy might have recognized him. They'd seen him, after all, in the woods just the other day. That might be moot though. Who else would attack the preacher in the woods, in *his* campsite?

James moved out from behind the root ball and eased down toward the river, keeping an eye on the woods in the direction of the clearing. He squatted at the river's edge and rinsed the clay from his face and arms. The stubborn goo yielded, but slowly, as he scrubbed at his shining skin. The river's muddy swirl matched the clay that ran from his arms. He rose, and turned to stride up the hill to the old camp. The sound of a cocking rifle froze him.

42 / Notes from a Stranger

Dylan sat at his desk, absently lifting the pages of a Hardy Boy adventure. The evening was still. The sound of a train somewhere in the distance, traveling south to Crisfield, or north to Baltimore, reached him as a low rumble. Dylan wanted to hate Cammy, but somehow he couldn't summon whatever it took. If anything, he felt sorry for the boy, in the way he sometimes felt bad for his own brother. James didn't belong with the likes of Stinger, or Scooter, or the kids who'd amount to nothing. But James seemed well on his way to closing a lot of doors. Just like Cammy. Dylan and Cammy would never be friends, he understood that much. Dylan just wished he had a better notion of why Cammy and James both seemed hell-bent on self-destruction.

He looked down again at the pile of notes James had saved from his mother. He knew James had kept the brief messages that came each birthday, just as he had. Nine notes in all. One for each year since she'd walked out.

He knew the notes weren't any of his business. They belonged to James. His mom was dead and James was gone, he'd rationalized, when he'd plucked them from the bottom drawer, and sat down at his desk, laying them neatly in front of him. He wished he could talk to Lois right now. But he couldn't tell her about Cammy's visit without telling her the reason, and she'd be steaming mad when she found out he was fighting Stinger.

As for the notes, he didn't know why he wanted to look, but after the visit to Mr. Thompson's house, it was possible that the story he'd been told years ago by Nana about his mom wasn't all the truth. He was curious now to find out more about the woman he'd never known, but he sure wasn't ready to talk to his dad about her. He didn't know if that time would ever come.

The notes were brief, the first three similar in size and pattern, evidently from the same card box. All wishing a happy birthday, all *love, mom*. A galaxy of hurt and recrimination brushed aside with a few pen-strokes, like dust under the corner of a rug. Dylan's were similar. Never a question asked, for there was no means to answer.

He thought about that for a moment. What purpose did the notes serve, except as annual reminders that this woman had not lifted the sentence she herself had imposed, to remain hidden from her own children. Dylan had heard once of a man in the state prison who came up for parole every two years like clockwork, and every two years it was denied, for the crime of killing a sheriff. He thought he knew how it must feel, not daring to hope, when denial deals such a heavy blow.

He knew each unopened envelope was a hope that the opening shattered. The evidence was piled neatly in front of him.

In only one note, written for his brother's 15th birthday, did his mother depart from her pattern. Within the simple card, all balloons and primary colors on the face, she had inserted a folded sheet of notepaper. It was undated and unsigned, but the handwriting was unmistakable. In places, it was smeared and the paper furled.

James —

My dear, sweet son. I miss you more than I can ever say. I worry for you too. You are growing into your own, and trying to parse your unique childhood. I cannot tell you to have no regrets, for I have a few that will be with me always. I cannot tell you not to follow your dreams whatever dark and lonely place they may take you, for I did that too. I cannot tell you to forgive me. But I can ask you to forgive yourself. What you think is so isn't always so, and sometimes life is bigger than our ability to understand.

Know that you were made in love and that I will always love you, even when I am away from you.

Love,

Mom

Dylan read it over several times. What did his mother mean, *forgive her*? Or that things aren't what they seem? It hurt him that he'd not received a similar note. If she had lived longer, would he have received his own message, written in this abstract code? And would he have wept, as James apparently had, on reading it?

He folded it carefully, and returned it to the card.

43 / His Name is Wayne

James turned at the sharp click of metal. A man stood twenty feet away, dressed in ancient boots, and overalls that were faded and torn. The coverings were stained with some dark, greasy substance. Leaves and bits of sticks poked from the defeated fabric. James would not have been surprised to see a squirrel poke its head from an overall pocket.

The man wore a shirt that may once have been white or light, but now was the gray-green color of thin pea soup. The remains of the sunset lit the man's lower face. The rest was shadowed under a broad, ragged-edged hat. What James could see made the hair on his forearms stand up. The man's chin was to the left of his nose, as James faced him, and the eyes followed the same diagonal fault, the left eye nearly jammed on the bridge of the nose, the right eye wide, the socket bulging from the side of his forehead.

James wondered how the deformation allowed the man to see at all, but as he straightened to show his empty hands, the rifle lifted a fraction. He waited for the man to speak, but the fellow just stood quiet. James also considered how the man had gotten the drop on him so easily, when the forest had seemed vacant of human life. This thing was human, right? What beast dressed like a, well, like a hayseed farmer?

James considered his situation. He felt, more than saw, the man's gaze on his midsection, where the barrel of the shotgun loosely faced. That was unnerving, but James wasn't particularly afraid, strangely enough. Maybe it was because the man he faced seemed to be unafraid as well. Then he noticed something that made his jaw clench. He lifted his arm slowly to point at the man's chest pocket.

"That belongs to a friend of mine," he said.

Without taking his eyes off James's middle, the man shifted the shotgun to rest in the crook of his arm, and reached up to lightly stroke the red ribbon that peeked from his pocket.

"And why take ye thought for raiment?"

The voice was young, a little garbled, and James studied the ruined face. The lips formed a smirk under narrow eyes. Whether the smirk was permanent from the horrific circumstances that had befallen this fellow, or a genuine disdain for him, James couldn't tell. He worked to recall the name he'd heard.

"I'm taking the thought that you might've taken what's not yours." James spoke with an edge.

"And the chief priests accused him of many things: but he answered nothing."

James looked at the man, mystified. "Okay, keep it! Are you saying you didn't take that ribbon from my camp?"

"And with him they crucify two thieves, the one on his right hand, and the other on his left." The man spoke without hesitation, but as if his throat were full of thick water.

"Who's talking about crucifying anybody?"

"And the scripture was fulfilled, which saith, 'and he was numbered with the transgressors.'" The man reached up with the hand that had stroked the red ribbon and wiped sidelong at his nose. James noticed a thin streak of blood come away on the back of his hand.

"Well, Mister Transgressor. Are you hurt?"

Transgressor seemed to consider the matter, but did not look away from James. "And straightway the fountain of her blood was dried up: and she felt in her body that she was healed of that plague."

James took a small step forward, his fists clenching. "I'd like to dry off if you don't mind."

"He saved others. Himself he cannot save."

"Transgressor, who is *he*?" James felt the river water dripping from the tips of his fingers, and shook them lightly.

The man gestured with the barrel of the gun at James's wet torso. "And straightway coming up out of the water, he saw the heavens opened, and the Spirit like a dove descending upon him."

James glanced over his head, a tiny joke. Transgressor wasn't smiling, but his eyes seemed to dance a bit. Or at least one eye did, and James realized that the other eye focused on everything and nothing at once.

"Not to seem unfriendly, but I sure would feel better if you'd point that shotgun someplace else," James said.

Transgressor seemed not to have heard him. He had a middle-distance gaze in the good eye. "Come ye yourselves into a desert place, and rest a while." Then he gazed around the wooded proximity, and back to James. James followed his wandering gape, then stared back, perplexed. Transgressor looked down for a moment.

"I hate to disappoint, but this doesn't look much like a desert to me."

The one good eye fixed on James's gaze now, Transgressor spoke again: "Blessed are they that have not seen, and yet have believed."

"Transgressor, what is your real name?"

Without missing a beat, the man responded. "Who do people say that I am?"

James slowly stepped to the side, giving the man a wide berth, and backed up toward the camp. "The ribbon? Did you take the ribbon from there?" James gestured at the fireplace. For the first time, the stranger looked perplexed, although it was impossible to register accurately a mood on the destroyed face. Once again, the man reached up to stroke the ribbon. James started to point at the tent, but it was long gone. He spotted the discarded cross, lying in the dust where the tent's imprint still showed faintly. Still facing the man, he backed up toward the spot, and bent to lift the small cross.

He turned to the man, who showed no signs of recognition. Despite this, James extended the rood to the man, who stepped forward to take it from him. The man gazed on the small cross with an expression unreadable, and then turned away from James.

"And Jesus answering them began to say, 'Take heed lest any man deceive you.'" Without another word, he disappeared into the underbrush, as silent in his departing as Benjamin managed to be.

James stood for a few moments, baffled and slightly chilled. The sun was disappearing in the west. He retrieved his shoes, then collected all the remaining camp items in a small pile, and eased them, heaviest items first, into the backpack. When he had everything loaded up, he spent a few minutes rearranging the fire ring rocks into a more natural state. While the scorched ground offered evidence there'd been fires here, Mother Nature would soon hide their passing.

What had brought the preacher in search of him and Anne, especially after he'd just seen them two days ago, not far from here in the company of CeCe? What had Benjamin been doing here? It was likely that CeCe had sent him to see if James and Anne had decided to move, and if they needed help. But why had the preacher been so mean to Benjamin? From the sounds of it, the old geezer was none too charming in his natural state, but something must have compelled him to threaten Benjamin. What would have happened if James hadn't intervened? And what was the man from Preacher Waugh's church—the one everyone thought was dead—doing here as well?

These questions gnawed at James as he grunted the bulging backpack onto his shoulders and cinched the waist belt. He started to set off back to the new camp, but turned, and plucked the sharpened cooking stick where it leaned against the ancient oak.

James strode into the new camp and unceremoniously dumped his cargo in the clearing. He rolled his shoulders, and slapped at a buzzing mosquito.

"Where have you been, you idiot?" Anne rushed over to him and grabbed his arms, shaking him like a rag doll. He tripped over the pack and landed with a thump on his butt.

He grinned thinly up at her, and then turned to Benjamin, winking. "Very nice to see you too!"

"You are such an ass. I mean it," she added, as he stared up at her, perplexed. "Are you trying to ruin everything?"

"Now hold on." James sat up on the backpack, and jumped to his feet. Casting an eye at Benjamin, he said, "Didn't you tell her what happened?"

Benjamin shrugged and looked away. "I don't rightly know just what happened. Was that you landed on the preacher?"

James looked at him cockeyed. "Who else do you know that would risk life and limb to save your bla—"

"What on earth were you *thinking*?" Anne brushed a strand of dark hair from her damp forehead. Her smudged fingers left a light trail, dimly visible in the gathering dusk. "We're not even relocated yet, and you *hand* that creepy man a reason for messing with us!"

James held up his hands, palms out. "Slow down. I didn't go looking for trouble from anybody." James turned and pointed at Benjamin. "He was about to skewer our friend here." He gave the boy a pleading look. "Did you happen to mention *that*? And by the way, do you have any idea why the preacher was looking for us?"

Benjamin stared back, his jaw set. James's features softened. "I could use a little help here, Benjamin. Did I have a choice if I was going to help you?"

Anne spoke: "For someone who charged in bent on destruction, there seems to be a lot you *don't* know!"

James expelled angry breath, exasperated.

Anne stepped forward, her arms crossed, toeing the pile James had dumped on the ground. "Benjamin said the preacher was just trying to scare him."

James looked from Anne to Benjamin. "That so? The preacher was so bothered that he couldn't get a rise out of you that he decided to *really* scare you?"

He turned to Anne. "The way *I* saw it, our friend Benjamin here was about as scared as a body could get." He swiveled back to the boy.

Anne lifted her face to the sky and growled. She swung on James. "When are you going to understand that violence is not the answer to every problem?"

He just stared at her, stunned.

Benjamin spoke, and James and Anne both turned to him. "What did you say?"

"Preacher Waugh he said you two are sinful, because you not brother and sister."

"How could he possibly know that?" Anne rubbed a palm over her eyes, smearing the light smudge further. "And how do you know you didn't kill that man?"

James rubbed his arm absently, grateful for the change in topic.

"I can't be sure he's not dead, but I didn't have to step over any corpse to collect this stuff." He gestured at the pile he'd recently carted over, then turned to step toward Benjamin.

"What do you think? Did I kill him?" He raised a questioning palm, fingers splayed, to the young black.

Benjamin was shaking his head vigorously. "I reckon you busted him up some, and he'll probably think of you first thing. But no, he wasn't dead when I saw those boys help him off."

Anne turned. "Boys? Who *else* was there?" She looked from one to the other. James started to speak at the same time as Benjamin.

"It was two boys from the church that's always with the preacher," said Benjamin.

"Great!" Anne looked skyward again, balling her fists. "So you go ripping into a situation without even thinking about it." She glared at James. "Tell me. How long did you spend concocting your assault plan?"

James remembered the feeling of his bare feet on wings, no recall of taking off his shoes, or picking up the club, or even crossing the distance to the clearing.

"I thought I had pretty good odds. I had the element of surprise." The silence that followed seemed to last for minutes.

Anne and Benjamin glanced at each other, as James awaited judgment. He was shocked when Benjamin grinned sheepishly, and Anne burst into a relieved laugh. She stepped in front of him, and slapped him, but not hard. He rubbed his cheek, and she leaned to him, and kissed him soft, lingering. Behind her, he saw Benjamin turn before James remembered to close his eyes.

***

The three sat around a low campfire, the last of the leftovers from Sunday filling their stomachs. The night sounds enveloped them in a primitive cocoon.

"Time you got to worry is when the crickets and such go still," Benjamin said when James remarked on the cacophony. He was glad the boy had stayed to eat. James had some questions, and he hoped Benjamin could provide some answers. And he realized with a pang that in this world full of people bent on disrupting his life, and in his search for a place to belong, he had just made another enemy. Probably several.

James sensed they were stepping around the subject of this afternoon, but there were things he felt he had to know before he tried to sleep tonight.

"Benjamin, do you think that preacher recognized me from Sunday afternoon?"

The boy returned his gaze with a look of puzzlement. "Benjamin wasn't with us when we passed that group Sunday," Anne said softly.

James nodded. "Yeah. Sorry. Well, did you recognize me when I—" He searched for the word.

"When you landed outa nowhere like a Seminole ghost?" Benjamin asked, then grinned a little. "Honest when you come up outa nowhere, I was more scared of you than the preacher."

The boys chuckled. James glanced at Anne. Her smile was thin.

"When I played it back in my head—I was halfway to here by then—I thought it had to be you. Or your ghost. You looked like you, but...different. Like some kinda banshee." He gazed at James, his face drawn up, confused.

"I um, put some red clay dirt on my arms. And face." He felt Anne staring at him. "My chest. It was part of my assault plan."

Benjamin laughed quiet, but Anne remained expressionless. James quieted, and then asked Benjamin, "Any idea how the preacher knew we weren't brother and sister?" But he suspected he already knew the answer. Benjamin just shrugged.

"What will the preacher do now, with you?" James asked. "What will happen since you ran away today?"

Benjamin looked up, for the first time his eyes betraying a trace of irritation, which he quickly blinked away. "The man is crazy," he repeated, as if that settled it. "He might decide you were the devil, and I ought to be hung for the devil's apprentice." Benjamin sat up, drew his knees up, and crossed his arms over them, clasping one wrist. He looked over at James, smiling.

"Or he might decide you were the Archangel Gabriel, and I'm God's anointed *other* son. The black one. Then he'll ask me to come speak at his church and lay hands on his flock."

"You don't seem very concerned about it," Anne said.

Benjamin shrugged, chastened. "My daddy used to say a man driving gonna get himself killed trying to cipher what the squirrel in the middle of the road gonna do."

James stared at the boy, his face twisted in thought. "And...?" he prompted?

Benjamin tossed a small twig in the licking flames. "...And so you got to travel not worrying too much over the squirrel."

Anne stepped over to the tent and retrieved her sweater. She draped it over her shoulders, and came back to stand close to the small fire.

"How did you come to be at the old campsite, Benjamin?"

The boy looked up at her, and then studied the fire. "Miss CeCe asked me to come see if y'all needed any help moving. I could tell right away y'all had already started. I sat down to wait. But 'stead of y'all, it was the preacher."

"How do you think he found our campsite?" James asked. "And do you think he's the one who left the cross and took the ribbon?"

Anne was shaking her head. "What?" James asked her.

"I know this'll sound weird, but I have felt watched for the last several days." She screwed her head around on her neck, stretching. "Funny thing was, I never felt scared, except for once." She looked steadily at Benjamin. "Could you have been followed?"

"No. I usually come at night, and I was extra careful today."

"Maybe they sent somebody to follow us Sunday after church. I remember seeing someone just behind us when we turned off the highway to come back here," James said slowly.

"The timing would be right. They must have come to the camp while we were at the Walker's, and that means they must have followed us before. And the only other time we left the camp was to go to church Sunday." Anne stared into the low fire. "But why?"

There was a thoughtful quiet for a time, as each considered the puzzle.

James leaned forward to arrange the unburned stick ends into the flame, and it leapt up warmly. "Why do you think the preacher came looking for us?" He asked.

"Been wondering that same thing," Benjamin spoke thoughtfully. "Reason I thought it was you, whoever it was walked right up like they knew exactly where they was going."

"Like they'd been there before?" Anne asked.

"At least one of them," Benjamin said. "Seems like they followed the string on in. I remember thinking at the time *why would you do that?* But before I reasoned it out, the men were there."

James glanced at Anne, but she hadn't reacted. James considered it odd that people he'd call boys, because they were his age or slightly older, Benjamin referred to as *men*.

"So you are at the camp, waiting for us to return. How long had you been there?"

Benjamin considered. "Don't know how long you was watching, but ol' preacher lit into me pretty much when they got there. Not too harsh at first. *What was I doing there, did I know where the boy and girl was.*" He raised his hand, fingers open, indicating James and Anne.

"When I said I didn't know who he was talking about, he got real mad. Asked if I came to steal. Had me empty my pockets." James could see the flicker of anger in the Negro's dark eyes, and he felt a pang of guilt at how he'd first reacted to seeing Benjamin in the new camp.

"What else did he say? Ask you?" James pressed.

"He mostly wanted to know where y'all were. One of the boys—Joey, I think—said 'Reverend—they all call him Reverend to his face—Reverend, it looks like they pulled up camp.'"

Benjamin ran his long, dark fingers over his face, from his forehead down across his eyes, his chin, and finally his throat. He sighed, and lifted his hand to rub the back of his neck. "That's when he got real mad. The preacher."

"So he came out in the woods, with those boys, just to find us," James mused. "Well I guess it's no secret we were camped out here somewhere. But why should he care?"

"Remember he warned us on Sunday about the prisoners on the

run?" It was Anne, who finally spoke. Both boys looked at her.

"Maybe he thought you were one of the convicts. Maybe he thought I was your girlfriend, and he was coming to take you in." She sat up, her eyes alight.

"Only one problem with that. Maybe two," James said, trying to dial down the doubt he felt. Anne looked at him, waiting.

"How did he know just where the camp was? And why would he come without a gun of any kind, if he thought we were desperate cons on a prison break?" James spoke quietly, but he could think of several other problems with Anne's idea. Anne seemed to sink down a little, and her gaze turned fearful, darting out into the surrounding darkness.

Benjamin seemed to notice too, and spoke up: "Well, y'all ought to be real safe here. You much further off the trail and hardly anybody comes back this far for fishing, 'cept by boat."

James followed the cue: "I was thinking that same thing. We are probably a mile further from town, and we can see anybody coming from up there, or hear them in the underbrush, before they can see us."

Anne seemed to relax a little, and her gaze returned to the fire. They were quiet for a time. Finally, James spoke: "I wasn't late just because of the time to pack up camp."

He let that sink in, and no one spoke. But Anne turned to look at him.

"I...met somebody else. I should have mentioned it before," he sputtered, as both his companions sat up, staring at him.

"Who?" asked Anne.

"Well, you remember CeCe told us about that guy that got bit by the snake. The one who belonged to the Church of the Crazy Signs?"

"You mean the one, the one who..." Anne's eyes fixed on something in the middle distance and her hand lifted involuntarily to her cheek.

"His name is Wayne." This from Benjamin.

"So he's alive?" Anne gulped. Both James and Benjamin nodded.

"Have you always known he was out here?" James asked Benjamin.

"I've never seen him. More like a feelin'. Once or twice at night, I seen a light out at the base of the Butler Mill chimney. Coulda been hunters, but it was sometimes real late. But how did y'all know about

Wayne?"

"A couple of days ago," Anne explained, "CeCe was telling us about Preacher Waugh's church. She told us about a boy—"

"—Wayne," interjected James.

Benjamin's eyes were as big as cherries. "Wayne Stiles? Snakebit Wayne?" His voice rose on the last. Both Anne and Benjamin looked at James.

"I'm not sure," James repeated. "But I think so. He looked like he'd been buried for a month out here, and had just dug himself up. And his face..." James shuddered.

"My goodness," said Anne.

"Sweet Jesus," Benjamin followed.

James relayed what he could recall of the encounter. "I wouldn't call it a conversation. I felt like he was trying to let me know something, but blanged if I know what it was. He just kept spouting scripture." He saw the dubious look on Benjamin's face. "The King James version, I'm pretty sure." Anne looked impressed.

"Did you just come upon him, or..." Benjamin clucked, rocking his head back and forth.

"Truth was, he got the drop on me, pretty as you please. He coulda easy plugged me if he'd had a mind to," James replied.

"What did he say to you?" Anne asked.

"That was the weirdest part. I was never sure he was actually talking to me. It was like I would say something, and it would start this recording in his head."

"A recording?" Anne asked.

"Yeah. Put in a dime, get a Bible verse. Funny to be quoted scripture by somebody who's pointing a gun at you."

Benjamin started. "Could you tell what kinda gun? Two barrels?"

James thought it over. "I'm not much for guns. But there were two barrels, yes."

Benjamin scratched at his nappy crown. "Some folks said when he ran off he took Preacher Waugh's shotgun. Boy never owned a gun before that."

"Was he trying to rob you?" Anne had screwed up her face, truly puzzled.

"Gosh no. Fact was, at first I thought he had." He explained about the red ribbon from CeCe's bonnet.

"And you don't think he took it?" Anne asked, perplexed.

"Nope. At first I did. I was fuming that we'd gone to all this trouble to move the camp over some retard." He saw the frown cross Anne's face, and regretted the word, but couldn't think of a better in the clutch.

"Anyway, I think he took it from whoever took it from us," James concluded, sitting back against his rolled sleeping bag.

Benjamin just sighed. "Mmmmm...mm."

Anne rocked back and forth, the light from the fire dancing on her high cheeks. "CeCe said that was a year ago," she said, almost in a whisper.

"Farther back than that," Benjamin sat up, studying the flames. "Funny how a boy can live secret out here, all that time."

"From what I saw, he's not living well," James answered somberly. "Although," he continued, after a few moments, "I know it sounds funny, but he didn't seem like he... he wasn't... I don't know. He seemed okay. Not like he needed anything in particular."

"How do we know you aren't making this whole thing up?" Anne asked, but her tone lacked any enthusiasm for the notion.

After a time James said, "I think he offered to give the ribbon back. Least ways, I told him to keep it. If I hadn't, I guess you'd have your proof."

44 / Down to the Sea

At the new camp, James decided that with so little traffic on the river, it would be safe during the week to venture out on the water to fish and explore. His first experiment was with a raft—really just several tree trunks lashed together. It floated just fine, but every time he mounted it, it rolled like a playful seal. He tried adding an outrigger log on one side, and got so badly tangled when the boat listed he worried he might drown. Benjamin stepped into the shallows to aid him, and they stared at the snarled branches. Davey Crockett used a dugout canoe. Anne thought she knew how they were constructed.

They didn't actually dig the wood. "They burned it out," she said

"Why do they call it a *dugout* then?"

She fixed him with a superior gaze. "They dig out the part they burn, silly."

James set to work. He found a candidate log about a quarter-mile further down Cat Head Creek, fifty yards or so in from the bank.

"Are you going to dig a canal next, or had you planned on another Great Flood? Should I start collecting animal pairs?" Anne asked, straight-faced.

"It's the best log for the canoe within five miles," James retorted. He planned to roll the log, using two other logs as casters. "Once I get it on the water, I float it on the tide to our camp," he said. Benjamin looked a little skeptical.

"I really do wish I'd thought to bring my brownie," Anne said. She mimed holding the camera to her face, and squinting into the viewfinder.

James said, "What I was thinking was I'll burn the log out here, away from camp. We'd have to do it at night, because of the smoke. You'd have to stay out here with me. I wouldn't want you back at camp after dark by yourself."

She stepped up to him and nuzzled him, her shoulders bent, her head against his chest. "Does the big strong man worry about his little woman?"

He groaned, exasperated, but stroked her back. "I just don't want you running around out here alone."

She lifted her head. "What was your plan for me when you're out sailing? Put me up a tree in a sack?"

He laughed. Anne had been in a good mood since they'd moved, but several times she'd mentioned that life after camping would be a pleasant change. They decided moving in and out of town so freely as before was not a good idea. Not 'til they knew more about what was going on. James looked forward to visits from Benjamin and CeCe.

Benjamin brought CeCe out to the new camp on Thursday. James helped CeCe unload a generous basket she'd prepared of fresh fruit, vegetables, and biscuits. "The bread is day-old. I didn't think y'all would mind, and it's cheaper that way." CeCe blushed, but Anne responded quickly.

"What you've been providing has kept us alive."

James whistled, lifting a chisel from the basket. "Thanks!" he gasped. "This is just what I need for the dugout!"

"How is that yacht shaping up?" CeCe asked.

James admired the gleaming chisel he turned in his hands. "I think the tree is a black gum."

"Bark like alligator scales?" asked CeCe.

James nodded.

"Most likely gum. They're usually found two and three together, real tall and real old. Is the stump on a hummock?"

James looked blank.

"A hummock." She smiled. "A kind of raised up piece of ground?"

James nodded.

"Black Gum Tupelo," CeCe agreed. "Figured out how to get it to the water yet?" She asked, glancing smiling at Anne.

Without pause, James gestured to Benjamin. "I'm rigging up a harness. May need to borrow your friend here for a day or so." The girls giggled.

"Want to see what I'm working on?" James asked Benjamin. "Oh, you all can come if you want," he added quickly.

The girls looked at each other, then back at James. "I want to catch up on town news," Anne said, and CeCe nodded too. They waved the boys away.

The two set off through the woods. James carried the chisel. He spoke over his shoulder. "So um, whatever happened after the other day? The preacher come looking for you?"

"No, sir." Benjamin chortled. "I think that old man have trouble finding me."

"Why's that?"

"Well, never mind about that."

James stopped on the thin deer trail and turned to face the boy. "Come on. He almost ran you through. How could he have trouble finding you?"

Benjamin looked at the ground, embarrassed. "Pa used to say, the reason whites chase us and don't let go when they catch us..."

James waited. "The reason?"

Benjamin continued, quiet. "Pa say we all look so much alike to them"—Benjamin glanced at James, embarrassed—"to y'all"—James laughed aloud.

Benjamin flushed. "You don't think it's true?"

James considered the question. "Well, when you come up on us in camp, do I ever say 'who're you?'"

They meandered down the dry creek bed and up the other side, finally reaching the area James was converting to a boat yard. Benjamin stepped into the small clearing and whistled. James watched his face, and suppressed a smile.

James ran a hand gently over the rough rounded trunk, slowly pacing the length of it.

"How'd you get the point on the...bow?" Benjamin asked. James nodded. "The original trunk was about 25 feet long. That was a lot more than I needed. So burned it through. I wish we could try to burn it now. I want to try out the chisel."

A fan of worry passed over Benjamin's face. "Smoke's easy to spot this time of day."

James sighed, and gripped the chisel handle in two hands. He pressed the blade into the area charred from his work the previous night. Prying, he flipped a blackened chunk up out of the shallow gouge.

"All I had last night was sticks," James grunted, reversing his grip and jabbing the blackened wood with the chisel. "Shaping wood with wood. I don't know how the Indians managed." They both chuckled softly.

After a couple minutes, James was perspiring freely. "This is harder than I thought. And why is this chisel point beveled on one side, not the other?" he wondered aloud, wiping his brow with his forearm.

Benjamin shifted, and James glanced up. "What?" he said.

"Well, my pa used to whittle up some rough furniture. That was his'n before he passed." Benjamin gestured to the chisel.

"Oh!" James slipped his kerchief out of his pocket, and stroked the handle of the chisel. "Why didn't you say so?" He made as if to hand the chisel back, but Benjamin raised his hand.

"I brought that for you to use. Remember you asked for it last time I came by."

James considered. "Yes, but I was only looking for a way to scrape this wood faster." James looked at the charred indentation, now marked with a few wounds of fresh, lighter-colored wood where he'd chipped it. "Am I doing this right?"

Benjamin was nodding his head, but it lacked conviction. "There might be another way to it."

James handed the chisel, handle first, across the trunk. He stood back to watch, as Benjamin stepped up to size along the great wooden block. Benjamin held the chisel with one hand, and laid the tip of the blade at the edge of the char, at a shallow angle.

Benjamin glanced up at James. "Like you is playing pool." He smiled, and pointed with his free hand. "Bevel side up." James nodded.

With a smooth glide, Benjamin passed the chisel across the black area, and a long, thin strip of wood curled up the blade and over his pressed fingers. He reached the end of the charred area, and flicked the curlicued shaving off to one side, then moved fractionally over, to shave the next black line. After three or four swipes, he'd already made more progress than James had managed the previous evening.

Benjamin straightened, lifting his eyebrows at James. James nodded, and Benjamin handed the chisel back over. James bent, and focused on what he'd seen. He felt a rising irritation, but couldn't put his finger on the bother.

"I still don't know how to make a burn, without burning the whole log," James said, frustrated.

Benjamin kept his eyes downcast.

"Look. I could really use some help. What are you thinking?"

"Tar."

James started. "Say again?"

"Resin?" Benjamin tried again, as if he were speaking to a foreign tourist. "Cross the river, where the rice fields are. Or any new-growth pine."

James still looked lost. Benjamin smiled. "You take the tar from the sapwood. You can make it up like paint, if you cook it right. Then you just slap it on your boat where you *want* it to burn."

James considered this. "But how do I get that stuff out of the tree?"

Benjamin nodded at the chisel. "Tap it." He made a slashing motion with his hand. "The young trees bleed. Closest to the bark."

"So I get some resin and smear it on here?" He pointed at the middle of the trunk, and then waved slowly back and forth.

Benjamin bent to wipe a place in the dirt, and used the chisel as a pencil to draw the top of the dugout. They did some erasing, and some sitting back on their haunches, studying the various effects. They glanced periodically from the drawing to the silent block of wood. James felt the excitement pulsing through him.

His earlier irritation at Benjamin had dissipated. As they hiked back to camp, James considered what it was that had got him so riled. Something about Benjamin recounting his own father's instruction had stirred the bile in James. All he really wanted, he thought to himself, was a family like other people had—a father who taught him what he needed to know in order to survive.

True, it wasn't Sam's fault that James had been fingered for a crime he didn't commit. But it all started to head south when his dad showed up. All James wanted was to be left alone. He was starting to feel like what he had with Anne, and even with CeCe and Benjamin, might be close to what he was looking for.

Back at camp, the girls had had great luck fishing. Benjamin and CeCe cleaned the fish. James tended a small fire while Anne busied herself preparing a biscuit batter.

"Yellow perch," CeCe replied to James. "They're common here in the creek. Fish them on the lee side of stumps and rocks."

Anne licked molasses from her fingers, chewing on the last of her fish. "Whatever they are, they're delicious!" she beamed. "I'm so stuffed I can hardly budge!"

James grunted. "When I get the dugout launched, we can eat like this all the time."

CeCe laughed. "And what will you do in the intervening years?"

Before CeCe and Benjamin left, Benjamin showed James how to bleed resin from a young pine. He promised to return later that evening to work with James on the canoe.

Anne shook the last of the rinse water from the cook pan, and wiped it with a towel. "Do you want to stay here in Darien?"

James sat back, eying Anne. "I thought that was the idea. To settle for a while. Stay here."

She nodded quickly. "Yes, that's what I want too. Only, I didn't mean—" she turned, gesturing in a wide arc "—here. I meant, you know, in town. With a house. With four walls. A bathroom."

James jabbed the chisel point absently into a log stacked at the side of the fire ring. "What about your dad?"

Anne looked off across the languid river. "I know he's out there." She turned and gazed intensely at James. "But my life is with you now. I feel like I'm discovering my soul on this trip."

James stared back, grateful she couldn't see into his head. He too was glad they were traveling together. He just didn't have the means to express thoughts as fancy as hers. He nodded. "I like the way you can say what you feel."

Anne smiled blushing. "I'm sure you can do that too." James shook his head emphatically. "I can't. I wish I could, but half the time, I don't know *what* I'm feeling."

She sat, waiting.

"I mean, I think something's broken inside sometimes." He hung damp dishcloths on a branch. "I must sound like I'm crazy."

He looked across at her. She was still, her hands folded in her lap. "It's as if what I'm feeling really isn't connected with what's going on in front of me."

Anne nodded, but didn't speak.

"Sometimes on a day just like this—quiet, peaceful—I just get in a black rage. I don't know where it comes from."

"Maybe you should talk to CeCe sometime," Anne said.

James lifted his head, startled.

"I mean it. She's talked about stuff that sounds like what you're saying."

James lifted a hand, palm up. "Not to *me* she hasn't."

Anne laughed, a melodic, warm sound. "I think you and she have a lot in common."

"Yea, I know. She tells dumb jokes and I don't laugh." He waited, but Anne was silent. "What else?"

Anne stared at him. "Tell me you're playing me. Tell me you are not really as dense as you pretend sometimes."

James stood up. "Now hold on. What call do you have to get so mad about a simple question? What do CeCe and I have in common?"

She clenched her jaw, and her hands were in fists. "How about you've both lost a mother. And a brother."

James stared back, stunned.

"Not to mention, neither one of you is particularly crazy about your fathers."

James mulled this over. Another thought occurred to him. "Well, doctor. Neither are you." She looked at him, puzzled. "Crazy about your dad."

"That's not the same at all. I love my dad. If I hadn't met you, I'd still be home."

James smirked. "Would you *really?*"

Anne looked at her hands in her lap. "Yes. But I'm real glad I met you." Her eyes narrowed. "That doesn't change what I said. You and CeCe might want to talk."

"I have something to tell you. I didn't want to say in front of the others."

Anne was already nodding. "I think I know what it is." She held up her hand. "The man in that hotel where we stayed. We left the Trojan wrappers, and he might've been a member of the crazy Preacher's church."

James slapped his forehead. "I completely *forgot* about that. What I was going to tell you was that when I packed up the rest of camp that day alone, I noticed something missing I hadn't noticed at first."

Anne waited. "Yes?"

James colored. "The rest of the Trojans. The pack was gone. That would have told whoever found them that you and I might not be what we seemed, but I could never understand why somebody would've gone looking to begin with." He shrugged. "Now I guess we know. That man at the hotel mentioned that church. Either he cleaned the room, or the maid told him about the condoms. I never connected the two when CeCe told us about the preacher."

James slung a shirt on, and tucked the chisel into his belt. "At least now we know why they came. To mete out God's justice, I guess. I'm going to collect some resin. I won't be far."

James moved quietly through the forest undergrowth. He sensed another presence. Something—or someone—nearby. Watching. He hadn't spoken of it to anyone, but ever since the day of the violence with the preacher, he'd had the feeling of being watched. Casually, he glanced about as he walked. He'd never seen anything to confirm his suspicions. Sometimes a shadow here, but when he'd look closer, just the foliage, batted by the wind off the creek.

Back from the creek's floodplain, he discovered a stand of new-growth pine on a low rise. He sliced across the thick bark with the chisel point, and waited for the sap to run. Feigning boredom, he glanced around. Nothing.

***

To their surprise, both CeCe and Benjamin appeared just before dusk. They'd brought potatoes and butter with them, as well as some corn. Good thing, Anne laughed, since she'd had no luck with the fish in the afternoon.

"They steal your bait?" CeCe asked.

Anne nodded.

"Night crawlers?" Anne nodded again.

"Maybe Benjamin can dig you out some crayfish from a shallow shelf. Perch like that meat, and they also like perch eyes." Anne blanched, and CeCe laughed.

"That's so," Benjamin agreed. "Perch feed by sight, is what Mr. Beck says. You catch a lot or none. That's their way. So daytime's good, and late summer's good, but, well, it's fishing."

After supper, James and Benjamin gathered the tools James had assembled for the dugout burn, and set off. The boys worked for several hours on the trunk of the tree. They experimented with how much to burn before they scraped off the blackened wood. James had shed his shirt and was sweating profusely from the heat from the charcoal and the humid summer evening. Even Benjamin had shed his flannel shirt and worked bare-chested, his overall braces dangling at his side.

James heard Benjamin laugh softly. "What's funny?"

Benjamin laughed again. Then he held his forearm up next to James's. "You about as dark as me." It was true. James's arms and chest were black from the coal scrapings.

"Is my...?" He raised a finger, pointing a claw at his face. Benjamin bent and studied James's face closely.

"More like a raccoon. Around your eyeballs is white. The rest, black as me." Benjamin laughed low and deep. Despite himself, James grinned widely.

Suddenly, he spun. Nothing there. Just a branch swinging lightly in the distance, in the breeze. But James noticed nothing else moved. The prevalent sea breeze that often wafted over the area in sunlight was absent this long after dusk. He turned back to the smoky log, and noticed Benjamin watching him.

"See something?" Benjamin asked, after a time.

"No." James said, slowly. "But that's just it," he exhaled. "You walk through these woods all the time alone. Ever feel like you're...not? Alone?"

Benjamin paused, chisel in hand. "I know there's others out here. Probably they's taking note of my passing. You mean like that?"

"I mean people see you, but you can't see them," James persisted.

Benjamin shook his head, eyes intently down. "Don't know what that means."

There was something in the way the boy avoided the question.

"I think you do know," James said quietly. "I think you know just what I'm talking about." He waited for Benjamin to look up, but the boy continued to scrape at the charred trunk.

"Who is it that's out here, Benjamin?" James raised his voice a notch. "Who's watching us?"

Benjamin mumbled a reply.

"Speak up! What's the big secret?"

Benjamin raised his head. "I surely don't know. I got no idea who is out here, besides you and me and Miss Anne and Miss CeCe." His sculpted face shown like mahogany in the flickering of the fire.

"Listen, I know I'm crazy, okay? But I am not imagining being followed. There is something out there, just out of my sight. Tell me you don't feel it!"

Benjamin shrugged. "I guess I don't." He looked around. "Whatever it is—whoever—it don't feel...mean. It's just a watcher. Like—my daddy used to call the whispering out here *memory voices*. He said you could hear people who were gone, but their voices still sounded sometimes, blown out from under a stump, or from down out the leaves, or wherever they got caught up."

Now it was James's turn to stare. "Memory voices," he repeated, skeptically. "Maybe we *both* crazy." The woods rang with the sound of boys laughing.

"Could be that Wayne boy you met up with," Benjamin said, almost as a question.

James contemplated the odd encounter, not for the first time since he'd met the boy in the woods. "Could be. I just still can't figure how, if you say that boy was kinda simple to start, he became this ghost walker. And I'm telling you. That boy had only one working eye!" He saw the puzzled look. "You know. Like in Daniel Boone. Ghost Walkers. They can pass through the forest without leaving footprints."

"Well, I think I seen his footprints. Maybe not. But maybe you could set a trap. Something that'd warn y'all when he's near."

James snorted at the suggestion. "How'm I gonna know which way he's coming from?"

The boys paused, both considering the problem. "What if you got some twine..." Benjamin said slowly.

"Even fish line might do," mused James. They both stepped over to the makeshift drawing board they'd created in the dirt. James bent and erased the draft of the dugout. He rooted about the ground, and produced a fistful of sticks. Wordless, he arranged the sticks in the center of the cleared ground.

"Camp," he said.

Benjamin squatted on his haunches, studying the scattered grouping of sticks. "Which one is you?" He asked, not looking up.

James looked from Benjamin to the pile. Then he shoved Benjamin's shoulder, so the boy rolled feet up onto his back, laughing soundlessly.

"Here," he said, as Benjamin recovered, and wiped at his shirt shoulder. "This is you." James gestured to a long thin piece of charcoaled wood.

Benjamin nodded approvingly. "Handsome cuss, ain't he?"

"So we surround the camp with this string. Pretty far out, don't you think?" James traced a circle on the ground, out to the edge of the cleared spot.

Benjamin stared at the ground, thoughtful. "What's going to keep deer and such critters from tripping your wire?"

James looked at Benjamin. "I come up with the great ideas. Anne can work out the details." He rose, and began to scrape the coals in the deepening scar on the top side of the dugout.

45 / Fighting Poet

The new sheet of blank paper mocked him. The borders seemed infinite to Dylan. So much space, so little to say. He folded the paper and carefully ripped it down the middle. Suddenly the size seemed a bit more manageable.

> *Getting to know you has been fun.*
> *When I think of special girls, you're the one.*
> *With you, I'd like to spend the day,*
> *To walk and talk and laugh and ~~play pray~~ stay.*

He groaned. This was worse than awful. He glanced at the clock: *2:35 pm.*

Lois of course had heard about the fight, and just as Sam said, she wouldn't listen to a lick of reason about it. She'd buttonholed him yesterday right at the end of his sidewalk. It was all he could do to ease her down Nash Street before Nana overheard.

"I thought you were different. I thought you had something besides muscle between your ears. Please tell me I'm wrong. Please tell me you are not going up the hill to get your brains knocked out."

He was flummoxed. Lois wagged a finger in his face. "You think you're just going to wait me out, you better have another think coming."

This was a side of Lois that Dylan had not run up against. He was not surprised she was mad. He thought fighting Stinger didn't seem too smart either.

"Lois, I don't have a choice. If I don't stand up now, I'll deal with it the whole school year."

By way of answer, she crossed her arms high on her chest and turned half away from him.

"Don't come," he said.

She gave him a look that would boil water. "Trust me on that one."

"I'm sorry," he said to her back. "I can take care of myself, Lois."

"I never did ask you. What religion are you?"

Dylan was baffled. "Religion? Catholic. Why?"

She walked away, pointedly tossing her hair in a flip. "I just need to know where to take the flowers."

The fight itself was anti-climactic. Thank goodness for summer. There were perhaps a dozen kids gathered at the water fountain. It had rained earlier in the afternoon, so no baseball game. Dylan hadn't mentioned the challenge to any of his friends, and Stinger didn't have many friends, so only a small group waited. Oddly, Scooter was not present.

True to his word, Cammy was there. He gave Dylan the barest of nods when he walked up. Stinger was strangely subdued, avoiding eye contact with him. Almost immediately, he said, "Let's get this over with," as if he were afraid Dylan would say or do something that would embarrass him.

Dylan was shocked to see Lois, with Lisa Haggerty, standing a short distance away. Lisa had a sour expression, as if she'd just heard some unpleasant news. Stinger tossed his baseball cap to his brother Doogie. Cammy, standing next to Doogie, said something to him, and Doogie started, nodded vigorously, and turned to watch the fighters.

Dylan turned away, and faced Stinger.

Stinger sneered, "You got one last chance—"

Dylan hit Stinger square in the nose with a hard right and pedaled back into his fighter's stance. Stinger lifted both hands straight to his face, and his eyes sprang tears. Blood dripped through his fingers, and he too backed away, tripping on a small gouge in the dirt. He dropped one hand to catch himself and Dylan was on him, hitting him twice in a blur, one a glancing blow off Stinger's large head, one squarely on the chin.

From the very first throb of Stinger's face on his fist, Dylan was back in the alley, and his mood was murderous. Stinger sensed it too, and his own eyes were wide with anger and fear. He was in trouble already and he knew it. The crowd was uncharacteristically quiet. Those gathered seemed to sense that this fight was about much more than a school bully and a kid who was tired of it. If they had been prepared to cheer for Dylan, and to step in as soon as he was in danger of being maimed, they were completely unprepared for the hate that drove the smaller and younger of the two fighters.

Dylan punished Stinger's upper arms, just as Cammy had done. Stinger was already winded and stumbling, less than a minute after the fight began. Dylan's lightning strikes backed him up continually, and he had yet to throw a punch.

Your opponent's eyes will tell you when he knows he's lost. That's the time to finish him. Don't hesitate. Stinger threw a desperate roundhouse from his back foot. Dylan stepped inside the swing, and pummeled Stinger's middle, following Stinger down to the ground.

The bigger boy tried to curl up to escape the younger boy's punches. He was openly sniffling, coughing on the blood pouring from his nose into his mouth. His eyes were squeezed shut, and he was trying to say something through his coughs.

"Dylan!"

His arm froze in mid-air, the fist pointed at Stinger's face. He turned to peer through the crowd, and suddenly relaxed.

"That's enough."

Dylan rose off Stinger's chest, breathing heavily, and eased through the crowd to follow Lois down the hill. She slowed as they walked past the shops, and he caught up to her. They walked in silence towards his house.

"I'm supposed to get together with the guys at my house to watch *Gilligan's Island*," he said quietly.

"I like that show. Do you watch Batman too? I like Robin. I like *That Girl* too. Do you ever have girls over to watch too?"

He turned to face her finally, and smiled. "Would you like to come? I have something for you."

At the house, he settled Lois on the front porch in the glider, and ran inside. His father called to him from the front room.

"Just a minute," he hollered, bounding up the steps to his room.

A moment letter, he clumped back down the steps. He waved at Sam. "Just a second," he said, before his father could speak.

"Here," he said, handing Lois a folded half-sheet of paper. "This is for you."

The door swung slowly open behind him. He turned, grinning, to wink at Sam. But something about his father's look stopped him. Sam nodded to Lois, who smiled at him. She started to say something, but he spoke to Dylan.

"Richmond. Remember? I'm sorry. But we have to leave soon as we can."

46 / Camp Intruder

Benjamin and James returned to the camp to find Anne and CeCe huddled over a magazine. *"Petticoat."* James smirked. "Find out the latest on Paul and Jane." He smiled at Benjamin, who returned a puzzled look. "Paul McCartney? The Beatles?"

"Jerry Lee and the King," Benjamin tapped his chest light, and lay the fire tools aside.

"So which is which?" CeCe asked serenely. At the same time, Anne chided, "Are you boys going to wash up?"

CeCe laughed. "Folks in town'll think it's some kinda plague. The night Cat Head Creek turned smoky black."

"Very funny," James grimaced. "I hope this soot comes off."

"You can always come live with us on Catpond Road," Benjamin smiled.

James gave him a look. "Catpond Road is it? Well, I'll keep the offer in mind."

The boys returned from the creek a few minutes later, freshly scrubbed.

Anne turned as they strode up the short hill. "CeCe thinks it's probably okay to come back into town for church on Sunday. Want to?" She looked expectantly at James.

"What about the preacher? We still don't know what he's likely to do next."

CeCe ground a few sparks outside the fire ring under her right shoe. "Preacher Waugh will be playing with rattlers at his own church on Sunday. Unless y'all stay for supper, or come back in town and he goes out fishing again, y'all shouldn't cross paths."

"'Sides," said Benjamin, "There's other trails to take to get here."

James bent to square up the fire. "Don't add any more wood, honey. I'm turning in soon," Anne yawned.

CeCe laughed softly. "And no more of that for awhile."

Anne looked at her innocently. "No more of what?"

James also laughed. "I think she means we need to behave like brother and sister."

* * *

The next several days passed uneventfully. Benjamin came every evening to help James with the dugout. After a few days, it actually looked like a canoe, and they spent the better part of one evening rolling it to the closest part of the river, several hundred yards from the camp. They decided to launch sometime in the next day or so, when Benjamin could be present for the ceremonial splash.

While James could still sense something tracking them, he was getting more at ease with the spirit, or whatever it was. With Benjamin's help, he had stretched a string completely around the campsite, at about 150 feet out from the center of their clearing. The fishing line was stretched low to the ground; in most places, just a foot or so off the forest floor.

James thought if someone approached from the creek, they should be able to see or hear the intruders first. If it was the dead of night, that was a different problem, but that didn't seem likely.

Last, they designated a faint deer trail as the route they would use in and out of the camp on the approach from town. The trail passed over an ancient shale outcropping before descending into a thicket. Just on the camp side of the thicket, they ran the trip wire, so that anyone who knew it was there could step easily over it.

The tripwire was a wide semicircle that had two terminuses, at the water's edge on either side of camp. The tripwire ran down to the water's edge from either end, and then looped back to the "alarm," which was the coffee pot, filled with river rocks and perched atop a stake James drove into the ground.

James had worried that any movement in the line would tumble the pot off its perch. But for the first several days, there was no hint of a breach. Early one morning, just before dawn, James was awakened by Anne.

"I think I heard a noise."

"The trap?"

"I think so," she responded.

James slipped quietly out of the tent and rose to his feet. He gave his eyes a few moments to adjust to the dusky pre-dawn. Off to the east was the faintest suggestion of a lightening. Breathing slowly, he listened, turning his head from side to side.

The coffee pot lay on the ground, rounded stones spilled from the dislodged top. The woods were quiet. Night peepers still sang in the deeper forest to the north, but here it was almost unnaturally quiet. His eyes tried to pierce the foliage surrounding him, but he could see nothing.

James crept to the rock outcropping at the bank's edge and stepped gingerly up the canted stone. Turning from the raised vantage point, he spied the forest for several hundred yards, but nothing seemed amiss.

As more light peaked through the trees, he walked the line of string, trying to determine where it had been disturbed. He began from the pot itself, moving east from the camp, looking for signs of disturbance. He slunk low, peering ahead into the forest on his left, and back to his right at camp. All was still.

Close to the end of his search, on the side of camp away from the approach from Darien, he finally found something. In a sandy wash, he spied a clear boot print. Up the side of the wash toward camp, several yards away, he saw a fresh smear on the wall, as if someone had been climbing, and slipped back. *No ghost walker made this*, he mused.

He clambered up the side of the wash. To his left, the creek meandered several yards away. At knee-level ran the trip wire, now hanging loosely. James peered intently in the direction of camp. Perhaps a hundred yards away, he could see the wisp of faint smoke from last night's dead fire, and the opening of the tent beyond the fire ring. The

tent was empty.

47 / The Vanishing

James froze, listening. A great quiet answered back. He felt the first icy tingles of dread. James raced barefoot across the forest floor, leaping finally over a low scrub into the middle of the clearing. He landed like a cat and turned slowly, waist bent, arms raised to ward off an attacker.

The camp felt deserted. He could sense the stillness in his pores. Every nerve felt alive, poised for an assault. But the only thing he could hear was the sound of a boat motor far down the creek.

The innumerable switchbacks on Cat Head Creek made it difficult to gauge the distance of boats by their engine noise. He raced down to the river's edge and craned his neck to the right, but all he could see to the next bend was the surface of the water.

Then he noticed the log that extended from the upper bank down into the water. He and Anne often used it as a kind of bench when they fished at the water's edge. It was wet several inches above the surface of the creek. As if the creek depth had fallen suddenly. He turned and stared at the bank. It had been so dry there was not much moisture to capture an imprint, and the terrain did not look any different than he remembered it. But as he stared at the ground, he saw a dull glitter. He bent and lifted Anne's hair clip from where it lay in the dust.

James scrambled up the bank and raced to the tent. As he approached the opening, he slowed, peering about the camp. Nothing seemed out of the ordinary, other than the upturned coffeepot, the string still attached. He bent and stared into the shadowy interior of the tent. All he could see was their rumpled bedding. He patted the folds, but there was nothing hidden in the sleeping bag. He reached under the pillow. His Bowie knife was gone.

James turned to ease back out of the tent. It was then he noticed Anne's sneakers, side by side where she always left them for bed, just inside the door of the tent. He had chided her more than once because she would not leave the tent, even to step behind it to pee, without slipping on her shoes.

James slipped on his own shoes and raced in the direction of town. At times, he lost sight of the creek. Its many bends and curves made it next to impossible to stay close to shore constantly. He also recalled that several tributaries fed Cat Head Creek from the abandoned rice paddies on the northern bank.

Who could have planned this? The more he thought about it, the more he marveled at the cunning. Someone had drawn him out of camp, then entered and seized Anne and escaped by boat. But could one person actually pull that off? How could anyone snatch Anne without her screaming aloud, or at least creating some kind of ruckus? And why would they try to pull off something so crazy so close to sunrise? Did they need some light to operate? Why wouldn't they just shoot him, and take Anne anyway? The more he considered what had happened, the more confused he was about how it had been done. Or why.

James felt panic rising. He couldn't go to the police. He should have searched camp more thoroughly. But how had her captors approached so silently? And in the dark? How had their camp been discovered again?

"Julie Rose ain't here at the moment. What you asking after her for anyway?"

James stood on the second step of the familiar house, looking up at the unfamiliar man. He was short and squat, with a round belly protruding under stained long johns, tucked loosely into a well-worn pair of dungarees. He was in stocking feet. His face bristled with a several-days growth of white beard, but his eyes, pink and watery, belied his gruff voice. They brimmed with curiosity.

"My name is Matt. My....sister and I are friends of Julie Rose, and Mrs. Walker."

The man was nodding. "Yes, yes, Julie Rose talked to me about you.

So you want to be a shrimper, do you?"

James was beside himself with worry about Anne, but he didn't know how much to say, or to ask. "It sounds like a better deal than working in the shrimp factory," he managed.

The older man nodded, a faint smile lighting his face. "Having done far more than my fair share of both, I would have to say that shrimping is a marginally more preferable pursuit. An aficionado of crosswords, are you?"

James started at the rapid change of subject and stared dumbly at his greeter. "Well come in, come in. A man of few words," the man mused as he stepped aside. "More for me, I say," he cackled, as James walked down the familiar hall, glancing up at the portraits on the wall. "An early riser too! I appreciate the hints of ambition!"

They moved on to the kitchen and Mr. Walker offered James a Coke, which he gladly accepted. They sat down across the linoleum table from each other. James looked around for a coaster. "Don't bother," the older man said. "A house is for living in, don't you think?" He sipped slowly at his own drink, smacked his lips, and set it down.

"So," Mr. Walker lifted his eyes. "You're not here to talk about shrimpin', are you."

James sighed, holding the cold bottle in two hands. "I guess not. I was hoping to find Julie Rose, or Mrs. Walker."

The man waited. "Truth is," James continued, "I'm really looking for CeCe. Julie Rose's friend."

"Kinda old for her, aren't you?" James started to protest, but Mr. Walker grinned, lifting a hand. "I'm just having it on with ya," he smiled. "But you seem like a lad with a load on his mind."

James wondered how to proceed. "It's kind of important I find her. She's..." James searched for the right words. "...CeCe kind of befriended my sister and me when we were passing through. From the north."

"Have you been by her place yet?"

"That's the thing. I don't know just where she lives. I knew your house," he added quickly. "Julie Rose and your wife and my sister and I all had supper here after church one Sunday. You were..."

"...tending the fleet?" He offered helpfully.

"Yes. That's what your daughter said."

"I can just imagine," he muttered wryly. "So how is it, out in these lovely woods of ours?"

"Oh, you know..." James shrugged, trying to act unconcerned. "Quiet mostly. Interesting sometimes."

Mr. Walker creased his brow. "So where is your—your sister, is it? She decided not to come today?"

James clenched his fists, willing his face not to respond. "Well, that's the thing. I...came back to camp, and she was gone. I was hoping she might be with the girls."

"Well, Julie Rose is off with her mother to the church for some nonsense, but I recollect they said they'd return in time for lunch. That's 11:30 around here."

Mr. Walker glanced at the clock above the fridge. "That gives you an hour or so, if you'd like to wait. Or I can give you directions around to CeCe's. Mind though, her father may be home and sleeping. Look for the truck tractor in the drive, and go quiet if it's there."

James nodded. "Thanks. If it's okay with you, I'll head over there. If she's not home, I'll come back here to wait for Julie Rose."

Mr. Walker dropped and lifted his head slowly. "That's fine. The words I'm missing will probably remain missing despite my most exhaustive linguistic efforts." At the last, he clamped his lips and raised his eyebrows, slapping a knee.

James looked at him, confused. Mr. Walker rotated the newspaper in front of him to face James. Glancing down, he understood. A half-complete crossword puzzle. "William James counseled that one should read something mentally challenging every day, just for the exercise." He turned the paper back to himself. "I know this doesn't really constitute reading, but it certainly feels like exercise."

Mr. Walker accompanied James to the front door and gave him the directions to CeCe's home, about three blocks distant. James raised a hand in farewell, and started down the steps.

"Oh, say," called Mr. Walker. "Have you an idea for a six-letter word for *bury?*" James finally shook his head.

"Neither have I," said Mr. Walker faintly. "Neither have I."

James studied the house on the small lot on the corner. It was a one-story cottage, with a small front porch and an even smaller side porch, which likely opened into a kitchen. The curtains on both front windows were wide, but the house felt still. A banded newspaper lay on the welcome mat before the front screen door. There was no sign of a truck or other vehicle.

James approached the door and rapped on the screen frame. He waited, listening, but there was no sound from within. Hurrying around the side, he mounted the steps and banged on the screen. The inner door was tightly closed. He assumed it was unlocked, but he didn't need to add to his troubles by entering a vacant house. He cupped his hand over his eyes, and peered through the screen and the door pane. Just what one would expect—a small, tidy kitchen, dishes holstered in the rack, a drying dishtowel draped over the top.

Where was everyone? Where was Anne? He wished he had asked Mr. Walker where he could find Benjamin's home. But he knew he was arousing concern on the part of the man as it was. *Catpond Road.*

James looked around. The street was deserted. It was midmorning on a Saturday, but he'd not seen anyone out. He turned back in the direction of the Walker's. Julie Rose might be home soon, and maybe she knew something. For the hundredth time, he replayed the events of the early morning. It was baffling, but he also vowed the person responsible would face some very bad consequences.

What made it most difficult was he had no idea what he was facing. He decided there must have been two people involved in the kidnapping, if that's what it was. Those tracks he had seen were probably not made by the same person who had eased the boat up to the bank.

So two people arrive by boat. A motorboat, but paddled, or he was sure he would've heard the engine. One person exits the boat a distance from the camp. That person left the tracks James had found, and perhaps spies on the camp. Maybe for quite some time.

The other person stays with the boat, and eases it into shore just beneath the rock outcropping that overlooks the water. James remembered clambering up the camp side of the rock this morning.

Could he have missed the boat? Unfortunately, yes. He had not been looking out at the Creek, and he'd not mounted to the top of the stone mound. If he had taken several more steps. If he had just turned, and looked down at the Creek.

Someone hiding in a boat could have seen him begin his reconnaissance of the trip line perimeter. That same someone could have eased up the Creek side of the rocks and watched him, out along the edge. Watched him while they also watched the camp. That someone could even have signaled to the other interloper. Were there two? Who were they? And how in hell had they gotten Anne out of camp without his hearing a sound?

As he hurried down the lane, it was all he could do not to raise his hands to clutch at his hair. He would not rest until he had the answers, and until whoever did this paid dearly. On the way back to Julie Rose's, he decided he had to get his hands on a gun.

As Mr. Walker swung open the screen to let him back in, James said quietly, "entomb."

"Eh?"

"Entomb. Six-letter word for bury."

Mr. Walker smiled. "Good lad. I think that fits."

Julie Rose and Mrs. Walker arrived a short time later. The smile on Mrs. Walker's face faded, when she said she'd not seen or heard from CeCe or from "Gwen." "What's wrong, Matt?"

"Where do I find Benjamin?" He asked, turning to Julie Rose. "CeCe's friend?"

"Well I don't know as they're friends," Mr. Walker spoke out, attempting to interpret the tension in the kitchen. "He and his mother help out at her place, since..." his voice faded, as James cut him off.

"I just need to talk to him. It is really important."

"Matt," Mrs. Walker said slowly, setting down her sack of groceries and moving toward him, "Where is Gwen?"

He swiveled, staring at her, his fists clenched, mouth thinly set.

"Did you leave her alone out in the woods? CeCe won't tell us much about where y'all are, but she did allow as how you moved your camp. Was there trouble?"

James put up his hands, pleading. "Mrs. Walker, it's really important. I need to find CeCe or Benjamin."

Mrs. Walker sat down heavily in the kitchen chair opposite her husband, looking up dazedly at James. "Why, child? What's happened?"

James spluttered, "They were the only ones knew where our camp was. The only—"

A low cry emitted from the girl. All eyes turned to look at Julie Rose. She'd been standing in the doorway from the hall, motionless, ever since they'd arrived.

"Oh no. Momma?"

Mr. Walker rose to slip an arm around his daughter, and led her to the chair he'd vacated. James circled to look full at her. He tried to keep the edge from his voice.

"What happened, Julie Rose? What do you know?" Mrs. Walker reached across the table to pat her daughter's hand and Julie Rose turned her wrist to clutch her mother's hand tightly. She looked up at James. Her eyes were red.

"One of the boys from school does chores for Mr. Bartlett next door."

"Roscoe. The Simmons boy," Mr. Walker prompted.

"Yes. Anyway, he was cutting the grass yesterday morning, before it got too hot." She paused, looking beseechingly at her mother.

"Go on, Julie Rose," her mother said softly.

"He asked if he could get water from our hose, since Mr. Bartlett was away in Savannah. I said of course." Julie Rose furrowed her brow, thinking hard.

"He asked did I know a new girl around town. I asked why, and he said up at the store earlier this week a man looked like a policeman—I guess a detective, suit and all—was showing pictures asking if anyone had ever seen this girl, or this boy."

"When was this, Julie Rose?" James asked sharply.

"I'm not sure he said. Maybe Tuesday or Wednesday."

Julie Rose wept quietly, tears spilling over her eyelids. Mrs. Walker reached back, and extended the corner of an apron. James groaned.

"I didn't really ask. I didn't want to sound like I cared. Not 'til I could talk to somebody." Julie Rose looked across the table at her mother.

James felt the room spinning beneath his feet. How could anyone track them here? "What else did he say?"

Roscoe said the man was showing the picture around, saying that this girl was in trouble, that she might've been kidnapped." Julie Rose glanced quickly at James, then dropped her eyes.

Mrs. Walker looked up at James. Her gaze was steady, sympathetic. Mr. Walker was looking down at the kitchen table, drumming his fingers on the red and white porcelain.

"Anything else?" James managed. "Anything else your friend knew?"

"One thing." She looked genuinely stymied. "Roscoe said one of the boys in the store at the time said he'd seen y'all."

The kitchen went silent, except for the ticking of the clock over the fridge. 12:08.

"Did Roscoe say who it was?"

Julie Rose nodded her head slowly. "Did you ever meet a boy named Samuel?"

"Anything you want to tell us, son?" Mr. Walker stroked his daughter's hair, and watched James. He seemed a bit older now. Stooped.

"Sir, you're probably better off not knowing too much." James was stalling. He needed to get away. To think.

Mrs. Walker spoke, addressing Mr. Walker, as if James were not there. "I think it's safe to say that those two aren't brother and sister." Julie Rose's head snapped up. She opened her mouth to speak, but glanced at her mother, and a dawning washed over her face. She closed her mouth and rested her chin on her hands.

Mrs. Walker looked up at James. "So *Gwendolyn* is missing?" He only nodded.

"Do you think she got tired of running, and decided to go back home?" Mrs. Walker asked slowly, trying to keep the question unemotional. He debated, and spoke, knowing he was confirming several things he hadn't wanted to reveal.

"No. She didn't leave on her own."

Mr. Walker looked up from his drumming. "How sure are you of that, son?"

James met his gaze. "Positive." He could sense Mr. Walker wanted to ask more, but he finally just gave a single nod.

"I think you know what you need to do, son." It was Mrs. Walker.

Truthfully, he did not have a clue. "What's that?"

Mrs. Walker didn't speak for a time. He could sense her getting her thoughts in line. Finally, she looked across at her daughter.

"Something as simple as love can get so blessed messy sometimes." She paused, then plowed on. "If Julie Rose were to disappear, I would do anything to find her."

James started to speak, but Mrs. Walker silenced him with a look. "Anything. Someday, I am sure you will know what I mean. For now, you just have to accept my word."

James dug his hands in his jeans and stared out the kitchen window. Mr. Potter occupied his place next to the garden, still as a sentry.

"It will be very hard for you if she is back with her father. He will be mad, and so will you. But given enough time..." She trailed off.

James waited. What Mrs. Walker said was true as far as it went, and he had known a day like this might come. But there was still one sickening doubt.

Mrs. Walker seemed to be reading his thoughts. "You need to make sure that she's with her family. If something else happened...well, you just need to know." She stroked her daughter's hand. "And frankly, so do they."

It all clicked into place now. "You think I should call her family?" Both the mother and father were nodding vigorously before he'd even finished the sentence.

He stood, staring at Mr. Potter. He half-expected the potted man to turn his chin, and nod a *no*. But no reprieve there.

He studied the faces of the two parents, and finally told them the whole story, omitting no details. Julie Rose stared at him, agog, for most of the narrative. At the end though, she spoke. "I'm kind of relieved. For being brother and sister, I thought y'all acted kinda mushy."

Mrs. Walker nodded, smiling sadly. "It must seem like a very hard thing. I know you and her father aren't going to be buddies anytime soon," she paused.

Mr. Walker took up the thread. "But time has a way...you may surprise yourselves. Oh yes," he exclaimed, as James shook his head. "But first things first. You need to know what happened. And soon."

"You're right," James said. "I'll call the family. Today. But why didn't they just barge into camp and take her? Why kidnap her? And how would her father track us *here*? If they don't have Gwen, I would at least like to have some answers, as well as questions."

He got directions from Mr. Walker to find Catpond Road. On the way out, Julie Rose called out a last question.

He stopped midway down the sidewalk, grinning shyly. "Anne. And James." He waved, and set off.

Almost as soon as he reached the end of the sidewalk, he broke into a slow trot. Though the family he'd just left now knew a lot more, he'd learned almost nothing new. That wasn't quite right, he amended. He now knew that someone had been tracking them. He also knew that he had to decide very soon how to handle the contact with Anne's father.

If Roy Sampson was *not* the person responsible for her disappearance, and James delayed before determining that, he would never be able to live with himself. If it *were* her father, at least James would know. He ran a few blocks off of the direct route to Catpond Road, to travel past CeCe's house again. No sign of life, and he didn't bother to approach and knock.

At the end of Old Cat Head Road, he turned just past the Mill Cemetery. A hand-painted sign read *Catpond Road*. The macadam yielded to a dusty red clay street. James heard the sound of kids playing. In the distance, he saw a group playing stickball in the street. He slowed and looked from house to house, as if seeking an address. He had no idea what house was Benjamin's.

As he got closer to the flock of kids, any pretense of a game dissolved, and they crowded around him, smiling shyly or grinning widely. A dozen hands pointed in answer to his question, and he squinted at the neat frame house on a slight rise from the street, several houses down. He thanked them and turned to go, but they crowded nearer, curious.

At the foot of the sidewalk, he faced a low picket fence. Too low-slung to provide an enclosure for any but the smallest animal, it appeared to be decorative. A neatly kept lawn separated the sidewalk from the house. Dotted with several small trees, the effect was spare, calm.

Not so the woman partially visible on the shaded front porch. Even from here, James could see the tension in her shoulders, and the way her arms crossed over her front, protectively. In one hand, she held a white tissue. He raised a hand to the gate as if to open it, and nodded to her. She made no move, either to welcome or discourage him. Slowly, he opened the gate.

Halfway across the lawn, she spoke over his head. "Go on with you now. Get about your business!" He heard the young protests behind him and the scampering of feet as his adolescent escort retreated to their play.

She stood up in the shade, watching him. Her face was unreadable. He realized suddenly what her last name was. Should he address her as Mrs. Pie?

Saving him the choice, the woman said, "What can we do for you, sir?" Her tone was neutral. Respectful, but not catering.

"Ma'am. I'm a friend of Benjamin's. You're his mother?"

If she was surprised, she didn't show it. "Do you know where he is?" She asked.

He felt the deflation. "No Ma'am. I was hoping to talk to him."

"He's not here right now." She made no move to say more. Then, when James was about to ask when he might be back, she said, "I don't know where he is right now."

Something in her voice made him pause. A slight break.

James nodded, as if she'd just said *come back in an hour.*

The woman took a small step forward. Her skin was shiny like Benjamin's, and her neck was long, emerging from her light collared summer dress. The dress itself was light blue, providing a pleasing foundation for her brilliant blue eyes.

James was surprised how young she looked. Her hair was tight and done up in a bun on the back of her skull. Her skin glowed, it seemed to him. He had assumed that Benjamin's mom would look more like... Nana.

The woman was twisting the hankie now in both hands, her arms straight down in front of her. "You say you're a friend of Benjamin's?"

"Yes. We met CeCe. My.. sister and I. Gwen. Out by the highway," he finished lamely. He had no idea how to get to where he or this woman needed him to go. She nodded, encouraging.

"So CeCe is our friend, and we've gone to church with her, and CeCe and Benjamin are friends," he finished lamely. She waited, clearly expecting more.

"I wanted to talk to Benjamin about something," he exhaled, coming full circle.

She didn't speak for a moment, but rather looked up, as if there was a sudden need to inspect the porch ceiling. When she looked at him again, her jaw was set. "Benjamin is the man of this house." She paused. "He often attends those who need help. At all hours. He doesn't always tell me where he's off to." She was speaking reasonably now, as if to a child concerning peeling a potato.

He nodded, and started to speak. "But..." she continued, "He's a good boy, and—" she bit her lip, her eyes straying again to the ceiling, "—I have a feeling."

She straightened, summoning some inner reserve, and clasped her hands, school-teacher fashion, behind her. "What is your name, if I may ask?"

James started at the change in topic. "I'm sorry. Matt. I'm Matt."

"Well, Matt. When is the last time you saw my son?"

"Last night." He thought to say more, and hesitated.

"My. And where did you see him, Matt?"

He felt himself squirming. It was hard for him to think so much about what he was saying. He was used to just speaking his mind.

"My sister and I are camped out on Cat Head Creek." This was clearly news to her, for she cocked her head slightly, as if to hear more clearly.

"Camping," she repeated, faintly.

"CeCe—and Benjamin—have come out to visit."

"More than once?" she pressed.

He nodded, feeling the earth widen under his shoes.

"Just what are they visiting for?" she asked. The last word she stretched into a roller coaster of tones.

He smiled, as if it were all very funny if you thought about it. "We don't really have much, and so CeCe was giving us food—rice and bread and corn—things like that."

The woman watched him, her gaze steady, lips thin.

"And some camping stuff. We really hadn't intended to camp. Or even to stay here in Georgia," he flailed. He started to recount how they'd traveled down from New York, after both their parents had passed. Benjamin's mother raised a dismissive hand. "So Benjamin came to y'all at night?"

James considered the question. "Sometimes. Not always. He and I were working on a dugout—it's this kind of boat."

The woman looked as if he'd just held up a dead rat. "A dugout. This was *Benjamin's* idea?"

"Oh no ma'am. It was something I wanted to do. But to tell you the truth, Benjamin seemed to know more about how it ought to be done. So he's been helping me."

Mrs. Pie looked at him for a long moment. "I'm completely forgetting my manners. Come up out the sun, and I'll fetch you lemonade."

She emerged from the house a minute later, carrying two glasses. She handed one to James, who was resting on a wooden chair. "No, don't get up. I'm sure you from the north, you probably not used to our weather quite yet."

Grateful, James took the glass and drank. It was delicious. He tried hard not to gulp.

Mrs. Pie seemed to have reached some decision. "I've not seen Benjamin since yesterday afternoon. That's unusual. He does come and go, but like I say, he is the man in this house, and I trust him."

"My sister is missing too." He swiveled at the noise she made. She was sitting bolt upright, eyes big as saucers.

"No, no. I don't mean—she went missing very early this morning, but Benjamin—I just thought he might've heard something."

She glared at him, but her eyes registered something more akin to fear. "Why you think that?"

"Truth was, I really thought CeCe might know something, but she's not home either. I know that CeCe and Benjamin are...friends too. So I was really hoping he might know where I can find her. CeCe."

Mrs. Pie sat back in her chair. James was sure that if it had been a rocker, it would be rocking furiously at this point.

"So your sister just went poof?" Mrs. Pie raised a hand in front of her, opening her fingers as if she were releasing a butterfly.

"Yes." He nodded, thinking just how apt that description was.

"Have you been over to the police office?" She asked casually, but again, James felt like he was about to fall into a large hole.

"Not yet," he replied, just as casually.

They traded a look laced with swirling meaning. *Nice try*, they both seemed to say to each other. He knew enough about Negroes here, or anywhere, to know that they'd sooner strike a bargain with Satan himself than to seek out the men in uniform for settling a grievance of any kind. For his part, not going to the police suggested that a lot of his story was fiction.

She seemed to reach another decision. "I went through his room this morning."

James stared out over the lawn, not daring to meet her eyes.

"I'm sure he didn't sleep here last night. So how late last night did you two work on this...?"

"Dugout," he filled in. "I'm not sure what time it was they left. Probably ten or so."

"He and CeCe?"

"Yea. He kind of...looks after people. I guess you know that. And he gets around the woods at night like he's got cat eyes." He glanced at her, and she was smiling slightly.

"Lots of us are *truly* scared of the dark," she said with a wistful grin. "Benjamin ain't never been. I guess that's good, all in all."

"Yes ma'am."

She took up the story thread. "So you saw him at ten last night and he seemed fine?"

James remembered the soot that had blanketed them both. "Yes, ma'am. He was fine."

"I pray to the Lord that he—and your sister—are still both fine.

Mmmmm…mmm."

James nodded, seeing Benjamin's features and expressions in this stranger-woman. He rose from his chair, and handed the glass to Mrs. Pie. "If I see Benjamin first, I'll tell him you're looking for him."

She rose, and walked him to the edge of the porch. "Likewise, Mr. Matt."

The ball game continued as James walked past the intent children. The kids didn't seem as interested in James on his departure. He shuffled slowly up the dusty lane, mulling over all that had happened since—was it only this morning? It now appeared that Benjamin and CeCe had both gone missing. Words spoken by Anne a week or so ago rang in his head: *I don't think you have any idea what or who you're dealing with.* But even if Roy Sampson were capable of harming their friends here, what was the point? And why had James been left alone?

He glanced up to the head of the road, where it joined the macadam. A car sat, pulled off the side, dusty and familiar. From where he was, James could see a man leaning against the car, legs crossed at the ankles.

The man appeared to be idling. Something was very familiar about him. He was white, but there was something else. Tall, thin. James stopped dead in the middle of the lane.

The man standing perhaps 200 feet away was Sam.

James stared, trying to assimilate this apparition from the Eastern Shore of Maryland, hundreds of miles north. He tried to conceive of how his father could be here, in this place. Waiting for him.

For what seemed like a long time, neither man moved. James couldn't see Sam's eyes under the brim of his felt hat, but he was sure his father was looking at him.

Finally, James crossed the remaining distance, squaring his shoulders. Whatever mad set of circumstances had brought Sam, he could just turn around and go back where he came from. James stopped a few feet from his father, his expression stony. Sam gave a slight nod.

His father finally broke the silence. "Awful hot down here. I'd forgotten."

James snorted. "You've been *here* before?" He gestured around him, wondering what anyone watching would think about these two white men at the head of Catpond Road.

Sam shook his head. "No, but I did take a turn on the shrimp boats out of Charleston a few years back. Gruesome work that."

James reflected briefly on the coincidence, but said, "Who told you I was here?"

Sam uncrossed his legs, and eased his hands into his own jeans pockets. "The Walkers."

James started. "Wha—? How did they know to call you?" He did a slow burn, replaying the time he'd just had with them, and them all along knowing—

"They didn't call me. I just showed up on their porch. Not more than 20 minutes ago."

James's brain reeled, not the first time this day.

"Wait a minute. You found *them*?"

"That's what I said. I explained who I was and why I was here, and they pointed me in the direction of Catpond Road. Is there really a cat pond, do you think?" His father glanced around, apparently done with his explaining.

"But how did you find the Walkers?"

Sam lifted his cap with one hand and ran his other hand through his thinning hair. "That part's not quite so simple. You want something to eat?"

James was about to protest, but thought for the first time that he'd not eaten a thing since yesterday. He wanted to say no, but his stomach was whispering *let's not be too hasty.*

A few minutes later, Sam and James were sitting in the shade of a large cedar tree in the nearby cemetery. Sam had produced several cold-cut sandwiches from a cooler in his back seat, as well as a jug of iced tea.

"Without the ice, I'm afraid. Hope you don't mind." James shook his head, his mouth stuffed with sandwich. His father laid a couple pickle slices between them on a paper plate.

After a few minutes, James wiped the back of his hand across his mouth. "So what are you doing here?"

Sam sat back against the trunk of the tree and sipped from a cup. "I guess we both have some explaining to do."

James didn't look at him. His insides were churning.

"I knew to contact churches, and right at the first one in town the minister remembered you. He was awful suspicious of me at first. Seems I wasn't the first to ask after you two there."

He paused and James nodded. That was pretty much how he'd figured it. He just had not expected anyone to realize which direction they'd headed so soon.

When James didn't speak, Sam continued. "I guess I convinced him I was your dad, because he finally let on as how you'd been guests of the Walkers for a Sunday dinner.

When James looked at him, brows arched, his father shrugged. "Small towns. Isn't it that way in Crane Ridge?"

James thought about it for a moment, and slowly nodded. Then he sat up, turning to Sam. "But how did you know to come here? To Darien? Did you check every church on the east coast?"

Sam set his cup down and pondered his response. "I'd like to think I would have, if it would have helped," he finally said. "But it turns out I'm not that good at finding people."

James knew his dad was talking about his search for David, and he sat, waiting.

"I'm here because somebody told me where to find you. And because you are not out of the woods yet. Not at all."

"What do you mean? Not out of the woods yet? I didn't bust into that store in town, but how do I prove I *didn't* do something?"

"Well, for the moment, that may be the least of your problems."

James ate a pickle, slowly. The light breeze lifted the longish thin grass around the headstones nearby. "What are you talking about?"

Sam turned to look at his son. "Unless I miss my guess, Anne is halfway back to Crane Ridge by now. Unless he wants to be here for the final scene, and has her stashed somewhere nearby."

James stared at his father, who continued calmly. "That little trick was orchestrated by the same man who wants to ensure *you never* come back."

James gaped. "Who? And how do you *know* all this?"

Sam studied his son for a long moment. "Let's just say it's someone who knows, who isn't as crazy as Roy Sampson."

James let it drop. "So he's here? Now? Was he?" James amended.

Sam shrugged. "I don't know. I didn't get the complete story from the Walkers. I thought it was most important to find you before…"

"Before what?"

"Before they do." Sam glanced around.

"What in the hell are you talking about?" James could feel his face flushing with anger. So far, his father hadn't made any sense, and his being here was making James feel pretty crowded. If there was information he had, so be it, but spit it out.

"Look," James said, breathing deeply. "Remember how you said you're not so good at finding people?"

Sam sat still, listening.

"Well, I'm not so good at running. It's just not my nature. The only time since this trouble started that I feel okay in my own skin is when I'm *not* running."

Sam gave a thin smile. "You're doing an awful lot of running for someone who doesn't like it." He held up a hand as James reddened. "Running works for awhile. But so does stopping and fighting. Wisdom knows when to do one, and not the other."

James stared out over the cemetery. "That supposed to be some nugget of fatherly advice?"

Sam laughed soft. "Fair enough. Let's just say I'm not in the business of dispensing advice. The best thinking I was ever capable of landed me in a mess of jackpots."

"You can say that again." In spite of himself, James smiled. "How is Nana? How's Dylan. Did you get my letter?"

"We did. I can't say about Nana for sure. Haven't seen her since Thursday evening. Your brother's been doing a lot of growing up in your short absence. But you can ask him yourself if you like. He's at the Walker's now."

James looked down between his feet. He felt the world spinning. Suddenly, it was simply too much to absorb. "He came with you?" He managed.

"Yes. We talked it over, and he wanted to. Your grandma thinks we're in Richmond counting service stations, or some such. We may make it there eventually."

"What did you bring him for?" James tried to make it sound offhand, but he strangled the last of the sentence.

His father answered off-handedly, "He wanted to help. We both want to, if we can."

James shook himself. "I appreciate it. Please tell him that. But seriously, If you just tell me what you know, you can head back where you came from."

His father looked at him and James could see the hurt, but he forced himself not to react. "Just tell me what you know. Please."

Sam reclined against the ancient cedar. "This might sound strange, but you probably know more than I do. All I have are the rough outlines of a plan. But I'm sure it's real. You," he looked intently at James, "have been living the plan. You just didn't know there was one. So what say we help each other?"

James nodded. "Okay. So what's the plan?"

His father sighed. "The first part's not complicated. Once they locate you two, take Anne back to Crane Ridge." He paused, and lifted a twig to his teeth. "I take it I got here too late to prevent that part."

James looked at him. "You were trying to keep her from being taken back?" Sam didn't answer. "But yes, she's gone as of this morning. Kidnapped."

Sam chewed the twig. "In answer to your question, I hadn't thought of it like that. Preventing something. I just thought you needed to know what the plan was, because there's more."

It was James's turn to wait. "The plan is not just to make sure Anne comes back, but to make sure that you *never* do."

They both sat in silence for several minutes. Finally James spoke. "If they were going to kill me…"

"We wouldn't be having this chat," Sam finished. "So no, I don't think that's what they have in mind."

"Well, what *do they* have in mind? And who are *they*, anyway?"

Sam examined the chewed end of the twig and tossed it away.

"As to the second part, besides his private investigator-friend, somehow Roy Sampson has managed to find someone from here to help him." He saw James mouth start to open. "And no, I don't know who it is. As to the first part, "I was hoping you could tell me. Besides your girlfriend vanishing, anything else odd going on?"

James gave a short laugh. "People are vanishing left and right," he said, remembering his visit with Benjamin's mother, and his trip to CeCe's. "People are vanishing…," he repeated softly.

"How's that?"

James looked at his father. "Yea, a couple of odd things…"

James filled his father in on events since Anne had disappeared. He started to explain about the name change too, but his father stopped him.

"I knew you were traveling as Gwen and Matt. Otherwise, the Walkers and I would have had an even more convoluted chat."

James's eyes widened. "How did you know?"

Sam spiraled a single finger, motioning for his son to continue the narrative. "That's not important right now. You were saying…"

"I can't be sure, but I think something's happened to Benjamin. I'm almost sure of it. Maybe CeCe too."

Sam sat back, gazing over the muted collection of headstones. He pursed his lips. "I don't know what that could have to do with making sure you don't come back. Maybe it's not connected at all. But it's a heck of a coincidence."

James rested his elbows on his knees, studying the problem. "What could Mr. Sampson do to make sure I don't come back?"

Sam shook his head slowly. "I hesitate to tell you this, but you need to know, if you don't realize it already. Roy Sampson isn't an evil man, but he's got it bad for you. Whether it's to protect his daughter, or because you made him look like a fool, it makes no difference. He thinks you're some kind of criminal, and he wants you to stay away from Anne."

James glanced at his father. "That supposed to scare me?"

Sam didn't speak for several beats. "It might help if you know who you're dealing with."

James snorted. "Are we talking now about Roy Sampson? Or about you?" Sam gazed back unflinching, but his eyes were filled with a deep sorrow. "Because with you, I have never known."

"Son-"

James rose to his feet. "You act like it was all your fault David disappeared. Big martyr. *'Feel for me, the ultimate screw-up!'*"

Sam's lower jaw opened in puzzlement. He started to speak, but James raised a hand. "We both know what really happened."

The perplexed expression spread on Sam's face. "I heard you tell it often enough," James continued. "*'James ran ahead. I chased after him.'*"

A dawning recognition lit Sam's eyes. "My God, son..."

James was backing up, fists clenched, face red. "It was my fault. You left because it was my fault David's gone."

Sam's face went slack, and he started to rise. "No. No. It wasn't that way."

Without warning, James charged, pushing Sam hard by the shoulders back onto the ground. In the distance, an older couple come to pay their respects to a loved one huddled together, peering at them.

"I probably killed him." James was weeping, hot angry tears now, and despite himself, his words were hiccoughing in his throat. He continued. "Do you know how many times I've tried to...tried to..."

Sam looked up at him. His eyes were red. "None of this was about anything you did, James. Not ever," he said, reaching out with one hand. "You were just a child." He dropped his hand as James turned his back, his fist pressed to his lips.

James said something into his balled fingers.

"Say it again, son. I didn't -"

James turned on him, spitting the words, his face a mask of pain. "I won't let it happen again!"

Sam stood warily, studying his son. He spoke slowly, choosing his words. "You've got to grab reality by the throat here, and you've got to do it now." He took a slow step toward his son, but James turned again, sitting heavy on a low headstone nearby.

Sam sighed, his eyes raised to the gnarled branches above him. "There'll be time to sort all this out later," he finally managed. "What's important now is for you to...breathe. Just breathe."

James's shoulders tightened, as if to ward off any more of Sam's words. But after a moment, his shoulders lifted, in a deep, lung-expanding breath. Sam waited several beats, and then spoke again.

"Let's assume Roy Sampson doesn't need to find you to carry out his plan." Sam said, bending to collect the trash from lunch.

James turned to look up. The change of subject took him by surprise, and they both moved tentatively closer, on safer ground. James gazed inward for a moment, struggling to recall something. "His plan is to make sure I stay away from Crane Ridge. And to make sure Anne doesn't leave?" With this last, he lifted a questioning gaze to Sam, like a student making a guess in class.

His father nodded. "I don't know how he ensures either, especially after that girl's of legal age. But I'm clear he'll do anything to keep you two apart. You need to be clear on that too."

James nodded slowly, wiping at his eyes with the front of his tee shirt. He sat back down heavily on the headstone.

Sam squatted in front of him, close but not touching him. He read the inscription of the headstone and smiled briefly. James noticed.

"What?"

Sam glanced down again, and read aloud:

> *Here lies Homer*
> *Killed by a Bee*
> *August 4, of '63*

Then his face took on a serious expression. "Anger," he paused, "does things to some men." He dropped his eyes to Homer's epitaph again. "Maybe to all men," he continued. "Roy Sampson is not rational. Heck, the truth is, Roy Sampson's not sane. Not right now. He's possessed by his anger. It runs his show right now, like jet fuel. When it will exhaust itself, I don't know. But I know the trouble he's gone to so far, and I'm afraid it's possible that your friends turning up missing may be connected somehow."

James picked up a clod of dry Georgia dirt next to the headstone base, and dropped it from one fist to the next, thinking. "If this is to try to scare me…"

"You need to *think*," Sam said sharply. "Use what you have," he said more gently.

"In case you hadn't noticed, I don't have much. Even my knife is gone. But I'll get what I need," he said quietly. "Right now, what I need most is nightfall."

Sam snorted. "Then what?" James remained silent. They both sat quiet for a time. Finally, Sam spoke again.

"I still can't worry out the business of Anne disappearing." He shook his head in confusion. "The way you describe it—is it possible she left with someone she knew?"

James tossed the small dirt clod, and considered. "Only Benjamin or CeCe. Besides, only they knew where the camp was."

Sam scratched the back of his neck, his face scrunched in thought. "What could force either one of them to spirit Anne away with you so close? Or force either of them to give up your location, come to it?"

James remembered his conversation with Benjamin's mother. He was brave, but he was only a boy, after all. CeCe too. Who would mean to harm them?

"Benjamin did have some trouble with a preacher here," James said slowly. Sam sat back on his haunches, silent, while James related the story of the incident in the woods with Preacher Waugh and Benjamin.

"Did you ever learn what this preacher was doing in your camp?" Sam asked.

James blushed. "I think it came to his attention that Anne and me weren't brother and sister," James answered. "I had kind of forgotten about it. You think there's a connection?"

Sam stared off into space for a minute. "I know this much. Roy Sampson found out pretty quick which way you'd headed."

James exhaled. "I see that now, but I don't see how. I thought we'd laid out a good false trail."

Sam smiled thinly. "Everybody thought you were headed to Cleveland. That is, until the good Father got a call about his car."

Sam related what had pointed Roy Sampson south. Several days after James and Anne had left the car, the mechanic at the garage had stumbled across a repair ticket wedged in the front seat, listing Father Mullenix and his phone number. The mechanic must've got to thinking there was a way to make more than the car was worth in parts by offering the car back to the priest. After, of course, the repair bill was settled.

"The man Father Mullenix spoke to described Anne to a tee. Seems like he took somewhat less notice of you." Sam grinned slightly. "He did remember you being a bit ornery."

Father Mullenix had called both Roy Sampson and Sam with the news. Unfortunately, he'd called Roy first. By the time Sam tried to contact Roy, Roy was no longer interested in maintaining the charade of trading information. It was only through a completely unexpected source that Sam had learned what Roy was planning.

"Roy sent a private investigator south to pick up the trail, starting with the garage. Someone with a reputation for playing fast and loose with the law, if he's paid. The mechanic remembered you two hitchhiking south. I guess the detective did what I would've done. He just headed down 301, showing your pictures in every gas station and coffee shop."

"And then he got lucky," James said quietly.

Sam nodded.

"Mr. Walker told me what his daughter said about the man in the store."

"So maybe that's why they came to the camp. Samuel told the preacher about us. But why would he care?"

"Maybe he objected to you two not being married, or pretending to be kin, or maybe Roy was offering cash for information leading." Sam shrugged. "Who knows? This preacher sounds like he and Roy Sampson could be brothers from the same nut house."

James grinned. It was hard to stay angry with this man who'd come so far to warn him.

"Thanks for making the trip down. I'm shoving off," James said, rising.

Sam gazed up at him resignedly. "Want to tell me what you have in mind?"

James looked around, squinting into the late-day sun. "I have to locate Benjamin and CeCe. Then I'll probably start heading back to Crane Ridge somehow."

Sam was already shaking his head. James thought he might be

upset that James hadn't asked for a ride back home. But when Sam spoke, it was with a different concern.

"There's something missing. I know Roy, and he's not going to let you waltz back into Crane Ridge. As long as you're there, you'll be a threat to him. As to the other, I think at least your legal troubles might be behind you." He related what Dylan had told him. Dylan wouldn't say where he'd gotten the information, but he thought it was sound.

James scuffed the red Georgia ground. "I can't stay here all day. I have to know what's going on."

Sam looked off for a moment. "Well, assume Roy is taking Anne home. Odds are, he won't trust anyone else to do that job. Put yourself in his position. We know he has at least one fella down here from Maryland working for him. Maybe more now. Plus, he has that preacher fellow who's pretty miffed at you. What's his play?"

At that moment, a car raced down Canal Road, and swung onto Old Cat Head Road in the direction of Catpond Lane. The car came abreast of Sam's Dodge on the street adjacent to the cemetery, and braked in a cloud of dust in front of the Dodge.

Sam rested a hand on James's arm, but James was already poised to charge the occupants. Before the car stopped completely, the driver's side door sprang open, and a head appeared over the hood. It was Mr. Walker. But James was staring at the occupant in the passenger seat. Dylan.

"They found Miss CeCe. She's at our home."

48 / It Just Sounded Like Inside

The two cars screeched to a stop in front of the Walker's graceful home. Sam moved quickly to accompany Mr. Walker up the steps to the door.

Dylan eased out of the door as James stepped up to greet him. "Hey," James said. Then, "What's the matter?"

Dylan raised a hand in greeting, but he was shaken by the scene he'd left in the house, when Mr. Walker had asked him to come along to locate his father.

"Your friend is pretty messed up. Upset, I mean," Dylan said.

A look passed over James's face. Gratitude? He lightly patted Dylan's shoulder as they fell in step behind the men.

In the living room, the girl was politely waving off Julie Rose's mother. "I'm okay, really." When she'd first arrived a half hour earlier, in the company of a Georgia State Trooper, she had seemed in a stupor, her eyes glazed, rubbing her wrists obsessively.

The officer had taken Mr. Walker aside in the parlor while Mrs. Walker whisked the strawberry-haired girl back to the kitchen, in the company of her daughter. Where Dylan had been the focus of this strange, warm family's attention a moment before, for the time being he was forgotten. He wandered into the hallway to give the two men a bit of privacy, and gazed up at the wall of photos. He heard snippets of the men's conversation, over the high-pitched exclamations of the woman and girls in the kitchen.

He gathered that the new arrival had been abducted the previous night, and held by people she did not know, before being released sometime early this morning. Mr. Walker and the state trooper stepped back out into the hall. Mr. Walker bid the trooper good day, and yes, he understood that someone else might be coming with additional questions, and yes, they would ensure that Cecelia would be closely watched here, until her father returned from his road trip. And yes, the Walkers would carry word to her grandparents immediately.

As soon as the front door closed, Mr. Walker whirled and dashed down the hall, brushing past Dylan. "Pardon me, my boy. With you again in a moment."

He began to speak with some urgency to the girl who'd just arrived. She was looking past him at Dylan. He looked back, not knowing what to say or do.

Ignoring Mr. Walker, she spoke directly to Dylan. "Are you related to James?" The girl spoke distinctly, as if shaking herself from a fog.

"He's my brother." Dylan stepped into the kitchen, smiling tentatively, but for some reason, she appeared suddenly alarmed.

"I need to see him." Her voice was rising and Dylan started to mention Sam looking, but the girl CeCe turned to Mrs. Walker, clutching her blouse sleeve. "Is he here? I really need to talk to him. Or Anne." Suddenly, she looked stricken, and dropped her head into her hand for a moment. Raising it again, she said, "I mean Matt or Gwendolyn."

Julie Rose gave her a small smile. "It's all right. James told us everything. He was here earlier. But Anne is missing."

CeCe gulped water from a glass Mrs. Walker offered. "Easy, lass," Mrs. Walker clucked, working the glass gently from CeCe's grip.

CeCe nodded her thanks, and then looked back to Julie Rose. "Anne is missing? When? We just visited last night." A confused look crossed her face again. "I think it was last night. Gosh. It *is* Saturday, right?"

Julie Rose shook her head vigorously. "Yes, Saturday."

"But where has James gone?"

Julie Rose rested a hand on CeCe's. "He's gone to Benjamin's, because you weren't home. He hoped you might know where Anne is."

Mr. Walker turned to look at Dylan. "Your father. Let's see if we can find him and bring him back here. Mother, we shouldn't be more than a few minutes."

Dylan followed Mr. Walker back down the hall. At the front door, Mr. Walker turned back. "Julie Rose!"

His daughter leaned out of the kitchen. "Yes, father."

"Lock the house behind us. All doors and windows. And open only for us or someone in uniform."

Now, as James entered the parlor with him, his brother stepped across the room and sat down next to CeCe. She smiled at him and started to speak. Behind him, she saw Sam, and glanced at him, clearly troubled.

"It's alright, CeCe. This is Sam. *My* father."

At these words, she looked relieved, but still confused. No one spoke for a moment, and then Sam cleared his throat.

"It is a pleasure to meet you, miss. I think everyone is eager to hear where you've been. The sooner the better, I'm afraid."

CeCe looked from Sam to James.

"You first," he said.

CeCe seemed to be gathering herself. "It is crazy, really. I was home asleep after Benjamin and I left you last night," she said to James. She paused.

"Go on," he said.

"Somebody—maybe more than one person—jumped onto my bed, and wrapped my pillow around my head, so I couldn't scream. I think it must have been more than one person, because my head was loose at first, and I banged it into someone, and they swore."

She sat, thinking. "I think that was when they put a sack over my head. My own pillowcase. And they wrapped me in my bed sheet."

James sucked in his breath. "You have no idea who it was?"

CeCe was shaking her head. "I couldn't see a thing, and I was sound asleep when they first attacked me. It was very dark. They just more or less rolled me up, after they pinned me with my face in the pillow, and tied my hands at my back."

"What happened then?" James asked, trying to sound patient.

She thought for a moment. "They picked me up. Yes, there must have been two, at least. They carried me feet first, like a battering ram." She smiled thinly, rubbing the side of her skull. "Even at that, they managed to smack my head somewhere."

Mrs. Walker said, "You poor, poor girl. What an awful thing!"

CeCe looked over at James, an enigmatic grin on her face. "You know the funny thing? At first, I thought it might be you and Benjamin."

James blinked.

"I know it sounds silly now, but at first they seemed like they were trying hard not to hurt me, or even scare me overmuch."

The group around her nodded.

"You said they carried you," Sam prompted. "To where?"

She dropped her eyes. "They put me in a car. In the back. On the floor." She looked up at James. "That's when I stopped thinking it was y'all."

"Could you tell how far they drove you?" Sam asked quietly.

"No. But there were a lot of turns."

Mr. Walker spoke for the first time since they'd returned: "Could be they were driving in circles to confuse you." Dylan noticed Sam nodding.

"I don't know how long it was. Maybe 30 minutes or so. Then they stopped and carried me out of the car, into a room."

Mr. Walker: "How could you tell you were in a room?"

CeCe: "It just sounded like inside."

Sam and Mr. Walker nodded again. "Go on," Sam said.

CeCe frowned. "I was so uncomfortable, but I couldn't talk. But after a while, someone lifted the hood enough to loosen the thing in my mouth. But they wouldn't take it off. I kept asking and asking what's going on, who are they, where am I, but they wouldn't say anything. But I knew someone was there the whole time. I could hear them breathing. Quick."

"They never spoke?" James asked.

CeCe nodded. Then, "No. Wait. Somebody said for me not to worry. They would let me go in the morning." She blushed crimson. "When they said that, all I could think was how bad I had to pee. But I wasn't about to tell them that."

There was an awkward silence. "We understand, dear," said Mrs. Walker.

"Nothing else?" Sam asked.

"Well, it sounded like somebody trying to sound different. The voice was deeper, like they were play-acting. But I couldn't tell who it was anyway. And cars. I heard cars leave, and once a car came. Might have been the same car coming and going for some reason. But no cars just driving by, so I don't think we were anywhere near a public road.

"Smells?" Sam asked.

CeCe thought for a moment. "Like a barn. Straw, but not a stable. A shed, maybe."

"Anything else you remember?" Asked James.

CeCe started. "Yes! I remember I thought once that they'd kidnapped the wrong girl, because a door opened, and there was this shuffling, like several men were entering. But nobody said anything."

"And?" Sam said, slowly. "You thought they made a mistake?"

"Yes, because they undid the hood again, and lifted it up, and shined a light in my face. One of them gasped, sounding all surprised." At this revelation, again she looked troubled, almost about to cry.

Julie Rose leaned toward her friend, taking her hand. "What, CeCe. What is it?"

CeCe looked up, first at Julie Rose, then at James.

"I remember thinking it was Benjamin. That's crazy, isn't it?"

Then her eyes widened.

"Where is Benjamin? Did you find him?" CeCe asked James. She sounded like she was on the edge of hysteria.

James shook his head. "His mother hasn't seen him since before you and he came out to the camp last night." He explained the events of the day, beginning with Anne's disappearance at camp this morning. Dylan stood at the outer edge of the group, listening in amazement to his brother's story. James ended with running into their father, and coming back here. There was a long silence.

Dylan had no idea what any of it meant, and wondered about this guy who was the center of discussion at the moment. He wished he and Sam could take a walk so he could ask questions. But it was clear he was not the only person confused at what was happening.

His father broke the quiet. "You have been through a remarkable ordeal," he said in his calming tone. "Just how did you get away?"

"Just about the time I fell asleep again—" She must have seen the look of disbelief on James's face, for she continued "—I was exhausted! It was a very long night!" Mrs. Walker rushed to soothe her, giving James a warning glance.

"Anyway," she went on, arching an eyebrow at James, "They picked me up again, and carried me back out to a car. Back on the floor. Another long drive, and then the car stopped. They pulled me out and lay me on the ground. Oh. Before they pulled me out, they tied a piece of rope on the outside of the hood, around my head, and ran it across my mouth." She mimed the gag, with her lips parted and pulled back in a rictus grin. "They knotted it in back."

"Then they pulled me out, and laid me down on the ground. Somebody unrolled the blanket I was in far enough to get to my wrists, and they cut the rope. Then the car drove off."

"Where were you, when you got untangled?" Asked Sam.

"I didn't know at first. Turns out, I was in the alley right down from the police station. I've been at the station since I was dumped. Oh, and that officer took me by my house too. Asked why I don't lock the doors at night." CeCe grinned at Julie Rose and Mrs. Walker, who smiled pleasantly back.

Everyone jumped, startled, at a sharp rap on the front door. Dylan was closest, but stepped aside for Mr. Walker, who strode grim-faced to the door and eased the curtains aside on the panes that bordered the door. He stared out for several moments, and then dropped the curtain back. He stood perfectly still for a moment or two. Then he unlocked the door, and swung it slowly open.

A Negro woman was standing on the porch. She kept glancing about her, as if she half-expected to be attacked by a dog leaping from nowhere.

She kept looking about even as she nodded absently to Mr. Walker. "Missus Minnie Pie sent me. Her son is Benjamin. He's in the clinic."

Besides Mr. Walker, only Dylan was in earshot of the woman, though Mrs. Walker rose to come see who it was at the door. Apparently, Mr. Walker had no idea what the woman was describing, for she said it again.

"The clinic. Over near the cemetery. Mrs. Proctor's front room."

"Please won't you come in?" Mrs. Walker said, finessing Mr. Walker back down the hallway.

The woman shook her head graciously, but with the kind of quick smile that said she doubted the invitation. "No, thank you ma'am. I should get back to be with the family. Missus Pie says I should go first to CeCe's house, and if nobody home come here. Missus Pie said to tell *Matt* to come if he can."

At the mention of the name, Mr. Walker took a step back further, to gaze into the parlor. He gave James a queer look, and James rose to his feet.

"She's looking for Matt," he said to James.

He colored slightly. "I'm Matt," he said to the woman.

Mrs. Walker repeated what the woman at the door had said.

"Is this Benjamin all right?" asked Mr. Walker.

The colored woman looked at him, askance. "My land no. He's been hurt bad. Stabbed."

49 / Walk With Me, Matt

Sam drove. Despite Dylan's protests, he was left behind again, with Mrs. Walker and Julie Rose. CeCe sat in front, giving Sam directions. In the back seat, Mr. Walker and a subdued James.

Sam responded to CeCe's curt directions. *Left at the corner. Just here around the cemetery. Slip on by this road*—James recognized Catpond, and the corner of the cemetery where Sam and he had been such a short time ago.

"Pull in here behind this station wagon. It's that small house with the calico cat on the front stoop." Sam glanced at CeCe for assurance, and slowed the Dodge to the side of the dusty lane. She nodded.

"I don't see a sign," he said slowly.

"There's never been one that I know of," Mr. Walker said from the back.

CeCe was opening the door before Sam had cut the engine. "This is where the colored go for doctor visits."

"But she said Benjamin's been stabbed," James blurted, grasping the seatback in front of him. Mr. Walker laid a hand on his arm.

"Perhaps your father and I should see what's afoot here first," he said, but all three of the car's occupants were looking on as CeCe hurried to the door of the small home and knocked on the screen. None of them moved as CeCe looked back at them to smile weakly, then to rise on tiptoes, covering her eyes, to peer through the ancient screen door. She started to knock again when it swung open.

"Needs a coat of paint," Sam said absently.

Next to James, Mr. Walker nodded. James gaped inanely at the weathered siding of the small house. It was barely more than a shack, and he wondered how it could have more than two rooms. It was hard to tell if the exterior had ever encountered paint.

The screen door swung out, and CeCe spoke earnestly to someone. She started to step in, looked up, and paused before nodding. The door closed slowly. CeCe looked back at the car. At James, he thought.

When it opened again, CeCe stepped back. A woman stepped out, and spoke to her. James immediately recognized Benjamin's mother. As they spoke, CeCe looked back at him, and then nodded quickly. Mrs. Pie turned, and looked at him too.

"Hold on," James addressed the other occupants of the car, and he eased out, gently closing the door. In the distance, he could see the backs of the houses facing Catpond Road. But the air was strangely quiet. No one playing in the middle of the day.

He moved toward the house. Mrs. Pie spoke to CeCe once more, briefly, and CeCe opened the screen and stepped inside. James made to step up on the small stoop, but Mrs. Pie stopped him with a hand.

"Walk with me, Matt."

They both turned, and continued down the road, which James saw ran parallel to Cat Head Creek as it meandered toward Darien proper.

"How's Benjamin?" James asked. He had been trying without success to interpret the set of her chin. She looked grim, but there was something else too.

She was looking ahead, out over the flatland beyond the creek. "You said it was called a dugout?"

It took James a second to understand what she'd said. "A dugout, yes. Benjamin was helping me to make it."

"And the last time you saw him was last evening, around nine or so? When he was leaving with Miss CeCe." She still gazed straight ahead.

"Yes, ma'am. But what—"

She stopped, and looked up at him. "So does that mean you have no idea how it is that my Benjamin ended up floating with the incomin' tide up Cat Head Creek, lashed to a homemade canoe?"

James stared at her, gulping like a fish. "Lashed?"

"Lashed," she said a little impatiently, her eyes fixed on his. "Tied."

It was clear to James that Mrs. Pie was not joking, but she was clearly talking craziness. Benjamin and he had hidden the dugout south from the new camp just last night. No one else even knew—

"It's impossible," he said.

She finally released her gaze, and pointed out over the field on the far side of the road. At the edge, where the bank dropped down to the creek, a stubby log with a blackened tip canted on the edge.

It was the dugout.

He blinked. It was still there.

Uncomprehending, he looked back at her. Mrs. Pie's expression had imperceptibly altered. She had tilted her head slightly, as if puzzling where they'd met.

"Can I see him?" he asked.

She regarded him for a moment, and there was something akin to a twinkle in her eye.

"I believe you should," she said finally.

As they walked back to the clinic, James noticed Sam and Mr. Walker, talking quietly outside the car.

Mrs. Pie smiled briefly at Mr. Walker and nodded at Sam.

"Um, this is my father," James said. When Mrs. Pie turned at this news, her entire upper body swiveled to study James. She was clearly waiting for more. "Oh. And my real name is James, not Matt."

Easing into the screen door behind Mrs. Pie, James found himself in a small front room. A woman he'd never seen before was scrubbing her hands in a sink of sudsy water. A hall led back to a set of doors. The ones to the left and right were closed. He guessed bathroom and closet. The one at the end of the short hall was open, and a small boy in cotton shorts smiled at him from the floor. He was stacking blocks.

To his left, a cot below an open window was occupied. James nodded, too stunned to speak. Benjamin lay on the cot, bare-chested. A rough woolen blanket covered his legs. His middle was wrapped in a huge bandage that cloaked over his shoulder and down across his chest like a sash three sizes too small.

He had been crying, and James wanted to look at anything but the swollen red eyes of his friend. But when he saw James, Benjamin attempted to rise. CeCe pressed his one bare shoulder, coaxing him back down, shushing him.

"It's my fault! I was so stupid. I couldn't think fast enough—"

James stared at Benjamin. "How—"

CeCe glanced back at James, and her look slowed him. He felt awkward, standing so close to the cot. He looked for a place to sit. Over the back of the closest chair, he recognized Benjamin's flannel shirt, and the boy's overalls.

Mrs. Pie stepped up next to him. "Let me get those things. They're soaked with blood." He watched as she lifted them and saw what he hadn't noticed before. Dark brown stains splotched the garments.

He eased into the chair and pulled up almost touching CeCe's knees with his. "What happened?"

James listened dumbstruck as Benjamin recounted the events of the previous night. CeCe evidently had heard some of it before he'd come in. James also listened to CeCe fill Benjamin in on what had happened to her. The two stories had started out eerily similar.

Benjamin had walked CeCe to her door and started home. It was perhaps ten o'clock or so. Down the street from CeCe's, a car had slowly come up behind him, and then alongside of him as he walked down Cemetery Mill Road. A man he'd never seen leaned across the front seat, and asked something Benjamin couldn't quite catch. It was a well-dressed white man, and Benjamin assumed he was seeking directions. Benjamin leaned down to find himself looking at the barrel of a pistol.

The man spoke very calmly, almost friendly, and told Benjamin to open the door and get in. As soon as Benjamin slid in, and closed the door at the man's instruction, someone from the back seat, who Benjamin had not seen, covered Benjamin's head with a hood. The driver drove just a short way, before pulling over to the side of the road. He'd had Benjamin turn to face the door, and put his hands behind his back.

The man had then tied Benjamin's wrists. He also lifted the hood just high enough to put a gag on the boy.

Then the man had gotten out, and come around to the passenger side. He'd helped Benjamin to his feet, outside the car. Immediately, he'd checked the rope binding the boy, then moved him to the back door, and opened it. Someone in the back had guided Benjamin to his stomach on the floor, and then the car was moving again.

He didn't know how far they'd driven, and all CeCe and Benjamin could agree on was that they might've been taken to the same place. The manner of the gags and the hoods had similarities as well. But Benjamin was in the car for several hours, guarded by someone whose foot rested on his back.

At one point, the polite man—the only one he'd actually seen— returned from somewhere and replaced the other man in the back seat. He explained what was going to happen.

The man knew that Benjamin and CeCe were friends, and that the two of them had befriended a couple, Anne and James, on the run from Maryland. The man did not care what happened to the boy, and wasn't interested in harming James. But the girl was underage, and her father had hired him to bring the girl home.

To make sure that Benjamin would help him, he was holding CeCe in another location. Nothing would happen to her, as long as Benjamin helped him to separate Anne and James.

"But how?" James asked.

"Me first," CeCe nudged him. She turned to Benjamin. "Why did you believe the man?"

Benjamin let out with a fresh burst of sobbing. "They took me to see you, where they was holding you. I believed them all the way to Jesus when they said they would hurt you if I made them."

CeCe soothed him. "You did what you had to do, Benjamin. You had no choice."

"But what did you *do*?" James tried to sound calm as well, but most of the pieces were already fitting into place.

"They took me to a boat. I'm not sure where it was kept. I was blindfolded, but I could tell it was deep night. All the crickets asleep, no breeze anywhere."

"I could tell we was traveling up river. I wasn't sure which river, but it felt like Cat Head Creek, from the echo of the motor on the riverbank. But I wasn't positive."

Benjamin looked around, and CeCe handed him a glass of water, with a straw. He drew deeply, and then sighed. "The boat stopped, and guess where we was?"

"Our new camp," James said immediately.

Benjamin dropped his eyes. "No. Not then. We were at your *old* camp."

Benjamin sniffled. "He wanted me to tell him where your new camp was. I couldn't think of a lie. All I could think about was you lying up there a prisoner." He looked in the general direction of CeCe, and began sobbing.

"Benjamin is so sorry. I'm just not smart. I couldn't think."

James moved a hand out to lay it on Benjamin's knee. "Don't sweat it. Nobody else would know what to do if it was them either."

Benjamin continued to sob, but slower, as if he was nearly spent. "I showed him. I would have done anything not to. If he had just come for me I never would have give you up."

James sat back, still confused. "So how did it go? Anne literally disappeared."

Benjamin looked ill. "He asked me how we signaled you when we came to visit. I got confused, and slipped up about the trip wire. Then he showed me how to start the motor, and steer the boat. Then he had me to row up near the new camp. It was dark as pitch, but I knew where we were. We sat across the river for awhile, him asking all kinds of questions about the camp, and the tent, and the tripwire."

Benjamin looked at James, pleading. "He promised that Anne wouldn't get hurt, or her father wouldn't pay him a dime for his trouble. And CeCe wouldn't get hurt, if I just did what he said."

"Who tripped the wire?" James asked.

Benjamin looked relieved to focus on the details of the raid. "He had me put in upriver from the camp, and he got out. He said to ease the boat in where y'all went fishing, up under that big rock overhang. He said when I heard a pig frog twice, I should call quiet to Anne. When she comes, I should tell her that you and me cooked up a surprise for her, and hop in the boat, and I will take her to see it, where you waiting."

James stared at the boy. "A pig frog."

CeCe said impatiently, "Like a bull frog, but it sounds like a hog gruntin'."

James and CeCe both turned back to Benjamin. He sat, seeming lost in his memories of the event. Just as James was about to ask him to continue, Benjamin looked from one to the other of them. "Does any of that scheme sound like it stood the least likeliest chance of working to y'all?" The boy was near tears, but James had an insane urge to laugh.

James gazed at his friend. "Well, *did* it?" he asked.

Benjamin was nodding philosophically. "Like it was destined. I kept trying to pray. But I didn't know what to pray for specific. So I just prayed for help, and please don't let nobody get hurt."

James could feel the expectation in the room.

"I hear the pig frog. And again. I call out soft, 'Hey Anne!' First nothing, then she comes edging over the lip of the bank, holding your knife." Benjamin shook his head.

"I motion for her to come down, all the time so scared she's gonna call out for you. I'm knowing I can't hide my guiltiness, she barefoot and just woke up. But I just keep talking like it's a fine morning and ain't this a big surprise she's gonna love, and ain't it just about the most excitement around here. And me all the time whispering thinking that man is laying for you, and maybe he was lying about that part too, not meaning you any harm."

"Where did you take Anne?" James asked.

Benjamin looked stricken again, but he gazed straight ahead. James glanced to the foot of the bed. He hadn't realized Mrs. Pie had pulled up a chair to rest a hand on her son's foot. James didn't know how long she'd been sitting there. But Benjamin seemed to draw some strength from fixing his eyes on his mother's. The look that passed between them was of a trust James could only dimly imagine. She patted his foot again, with a touching gentleness.

Benjamin inhaled deeply. "I rowed for a minute or two, then started up the motor, just like he showed me. ' Is this your boat?' Anne asked me. I pretended I couldn't hear over the motor, but I just couldn't look at her. She asked me why we were crossing the creek, heading up the Altamaha Branch. I said it was part of the surprise. We traveled maybe a half mile up the branch. Just before I pulled up to the ramp runnin' down through the cat tails, out on the Butler plantation, she asked me to take her back. That's when her pa stepped out of the reeds, and grabbed the rope on the front of the boat."

A light knock at the door and the woman-doctor glided quickly to open it. She spoke to someone outside.

"Gosh where are my manners," Mrs. Pie suddenly exclaimed. "James. That is your name now for the rest of the day?" Her eyes twinkled. Then she nodded to the woman by the door.

"This is Mrs. Mabel Chesley. She is our guardian angel—our Florence Nightingale—here in Darien. Mrs. Chesley, this is James." Greetings were exchanged. He noticed Mrs. Pie had slid her chair closer to take Benjamin's hand in hers.

Then Mrs. Chesley spoke. "It's Mr. Walker outside. He's asking after the boy, and says his wife will be crazy if she don't hear from him soon. He's with that other gentleman."

Benjamin stirred. "Other who?"

James spoke quietly. "It's my dad." At this, Benjamin looked more alarmed, and tried to sit up. "It's okay. He wants to help." Benjamin sat back, wincing in pain. James turned to Mrs. Pie.

"Can I have my father meet Benjamin? Just for a minute?"

Mrs. Pie thought for a moment, studying James. Finally, she nodded *yes.*

Mrs. Chesley held the screen wide, and in slipped Sam and Mr. Walker. James watched his father take in the strange scene. He introduced himself to Mrs. Pie and Mrs. Chesley. He nodded to CeCe, and James slid his chair back as best he could in the cramped space.

His father bent down, almost to eye level with Benjamin, and spoke softly. "Sam Paxton. Pleased to make your acquaintance. How're you feeling?"

Benjamin and he talked for a moment, as Mrs. Chesley filled in Mr. Walker, in a businesslike tone. She was explaining that she had checked the bandages over the entry points of two stab wounds, one high on Benjamin's back just behind the shoulder blade, and one on the same side of his body, just below the ribs. He also had a bump big as a hen's egg on the crown of his head, but it hadn't broken the skin, so he would be woozy for a day or two.

Sam turned from Benjamin. "You sure do fine work on your clients," he said respectfully, looking back at the boy.

Mr. Walker chimed in. "Julie Rose has been a patient of the Widow Chesley on occasion. Savannah is too far sometimes."

"Me too," CeCe spoke. "Remember that hive of bees I intruded on?"

Mrs. Chesley blushed, poking her glasses back up on her nose. "I do what I can." Then she looked down at Benjamin, shaking her head slowly, and her expression softened. "But I didn't bandage that boy."

Mrs. Pie had been speaking to Benjamin, but now she too paused. Sam looked at her, and she nodded too, her face set in an almost reverent look.

"That's how we found him, Mr. Paxton. Lashed to your son's dugout. Bandaged just like you see him. Floating on the current just like Moses, right beyond the field outside that door."

Sam looked back at Benjamin, but now he examined the bandages. "Poultice direct to the wound?" he asked the room.

Mrs. Chesley spoke up. "Neat as you please. Dressed out with pepper direct on the wounds. Then a poultice, charcoal. Then the wrapping."

"And the wrapping?" Sam asked.

"It's Benjamin's own tee shirt, cut into strips. The poultice was a sleeve of his red flannel shirt, where it wasn't blood-soaked," said Mrs. Pie.

"Where did the charcoal come from?" Asked Sam.

"The dugout," said James, promptly.

Sam raised his hands as if he were being robbed. "Hold on just a second. I know I'm Johnny-come-lately here, but—" He looked over at Mr. Walker. "Are you as lost as I am?"

Mr. Walker scratched the back of his head. "More so, if that's possible."

James quickly filled in the two men on what Benjamin had related. CeCe interrupted occasionally to add pieces from her own adventure the previous night. Sam listened without interruption. But when they were done, he was chewing his lower lip, frowning.

"Benjamin, who stabbed you?"

Benjamin shrugged. "Honest, I don't remember being stabbed." While those in the steamy room listened quietly, he related how Anne's father had instructed him to return to pick up the man he'd left on the shore, at the new camp. Anne had been hysterical, but a man with her father had led her away by the arm, while the snarling parent had issued his last instructions.

Anne's father said as soon as the other man was returned to the ramp where they stood, CeCe would be released safely, and Benjamin was to tell James never to come back to Crane Ridge. He had motioned for Benjamin to get back up river, and had turned on his heel to deal with his daughter.

As Benjamin slowly motored the skiff back up the river, he glanced down in the bottom of the boat. There lay James's knife, forgotten by Anne.

He picked it up, and gripped it in his free hand. As he cruised up to the new camp, the man stepped down to the bank, waving slowly. He leaned down as Benjamin eased the boat into the narrow shelf of a shore.

"Say, what's the knife for?" The man had asked, guarded.

Benjamin had looked down, remembering, and explained the knife belonged to James, but Anne had brought it with her. "Toss it," the man said, and Benjamin had flipped it up on the bank.

"Her father has her back then?" Benjamin had nodded.

The man stepped aside as Benjamin cut the motor and stepped forward over the bench amidships. He even gave Benjamin a hand up, and Benjamin stepped clear, and clambered up the short bank. Then everything had gone black.

The small room was completely silent, except for Benjamin's ragged breathing. Finally, the widow spoke.

"Why does a person knock a boy out, stab him, and then tend to all his wounds, and send him floatin' into town, where he's sure to be found, and to tell the story?"

James glanced at Mrs. Pie. He could see that her only care right now was that her son was alive and safe.

Mr. Walker looked at the ceiling, thinking, then lowered his head, shaking it. "Damnedest thing—" He raised his eyes. "Please excuse me, ladies and children."

CeCe sighed, looking at Benjamin. "But Mr. Walker's right. It doesn't make any sense at all!"

James eased his chair back. "Well, what's sure is that Anne is with her dad, and I have to find them."

He was stayed by his father's hand on his arm. "There is another possibility," he said slowly. He had everyone's attention. "What do you remember next, after getting banged on the head?"

Benjamin thought carefully. "Just being carried up from the river, and my back burning. They were as careful as they could be—"

"Maybe there were two different people," said Sam.

Everyone stared at him again. "What do you mean, sir?" asked CeCe.

Sam looked out the window, down toward the river, for a minute. "Maybe one fellow knocked the boy out, and stabbed him, leaving him to bleed out."

"With my knife!" cried James. He looked stricken.

"Hold on. Maybe so. We don't know," said Sam.

"But what's the rest of it?" asked Mrs. Chesley.

"And why stab Benjamin? He didn't know these men anyway," sputtered Mr. Walker. "And forgive me for saying so, but these men are white."

The reality hung in the air, in the center of the room. The stabbing seemed so superfluous. "I mean, why complicate what they'd done up to then?" Mr. Walker finished.

"The plan." said Sam quietly. James stared at his father.

"What plan?": CeCe.

"The plan," James repeated slowly. He turned to Benjamin. "Taking Anne was only half of it." He looked at his father for confirmation, and Sam slowly nodded. James spoke, almost to himself. "They also had to make sure I never came back to Crane Ridge."

Benjamin looked tired, and confused. "How could they do that?"

Mrs. Pie spoke, for the first time in several minutes. "Make it look like James here," she paused, glancing at James, "stabbed you and left you for dead."

Sam nodded. "Not what you'd call elegant, but an opportunity presented itself, and Roy Sampson's hired muscle freelanced a little."

"What's one dead Negro boy, to protect a whi—" Mrs. Pie pressed her fist into her lips, shaking. Sam looked at her with understanding.

"But then who—" The Widow Chesley stepped over behind CeCe, staring at the bandaging on Benjamin, willing it to give up its secret.

"No one else knew where you were," CeCe said. "And the nursing, had to be someone knew herbs, and field dressing. And who else knew about the dugout?" Her words faded to a whisper. James sensed CeCe coming to the same thought he was having. He looked at Benjamin, who nodded a little.

James sat back, considering this development on his most recent plan to chase Roy Sampson up the coast. But Sam slapped his knees, and stood abruptly.

He looked around the cramped room. "If we have it right, this boy is in real danger."

Benjamin looked up at him. "Who want to hurt me *more*?"

Sam studied him with soft eyes. "It's a safe bet at least one person out there thinks you're dead. My guess is he was improvising on the spot. Even Roy Sampson isn't the murdering kind. But this man he sent down here was hired because he's ruthless." He gave Mrs. Pie a thin smile. "...And because he gets the job done. My guess is he's going to be none too happy when he learns news of your death was premature." He winked at Benjamin.

Without a word, Mrs. Chesley stepped out the screen door. She returned several minutes later, as the rest were discussing what to do next.

"The men are all about the house. No one will get near here before Benjamin is fit to be moved someplace safe." She fixed her only current patient with a steady stare. "Sunset should be ample time," she said.

50 / Slight Change of Plans

"I still don't see why we don't go to the police," Dylan said, as the boat edged upstream out of Darien, up Cat Head Creek. He spoke low, and the quiet black man standing at the controls appeared not to have heard.

James, Sam, and Dylan sat on benches at the back of the workboat, so close their knees touched. Dylan looked out at the small wake spreading behind them on the smooth surface of the creek. The odor of sea and catch was tangy, so strong it played at his nostrils.

"They don't trust police very much," James said softly to his younger brother. Sam too nodded.

"How much stuff do you have up at camp?" Sam asked.

James shrugged. "We carried it in about a trip-and-a-half," he said as the boat eased past the field, beyond which lay the cemetery, and the clinic, and his friend Benjamin.

"How far to your camp?" asked Dylan.

"We had two camps on the river here. We had to move because of some trouble about a week ago. I'll point the first out going past," James said. After a while, James spoke again. "I recognize that sunken tree. That was the first camp," he pointed, standing.

After they'd assured themselves Benjamin was safe for the time being, Mr. Walker had spoken briefly to Mrs. Chesley. Turns out Lucas Smallwood had injured his back and wasn't doing his usual runs out into the Gulf Stream for shrimp this week.

He had his own boat, small enough for eel and shad fishing on the Altamaha and Butler Rivers and Cat Head Creek. The plaque behind the captain's bench read Whaler 16 Eastport.

James pointed up the bank. "Just this side of the big oak," he said to Sam. "We had our camp. That's where Benjamin was attacked the first time."

Dylan stared at the bank, his face expressionless. He looked back at James. "You were living there since you left Crane Ridge?"

James shook his head, and related briefly the time from leaving Crane Ridge until his arrival in Darien.

"Lois Mast saw you the morning you left." Dylan had to repeat it over the low churning of the boat's propeller. James looked startled, but just nodded.

"She's an early riser summers," Dylan spoke louder. James nodded again.

Off the starboard side now, they stared down the tributary that led to the ramp that Anne had traveled with Benjamin. It seemed weeks ago. Lucas suddenly turned and bent, lifting several crab nets that had been lying on the deck floor and handing them to the three passengers.

"Fishin's been poor, if y'all are asked," Lucas said quietly, then stood and turned back to the wheel. The three in the stern looked at each other mystified. Dylan craned his head out and saw a similar workboat approaching from up river, on their side. In front stood a police officer.

"Oh no," said James. Dylan turned to see him ducking low, his face averted from the oncoming boat. Lucas raised a hand in greeting.

"Afternoon, Tom," he said to the driver of the other boat.

"Catching anything?" was the reply. A portly, dungareed angler came into view. "Fishing's slow," Sam said, standing in the stern of the boat. Did he sense something amiss, James wondered?

"Officer. What brings you out on the Cat Head on such a hot day?" Lucas drawled, idling back the throttle. The two boats sloshed to a stop, slowly easing by each other.

"Afternoon. Damndest thing—oops sorry." The officer colored.

"No problem, officer. He's heard worse from me on occasion," Sam replied.

"Anyway—dispatch gets a call. Says we'll find a dead colored boy, with a knife in his back, up river here in a camp."

James half-turned. Dylan could see he was trying to hide his face.

"Caller said a white boy did it. Some kind of fight."

"Hmmm," Sam responded, nodding. "How would somebody know a thing like that?"

The officer grunted. "Guess we'll never know. Caller hung up without saying who he was."

"Couldn't find the camp?" Sam asked, nonchalantly.

"Couldn't find the body," the officer said. "There's a camp up further alright. Just where the caller said. No body, no blood, no knife, and—"the officer slapped his smooth head under his uniform cap "—no mosquito spray."

Sam chuckled. "Some kids having it on with you, you think?"

"Dispatch didn't think so, but it was a waste of an afternoon. Y'all seen anything odd coming up out of Darien?" Sam and Lucas looked at each other and responded negatively in unison.

The driver of the policeman's boat called out, "Lucas, you hear any news of anyone out Catpond way missing or hurt? Anything strange?"

Lucas considered briefly. "No suh. Nothing but the usual out our way."

The officer addressed the three in the stern. "Where you all visiting from, hoping to take home some of our fine fish?"

"Fayetteville," Sam said promptly.

"Oh!" replied the officer. "Army family?"

"Nope," Sam said, and left it at that.

There was a pause. The occupants of the other boat waved, and Sam and Lucas lifted desultory waves back. "'Afternoon to y'all then," the police officer said The engines of both boats whined as the Whaler's bow rose.

Dylan looked at James, who was exhaling with relief.

Less than five minutes later, James tapped Lucas on the arm, and pointed at a spot on the left bank ahead. They stared at the outcrop as they approached, imagining how Benjamin had eased in just downriver. Benjamin would have known that someone atop the rock ledge would not have been able to see the bank or water immediately below.

Lucas nudged the bow in under the outcrop, and eased the boat in reverse, and then neutral. He turned to James. "Need help loadin' up?" he asked.

James shook his head. "The three of us should be able to make pretty short work of it." He vaulted over the gunwale and extended a hand to Dylan, who waved his big brother out of the way with a gesture. Dylan too vaulted agilely over the side, landing next to James.

They both looked up at Sam, who placed his hands on the gunwale, making as if he were going to vault as well. Then Sam laughed quietly, sat down on the edge, his legs outside the boat, and dropped easily onto the shore.

The three of them clambered up the bank. As they walked slowly into the camp clearing, Sam and Dylan let James lead, awaiting his direction. Dylan could almost hear his brother's brain trying to piece together what had happened here. James turned slowly. Dylan glanced around for the tripwire, but could spot it only near the coffee pot. He started to retrieve it, as James searched the ground. Then James stopped. Just outside the clearing, perhaps fifteen feet into the underbrush, stood a sapling with a red ribbon tied to its trunk, a foot or so off the ground.

As Sam and Dylan watched, James peered into the forest on all sides, and then approached the ribbon. He untied it gently, and then dug his fingers into the dirt below. The soil was loose, and gave easily. About six inches down, he paused, then worked his fingers around something, and slowly drew his Bowie knife out of the hole.

"Should have wrapped it in something before you bury it like that," Sam said from behind him, with a faint note of disapproval.

"I didn't put it there," James said, rising and raking the forest with his gaze.

A slow smile spread across Sam's face. "Another gift from whoever treated Benjamin here, and loaded him up on your canoe thing?"

Dylan spoke up, in a frustrated tone. "I wish you two would talk English sometimes."

James laughed, a loud, careless laugh. It sounded good in his ears. "It's called a dugout!"

***

Dylan watched the low fields of summer vegetables slip by out the window of the Dodge. He sat in the front seat alongside Sam. Sam had given him the map, but there wasn't much directing to do.

Lucas had taken them back down river, where Mr. Walker had met them at the pier in Darien with Sam's car. Furtively, they'd loaded the camp gear in. The items they'd gotten from CeCe and Benjamin were slipped into the back seat. When they were done unloading, they all thanked Lucas. Sam had drawn out his wallet, and tried to press some bills in Lucas's hand, but the older man had just waved him off. "Pass it on," was all the spry Negro had said, and Sam nodded in understanding. Dylan's eyes had widened at the sight of a thick wad of currency in Sam's pocket.

James and Dylan had squeezed into the back seat together, laughing. They were wedged in next to the camp gear like a couple of sardines. When they'd gotten to the Walker's and unloaded the gear, Sam and Mr. Walker had spent a few minutes talking in the parlor. Dylan had sat with Julie Rose and Mrs. Walker in the garden out back, with the quirky scarecrow made of pots. At first, CeCe and James had sat with them, but at some point, they'd both risen, and gone to the porch. Whatever they were discussing was something earnest, for James's voice would rise occasionally, and immediately drop again.

At first, they seemed to be fighting. But after a time, CeCe was sobbing, and grinning. When Sam had called for James and Dylan to get in the car to head north, CeCe was crying, and Dylan could tell James did not trust himself to speak.

He and CeCe rose, and clung to each other. Then, as CeCe gave Dylan a shorter, friendly hug, James disappeared in the back door. Sam shrugged, thanked the Walker's for all their help, and held the door for Dylan.

In the driveway, James was in the back seat, hunched down. The Walkers gathered at the top of the stoop to wave, but CeCe did not appear again.

On the drive north, James had not spoken until well after dark, and then only in answer to a question or two from Sam about directions. In a small town, several hours into their drive, Sam had pulled over opposite some kind of auto shop on Route 301. He'd conferred briefly with James, and then disappeared.

Dylan and James had sat, wordless, in the car, listening to the pinging of the cooling engine, the chatter of cicadas, and the low bass of the bullfrogs. Dylan busied himself swatting at mosquitoes that seemed to favor his ears the most.

Thirty minutes or so later, the driver's door opened and Sam slid in.

"I'll pay you back. Soon as I can." James said quietly.

Sam half-turned in the front seat. "George says hey." Sam laughed weakly at his own joke, and James lapsed into a loud silence again. Whoever George was, he and James were evidently not on friendly terms.

"Don't worry about the money," Sam continued. "Mr. Latham found us a buyer for Mr. Thompson's place, and I got a handsome down payment for it." He paused, glancing at Dylan, then back at James. "Way I figure, some of that money goes to each of us." He chuckled. "So James, you get to spend some of yours right away."

"That why you have such a pack of cash on you?" James asked. So he, too, had noticed.

"Well, I wasn't sure what we'd run into on this trip," Sam had said, to end the subject.

The three of them sat, exhausted, in a hotel room a few minutes north of the garage. Sam explained they'd have to arrange for a tow bar in the morning to tow Father Mullenix's Plymouth, using the Dart.

"We stopped on the way down and I told George to go ahead and fix what need fixing. He said it still needs a tune up. Just to be safe, we'll tow it back. He paused, but James didn't speak. "Either way, looks like we can get the good Father back his car," Sam went on.

James now sat with his back against the headrest of one of the beds, feet crossed and hanging off the side of the mattress, arms cupped behind his skull. He seemed a million miles away.

"James. I know you've been through a lot here," his father finally said. "But there's some items we need to discuss before you're back in Crane Ridge." Sam ran a hand through his hair.

"Like what?" James finally said.

"Well, for starters, how we avoid keeping you out of jail." James started to sit up, but Sam held a hand out. "I talked to Mr. Walker. There is no way on God's green earth that Benjamin and his people will ever bring charges, or even talk to the police. Maybe if they had a lick of proof—but they don't. So they won't. The good news is that everyone in Crane Ridge knows you didn't break into Wilson's Hardware. Or beat up that boy."

He waited, but James didn't speak. Dylan felt like James, even though he had not moved a fraction in the last few minutes, was falling. Falling away from him. Maybe even falling away from himself.

"The other thing is this file I found in Mr. Thompson's house. It—" he chewed his lower lip, regarding James for a long time, and then turning his eyes to Dylan, "—concerns your mother. I don't know what all it means, but it might—" he rubbed his eyes roughly, for a few moments, "—change things."

No one had bothered to turn on any but the bathroom light. Sam reached to turn on the light between the beds. "I brought it with me. Maybe we can decipher it together." Suddenly, he sounded much older.

He rose, creaking, and unbuckled his suitcase. "If you boys don't mind, I need a long shower." He turned, expectant.

James did not move. "Sure," said Dylan. "Go on ahead."

Sam gathered his shave kit and other sundries and eased into the small bathroom, closing the door. As soon as the shower sounded, muffled behind the door, James rose.

As Dylan watched, James gathered Sam's keys quietly, studied one key that was separate, and laid that back on the nightstand. He lifted Sam's wallet and fanned it, then withdrew a fistful of currency. Finally, he lifted items from Sam's suitcase until he held up a thick, yellow file.

Only then did he turn to Dylan. "I want you to come with me. She was your mother too," he said.

Dylan stared at James, wide-eyed. Perhaps it was the lack of sleep, but he felt like he was going to cry.

"Go where?" he asked, though he already knew.

51 / Sugar Land

Despite his distress at abandoning Sam, Dylan had fallen asleep in the Dodge almost immediately. When he awoke, the car was humming into the darkness. He sat up stiffly and noticed a faintly clearing sky behind them.

"What time is it?" he asked, feeling an overwhelming need to pee.

"Got me. I'm guessing around six."

James stopped for gas a few minutes later, and Dylan hurried around the corner of the station.

"Any chance Dad'll try to follow?" he asked his brother, sliding back into the Dodge.

James offered a crooked smile as he started up, and eased the car into first. "I don't think so. We have something he doesn't," he said, patting the dashboard. "A car that actually runs."

For the first full day or so, James was careful to stay to back roads, heading generally west when the sun was out, and venturing onto the state highways westbound after sunset. James didn't think Sam would call the police.

He asked Dylan about books he'd been reading.

"I finally finished Treasure Island," Dylan responded.

"One of my favorites. What did you think?"

"I think we're on our own treasure hunt. But we don't have a map."

James laughed. "Don't you remember geography? We just head west, then south. Right?"

"To where?"

"That's easy, if Nana had it right. Sugar Land. I think she said it's near Houston, where those guys talk to rockets."

Dylan grinned. "But what do we do when we get there? What if she got married again?"

"That's part of a treasure hunt. We don't know all we need to know, but we know how to start." He shrugged. "I guess if it gets to it, we can call our father." After a moment, he glanced at Dylan. "So did you find a hero?"

Dylan thought. "Not really. Jim the cabin boy, maybe. For some reason he reminded me of you." Dylan colored, then continued. "It just seemed like no one was better off after the treasure was found, and that looking for it just led to a lot of mess," he said.

James looked over at him. "Say more," he finally said.

"Well, in Treasure Island, Jim and Captain Smollett almost end up killed, and Ben Gunn, I guess he got off the island, but the treasure, it seemed like it drove him mad." Dylan shrugged. "And Long John Silver, it's hard to picture him changing much when he finally got all that gold and whatnot."

James considered this. "I never thought about it quite like that."

Dylan didn't reply, and several miles slipped by quietly.

"Listen," James said, "I guess things might have gone hard for you when I left. I guess I wasn't thinking about how it might leave you in a bad spot."

Dylan shifted, looking out at the pecan groves, lush in the deep green of late summer. He wished they could talk about something else.

Several more miles ticked by, with no conversation.

"Maybe I'm my father's son after all," James finally managed.

Dylan glanced over at his brother and sipped from his Orange Nehi. "What's that supposed to mean?"

Another several miles slipped under the car before James spoke again.

"Do you remember how Long John Silver had the chance to help or kill Jim at the end, in Treasure Island?"

Dylan wondered about the change of subject. "Do you mean when they found the place the treasure was supposed to be, but Ben Gunn had moved it off?" Dylan asked.

"Yea. Remember how the treasure pulled at Long John, how it drove him to kill and to switch sides from the good guys to the pirates and back again?"

Dylan nodded. "But what are you talking about?"

James didn't answer for a few moments. From the side, Dylan was a little startled how much James looked like Sam. "I thought about dad when I read the book. I thought I was Jim, of course, and alternately I liked and despised Long John, who saved my life, but also almost got me killed."

James glanced over at Dylan as the afternoon sun eased down behind the trees along the road leading through Mississippi. "I thought of Sam especially because of how the pirates and Long John liked their grog. 'Drink and the Devil had done for the rest,'" he sang, swinging his right arm, hand in a fist, in the manner of Robert Driscoll in the Disney movie that Dylan and James had seen with Nana.

James abruptly stopped singing, and his mood darkened. "I wish I could talk to Anne. Just to know she's all right."

"Isn't there somebody you could call?" Dylan asked. He thought about how much he missed talking to Lois, and wondered if she was worried. He hadn't had a chance to ask her what she thought of his poem.

James drummed his fingers on the steering wheel. Dylan remembered how Sam had done the same tattoo on the wheel when he was thinking about something on the trip to find James.

James paused, and looked over at Dylan. "What about your friend Lois?"

Dylan shrugged. "What about her?"

"Does anyone else know you two like each other? Billy? Ryan? Tink? Any of those guys?"

Dylan slowly shook his head. "Don't think so. Why?"

James reached down and lifted his Nehi, gulping some. He set it back down. "Maybe she could find out how Anne's doing back in Crane Ridge. I don't even know for sure that she's there."

"But if I call her, her parents will know she talked to me. What if they know we're runaways?"

James considered this. Finally his brother spoke. "Well, the first thing is, Sam may not even be home yet. We left him last night. And he had to get the car tuned."

Dylan thought this over. "Gosh, you mean it was just yesterday..."

James nodded. "Yep. I'm not even sure Anne would be back yet. I just have to know if she's safe. But I guess there's nothing to be done for it now. We're making good time."

Dylan watched the groves of stately trees roll by, seeming without end. He was glad for the change of subject. He was trying not to think about home, and Sam. "Where are we?"

"Coming up on Mobile, Alabama, from the signs. Thank God Mr. Thompson took such care of this old heap. We must be close to Florida, to the south. I saw a sign for Pensacola."

They drive on in silence as they crossed into Alabama. By the time they hit Mobile, it was dark. James shook his head vigorously a couple times. "It won't do to get pulled over here. We might need that money to get home. And I need to get a little sleep."

They passed much of Monday with Dylan reading to James from the file Sam had been carrying. In the clippings Dylan read, Sam and David and even James were mentioned numerous times. Especially David. The missing toddler. Repeatedly, beginning with an article from a Wednesday.

Dylan hadn't realized at first that the clippings were in order, from the back to the front of the file. The last one in the file was from April 7, 1954. It was the earliest dated item. David was two, and it was a one-column piece barely larger than a bookmark. Berlin Child Disappears, it said. James had Dylan read each clip to him. There were perhaps fifteen in all, from the local daily, and two weekly newspapers. The second and third days after the disappearance had the largest articles. Sam Paxton at first was a Master Carpenter between jobs. But by the following day, the Friday edition, he was the unemployed father.

By Monday of the week following, the articles had shortened again, as police report no new leads. David had simply vanished without a trace. No witnesses. No apparent motive. No one else hears auto allegedly fleeing scene. Family members are not suspects at this time. James had laughed humorlessly at this line, which appeared in some form almost every article. "One of the few things I haven't been suspected of doing," he snorted.

Several of the clippings had names underlined. People who the reporter had interviewed, Dylan assumed. After the first small article, each story until the last one had been written by someone named Tom Paris. In neat handwriting, in the margins, Mr. Thompson, apparently, had written tiny notes. Why leave blanket? appeared next to a reference to the empty stroller, with a "poignant cast-off baby's blanket." Another note read, No one saw car?? with a pen-line pointing into the text where Sam is quoted as hearing a car allegedly fleeing from near the scene of the disappearance. Finally, the note on the last page, which had been the second from the top in the file, the one Sam had spoken aloud the day he and Dylan had gone to Mr. Thompson's. Check date Godfrey Winter left town.

James had looked at him, then drummed his fingers for a long time. "Winter. That name familiar?"

Dylan reached back into his memory. It seemed like his father had said something about the name, but he couldn't remember for sure. "No," he said.

James had managed to drive them through the "M" towns, as he called them: Macon, Montgomery, Mobile. They slept briefly in a park near New Orleans, before the heat and the mosquitoes convinced them to move on. Every time they bought gas, they would buy a snack and a pop. When they passed through Lake Charles, finally crossing into Texas, more than a thousand miles from where they'd left their father, Dylan finally asked James just what he had in mind in Sugar Land.

James shrugged. "I think we should pay our last respects. Visit the grave. See if we can find anyone who knew her."

Dylan looked at him, as he chewed a mouthful of Twinkie. "Why try to find someone who knew her?"

James shrugged, and put out his hand. Dylan passed him an unopened package of Twinkies. He glanced down, and his eyes widened. "These were a Dime?" James sputtered.

They arrived in Houston Monday in the early afternoon, and James headed straight south and west toward Sugar Land. When they reached the small town, Dylan stayed in the car while James ran into a general store. "Down on this street, two blocks," James said, sticking his head in the driver's side door. "Want to get out? Look around?"

Dylan opened the door. James had already stepped up on the sidewalk and was walking slowly down a row of mercantile fronts. "Are we going to leave the car here?" Dylan called. For an answer, James raised an arm without looking back, motioning for his brother to follow.

The librarian at the Fort Bend County Library, Sugar Land Branch, was very helpful. James explained they were seeking microfiche of the Houston Chronicle for the months leading up to September 1966. That was when Nana had given them the news about their mother's passing.

To Dylan's surprise, James had told the librarian the truth. Maureen Paxton was their mother. It was possible she'd remarried, and she had been living in Sugar Land. Dylan thought about what Cammy had said, the night they'd talked. Stinger said something about your mother going off to be with his uncle and James just went insane. If James remembered it, he never mentioned it to Dylan, and Dylan thought better than to bring it up now.

No, they didn't know how long their mother had lived in Sugar Land. They'd had no word from her at all since she'd left Berlin in February 1956, other than the short notes, no return address, that accompanied the gifts she'd sent, every birthday.

Dylan felt the room temperature suddenly rise, and he looked for a place to sit down. He eased into a chair at a desk nearby, and laid his head on his arm.

"The heat can do that to you if you're not used to it down here," the librarian's voice had sounded from far away. A year old. He had been just over a year old when his mother wandered out of town. He lifted his head and stretched, trying to shake the poison from his mind.

"Yea, I'm okay," he assured his brother, waving an arm diffidently.

At first, the librarian hadn't known how to narrow the search. Maureen was not common, but it wasn't rare either. She asked several questions, and James remembered her birthday: May 3, he was sure. He wasn't sure of the year though.

"This may take some time, since some of this will be on microfiche, but the papers less than a year old will still be in storage," Mrs. Waverly, the soft-spoken librarian, was thinking aloud.

Dylan thought it would be nice if she worked at the Wicomico Library in Crane Ridge. She was dressed severely in a high-collar blouse and a skirt that fell well below her knees. But there was something about the way her eyes danced that made her appear much younger than the Crane Ridge librarians.

She glanced up at the wall behind her. "We are closing soon," she said, frowning. "Can you gentlemen come back here in the morning? Say, 10 o'clock?"

They both nodded, and thanked her for her help.

That night, they slept undisturbed in the car outside of town on a country road.

The next morning, they returned to the library. Mrs. Waverly was at her post at the circulation desk. The library was quiet. "It gets much busier when summer ends next week," she said.

"Next week?" Dylan repeated, stunned.

"Well, today is Tuesday, and we start the day after Labor Day, so yes, a week from today. You?" she asked with a trace of misgiving.

"Yes, us too," James quickly replied. "Tuesday after Labor Day."

In answer to her question, Dylan said he was going into seventh grade, while James acknowledged he'd be a senior in high school. She nodded, absently. She seemed to be hesitating, and James prompted her.

"Any luck with Maureen? Paxton or otherwise?"

She nodded. "It was actually easier than I thought it would be. I located one candidate almost immediately and then looked for others, but there really weren't any in your mother's age range. From Sugar Land." While Mrs. Waverly spoke, she'd eased her chair back to open a desk drawer. She extracted a file from the drawer and laid it on the desk. Her hands rested on it, primly folded.

Dylan glanced at James, who noticed too. "We want to thank you very much for your time and your help," he said, glancing at her hands. They hadn't moved.

She nodded, acknowledging his words. Then she looked back and forth from Dylan to James, and back. "You've had no word about her at all, from the day she left until the day she died?"

James and Dylan both nodded. "Notes she would send with birthday gifts. But no return address, and she just signed them mom," James offered, a little impatiently.

"Nothing else," Mrs. Waverly repeated.

The boys nodded again.

"Well," she said, her mouth a strange mixture of smile and pucker, "It appears you may have a sister. And a brother. Half-sister, half-brother," she amended quickly, with the same pleasant-sour blend in her lips. The windows behind her were open onto a schoolyard, but it was deserted now. The clock high on the wall between the windows was the only sound for a few moments. 10:13.

52 / Maureen

Dylan felt the hot breeze on his face, lifting his hair. He stood in the comfort of the shade, gazing down at the flat marker.

Maureen Winter

B. May 3 1927

D. Jul 8, 1966

Next to him stood his brother. The dirt before the marker was bare and slightly mounded. The marker itself was skewed as if the earth around it had not wholly accepted its presence. It looked more like a heavy weight that had dropped from a great height and had heaved the ground immediately around it, rather than nestling as part of the landscape. Dylan imagined in another year or so, it would look as if it had been here forever. A large wilted bunch of unidentifiable flowers spilled from the neck of a cardboard vase at the foot of the bare earth patch. There was a faded card tucked inside a yellowing plastic sleeve.

Dylan was glad to be out of the car, and glad they had the cemetery to themselves, or at least this section of it. He tried to imagine the woman who lay here. But all he could remember were the several photos, and the eyes he couldn't see. She was 39, he reckoned. That seemed old to him, but still very young to die. The hot draft of air lifted the leaves on the underside of the chestnut, and Dylan wanted to imagine the spirit of his mother was somehow awakening.

James was as quiet as he'd been since they'd thanked Mrs. Waverly once again, eased out of the library, and trudged around the side to the Dodge.

Yesterday, as they'd walked down the main street in town to find the library, Dylan had briefly imagined his mother, coming out of a store, getting in a car, carrying groceries, glancing at envelopes as she walked into or out of the post office. But he could not see her eyes. Wherever he imagined her, her head was bent, her eyes were cast down, or she was turning away just as he saw her.

A short time ago, before they'd driven to the cemetery, Dylan had imagined a woman with two children hustling out of the *Ben Franklin's* store on the corner ahead. He realized he knew even less of her than he'd imagined. It wasn't *family* she hated, after all. He reached up at the coolness on his cheek, as the wind whooshed over his arm and the side of his face, and was shocked to find he was crying.

"James."

No answer.

"James."

"James. Let's go home." Dylan hadn't been sure James had heard him, and a few moments later, James had jogged up to ring the doorbell at the rectory of *St. Theresa of the Little Flower* parish. Someone opened the screen for him, and he disappeared inside. Less than two minutes later he emerged, followed by an elderly priest dressed in black slacks and a short-sleeved black shirt with Roman collar, who gestured as James nodded. Apparently, the priest was repeating himself, as James continued to nod, backing up toward the car. The priest spotted Dylan and lifted a hand in greeting, smiling.

James slipped behind the wheel and continued to smile and nod at the priest, until he stepped back in the rectory. Then James let out a sigh. He finally looked over at Dylan. "Don't worry. We'll be headed home soon," he'd said.

Now, as they stood before their mother's marker, James had reached into his back pocket. "Do you want to read it, Dylan?"

"Is there a picture of her?" Dylan asked.

"No."

"That's okay. Does it mention us?" Dylan already knew the answer.

"No." James stepped closer to Dylan, as if to shield him, or slip an arm around him. Dylan would have allowed that, but James just stood, waiting himself.

"Jennifer and Godfrey."

James bent and lifted the vase of flowers. He read the card inserted in the plastic sleeve. Then he lay it back on the ground gently, on its side, the way he'd found it.

"Sorry?" said Dylan.

"Jennifer and Godfrey. We have a sister named Jennifer. Half-sister, I guess."

Dylan looked across the parched Texas field beyond the slightly greener turf of the cemetery, but did not speak.

"Do you remember that flower shop we walked by yesterday?" he asked, turning from the grave.

Dylan turned to watch him walk away. "Yea. What about it? And where you going?"

James stopped and stood, hands at his sides. "Did you want to say a prayer or something?"

Dylan shrugged. "Don't you?"

James looked off toward the car, then walked back, and draped an arm around his brother's shoulders. They both stood, looking down at the nondescript mound of dirt and the clay and metal-colored stone with the brief epitaph. The breeze was hot but gentle, and stirred the small tufts of grass that ventured to grow in the hardscrabble bare earth leading to the stone.

Finally, James spoke. "I wish you hadn't left."

Dylan nodded, waiting respectfully. After a short time, all he could muster was, "It would have been nice to see your eyes."

After a few moments, James squeezed Dylan's shoulder briefly, and the two boys turned and walked away.

53 / Black-Eyed Susans

"This is it," James said, easing into the diagonal space on Main Street, Sugar Land. *Graham Florist: Deliver Joy Today,* emblazoned the plate glass on the storefront.

Dylan debated a moment and then followed James in.

"I was looking for something for a relative out at St. Theresa's Cemetery, and a friend of my dad's mentioned some flowers he'd gotten from your store." James was speaking to a matronly woman at the counter. She'd removed her glasses to lay them on her ample chest. They hung by a dark brown cord around her neck.

Dylan stepped over to a display window. He looked at a collection of flower arrangements displayed on several glass shelves behind a glass door. There was a slight hum from behind the display.

"I can't remember his name, but I know he got it back in July. Around the eighth." Dylan glanced over at them. The woman reached under the counter and emerged with a folder, like the one Mrs. Waverly had presented this morning, only this one was green. She was giving James a thoughtful nod.

"If I gave you the name it was inscribed to, would that be enough to tell me what arrangement you did for him?" James asked politely.

Dylan bent to look at the small arrangement on the bottom. It was a burst of yellow and black flowers, neat and muted.

"Let's see. The date may be enough, if it was one of our memorial arrangements. There. That must be it." Dylan glanced up. The woman had turned to consult another book on the counter behind her. James was studying the upside-down folder in front of him intently.

"I can do that up for you if you want to wait, but it will take me several hours. Or you could come back," she offered, encouragingly. James was smiling at her with a vacant grin.

"James. What do you think of this one?" Dylan said. He caught the proprietor's eye and bent to point at the arrangement on the bottom shelf.

James bent too, and then rose. "Black-eyed Susans. Is that something we could take now?"

The woman smiled a half-smile. "Well, they are an unusual choice for memorial, but yes, of course, those are available for purchase."

Her smile widened, and she moved from behind the counter, lifting her glasses back to her nose. James and Dylan waited while the woman busied herself preparing the vase for transport.

At one point she looked up. "What should the card say?" she asked. "Or do you want to write it yourselves?"

Dylan carried the box with the upright vase carefully to the grave. James followed behind him.

"What do you want the card to say?" James asked as Dylan bent and set the box down.

"Do we have to leave one?" Dylan rose.

"Nope. Nice flowers though."

Dylan glanced up at James. "Why did you want to get those flowers for her anyway?" he asked, gesturing at the cardboard vase, lying where they'd returned it.

"I didn't want to get flowers at all. I just needed the address for Godfrey." He grinned at Dylan, and for the second time that morning, the boys turned from Maureen's grave, and walked away, together.

54 / David

The house was small and well-kept, at the end of a cul-de-sac at the edge of town. It looked like a newer neighborhood. The trees were few and they were short, decorating a front yard here and there.

James and Dylan had parked at the end of the street where it joined Main Street. They walked slowly down the lane. It reminded James of walking down Catpond Road a few days ago. Only this road was paved, and most houses had neat, bright silver chain-link fences, or short, gleaming pickets.

James stopped at a green-shuttered white house, and gazed at it.

"This is where mom was living when she died," he said quietly. Then he smiled slightly. "That came out wrong."

At that moment, a girl of about nine or ten appeared on the porch and turned left to retrieve a bike with a pink basket on the handlebars. It was leaning against the inside of the porch railing, and she walked it to the steps. When she saw Dylan and James, she smiled.

"Hey," she said.

"Hey," replied James. "Is Godfrey home?"

She laughed. "You mean my brother, not my dad?"

"Yes," James said. It wasn't all in place yet, but he felt close. "You must be Jennifer." He pushed open the fence gate, and eased into the yard.

"Why yes I am! And you are?"

James half-turned. "This is Dylan, my brother. I'm James."

She nodded. "Nice to meet y'all. My brother's in back, cutting the grass." She waggled a finger at them, teasing. "My daddy said he's not to play until it's done. But he should be finished shortly. Grass doesn't really grow around here yet."

"Is your father at home?" James tried to sound casual, but his stomach knotted.

"Nope. Not til late this afternoon. Come on in."

James had looked for any sign of recognition at their names. There was none. He glanced behind, and then stepped up to the porch, following Jennifer.

She leaned the bike on its kickstand and opened the screen door, ushering the boys into the cool interior. When they were all in the front room, she said, I'll go let him know you're here."

James abruptly spoke. "We don't mind waiting. But is there a chance we can get a glass of water?" He fanned himself.

"Why sure," she replied, with a lilting southern accent. "Want lemonade instead?"

They both nodded, smiling. While she disappeared through the dining room on the right front of the house, the boys looked around. On the back wall of the room sat an upright piano, covered with variously sized frames. The two boys stepped over and gazed at the pictures of a family they did not know, at Christmas in front of an electric tree, on a beach somewhere with squinting eyes and wide smiles.

"That's your mom," James whispered, pointing to the prim woman posed in front of a car, with what looked like the Grand Canyon in the background. She had on a sleeveless blouse with high shoulders, and a pair of shorts, in the monochrome photo. She was not smiling, and her hands were at her sides, almost rigid.

"Godfrey Junior is the spitting image of his father, that's for sure." Dylan said under his breath.

James nodded. The resemblance was striking between father and son. Both tall and slender, with hair raked back and blonde, and smiles wide and easy, framing perfect teeth above deep blue eyes. There was something else familiar about the boy.

Something.

Jennifer emerged behind them, carrying two tall glasses of lemonade clinking with ice. She handed them the glasses, her face a delightful innocence, and asked, "So which of you is in Godfrey's class?"

James and Dylan gulped from the glasses, nodding appreciatively. "This is delicious," James said. "Thanks so much." His mind raced.

She nodded her thanks, waiting.

"Sorry to hear about your mother, by the way," James said somberly.

"Thanks. Did you know her?"

James shook his head. "Not well."

She sat up. "So have you known my brother long?"

James lifted the glass, draining it. "Not long. I mean, we both know Godfrey from school."

Jennifer eased back into a chair in the dining room, her ankles crossed, legs swinging.

"Why do you keep calling him that?" She burst out with a laugh. "Godfrey David Winter is his name. But nobody calls him Godfrey. I was surprised you even knew his first name." She laughed again, but her raised brows said she still expected some kind of answer.

"We were just kidding around. Do you know David's birthday?" James said pleasantly.

Jennifer's legs stopped rocking, and she sat up, confused. "Of course. But why are you—"

"See, Dylan's is in February, and I was just wondering if they have the same day," James said easily. Dylan was staring hard at one of the photos, and James could tell Dylan was working hard not to look at him.

"Dylan's is the 3rd of February," James continued. He noticed Dylan's shoulders tense. "What about David?"

Jennifer was shaking her head. "Sorry. February the twenty-first."

"Bet you don't know what year," James needled.

Just as quick Jennifer replied. "Nineteen Hundred and Fifty...TWO! So there!" She stuck out her tongue a little. For an instant, James saw his mother in the small gesture. He turned away.

"Your brother sure looks a lot like your dad." He said in a voice that shook.

"Everybody says that," she grinned. James stared at his brother, now tall and perhaps fifteen, looking back at him from a sandy beach, skim board tucked under his arm.

He moved toward the hall leading to the back. "Mind if I see how much he's got left?" She wordlessly shooed him down the hall, and he stopped at a screen door that led onto a small back porch.

He laid his hand on the frame of the door, and watched a younger version of himself pushing a mower confidently in the almost-peaked Texas sun. For some reason, when David turned at the end of the yard, and made his way back down the next row, James thought of Stinger. His hand pressed the frame, and it opened a fraction. A long-forgotten memory bubbled to the surface. The time he'd fought Stinger, trying to kill him.

So this boy and he shared a mother, but not a father. And then she'd become pregnant with Dylan. *No wonder she's never smiling in her pictures*, he thought. He watched David move easily up and down the yard. In a moment, he could be at David's side again. Restored. Would it make up for all that had happened since? Would it fix anything?

No one was better off after the treasure was found, the only brother he'd ever really known had said yesterday. He drummed his fingers for another moment on the door.

James walked slowly back down the hall, pausing at an open bedroom door. He peeked inside. A small bookshelf overflowed to the side of the twin bed's headboard. Many of the book titles were familiar. Over the board, a banner from the Houston Oilers. Discarded jeans on the floor.

Dylan and Jennifer were chatting in the dining room. At least he'd heard Jennifer's animated, friendly voice in the distance the last few minutes. Dylan turned to his brother, seeming relieved.

"Looks like David's gonna be awhile. Tell him Dylan and James stopped by, would you, Jennifer?"

She frowned. "You sure? Bet you he'll be sorry he missed you."

He nodded as Dylan stared at him, anxious. "I'm sorry we missed him too. But we should probably be heading home."

55 / Deal Sealed While Fishing

Dylan flicked the tackle out over the quiet waters, then drew his arm back, dropping the bait several feet from the opposite bank. Labor Day Monday was young, but it already promised tropical humidity and heat that would leach perspiration. Any fish still feeding would be cruising the deep channel.

When he'd slipped out the back door, a small noise behind him caused him to turn. In the shadows, Nana stood, arms wrapping her threadbare bathrobe. She motioned him back, and he was sure he was in for another tongue-lashing. Instead, she raised her hand, and slipped his hair back off his forehead. "By next week you'll be as tall as your father," she said softly. Then her brow furrowed like a thunderhead out over the flat Eastern Shore delta. "And if you ever scare me like that again, off with no word, you won't live to grow another centimeter." Then she drew him close, hugging him fiercely.

He turned at the footfalls behind him. "Any fish left?" James asked. Dylan grinned.

"A whole river full," he said pleasantly, gently reeling his line back across the channel. He glanced back up the hill to Mr. Thompson's. The silent house stood watch on the crest of the hill, shading them for another hour or so from the full weight of the summer heat.

"Saw you two talking in the kitchen. What've you told him?" Dylan handed James the tin of worms.

James rooted in the tin, coaxing out a fat bloodworm. "Thanks. I told him she had a real nice plot."

Dylan turned to his brother with a blank expression.

"Plot. Cemetery plot." James baited his hook. "I think he may be coming over. He was going to root through the garage for a fishing pole he used to have."

Dylan slowly reeled in the last several feet of line. Live, lonely worm. He cast again, deep into the channel. "You didn't mention…" James and he had had many miles and time to discuss what they'd found in Sugar Land, but after an initial burst, driving out of town, there hadn't been a lot to say, after all. The mother they never knew became a creature with motives they couldn't understand, and there was no one left to try to explain. And no explanation that would do.

And no, James was not sure what, if anything, they should say to their dad about it when they got home. Dylan had been furious when he realized they were actually leaving Texas, without at least telling Jennifer and David that they were related.

"So tell me. Pretend I'm Jennifer. What do you say?" James hissed. Dylan had turned in the seat, arms crossed, staring fixedly out, watching the wide Texas prairie break up into the Houston suburbs.

Finally, Dylan had turned back. "They have a right to know, just like we do."

James considered, chewing on a day-old doughnut. "We waited twelve years," he said quietly.

Dylan looked ahead. "If somebody kidnapped David, and mom found out later, why would she…" Dylan's voice trailed off. The question hung between them through Houston, and into eastern Texas.

Finally, James said, "Mom didn't find out later. Something tells me she knew about it all along." The miles clipped under them, each brother absorbing the notion.

"It explains a lot," James mused. "She meets someone while she's married. Gets pregnant. Can't tell a soul. Has the baby. Gets pregnant again with her husband, decides to run…" He tapped the steering wheel. Dylan sat still as a post, waiting for the explosion, but it didn't come. "How do you make that choice?" he said to the streaming highway.

"What are you going to tell dad?" Dylan had finally asked. James had just shrugged.

James stepped upriver from Dylan and cast out to land his rig cleanly in the channel, up from his brother's bobber.

"No. I didn't tell him. Not about mom being involved. Not about finding David. Not about telling him David wasn't his."

Dylan stood next to his brother, frowning. "I don't like it."

James nodded in agreement. "I know. I don't either. But a lot of people have been hurt already." He reeled in slowly. "I think you and me have to decide what the real treasure here is. Like Jim Hawkins. He was about your age, but he had to make some hard choices. This is our Treasure Island, Dylan."

They turned at a shouted greeting from the top of the hill, and Ryan Daggert came flying down the steep knoll, the Hobbitmobile shaking in protest. He skidded to a stop, just feet away from Dylan and James.

"Nana said you were back," he grinned. "She didn't say it like she was swooning with joy about it either." Ryan waited, but Dylan just nodded, and said, "What's new?"

Ryan spluttered, looking from one boy to the next. "Well, forgive me if I want to ask you the same thing. I just spent your dull average Crane Ridge summer. I'm thinking you two might have some stories of your own."

"I went to Georgia, then Texas," James said, flicking his reel out over the shimmering Wicomico River with a practiced ease.

Ryan's face reddened, and he looked ready to burst. "Your father's gonna be over in a minute. Give me *something!*" He looked desperately from James to Dylan. "Stinger hasn't shown his face since the day you left," he continued, looking at Dylan.

"Say. Do you know anybody named Winter, here in town?" James turned to Ryan.

Ryan stared back. "What of it?"

James sighed, and changed his tone. "It's important. And between us. Do you?"

Ryan shook his head. "No live ones."

"What's that mean?" James asked.

"There's a few in the cemetery at St. Joseph's. Up next to the Owens's." He made a face at Dylan. "That's where I used to practice my bike slide." He grinned again. "Nobody complained about the racket!"

Dylan shrugged. "So what you been up to?"

Ryan slapped his handlebars in exasperation. Then he brightened again. "Coming out to the picnic later?" Crane Ridge sent summer off with a town festival at the fairgrounds each Labor Day. "Lisa Haggerty's gonna burn her chain," he said. "It's supposed to stretch from here to Salisbury, but nobody believes that."

"Who's she burning it for?" James asked casually.

"You will never guess. Ever ever try." When the boys ignored him, leisurely working their fishing line, he grinned as if they'd been begging him to spill the beans. "Billy Bergin. Do you believe it? You'd think he discovered *Mars* bars."

"Pleased, is he?" Dylan grinned to himself, then wondered again what Lois Mast was up to.

"Hey boys." They turned to see Sam traipsing down the hill, ancient tackle box and a bamboo pole balanced in one hand. Ryan waved and Dylan and James nodded.

The mood quieted as Sam rigged his line. "Any worms in that tin?" was all he said. James handed the tin over without speaking. Ryan seemed to sense a closing up that didn't include him, and he said he hoped to see them all later at the picnic.

"Lois will probably come with Lisa?" Dylan said, when Ryan turned to hike up the hill.

Ryan turned back to give him a probing look. "Funny thing," he said slowly. "Lisa and Lois don't spend so much time together lately. But yeah," he continued, his gaze on Dylan narrowing, "I imagine Lois will be there."

Then he laughed, again slapping his handlebars. "I guess that explains something."

"What?" Dylan asked, as innocent as he could muster.

"Why she keeps askin—" He stopped, shaking his head slowly back and forth, smiling. "Tell you what. We'll *trade stories* later today."

Ryan winked at Dylan and turned to make his way up the hill.

His father said something Dylan didn't quite catch. "Sorry?"

Sam smiled. "She was just this side of pesky, stopping by the house every morning since I got back, to ask after you."

Sam and James laughed, and James elbowed Dylan. Dylan watched the shade creep across the river's surface. Though it still felt like deep summer, Dylan realized it was a time passing.

"The folks that bought Mr. Thompson's, will they still let us fish here, you think?" Dylan turned to Sam, looking up.

Sam eased his hat back on his head, and wiped at the perspiration with a handkerchief. "I did broach the subject with him. I said some rowdy neighbor boys favored this spot for their fishing escapades." Dylan waited, still looking up at his dad.

"I said they would probably be delighted to help with some of the mowing summers if they could still have access."

"And?" Dylan prompted.

"And he seemed very amenable."

They fished in silence for a few minutes. Then James spoke to the river. "I was thinking over what you asked me." Dylan looked at James, and then Sam. His father was nodding slowly.

"Me going to Richmond makes sense," he said. Dylan looked at Sam.

Sam cleared his throat. "I stopped on the way back home and looked at some places in Richmond. Turns out a man has a station with an apartment above for sale, right off Monument Avenue. That might do 'til the bypass opens up."

James looked at Dylan. "Dad and I've been talking. It might be better for me to be out of Crane Ridge for a little while, til Roy Sampson cools off. Dad…talked to him."

Dylan looked at Sam, who only nodded. "Dad told him what that man of his did in Darien," James continued, "and he said he was prepared to let it drop, if Mr. Sampson would leave me alone until Anne is 18."

Dylan stared at James, openmouthed. Was this really his hot-headed brother, who was usually spoiling for a mix up?

"That's only a little over a year off now," he said. "It sure isn't going to work for me to be in the same school with that man this year. But he did let me see Anne. Him on the porch the whole time, of course."

"How did you work *that* out?" Dylan asked, amazed.

James stared out over the river. "I told him I understood his wanting to protect her, because I felt the same way. For some reason, I guess that set right with him."

"What did Anne say about all that?" Dylan blushed a little. "You don't have to—"

"It's okay. She said she'd wait as long as we had to," James said wonderingly.

"So," his father picked up, "I was saying maybe we buy this place in Richmond, and James can fix it up part-time, maybe start school when he gets settled down there."

"Um, there's something else I have to do first." James dipped into the tin, and lifted out a stringy worm. "I'm going to back to Darien, maybe get some work for a month or so, help Benjamin get back on his feet. It has to be hard right now, just him and his mom. I also," he hesitated, then pushed on, "…have a conversation to continue down there."

Dylan raised a hand in exasperation. "Wait a minute. Just like that?" Sam and James both looked at him. Dylan looked from James to Sam. "When are you going to start screaming about us leaving you in Georgia with no car?"

His father chuckled. Dylan wondered briefly if he'd just woken from a long, incredible dream. "Well, I was pretty testy at first, when I realized what you two whelps had done." His face changed, softening. "When I figured where you were headed, and why I wasn't consulted, or invited, I understood. And George the mechanic, turns out, is pretty handy after all. Got the car running in just a few hours."

The three of them turned at a commotion. Buster barked merrily, then loped down the hill, alongside Nana. Carefully, she eased down the incline, carrying a jug of lemonade in one hand, her other arm cradling plastic cups, and a paper sack. *Cookies,* prayed Dylan.

"I wouldn't say we're even," Sam went on quietly. "I'm just glad you're home again. Glad I am too, for all that."

He winked at Dylan. "Glad somebody can attend to that lady friend of yours. I think she missed you most of all."

Dylan grinned. Then he said, "I'm not sure about Richmond anymore…for myself." James and Sam simply nodded, as if they understood.

The sun finally rose above the peak of Mr. Thompson's house, lighting the Wicomico and the family on the bank, in a blaze of late-summer brightness.

THE END

About the Author

Jack Downs lives wtih his wife and three children in Eldersburg, MD. His next book, Cattails — *The Edenmist Affair*, will be released in late 2013.

Visit him at www.jackbdowns.com

Apprentice House is the country's only campus-based, student-staffed book publishing company. Directed by professors and industry professionals, it is a nonprofit activity of the Communication Department at Loyola University Maryland.

Using state-of-the-art technology and an experiential learning model of education, Apprentice House publishes books in untraditional ways. This dual responsibility as publishers and educators creates an unprecedented collaborative environment among faculty and students, while teaching tomorrow's editors, designers, and marketers.

Outside of class, progress on book projects is carried forth by the AH Book Publishing Club, a co-curricular campus organization supported by Loyola University Maryland's Office of Student Activities.

Eclectic and provocative, Apprentice House titles intend to entertain as well as spark dialogue on a variety of topics. Financial contributions to sustain the press's work are welcomed. Contributions are tax deductible to the fullest extent allowed by the IRS.

To learn more about Apprentice House books or to obtain submission guidelines, please visit www.apprenticehouse.com.

Apprentice House
Communication Department
Loyola University Maryland
4501 N. Charles Street
Baltimore, MD 21210
Ph: 410-617-5265 •F ax: 410-617-2198
info@apprenticehouse.com
www.apprenticehouse.com

CPSIA information can be obtained
at www.ICGtesting.com
Printed in the USA
BVHW042235300720
585118BV00015B/443